HUNT
IN THE
DARK

Hugh Wheeler (left) and Richard Webb (right) with unidentified woman at Steel Pier, Atlantic City, c. 1935

HUNT
IN THE
DARK

Q. Patrick

Edited by Curtis Evans

P. O. Box 532057
Cincinnati, OH
2021

FIRST EDITION

ISBN (cloth edition): 978-1-936363-52-0

ISBN (trade softcover): 978-1-936363-53-7

Printed in the United States of America on acid-free, recycled paper

Crippen & Landru Publishers
P.O. Box 532057
Cincinnati, OH 45253
USA

Jeffrey A. Marks, Publisher
Douglas G. Greene, Senior Editor

e-mail: info@crippenlandru.com
web: www.crippenlandru.com

Contents

Introduction

*H*unt in the Dark and Other Fatal Pursuits collects a half dozen short works of crime fiction (two novellas, two novelettes and two short stories) by Q. Patrick, aka Richard "Rickie" Wilson Webb and Hugh Callingham Wheeler, two of the greatest Anglo-American masters of mid-century murder. Included are the presumably final recovered tales of the criminous adventures of Rickie and Hugh's series characters Peter and Iris Duluth ("Hunt in the Dark") and Dr. Hugh Westlake ("The Frightened Landlady"), as well as four other tales of deathly doings: the ingenious shorts "Killed by Time" and "The Woman Who Waited" and the noirish novelettes "The Hated Woman" and "This Way Out." Within the pages of this fine volume, readers will find dark fantasies of murder, full of flawed men and fatal women, as they walk the wilder, pulpier side of Rickie Webb and Hugh Wheeler's rich legacy of short crime fiction.

****

Initially in the 1930s Rickie Webb and Hugh Wheeler lucratively tapped diverse markets for their short fiction in *Street & Smith's Detective Story Magazine*, one of America's premier purveyors of "pulp" crime fiction (so named for its cheap pages made from wood pulp), which aimed primarily at a male audience, and in *The American Magazine*, a so-called "slick" (so named on account of its more expensive, glossy paper) with a readership composed to a great extent of middle-class women. Among the pulp detective fiction which Rickie and Hugh published at this time were three serial novels and a novella, all of which appeared under the pseudonym Q. Patrick in *Detective Story Magazine*, about Dr. Hugh Cavendish Westlake, a widowed New England country doctor with an irrepressibly rambunctious young daughter, Dawn, who manages, albeit usually inadvertently, to help her bemused father solve, with the considerable help of folksy series policeman Inspector Cobb, the myriad fiendish murders which cross his path. That Hugh Cavendish Westlake shares the same initials—H. C. W.—with Hugh Callingham Wheeler surely is no accident.

The serial Dr. Westlake novels--*The Dogs Do Bark, The Scarlet Circle* and *Murder or Mercy?*—all were later published in hardback editions by "Jonathan Stagge," albeit in the case of *The Scarlet Circle* only after a lag of seven years, due perhaps to the possibility that the pulp novel in 1937 may have helped inspire two horrific real-life copycat murders in Queens, New York. (See my article "Jonathan Stagge's *The Scarlet Circle* and the Scarlet Circle Slayer" at my blog *The Passing Tramp*.) However, the second Hugh Westlake adventure, the novella "The Frightened Landlady," which was originally published in *Detective Story Magazine* in December 1935, a month after *The Dogs Do Bark*, was never expanded as a novel. It now appears here, in print in English for the first time in eighty-five years—an exciting event indeed for admirers of Jonathan Stagge's ingenious murder cases.

Dr. Westlake's daughter Dawn does not put in an appearance in this exceptionally grim story, happily for her being "away at the shore with friends." However, the doctor's investigative partner Inspector Cobb, Chief of Police of Grovestown (where the doctor, who normally resides twenty miles away in Kenmore, is substituting for his vacationing colleague Dr. Hammond), provides some timely assistance. Young Dawn, who is present in spirit if you will, manages to do her part as well to help her father and Inspector Cobb crack the weird and gruesome case, which turns extremely nasty. "The affair ended with a brutal murder and the unearthing of another crime so fantastic in its twisted abnormality that I cannot help wondering whether I am violating the ethics of my profession in setting it down," Dr. Westlake forebodingly announces in the first lines of the novella. What stouthearted mystery fan could resist?

In an opening reminiscent of the strange consultations once held in London by a certain eminent detective at 221b Baker Street, Dr. Westlake is visited by Mrs. Eva Bellman, a highly respectable sixtyish Grovestown landlady who believes she must be suffering from some malady of the eyes (like Hugh Wheeler in real life), on account of the seemingly impossible transformations which she imagines have been taking place around her in her building. Gladioluses in a vase have turned into zinnias and back again, for example, while a pet canary has gone from life to death (stabbed with a paper knife and pinned to a pillow) to life again. Dr. Westlake assures the frightened landlady that there is nothing physically wrong with her, yet he is highly intrigued all the same by her problem. "Possibly my recent connection with the unpleasant series of murders near my home in Kenmore had given me a taste for the bizarre," he speculates, recalling the ghastly case earlier detailed in *Detective Story Magazine* in *The Dogs Do Bark*.

It is not long before Dr. Westlake calls upon Mrs. Bellman at her building, where he finds that things are even queerer than he had imagined. "The Frightened Landlady" is a fine baroque mystery tale with some classic twists and a twisted crime. To be sure, it shares affinities with another Webb and Wheeler work, "Danger Next Door," a non-series Q. Patrick novel which appeared in *Detective Story Magazine* in May 1937 and fourteen years later was published by Q. Patrick in hardcover under the same name (now long out-of-print); yet Hugh Westlake fans will by no means want to miss "The Frightened Landlady." It makes a fine (and presumably final) addition to the distinguished Hugh Westlake crime canon.

"Killed by Time" and "The Hated Woman" like "The Frightened Landlady" are among the earliest pulp crime pieces published by Rickie and Hugh. They appeared in *Detective Story Magazine* in, respectively, October 1935 and February 1936. The former is a pure problem detective story, though a rather memorably gruesome one, along the lines of something mystery genre master John Dickson Carr might have devised. In it Inspector Groves (of Grovestown perhaps?) is summoned on the scene to investigate the murder, at the home of esteemed brain surgeon Doctor Cobden (shades of Inspector Cobb), of Cobden's son-in-law, Julius van Holdt, a woman-chasing wastrel. The dead man was discovered gruesomely slain on the couch in Doctor Cobden's office, his face "no longer calm or handsome": "One eye was closed as if in sleep, but the other—or rather, the place where the other had been—was a hideous red gash, a gaping void. It was as though someone had stabbed persistently and accurately at the eye with a sharp, thin weapon." "[P]ossibly an ice-pick," speculates the phlegmatic medical examiner. Steel yourselves, readers!

The novelette "The Hated Woman" presents one of the most unsympathetic titular in the Webb-Wheeler canon in the person of

Lila Trenton, the eponymous hated woman. Lila, it soon becomes manifest, is very hated indeed, and deservedly so, being a self-ish, spiteful individual concerned only with preserving her own diminishing physical charms (past forty, Lila's looks are being "killed by time"), so that she can continue successfully to pursue handsome young men, her longtime marriage notwithstanding. When she is discovered dead in the kitchen of her apartment at the Vandolan Hotel, her head bloodily battered by blows from a wood hatchet, there is no shortage of suspects in her murder, including her long-suffering husband, Paul Trenton, a chemistry researcher at the local university; Larry Graves, a strapping yet weak-willed blond whom the smitten Lila had loaned five thousand dollars, with sexual conditions attached, to start an auto garage; Larry's girlfriend Claire French, the coolly attractive and determined owner of her own beauty parlor; and Sam Nolan, the Vandolan Hotel's strapping brunet electrician, patently on the make. ("If you ever need me, Mrs. Trenton, it's easy to get me," he pointedly advises Lila.) The police are stymied by the multiplicity of suspects (truly Lila and Paul's apartment was something like Grand Central Station on the night of the murder), leaving Paul Trenton's likeable colleague in the chemistry department at the university, Professor Gilbert Conroy, to bring the crime home to its perpetrator.

Like "The Frightened Landlady" and "Killed by Time," "The Hated Woman" has the fingerprints of Rickie Webb all over it, in its depictions of nasty people and grisly murders and its trans-gressive gay subtext, among the most prominent in the writing of Webb and Wheeler. In Lila's relationships with Larry Graves and Sam Nolan, it is easy to discern what Marc Fisher in "The Life of a Trophy Boy" termed the "gay paradigm" of an older gay sugar daddy, his looks fading, avidly pursuing hustling young hunks.[1] "You're nothing but a gigolo—a gigolo," a dis-gusted (and somewhat priggish) Claire castigates Larry at one point, while studly Sam Nolan, clad in his overalls, provocatively comments to Lila, "Geez...I wish I was a girl. Maybe then you

---

1. See Washington Post, 25 July 1997, at https://www.washingtonpost.com/ar-chive/lifestyle/1997/07/25/the-life-of-a-trophy-boy/f978dd1a-2f2e-4439-b645-4ede046c78e7/?noredirect=on. The article is a meditation on the life and death of Andrew Cunanan, a "high-class gay prostitute" and serial murderer who infamously slew fashion designer Gianni Versace in 1997.

could use me around this place, Mrs. Trenton. I'm pretty good at housework, too. Used to be a houseboy when I was a kid." A positive portrayal in the novelette of a same-sex relationship can be seen with middle-aged academic colleagues and best friends Paul Trenton and Gilbert Conroy, who resemble pals of Rickie's from the University of Pennsylvania and other colleges. Seven years after the publication of "The Hated Woman," Rickie Webb ironically made a disastrous five-month marriage with a noted woman author, Frances Winwar, starkly contrasting with the years of contentment he enjoyed with his writing partner Hugh Wheeler, who also was his companion of many years.

A much happier depiction of a heterosexual couple is found in "Hunt in the Dark" (published in October 1942 in *Short Stories*), which—like "Death Rides the Ski-Tow" and "Murder with Flowers," both of which appeared in *The American Magazine* the previous year (and have since been collected in Crippen & Landru's 2016 volume *The Puzzles of Peter Duluth*)—is another madcap wartime adventure of theater producer Peter Duluth and his charming and glamorous actress wife Iris, lead characters in Rickie and Hugh's Patrick Quentin "Puzzle" series of novels. Even here, however, some gay subtext is slipped in when Peter tells us that on a sleuthing visit to a Manhattan book and record shop, he pauses occasionally to pretend to glance at something, like "an old copy of *Leaves of Grass*" and "a *Strength and Health* magazine from 1936."

This time Peter and Iris run afoul of a deadly terrorist plot against the United States, recalling the "Black Tom" explosion of 1916, an act of German sabotage at a major munitions center at Black Tom, an artificial island adjacent to Liberty Island in New York Harbor. (Peter specifically mentions the Black Tom attack.) On the side of Peter and the irrepressible Iris in their valiant against-the-odds attempt to foil the Nazis' deadly machinations (Iris has "always been the Lady Macbeth of our team, taking danger and disaster in her stride," observes Peter), are the couple's indomitable black cook Aloma and her hulk of a husband, Rudolph, the latter, we are cheekily told, mysteriously returned "after a long absence upstate." The ultimate moral of "Hunt in the Dark" seems to be, "Good help is hard to find," so hang onto it when you find it. Within a few years, Rickie and Hugh at their home at Twin Hills Farm in Monterey, Massachusetts would hire a handsome black male cook, Johnny Grubbs, a move which ironically would help lead to the irrevocable sundering of Rickie and Hugh's companionship, something which had not happened when Rickie had been briefly married to Frances Winwar.

We return to the formal problem detective short story with "The Woman Who Waited," a fine brief tale of detection which would have melded perfectly with the lauded Lieutenant Trant short stories that Rickie and Hugh published over the decade from 1945 to 1955 (and which have since been collected in Crippen & Landru's 2019 volume *The Cases of Lieutenant Timothy Trant*). In "The Woman Who Waited," which first appeared in *The Shadow* in January 1945, Trant stand-in Inspector Macrae is tasked with determining the identity of the mysterious woman in black who shot and killed Ellery Trimble with his own gun in his parked car outside his Twin-Town Department Store, "the one big league emporium in the dual community of Stuart-Cartersville." Left bizarrely sprawled across the dead man's corpse are a dozen "pairs of silk—real silk—stockings," resembling nothing so much as "grotesque, elongated caterpillars." Macrae manages to pin the guilt for a truly audacious act of murder on the correct culprit, doubtlessly one whom Lieutenant Trant, with his well-known penchant for murderesses, would have relished encountering.

Like "Hunt in the Dark" and "The Woman Who Waited," "This Way Out," published in *Mystery Book Magazine* in March 1947, has sophisticated touches reflective of the fine hand of Hugh Wheeler, a still youngish man of thirty-five when the novelette was published. Hugh's writing talent had burgeoned over the years while that of Rickie, who suffered from various debilitating physical and mental maladies after his return from wartime service with the Red Cross in Hollandia, New Guinea, had decayed. (Hugh, who suffered from diplopia, or double vision, served stateside in the Medical Corps at Fort Dix, New Jersey.) In Hugh's hands "This Way Out" rises from the pulpish danses macabres of the "The Frightened Landlady" and "The Hated Woman" to the operatic heights of the tragically doomed romances of Forties film noir.

As in many of the postwar film noirs, the protagonist of "This Way Out" is a disillusioned World War Two veteran returned home, like Rickie Webb, from overseas service into a world of hurt. In this case it is Steve Glenn, who when he beats up playboy Tony Dort at the beginning of the story has been officially honorably discharged from the Army for but a few hours and symbolically is still wearing the uniform he had donned to fight the Japanese. Getting even with Tony was something Steve had been living for over "eighteen long, bitter months" of combat in the Pacific, at New Guinea and Leyte, since Steve's beautiful blonde ex-wife, Celia, had commenced a wild fling with Tony and persuaded Steve to divorce her. The embittered vet exits Tony's apartment, having left the playboy knocked out and flat on his back, and he heads for liquid consolation to a bar. Later, however, with the assault and the drinks having failed to make him feel any better about the situation, Steve decides to check up on Tony at the apartment, where he discovers to his mortification that in the interim someone has shot Tony–dead.

Finding Celia's small white-gold, emerald-encrusted compact, a gift from him during their marriage, at the scene of the crime, Tony jumps to the conclusion that Celia must be Tony's killer, and he sets out at all costs to protect her from the consequences of the crime he thinks she committed. However, Steve soon learns there are other promising candidates besides Celia for the role of the odious Tony's murderer, including Celia's virginal younger sister Dennie, who during the war has blossomed into a lovely blonde simulacrum of her sibling; Virginia Dort, Tony's cynical estranged wife; 4-F Roy Chappell, who fashions metal into jewelry and trinkets of exquisite beauty, like Celia's compact; Goody Taylor, an aging man-about-town ("Goody Taylor? I thought he'd been embalmed years ago."); and a "cool, metallic blonde" named Janice, the latest of Tony Dort's flings.

Things get so very complicated, Steve reflects morosely during the course of this twisting tale: "[T]he perversity of life got under his skin. Celia loved Tony; Steve loved Celia; Dennie loved Steve. He felt a sudden, savage hunger for the old world of mud and death in the Pacific. At least you knew where you were in a foxhole. Nobody loved anybody there." Like Roy Chappell's intricately bejeweled creations, "This Way Out" is exquisitely fashioned, a moving tale of fatal misunderstanding that, though it likely was mostly composed by Hugh Wheeler, seems to have been informed by some of Rickie Webb's recent disillusioning experiences, as the two men's own relationship, like the fictional one of the seemingly imperishably insouciant Peter and Iris Duluth, became more "complicated" during the postwar years.

Rickie and Hugh had permanently parted ways by 1952, with Rickie leaving the house at Twin Hills Farm, which they had shared together since the war, for France, never to return again except for occasional visits, when his failing health permitted. He passed away in obscurity fourteen years later, at the age of sixty-five. Hugh, on the other hand, remained with Johnny Grubbs at Twin Hills Farm for the rest of his life, surviving Rickie by twenty-one years, during which time he kept up the acclaimed Patrick Quentin mysteries and worked with entertainment world giants Stephen Sondheim and the late Harold Prince, among many others, attaining greater prominence than he ever had before as a writer for stage and screen. Among other things, he won three Tony Awards for his books for the musicals *Sweeney Todd*, *A Little Night Music* and *Candide*.

Many of Rickie and Hugh's stories in *Hunt in the Dark and Other Fatal Pursuits* are far removed from Hugh's rarefied world of shining, richly rewarded achievement, in the way of noir capturing, rather, some of the darkness which in his later years Rickie often felt in his own melancholy heart, never more bleakly than in "This Way Out," when the narrator observes: "During the evening there had been moments of wild racing hope. Moments when he thought he was on top and could thumb his nose at doom. They hadn't been real of course….He'd been licked from the start." In this latest volume from the devilishly good Crippen & Landru, cross over for a few twilight hours to the dark side of life with Rickie Webb and Hugh Wheeler—if you dare!

Curtis Evans
thepassingtramp.blogpsot.com

The Frightened Landlady

I

FEAR IN HER EYES

The affair ended with a brutal murder and the unearthing of another crime so fantastic in its twisted abnormality that I cannot help wondering whether I am violating the ethics of my profession in setting it down. The ending, I repeat, was fantastic and rather beastly. And yet the beginning was so simple, so routine and—though I hesitate to use the word — almost humorous.

It all started when a small, shabbily respectable woman marched into Doctor Hammond's consulting office. She was well over sixty, and at first there seemed nothing to set her apart from the other patients, unless it was that she obviously possessed the vitality of a woman much younger than her years. All her movements were quick and alert. She glanced around her and perched herself on the extreme edge of a chair like an old-fashioned, untidy doll.

"I want to see Doctor Hammond, young man," she snapped.

I explained that Doctor Hammond was away on vacation and that I was taking care of his patients. She glanced at me suspiciously as though she were sizing me up in her mind. Then she laughed—a high, rather startling laugh.

"Well. Doctor Westlake, the last time I went to a doctor was thirty years ago. You were running about in short pants then." Again her laugh rang out almost defiantly. "But I'm sick now, and I want you to tell me what's the matter."

At the advanced age of thirty-eight, I found it flattering to be treated as a boy. I was prepared to like this indomitable little woman.

"What's the trouble. Mrs.—"

"Bellman. Eva Bellman," Her voice suddenly faltered. "And don't ask me what's the matter. Find out for yourself."

She did not look like an ill woman, nor did she seem the type that goes in for malingering or invalidism. I gave her a thorough physical examination. Except for a slight systolic murmur and rather low blood pressure, I could find nothing wrong. I told her so.

For some reason, this reassurance seemed to aggravate rather than calm her.

"You young doctors!" she exclaimed with curious vehemence. "Full of newfangled nonsense! If you can't find out what's the matter, I shall have to go to someone who can. You see, whatever you say, I must be sick." She laughed—this time more shrilly than before. "You—you didn't examine my eyes, did you?"

"I'm not an eye specialist, you know."

"You must look at them." There was a note of finality in her voice. "If it's nothing else, it's my sight."

I gave her some simple tests with colors and letters. Then for the first time since she entered, I looked straight into the small, deep-set eyes. I could see nothing wrong—that is, nothing organically wrong. But as I examined those dilated pupils with their border of faded iris, it was as though a veil were lifted, and for an instant I saw into her very soul. In that brief examination, I realized that I was dealing with a case which did not belong within the normal sphere of medical activities. There was no doubt as to what was wrong with Mrs. Bellman. She was afraid—blindly, desperately afraid.

My expression must have betrayed my surprise at this discovery, for she exclaimed abruptly.

"What is it, young man? There is something wrong, isn't there? Am I going blind?"

Frankly, the case bewildered me. I told her that her eyesight seemed normal and tried to encourage her to talk, hinting that perhaps her nerves or overwork—

"Overwork," she snapped. "When a woman's been on her feet fourteen hours a day for thirty years, she gets used to a little work." She broke off and glanced away. Then she added suddenly, "I'll tell you why I'm sure it's my eyes, young man. I've seen things—horrible things—things that couldn't possibly have been real."

As a doctor, I am used to hysterical women with their dramatics and exaggerations, but there was a basic sanity and matter-of-factness about Mrs. Bellman which had to be taken seriously. Here was no mere old woman's neurosis. I felt I was on the threshold of something more complex—something far less easy to diagnose.

She was talking rapidly now—talking about herself as if to regain her confidence. It seemed that she owned a rather superior boarding house somewhere downtown. As soon as she mentioned it, a change came over her. She became the very essence of all landladies with their pride in the house, their strict code of respectability and correctness. Yes, she had run No. 12 Potter Street by herself for many years, and hoped to do so for many more. Of course, it was in a very good section of town. There would be no difficulty in selling out if she wanted to. Why, only the other day she had had a very satisfactory offer. But she would never consider retiring.

"I've always been a working woman, Doctor Westlake," she said, twisting a plain gold wedding ring on her finger. "And I hope to go on working as long as my two legs carry me. That is, provided I keep my health. But if things don't get better—"

I could tell that she was pathetically eager to confide in me and yet afraid lest I should fail to believe her. Again the strange laugh as she leaned impulsively forward.

"It began a few weeks ago, young man. At first it was just little incidents and I was too busy to pay any attention. Then things began to happen. Well, there just wasn't any explanation. It was as if the devil himself was playing spiteful tricks on me."

Her small, deep-set eyes met mine for a moment and then flicked away. "It was the flowers that I noticed first."

I nodded sympathetically.

"I hate zinnias!" she exclaimed with seeming irrelevance. "Nasty things—the color of blood! I know I never bought them. You see. I always have a vase of flowers on the table in the vestibule to keep it fresh and dainty. One morning I bought some lovely gladioluses from a man on the street. I set them up in the hall and went to my room to take off my hat. When I went back to the hall, those flowers had changed. They were zinnias. I stared at them and just couldn't believe my eyes. I was so worried that I ran out to the street to find the flower man. He'd gone, but when I got back to the hall,"—she paused and then whispered—"they were gladioluses again. And yet I had seen those zinnias. I swear I had."

To me, this incident seemed amusing rather than sinister.

"And that's only the beginning, Doctor Westlake. The very next day something else happened. In my bedroom, I have a photograph on the wall—an old wedding group of myself and my husband." For an instant her eyes flashed with an expression other than fear. "I turned him out of the house five years ago, but I still keep the photo there. Guess I never bothered to take it down. Well, on Wednesday, I was tidying up when I happened to glance at the picture. It—it had changed." The laugh rang out again suddenly. "It had changed to a photograph I had seen in the paper —a nasty picture of a dead woman all smashed up after a motor accident.

"I touched it. I know I touched it. Then Mrs. Brown called me upstairs saying the mosquitoes had got into her room. I was away about twenty minutes fixing one of hall screens, but, when I got back, there was the old wedding group just like it had always been."

I must have been looking at her in a rather tactless manner for she added immediately: "And don't think I drink, young man. I haven't so much as touched a glass of beer since I—since my husband went. I hate the stuff."

I started to ask a question, but a gesture of the thin arm stopped me.

"Ever since, it's been going on. Things changing and then changing back again before my eyes. I'm not the fanciful sort. And I'm perfectly capable of running my own house even if I do have tempting offers. But I can't tell any more what's real and what isn't. I see ornaments and pieces of furniture in the wrong place—and when I come to move them back, they're already there."

Her hands were fluttering around the meager bosom, "But it was yesterday that it happened—the thing that made me decide I had to come to a doctor." Her lips were tightly pressed together, almost invisible. "There's a canary by the desk in the hall. It's been there for years, and no one pays much attention to it except Miss Clymer who feeds it and gives it water. Yesterday afternoon when I'd got through with lunch, I went to my room to rest. I crossed to the bed." She glanced up fiercely. "And you must believe this. I saw that canary stabbed with my paper knife and pinned to the pillow. It was bright yellow and there was a long trickle of blood on the slip."

She looked down. "I ran along the passage to the hall—and, oh, of course, you know what I found. The canary was still in the cage, singing its head off. Miss Clymer was there giving it a bit of sugar. She—she saw me and started to talk about her hot-water faucet being loose."

"And when you got back to your room?"

"Yes, the canary wasn't there. The paper knife was on my table where it always is. And—and there was no blood on the pillow slip, young man."

She broke off abruptly. There was no hysteria in this sudden silence.

For a moment I did not speak.

"You've told your lodgers about this, Mrs. Bellman?"

"Of course not. What do you suppose they'd say? Besides, nothing ever stays the same. I don't believe I saw those things at all. I'm sure—I know it's my eyes."

I was equally sure it was not.

"I don't doubt for a moment that you saw what you say you saw, Mrs. Bellman. Surely, the solution is obvious. Someone in the house is doing it—one of your boarders—practical jokes."

Instantly I came up against the landlady in her. I could tell exactly what my patient was thinking. Hers was a respectable house. It was impossible to suspect one of her lodgers. Did not she always look prospective tenants over personally? She gazed at me coldly.

"Why should they?" she asked.

That was a question which seemed difficult to answer, but I continued with my argument.

"Boarding houses, you know—people get peculiar. Isn't there someone you might suspect of having a grudge against you?"

"Grudge! I guess they all have grudges. Never knew a boarder that didn't. I've been renting out rooms forty years, young man, and I know boarders gossip and complain, but they don't do things like that. Not at my house. They know they get their money's worth at 12 Potter Street. Why, Miss Clymer—she's always behind with the rent. And I don't turn her out, do I? And Mr. Washer, saying he has a right to play that piano of his all hours of the night as though no one else was trying to sleep!"

I encouraged her to talk, hoping to find in her random remarks a clue to these strange happenings.

"Yes," she continued, "and those two Furnivall women complaining about the meals or the service. But I always say that you can't expect the Ritz for twelve dollars a week inclusive. The Browns—they're the only good tenants, but they're always asking for my best suite. As for that Davenport girl, painting her lips and nails, and running in and out of men's bedrooms. And there's Mr. Jay. He's a fresh boy, but that's only when I complain

about his chemistry and the smells he makes about the house."
She broke off suddenly as though she had been caught out in
depreciating the reputation of the house. "But they wouldn't do
a thing like that. No, Doctor Westlake."

I saw it was merely a waste of time to try to shake her convic-
tions on this point. There seemed nothing for it but to tell her
to take things a bit easy and gave her a prescription for a boric
eyewash. She snatched it eagerly and put it in her dilapidated
pocketbook.

"Well, Mrs. Bellman." I said, as I crossed with her to the door,
"you can take it from me that you are perfectly sound physically
and—er—mentally. My suggestion is that someone is arranging
all these things to frighten you. If anything else happens, please
call me up, and, if necessary, we can put the police onto them."

She did not seem to hear the last part of my sentence. She had
turned and was staring unseeingly across the room.

"Of course," she muttered, "if she was still there, I could
understand." There was a strange emphasis on the word: "she."
"But it couldn't be Agnes. Mrs. Salt took her to Arizona to try
and cure her, poor thing."

Then her mood seemed to change and she broke into genuine
laughter for the first time.

"Jo—that soft, spineless, no-good Jo. He couldn't. No, it's
impossible."

Before I had time to question her, she was gone. I saw her
back as she hurried into the street—a thin, erect back carrying so
defiantly its burden of bewilderment, suspicion and fear.

II

A COCK-AND-BULL STORY?

Doctor Hammond's practice was not a large one. A few more
patients trickled into the office after Mrs. Bellman's depar-
ture, but they were all routine cases. When lunch time came,
I found myself still thinking of the frightened landlady. The case
intrigued me. Possibly my recent connection with the unpleasant series of murders near my home in Kenmore had given me
a taste for the bizarre. At any rate, I gave way to an impulse and
called up my old friend Cobb of the Grovestown police.

Without violating professional confidences, I told him something of my interview with Mrs. Bellman, pleaded vulgar curiosity, and asked him if he knew anything about her boarding house at No. 12 Potter Street.

Cobb is a very methodical individual with a prodigious memory. He considered a moment and then said:

"Come to think of it, I do remember a little thing—just one of those cases of a frightened, hysterical woman."

"Frightened?" I echoed swiftly "You mean Mrs. Bellman?"

"No, sir. It was one of her neighbors. That Bellman woman's got her head screwed on pretty tight. Nothing could scare her."

I could have contradicted him, but I didn't. "What was it all about?" I asked.

"Just a cock-and-bull story. Sometime last spring this woman came running into the police station and said her little boy had been scared half out of his wits by something he saw in one of the windows across the way. The woman said she caught a glimpse of it, too."

"You mean something in No. 12 Potter Street?"

"Yeah. She described it to me, but she was all het up and didn't get her story straight. What she said first didn't make sense. She accused Mrs. Bellman of running a sort of menagerie—swore she'd seen a queer-looking animal in one of the upper rooms. A kind of baboon, she said, only it was much too large and the face was sort of bluish-purple."

"She must have been crazy."

"No, she calmed down after a bit and admitted it might have been a person. There was no hair on the face, but her little boy said he had seen it crawling around on its hands and knees. Once, she swore, it sprang at the window as though it was catching flies or something. Heaven knows why I remember these darn things."

I thought of Mrs. Bellman sitting opposite me, so small, so rigid and so afraid. Then for some reason or other, I remembered one of her last remarks: "If *she* was still there. But it couldn't be Agnes."

"What did you do?" I asked Cobb.

"One of my men went round and talked to Mrs. Bellman. She was perfectly sensible. Said that one of her lodgers had a sick child. She promised to have them keep the shades drawn."

"And you heard nothing more?"

"No." Cobb seemed bored with the whole affair. "What you so interested for, anyway? We get that sort of case coming in every day."

"I wonder," I murmured and rang off.

I sat a moment, turning over in my mind another of Mrs. Bellman's remarks. "I've seen things—horrible things— things which couldn't possibly have been real." It looked as though there were other people in Potter Street who had seen strange things too.

III

THE GRIM APARTMENT

Doctor Hammond was a very old friend of mine, and it had been out of friendship alone that I had offered to look after his practice while he snatched a much deserved vacation. I found my life at the Regent Hotel extremely dull. My own house in Kenmore was only twenty miles away, but I had shut it up for the summer, and my eight-year-old daughter, Dawn, was away at the shore with friends. At this stage I think it was largely a sense of boredom that kept alive my interest in Mrs. Bellman. I am sure it was the depressing anecdotes of the traveling salesmen at the Regent that finally drove me to visit her.

There was still a month before Doctor Hammond returned. A month was long enough to make it worth my while to rent an apartment, and, judging from what I had heard, No. 12 Potter Street seemed interesting. Dreary it might be—but certainly not dull.

By five o'clock next evening, work at Doctor Hammond's office was over for the day. I strolled through the late August sunlight to Potter Street, which was located in one of the older sections of the town. The buildings were tall and dignified and, like Mrs. Bellman, possessed an air of decayed respectability. No. 12 was typical of the street, except perhaps for a rather exaggerated neatness. Any visions I might have had of a sinister, cob-webbed mansion were immediately dispelled. The windows were painted a fresh green, and their muslin curtains were bright and crisp. Mrs. Bellman's troubles, I reflected, had not made her neglect her duties as a neat, progressive landlady.

The sight of the actual hall confirmed this belief. It was scrupulously tidy without being arty or pretentious. There were the
usual pot ferns, and on a table by the deserted desk stood a large
vase of gladioluses. I wondered if they were the ones which had
achieved the remarkable transformation into zinnias.

By the window was a small wicker cage, in which perched a
very yellow canary. I crossed and regarded it with interest.

As I did so, I heard a vague fluttering sound behind me as
though a larger and heavier bird had broken loose. I turned to
see a plump woman of about fifty. She was smartly dressed in
a frilly, flouncy way—too smartly dressed, I thought. The blue
eyes that gazed into mine were pleasant—a little too pleasant.
This must be Miss Clymer who spent all her money on clothes
and got behind with her rent.

"Isn't he a tweetsie?" she crooned at the canary. She smiled
coyly. "Were you wanting to see someone?"

I asked when the desk clerk was likely to return. The plump
shoulders shrugged beneath the frills.

"Poor Jo! He has to do everything. She treats him more like a
slave than a nephew. It's no wonder that—"

She broke off. I remember Mrs. Bellman's cryptic remarks
about Jo—soft, spineless, no-good Jo.

The woman was still looking at me, and the blue eyes had
hardened "You're—you're not taking a room here, I suppose?"

There was something in the tone of her voice which suggested
vaguely that she was advising me against the step.

"Why—" I began, but she had turned away.

As she moved toward the passage beyond, she knocked
against one of the pot ferns. Out of the corner of my eye, I saw
something drop. When Miss Clymer had fluttered out of sight,
I bent to pick it up, and, as I did so, I felt a curious sensation—
a sensation which seemed far stronger than the occasion war-
ranted. In my hand I held a withered flower. I am no botanist, but
I needed no expert knowledge to tell me that the dried-up scrap
in my hand had once been a zinnia. I glanced across at the vase
of gladioluses. There was no question now as to the normality
of Mrs. Bellman's eyesight. Someone had been trying to frighten
her, and that someone, in removing the zinnias, had accidentally
dropped one of them into the pot fern.

I was just about to make a closer inspection when I heard footsteps on the stairs behind me. Two young people were entering

the hall. The boy was dark with a smooth, sallow face. The girl was a striking blonde—young, intense, and rather bold-looking. They were talking animatedly. At least, the boy was.

"We perforated a frog's viscera this afternoon," he was saying. "The experiment was a flop." He glanced at the letter rack and added, "No mail. Hell!"

"No mail. Hell!" repeated the girl with a glance at me, which made me feel uncomfortably conscious of my advancing years. "Come on. If we're late for dinner again, the old bag will say there's nothing but lunch left-overs."

They disappeared down the corridor, the dark boy talking incessantly.

Mr. Jay who makes smells about the house, I thought. And Miss Davenport who paints her face and runs in and out of men's bedrooms. Ever since I had found that withered zinnia, the boarders at No. 12 Potter Street had taken on an intense interest for me.

I lighted a cigarette and waited patiently. Soon there was a slow shuffling in the passage, and a tall, spectral man shambled in. His graying hair straggled across his low forehead, and his cadaverous cheeks moved slightly as though he were chewing something with toothless gums. Mrs. Bellman's nephew, Jo, looked much older and far more disintegrated than his aunt. So far, he was the only untidy thing I had seen in No. 12.

"Is Mrs. Bellman in?" I asked.

Instantly, a furtive expression came into his faded eyes. He pushed back the hair with a limp hand. "Sure, boy, sure. She's upstairs. She'll be down soon."

As he spoke, there was a sharp clatter of feminine heels on the stairs. I glanced around to see Mrs. Bellman herself, very brisk and landlady like. She looked like a perfectly normal, busy woman.

"Just a minute, Doctor Westlake," she called. "I will be right with you."

I saw her turn down a passage and then heard a door open. For a while there was silence, then once more I heard the footsteps hurrying toward me.

When Mrs. Bellman reappeared, she was an utterly different person. Her face was pale, her back stooped. She ran to my side and gripped my arm. She seemed utterly unconscious of her nephew's presence.

"Doctor Westlake. Thank God you're here. Quick, quick!"

She had turned and was almost dragging me after her down the passage. As we passed the stairs, I heard a woman's voice, high-pitched and querulous, calling: "Mrs. Bellman, Mrs. Bellman." But the landlady paid no attention. Her grip on my arm tightened as we turned a corner and drew up before a door. She pushed it open and ran in.

"Doctor Westlake. Is—it there? Can you see it?"

She was pointing to a table by the window.

I do not know what it was I had been expecting to see there, but it could hardly have been more bizarre than the actual truth. A small electric cooking plate stood on the table. I could see it was red hot, and on it perched the most ludicrously unlikely thing—a bowl of goldfish.

I say "ludicrous" because that was my first reaction. It did not last, however. Whether it was some of Mrs. Bellman's panic being transferred to me, I do not know. But suddenly the bowl, that neat room, the whole scrupulously tidy house seemed charged with a macabre, nightmarish quality.

I stood staring at the cheap, bubble-shaped bowl. The water must have been very hot for the fish lay flat and listless on the surface—all except one. It cambered blindly about—round and round in helpless, desperate circles. Then it lurched, and its fins flapped and collapsed as it showed its silver belly and floated up to the top of the bowl like a thin strip of silver gilt paper.

Mrs. Bellman was watching it, fascinated, I moved forward and snapped off the switch.

"Lucky I came," I said. "There's no question of your seeing things now, Mrs. Bellman."

The small eyes flashed to mine. "I don't know, Doctor Westlake. You see, I can't be sure I didn't do it myself."

I gazed at her in surprise.

"Yes. I was in here just a moment before I went upstairs. Why—why couldn't I have done it? Why couldn't I have done all these things and not known it? Lately, I've had almost too much to—"

She broke off, just as she had broken off the day before in my office. By a supreme effort of will, she seemed able to drive the whole matter from her mind.

I took the withered flower from my pocket and handed it to her. "Listen, Mrs. Bellman, I found this in one of the pot ferns.

It's obvious that someone in this house is trying to scare you. Don't you see? They would have taken away these goldfish, only we came in too quickly." Then a thought struck me. "By the way, who was the woman that called to you?"

Mrs. Bellman frowned. "What woman?"

"Just now someone called 'Mrs. Bellman' down the stairs. I wonder why she chose that particular moment."

"I didn't hear any voice," murmured the landlady wearily. "I guess I was too worked up."

I racked my brain trying to recall the exact tone of that voice. If it could be recognized, I felt, the mystery of No. 12 Potter Street might be well on its way to a solution. Mrs. Bellman had crossed to the table. I followed her.

"You're sure those fish are yours?" I asked.

"Why, of course." She peered at them. "I only bought them the other day. They're the sort everyone can get, but—" She paused, staring at me in surprise. "Come to think of it, I didn't have one with that black spot on it."

I smiled. "Well, that proves it once for all. Whoever's playing these tricks on you bought a canary like yours and a bowl of goldfish. They knew you wouldn't look at them closely. Then afterward they intended to replace your original ones."

She turned on me like a flash. "You mean—it *is* one of the lodgers? Then they'll still have them—my goldfish. We can find who it is."

"Too late," I grunted. "I'm afraid your goldfish will be as dead and gone as these by now. My suggestion is that you call in the police."

She looked like a brave little general after a lost battle. "There'll be no police here with their dirty boots," she snapped. "I've the reputation of the house to consider."

It was obviously no good pressing the point. Besides, as far as the authorities were concerned, there was nothing so particularly important about the murder of a canary and a few goldfish. I changed the subject and explained my plan of renting an apartment for a month. I saw an expression of relief pass across her face, but it quickly changed to one of doubt.

"Ye-es, certainly," she said at length. "I have the best apartment vacant. That is, I've been making some alterations. The men have only just stopped working. The rooms aren't exactly ordinary, but you're a doctor. You'll understand."

Before I had time to question this curious remark, she had produced a key and was moving to the door.

"I always keep this apartment locked," she murmured as we ascended the stairs. "You see, I don't want the boarders running in and out."

Before a room on the top floor she paused, and, as she did so, a door farther down the corridor opened.

"Oh, Mrs. Bellman."

"What is it, Mr. Washer?"

I turned to see a man standing in the passage. He was middle-aged and rather plump. His face was very brown but he looked puffy and not particularly healthy. He wore a dark-blue shirt and a white tie. His gestures were curiously mincing.

"There've been no clean towels today, Mrs. Bellman. That's the second time this week."

Mr. Washer was eying me with strange interest. A soft, rather feminine hand fingered the tie.

"All right, all right," Mrs. Bellman said rather testily. "I'll have some sent up."

"Thank you. Thank you indeed." Mr. Washer was still looking at me. He glanced once more over his shoulder as he retired into his room. So this was the gentleman who played his piano while the rest of the world was sleeping.

"It's my best really," said Mrs. Bellman as we entered the apartment. "But the rent will be reasonable—to you, Doctor Westlake. There's an outside phone, too, in case you are expecting calls from your patients. With the other rooms you have to call down to the switchboard in the vestibule."

It was a remarkably luxurious suite of rooms—far larger and more modern than one would have expected in this otherwise rather modest establishment. Even so, I did not like it. There was something cold and depressing about its very modernity. As the landlady closed the door, I saw to my surprise that there were two heavy iron bolts on the inside.

Mrs. Bellman was pointing to an untidy heap of bricks and mortar in the fireplace.

"The workmen have been opening up the hearth," she explained apologetically. "We used to use it as an outlet for hot-air heat, but we've changed to steam now and I think an open fireplace makes a room so much more cheery—particularly as it's one of those wide, old-fashioned chimneys."

I nodded absently, thinking it would take more than a fireplace to cheer up this particular room. As I tried to analyze what it was that depressed me, I noticed an enormous electric fan hanging down from the ceiling above my head. It was of the type that usually is seen only in large halls or workshops. The shaft was thick and strong. The blades looked as large as an airplane propeller. There was something cruel and relentless about it.

Mrs. Bellman switched it on, and it stirred the musty, prisonlike air. Even so, it was still stuffy. I crossed to open one of the windows and noticed that they were guarded with thin iron bars.

As I looked out, I found that I commanded a close view of the house opposite. I could see inside one of the windows across the way. A little boy was eating his supper.

Instantly, my mind flashed to the bolts on the door, to the conversation I had had the day before with Cobb. One of the neighbor's children had been frightened by something he had seen in a window at No. 12—some strange misshapen creature with a bluish-purple face. My instinct told me at once which window it had been.

Mrs. Bellman was laughing—again, that strange, humorless laugh. "This apartment has been rather a problem. Every one in the house wants it."

Something in the tone of her voice made me turn. "They do, do they?" I asked.

"Miss Clymer says she wants it because there's a roof garden attached and she likes the sun, though Heaven knows how she supposes she can pay the extra rent. Mr. Washer wants his sister to come and live with him here and thinks there'd be more room for his grand piano. Mr. Jay thinks he could use that back room for his chemistry experiments. I believe the Browns want it, and so does Miss Davenport. They all want it, but they're not going to have it."

"Don't let me interfere with any other plans," I said hurriedly. "After all, I'll only be staying a month."

"You couldn't stay for longer," she said bluntly. "My previous tenant is coming back. At least, I think so. It's to have things brightened up for her that I'm getting the hearth fixed."

At this point, a sleek ginger cat entered the room, its bushy tail erect. It ran toward Mrs. Bellman with a little miaow. Then it jumped onto a chair and started to claw at the front of her dress.

"Go away, Hilda—shoo." The tone was sharp but not unkind. As she spoke, Mrs. Bellman tried to tilt the chair to dislodge the cat. Neither of them budged.

"I'd forgotten," she said, as she picked up the cat and put it outside. "All the furniture is fixed to the floor. I hope you won't find it inconvenient. I can't have things altered—not if my previous tenant is coming back."

"And who," I asked, "used to live here?"

Mrs. Bellman glanced at me sharply and threw a swift look at the half-open door. "None of the others know, but I can tell you since you're a doctor. A woman called Mrs. Salt rented the apartment over a year ago. It was for her stepdaughter." Her voice lowered. "She was—afflicted. You know, doctor, one of those children that have to be kept out of sight."

I sat on the arm of one of the immovable chairs and lighted a cigarette.

"'Yes," continued Mrs. Bellman, "Agnes, her name is. She's fifteen but you couldn't tell how old she is. It's—it's just like an animal. She can't talk, can't do anything for herself. She even has to be fed by hand. And sometimes she's difficult—destructive. That's why the furniture had to be fastened down. Mrs. Salt had that great big electric fan put in because the doctor said the heat made Agnes worse. It's a terrible thing—terrible."

"But she ought to have been in an institution!" I exclaimed.

Mrs. Bellman nodded. "That's what I always said. But there was something in her father's will. He was rich and he wanted his wife to give the child a chance. They spared no expense, but after all—"

"Wasn't it rather hard on the other boarders?" I asked.

"Oh, they didn't know. You see, the girl didn't make any sound—not even when she had one of her fits." Mrs. Bellman crossed to the wall and indicated a dumb-waiter. "We sent the meals up in this. The others just thought there was an invalid here. Of course, Agnes never went out."

"But how did she get air?" I asked, moving to the open window.

Mrs. Bellman indicated a door. "There's a special roof garden made for her up there. Up those steps.

"Miss Furnivall—the elder one—she used to live here with her. She acted as a sort of nurse. Mrs. Salt never came here herself. It was as though she couldn't bear the sight of the child. And I don't blame her."

Mrs. Bellman kicked a piece of brick off the carpet.

"And she's returning—this—this unfortunate creature?" I asked.

"Yes. I heard from Mrs. Salt's lawyer a week or two ago. She had taken Agnes to Arizona for some sort of treatment, and he told me that she was coming back next month."

Mrs. Bellman had crossed to draw the thick green curtains. "She paid the rent here for three months after she left. Didn't want anyone else in the apartment, she said. So you see why I couldn't let any of the others have it. But the three months are up now and she can't object to you—especially since you're a doctor." She moved to the door. "I'll send Jo up to clean the fireplace."

"Thanks."

Mrs. Bellman had paused. Her voice was curiously altered. "I'm glad you're staying, young man. Somehow, with you here, it'll seem safer. I've been thinking out what you said about things that have been happening. Someone is trying to frighten me out of here. I'm practically sure." She stood on the threshold, very small and determined. "But they're not going to succeed—not if they have to kill me."

With this remark, she was gone. I heard the hard, mirthless laugh echoing along the passage outside.

IV

THE BOARDERS LOOK ON

The boarders at No. 12 Potter Street had dined early, it seemed. When I went downstairs in search of food, I had the dining room and one silent Negro waiter to myself. There was a dreary, deserted air about the white-clothed tables. It lingered on in the passages as I returned to my room.

Jo had cleaned up the hearth in my absence. Someone had dusted the place, too, and made the bed. I was glad to see that my bags had arrived from the Regent Hotel. I started to open them and sort things out. The steady whir of the huge electric fan annoyed me, but I did not switch it off, for the night was close, and the stale, musty odor still lingered in the air.

A few minutes later, there was a loud, single knock on the door. I called to come in and turned to see the blond Miss Davenport standing on the threshold. She was leaning nonchalantly against the doorpost, a cigarette dropping from her red mouth. The gaze from her violet eyes moved slowly around the room and then rested on me.

"Unpacking!" she said. "Quite domesticated already, aren't you?" She moved and stood with her back to the fireplace. "I came to see if you were going to object to smells."

"Smells?" I echoed in mild surprise.

"Yeah. Jay's room's underneath this one. He's in chemistry and I'm physiology—both at the Tech. We do experiments together and sometimes they smell terribly. Wondered whether they reached up here. Not of course that we could do anything about it, if they did, but we thought we'd let you know what it was."

Once more the violet eyes traveled round the apartment. I had the distinct impression that it was the rooms that interested her rather than myself.

"As it happens," I remarked, "there is rather a musty smell about the place."

"Too bad." Miss Davenport grinned and puffed smoke through her nostrils. "You'll get used to it soon. I have. In fact, my nose is so hardened by the chem. labs that I couldn't tell B. O. from eau de Cologne any more." She pushed her herself away from the fireplace and strolled toward the bedroom. "Nice place you've got here. Frankly, I wish Jay and I could turn you out, then the old hag might let us have this place. We could make that back room into a swell lab."

I followed the surprising Miss Davenport into the bedroom. Despite the unpleasantly chemical turn of phrase, she was distinctly attractive—even if the attractiveness itself was a trifle chemical. Her hair, I suspected, was not innocent of chemicals, while her lips and cheeks were frankly martyrs to science.

I had started some banal remark when a sound from the next room made me break off. Someone had begun to play the piano—very softly and sweetly. I recognized the piece as one of the well-known Chopin preludes.

Miss Davenport had been fixing her hair at my mirror. She turned around swiftly. "Heaven! That Mr. Washer! He plays Chopin all day, all night. And have you seen him, my dear?" Her voice mocked mincingly. "He's just the sweetest thing with a green tie and rings. Give me a good old healthy smell any day."

She moved back to the living room. "He's got a sister who's always visiting him. If you ask me, she's the only woman that's ever likely to get into that room."

Miss Davenport threw her cigarette into the fireplace and crushed it beneath her toe.

"Well, I've got to be getting back. Jay's got a couple of experiments started." At the door she paused and jerked a thumb at the wall of the next room, from which the strains of Chopin were still issuing. "If you get any trouble from that fat old sissy," she said, "just call on me. I've got a pretty good command of the English language."

I needed no reassurance on that point.

She had been gone hardly a minute when the music stopped and there was another knock on the door. This time it was Mr. Washer.

He paused on the threshold, rubbing his plump hands together. "I'm sorry to trouble you, sorry indeed. I just wanted to ask you whether my piano annoyed you. I love Chopin at night, but I always stop at eleven."

I assured him rather curtly that I liked music, too. He hesitated and then stepped in. Just as with Miss Davenport, his eyes flashed instantly around the room. The well-manicured fingers went to his tie.

"There was another little point. Mrs. Bellman tells me you are a doctor. I wonder if you could give me your opinion of artificial sunray lamps."

It hardly seemed a topic of grave importance, but he kept me talking about it for some twenty minutes.

"Yes, doctor, I have a lamp of my own. I like a sun tan, you know. More becoming, I—"

He broke off as though he were listening. I listened, too. Outside the door there had been a faint metallic sound. It came again and then again until it developed into a slow, steady noise that was halfway between a creak and a clank.

"Sounds like the family skeleton dragging its chain," I said.

He laughed again. "Oh, that's just the younger Miss Furnivall. She's a cripple, poor thing." He glanced at me swiftly. "I often think there's something funny about those sisters. But then, when you've been here longer, you'll realize there are a lot of funny people in this house." An inquisitive look came into his eye. "I wonder why a successful young doctor like you chooses to live in this sort of a place."

For the second time that day, it seemed, someone was trying to warn me against No. 12 Potter Street. I made some banal remark about its being a pleasant apartment.

Mr. Washer rose and started to walk about the room. "It is very attractive. I have a sister, you know, who's very close to me. She travels for a piano firm and isn't often in town. I wanted to have these rooms myself so that she could always come and stay with me"—he poked his head into the bedroom—"but oddly enough Mrs. Bellman wouldn't rent them to me. I wondered if perhaps—" He broke off. "I've had to get a room for my sister in the house over the way. Just a little attic, you know. It's most unsatisfactory."

By now he had made a complete round of the apartment. He smiled and patted the back of his neck. "Well, I must be getting along." He paused and then added: "I'm expecting my sister any minute. Perhaps you'd let her come in some time and look around. I know she'd love it."

I told him that, as far as I was concerned, the apartment would be free in a month, and ushered him out as politely as I was able.

I did not have to wait long. The piano had just started once more when my door was thrown open. A dark, very athletic-looking middle-aged woman stood on the threshold. She remained absolutely motionless, her handsome brown eyes fixed on me.

"Oh, I—that is, I'm sorry. I saw the lights and wondered. You see, I—er—used to occupy this apartment. The name's Furnivall—Constance Furnivall."

"Won't you come in?" I sighed. "You might like to take a look around, too."

Her piercing, restless glance swept across the room, pausing, it seemed, on the great electric fan.

For a moment, I thought an expression of horror passed across her face, as though there were something about that propeller-like device which brought back awful memories. I remembered that this was the woman who had acted as nurse to the unfortunate Agnes.

"Please come in," I repeated.

She shook her dark hair. "No, I wouldn't bother you. Silly of me. I didn't know this apartment was rented."

I did not believe her. I knew that her sister had been clanking about outside. I could tell, too, from Miss Constance's eyes that she was withholding something.

"Well," she said curtly. "I'm sorry. Good night."

She turned abruptly and disappeared.

After she had gone, I sat down in one of the immovable chairs, listening idly to the rapid Chopin prelude and wondering what in Heaven's name was wrong with the boarders at No. 12 Potter Street. I found myself reviewing them in my mind: Miss Clymer, the fat inquisitive spinster who was behind on her rent; Mr. Washer, an obviously effeminate man who played his piano at all hours of the night and used a sun-ray lamp; Miss Constance Furnivall, the abrupt, muscular ex-nurse with her crippled, eavesdropping sister; Mr. Jay, the ardent young chemist; Miss Davenport, his outspoken and attractive assistant; and finally the mysterious Browns whom Mrs. Bellman had described as her "only good tenants."

For all their oddities, they seemed a fairly typical cross section of almost any boarding house in America. It was even possible that their interest in my apartment was based purely on curiosity. But I did not believe it. One of them, I knew, had something vital to conceal. One of them was doing his utmost to scare Mrs. Bellman out of her wits. I wondered how long it would be before they tried to frighten me out of my rooms.

V

STEPS ON THE ROOF

With the Chopin still rippling in the next room, I began to complete my unpacking. Stuffed under some shirts, I discovered a photograph of my daughter, Dawn. As I looked at her sane, smiling face, I thought of that other child—the child who had recently lived in this apartment with its fixed chairs and its enormous electric fan. I am not normally sensitive, but there was something about the contrast between the two girls that made the room seem suddenly repulsive to me. I thought of Agnes being fed like an animal, being taken up on the roof for air, having her meals sent up on the dumb-waiter so that the world should never see her. The whirring of the electric fan seemed to become louder, drowning the sweet strains of music and making them harsher, more mechanical.

My mind was still running on these thoughts when it happened—the last of the amazing serio-comic incidents which were so soon to culminate in real, brutal tragedy.

I remember a clock downstairs striking ten, and then, suddenly, there was a violent knocking on my door. I hurried into the living room and opened to Mrs. Bellman. She was dressed in an old Japanese kimono wrapped very tightly around her sparse figure. The gray hair straggled across her forehead.

"Again," she whispered, and this time there was no fear in her voice, only anger—a grim, smoldering anger. "Again it's happened. Come, you can see for yourself."

Leaving the door open, I hurried after her down the stairs. Behind us, the Chopin grew fainter and fainter, fading to a whisper as Mrs. Bellman drew me toward her room.

"Look, look!" she exclaimed, pointing to the lintel above her door. Then suddenly, she broke off. "She's—she's gone, but I saw it. I swear I saw it. She was there."

There was something horrible about the sight of that small, fierce woman pointing upward—pointing at nothingness.

"What is it?" I asked.

"Hilda." Mrs. Bellman clutched my arm. "I was just going to bed when there was a knock at the door. I went to answer it, but there was no one there—nothing except Hilda." She gave a curious dry little sob. "She was hanging from that hook by a piece of ribbon—red silk ribbon."

"Hilda!" I exclaimed dazedly, half supposing for an instant that she must refer to some person.

"Yes, yes, my cat. You saw her this afternoon. She was dead. I tell you. Hanged."

My mind was still confused by the swiftness of this latest happening.

Then my eyes caught something red against the white paint of the lintel. I reached upward toward an old iron hook. Twisted around it was a fragment of ribbon. I pulled it down and stared it. Then I glanced at Mrs. Bellman.

"Yes," I exclaimed, "it was there all right. Someone must have taken it away when you came up to find me. They couldn't have passed us up the stairs. If we're quick, we can catch them."

I started down the corridor and heard Mrs. Bellman hurrying after me.

"It's no use," she called. "There's the back stairs. Any one could have gotten up to their rooms by now."

We searched, but found nothing. When we returned to her room, I took hold of Mrs. Bellman's arm.

"Listen," I said. "I have a friend in the police force. This thing is getting beyond a joke. Don't you think you should put him onto it?"

Mrs. Bellman wrapped the kimono more tightly around her and drew herself up. "There'll be no police here," she snapped. "As I told you this afternoon, I have the reputation of the house to consider. If an officer set foot in here, I should be ruined. Besides, I'm not afraid any more—not now I know for sure that it isn't my imagination." Her thin lips broke into a smile, "I'm not scared of people. Give 'em rope and they'll hang themselves. There's nothing to fear so long as we have locks on our doors."

She turned and walked into her room, shutting the door behind her. I heard the hard scrape of the key in the lock. "Give 'em rope and they'll hang themselves."

I moved back to the stairs. As I did so, I heard footsteps. A young man was slouching toward me front the hall, his head down, one hand thrust deep in his trousers pocket. For an instant, his eyes gazed into mine, and he gave me a gruff good night. Then he strode on up the stairs.

As he passed me, I caught a glimpse of something white in his hand. At first I thought it was a piece of paper. Then it moved and I saw a small, beady eye. It was Mr. Jay, and he was carrying an albino cat.

"So," I reflected, as I followed him upstairs, "our young friends' experiments aren't just pure chemistry."

The music still floated out from Mr. Washer's room as I returned to my apartment. Apparently, all the excitement in the world could not keep him from his Chopin. I was beginning to feel rather bored with Chopin—bored, too, with the pointless monotony of events at No. 12. After all, if Mrs. Bellman was not willing to have the police help her, there was very little that I could do. Besides, I had had a hard day and I need sleep.

As I paused a moment outside my room, the music stopped and I heard Mr. Washer saying:

"Well, my dear, that's all for tonight. I'm sure you're tired."

Feeling no desire to eavesdrop, I was moving into my room, when Mr. Washer's door opened.

"Good night, Grace," I heard him say.

There was a soft feminine reply and a woman stepped out into the corridor, shutting the door behind her. She gave me a casual nod and walked briskly toward the stairs. It was dark in the passage, but sufficient light fell from my room for me to catch a glimpse of this woman's face. She was delicately dressed, delicately powdered and looked like an even more feminine Mr. Washer. Obviously, this was the piano-selling sister of whom he had spoken.

She had hardly reached the top of the staircase when the music started again. Those quiet, flowing melodies were becoming ineradicably associated in my mind with the house.

I entered the apartment and closed the door behind me. At first everything seemed perfectly normal. The electric fan was roaring. The heavy green curtains flapped slightly in the breeze. That strange, musty odor still lingered, striking my nostrils as I moved toward a chair.

I was about to sit down when I saw something which was so fantastic that, for an instant, I felt that Agnes Salt must once more have come to take possession of her dwelling place.

Propped on the white wooden mantelpiece was the body of a large ginger cat. Around its neck, in a garish, chocolate-box festoon, was a piece of wide red ribbon. The bow had been arranged with meticulous care, but, as I stepped over to examine it, I saw at once that the ribbon had been pulled so viciously tight that the animals head did not seem to belong to its body.

Gradually, my thoughts collected themselves and I realized what had happened. As I had anticipated, the campaign to frighten me out of my rooms had begun. The person who had worked on Mrs. Bellman was now starting on me.

For a moment I stood staring at the cat, revolving various lines of action in my brain. I could call Cobb and turn over to him the whole preposterous affair. I could leave No. 12 and let whoever this maniac was do with it what he wished. I could go down and discuss the matter with Mrs. Bellman. But, as my reason reasserted itself, I felt a growing determination to stay. After all, it takes more than a dead cat to frighten a hard-working doctor out of his rooms. My friend would have to try harder than that. As Mrs. Bellman had said, there was nothing to fear as long as we had locks on our doors. I crossed and shot the heavy bolts.

It was not until I had locked myself in for the night that I remembered the cat. It could hardly be left on the mantelpiece. Finally, I picked it up, dropped it into a scrap basket and lowered it to the kitchen by the dumb-waiter. It was only after I had done so that I reflected, almost with amusement, that I was probably providing another scare for Mrs. Bellman on the morrow.

While I was undressing, I became conscious of the steady whirring of the electric fan. I went to turn it off and, as I did so, I heard in the passage outside the sound of limping footsteps, accompanied by that strange metallic creak on which I had remarked to Mr. Washer earlier that evening. Outside my door, I fancied the footsteps paused. The younger Miss Furnivall, it seemed, kept later hours than the other boarders at No. 12.

Despite my physical weariness, I did not fall to sleep for some time. The Chopin still filtered through from the next room, but it was not that which kept me awake. In fact, I found it rather soothing. I recognized a tune which my daughter, Dawn, had been struggling with in her second year of piano lessons. It was pleasant to think of her, biting her tongue and bending earnestly forward over the keys. I began to feel drowsy.

I had just dropped off into a light doze—the type which is broken by the least unfamiliar sound—when something awakened me. I pushed myself into a sitting position. Then I heard it again—the sound of stealthy footsteps above my head. For a moment, my tired brain was at a loss to discover why these noises should have disturbed me. Then I realized that my room was on the top floor and that the footsteps must be moving about on the roof.

There is something primitive in one that is instinctively alarmed by the sound of footsteps on a roof. I sat up in bed, straining my ears, feeling my heart beating unnecessarily faster. Above me the noises continued with slow, muffled monotony. I lay down again, trying to sleep and telling myself that the whole business was no concern of mine. Even so, I could not rest.

At length I could stand it no longer. Pulling on a bath robe, I hurried into the main room and opened the door which Mrs. Bellman had told me led to Agnes Salt's roof garden.

As the door swung back, a blue patch of moonlight fell at my feet. At the head of the broad flight of wooden steps, I could see a pale strip of August sky, studded with a few stars. A train hooted, and in the moment of quiet that followed, the footsteps sounded again—moving, it seemed, away to my right.

Slowly, silently, I began to creep upward, the soft notes of Mr. Washer's Chopin following after me. As I climbed, I had a vivid mental picture of Miss Furnivall, her muscular arms carrying her strange patient up those steps. It added to the mad, nightmarish quality of the escapade.

Within a few seconds, I had reached the top of the stairs. I paused there, listening. Then, slowly, I pushed my way up and crouched low on the roof at the foot of a chimney stack.

At first it was difficult to make out my bearings. The moon had slipped behind a cloud and I had only the dim starlight to guide me. Gradually, I took in the details of the roof garden. It was hardly a cheerful place. A fence of stout six-foot iron railings surrounded it on every side, and the surface of the roof was slightly sticky with tar.

Keeping in the shadow of the railings, I made my way in the direction of the footsteps, which sounded louder now, and heavier. Slowly, I straightened, and, as I did so, the moon broke out from behind the cloud. It must have struck directly on me, for I heard a confused scuffling, and, for a second, I caught a glimpse of a figure scrambling away between the broad chimney stacks.

"Who's there?" I shouted. "Who is it?"

My cry echoed hollowly across the tiles. There was no answering sound. Once more I saw the figure, this time, silhouetted against the sky. I could tell it was a woman. A fragment of skirt blew out in the night breeze. It was obvious that she had seen me, for she started and something fell from her hand. Then she slipped into the shadows.

Mrs. Salt had taken good care that her daughter should not escape across the roof. The iron railings were pointed and bent inward. It was the devil of a job scrambling over. I managed it finally and dropped down onto the other part of the roof, but I knew that my chances of catching the night prowler were small.

Mechanically, however, I started forward. The roof sloped steeply and dangerously to the street below. I clutched onto a chimney stack for support and, as I did so, my foot struck against something soft—the something which this unknown woman had dropped.

For one moment I stopped dead, expecting to find there I know not what. But soon I shook off all nightmarish notions and bent to pick up the thing at my feet. At first I thought it was some sort of feminine garment. Then, as I lifted it more closely to my eyes, I saw what it was. In my hands I held a large, cretonne laundry bag.

This seemed the final touch of fantasy in this incredible evening. Mysteries toppled over one another here at No. 12 Potter Street, and yet there was in them all an element of wild, almost humorous craziness. A canary is stabbed with a paper knife. A cat is strangled with a red silk ribbon. And now a woman creeps about the roof and leaves behind her —a laundry bag.

I took the thing back with me to my room and sat gazing at it. The name, "E. Bellman," had been worked on it in green cotton. This hardly surprised me, since so many mad, disconnected things were happening in this respectable boarding house. So many strange people were doing so many strange things. Something was afoot, I know. Something complicated and dreadful—yet something which would be perfectly logical if only one could find the key, if one could fit together all these crazy scraps of puzzle and arrange them into one complete, unified picture.

Before going to sleep I decided to telephone Cobb and tell him unofficially, at least, all that had happened since my last call.

His clear, matter-of-fact voice reassured me somewhat, and I found it a relief to be laughed at and called an old woman.

Yet, despite his flippancy, I could tell that he did not take the matter altogether lightly.

VI

THAT DREADFUL REVELATION

In the bright sunlight of the next morning, the uncanny incidents that had taken place at No. 12 seemed rather remote and trivial. After all, I was responsible for Doctor Hammond's patients, and sick people are of more importance in the scheme of things than problems involving dead cats, goldfish, laundry bags, and frightened landladies. I was working hard all day, and it was not until dinner time that I put in an appearance at No. 12.

All the boarders were at their tables when I reached the dining room. It was quite a relief to see that the mysterious Mr. and Mrs. Brown were a stolid, middle-aged couple whom one could not possibly associate with anything disagreeable or sinister. As to the others, they were all doing what would be expected of them. Mr. Jay was gesticulating over his soup plate and describing some unpleasant anatomical experiment to Miss Davenport, whose violet eyes were alight with scientific interest. Miss Clymer, pink and frilly, was shuffling her salad and half cricking her neck in the hope of gleaning some tidbit of scandal from all quarters of the room at once. Mr. Washer was playing an adagio movement with his fingers as he waited for his next course.

But most of all, I was interested in the Furnivalls who sat at the table next to mine and who gave me a frigid "Good evening," as I took my seat. I tried not to stare at the crippled Miss Sophie, but, having once looked, it was difficult to keep my eyes away. For a woman no longer young, she was one of the most beautiful I have ever seen. Her fragile feminine charm was in marked contrast to the heavy, rather masculine handsomeness of her sister. It was hard to believe that these two strangely dissimilar women were related. It was hard, too, to believe that the pale, Dresden china Miss Sophie was an incurable cripple.

The meal was plain but well cooked. By the time I had reached my dessert, people were beginning to drift out of the room. The waiter had just vanished into the kitchen when a rather extraordinary incident happened—one which reminded me that the unusual could invariably be counted upon at No. 12.

Miss Davenport left Mr. Jay at the table and strolled across to the Furnivalls. She laid a newspaper at Miss Constance's side.

"I brought you the *Grovestown Times* just to let you know you aren't missing anything." She shot me an impudent glance and added, as if to shock the two spinsters. "I hope you've got your underwear straightened out, doctor. Or did Chopin come in to help you?"

She grinned, produced a cigarette, and wandered away.

After she had left, I saw Miss Constance Furnivall pick up the paper and glance through it as she sipped her coffee. My seat was directly facing hers so I could not help seeing everything that happened. For a while she rustled the pages absently, then suddenly her eyes hardened in a fixed stare. The strong line of her jaw slackened.

"Sophie." she gasped, pointing to one of the columns. "Sophie, did—did she do it on purpose?"

A hand went to her throat and she half rose from her chair. Her head moved from side to side in a little helpless gesture that seemed quite out of keeping with her neat, efficient appearance.

"Sophie!"

I jumped from my chair and reached her side just in time to catch her as she collapsed.

Miss Sophie seemed at a complete loss. She stood gazing blankly as her sister.

"It's only a faint," I reassured her. "Let's get her up to her room."

With the help of the waiter, I supported Miss Constance upstairs. Miss Sophie walked behind, dragging her crippled leg and clutching tightly to the newspaper.

The two spinsters occupied a small room containing divans which were converted into beds at night-time. Having explained that I was a doctor, I did what I could for Miss Constance through it was obvious to me that nothing was seriously the matter. At length her eyes flickered open and played unseeingly on my face.

"Feel better?" I asked.

"Yes, yes. I'm so sorry. Where's that newspaper?"

Miss Sophie fussed forward with a glass of water. As she bent over her sister, I took the opportunity of glancing at the *Grovestown Times* which had been laid on a chair at my side. Here, I thought, must lie the clue to Miss Constance's unexpected collapse. The paper was turned to a middle page. One column caught my eye particularly. It was headed: "TWENTY YEARS AGO TODAY." Beneath it there was a photograph of a striking looking woman who, despite her old-fashioned clothes and style of couture, was unmistakably the woman I knew as Miss Constance Furnivall.

Swiftly I picked up the paper and read:

Twenty Years ago today, the notorious Mrs. Constance Farrar was sentenced to fifteen years penal servitude for the killing of her husband. It will be remembered by those who—

But I did not get any further. Miss Sophie had snatched the paper and was glaring at me angrily. In the hard illumination from the ceiling light, she did not seem as pretty as she had at dinner time. The Dresden china features were coarser, the white skin rougher.

"It's no use, Sophie." Constance Furnivall had risen from the couch and was staring dully in front of her. "It's no use. He's seen."

Not only had I seen it, but I remembered the case clearly as indeed any one must have done who lived any length of time in the neighborhood of Grovestown. The Farrer murder case had been one of the most sensational crimes in the annals of the country.

It had never entered my head to wonder what had happened to that glamorous, tragic woman who had shot her husband in a fit of passion on discovering his infidelity. There was something infinitely pathetic in finding her here in a boarding house, poor, masquerading as a spinster, and obviously living in dread lest someone should piece together the truth and reawaken for her the horrors of the past.

Both sisters were staring at me—Miss Sophie with a shrewd, bitter expression in her eyes, Miss Constance, dark, smoldering, and defiant.

"There's no need to tell me, Miss Furnivall," I murmured as kindly as I could. "The past is none of my business. I'm sure no one else will recognize that photograph. With me it was merely chance—the association of your fainting and the newspaper."

Miss Constance's powerful hands lay in her lap. "It's no use," she whispered bitterly. "You can't live things down. They all find out in time—just like that Davenport woman did tonight."

"Constance!" Sophie was bending fiercely over her sister. "You mustn't talk that way. You mustn't. You know I can't bear it."

Constance gazed at me. "Poor Sophie. It's just as bad for her."

"Stop it." Sophie's voice had risen to a hysterical scream. "If you're going to say those things, I—I won't stay."

The Dresden china face was livid with anger. She shot me a glance almost of hatred and limped out, slamming the door behind her.

Constance followed her with grave eyes. "She can't bear talking about the trial," she said simply. "You see, that was how her leg was injured. She was crushed when the mob crowded around me coming out of the courthouse after the sentence."

So many strange things had happened at No. 12 that the presence of a convicted killer in the house no longer seemed unusual. Besides, there was a certain courage and defiance about Miss Constance which I rather admired. I waited in silence, for her to continue.

"I've been out of prison for five years now," she said at length, "and no one would give me a job. That is, no one until — Mrs. Salt."

"Yes," I said quietly, "I know about Mrs. Salt."

Constance Furnivall started. "That child? You know about — er — Agnes? It was ghastly, but I had to take work. The money was good, and I needed money terribly."

"You acted as a kind of nurse, I gather?"

"Yes. I put an advertisement in the paper saying I would do anything. There was only one reply. It was from Mrs. Salt. I had to live with Agnes for nearly six months. Sometimes I thought I couldn't stand it any longer."

"What was this Mrs. Salt like?" I asked curiously.

The dark eyes widened slightly. "I never saw the stepmother. I was sent here with instructions that an apartment was already prepared. The next day a trained nurse brought Agnes. And then, at the end, when Mrs. Salt took the child away to Arizona, I was sent my salary and two hundred dollars extra and told to go."

The elusive Mrs. Salt was beginning to intrigue me. I felt more and more strongly that either she or her unfortunate stepdaughter was somehow involved in the strange happenings at No. 12.

"But Agnes—" I began only to break off at the sound of a knock at the door.

Miss Furnivall called a rather shaky "Come in," and Jo stood on the threshold, tall and spectral, pushing the shaggy mane of hair from his low forehead.

"Doctor Westlake," he said in his thick, almost unintelligible voice. "There's a woman on the phone wants to talk to you. I heard your bell ringing as I went by," he added by way of explanation, "so I got my duplicate key and answered it."

With a few parting admonitions to Constance Furnivall, I hurried along the corridor to my room. The thought passed through my mind that Jo had no business breaking into my apartment and answering my telephone calls. Had it, I wondered, been mere officiousness on his part? Or was he, like every one else the house, finding an excuse to be alone in those extraordinary rooms?

A woman's voice spoke to me over the phone. Her mother was dangerously sick. She was, she said, one of Doctor Hammond's regular patients. Would I please come quickly? She gave an address.

There was something curiously familiar about the voice. I had the vague impression that I had heard it somewhere before— quite recently. But I was too hurried to give the matter much thought.

I picked up my emergency case and went downstairs. As I passed through the hall, I saw Mrs. Bellman for the first time that evening. She was standing by the desk, talking to a plump nondescript woman whom, I recognized as Mrs. Brown.

The landlady glanced at me as I crossed to the door. "Going out, Doctor Westlake?" she said. "You'll need your coat. It's a raw evening."

"Haven't time," I said. "Someone's ill."

Her voice followed me out into the street. Vaguely I heard something about a fire—the open fireplace—and that "things would be more cheery."

It was raining hard. By the time I reached the address, I was soaking wet. I rang the bell and explained my business to a maid who informed me none too politely that no one of the name I mentioned lived there and that no one was sick. I tried several other houses with the same result. Like Mrs. Bellman, it seemed, I had been the victim of a practical joke. At first it infuriated me, then I began to feel a sensation of alarm. Someone had wanted to get me away from No. 12. Why?

I arrived home, soaked to the skin. In the hall I found Miss Clymer, crooning over the canary. She eyed me sharply, but I did not stop. I hurried upstairs and along the dark passage to my room, strangely uneasy.

The apartment was in darkness. As I entered, I noticed that the windows were wide open, but the strange, fetid atmosphere still lingered in the room. It was, if anything, more marked.

I fumbled for the switch. As I did so, I could hear the purring of the electric fan. There was something about the sound I did not like. It seemed slower, more jerky—somehow sinister. Besides, I had not remembered turning it on before I left.

At length, my fingers found the switch, and the whole room was flooded with vivid illumination.

If I live to be as old as I sometimes feel, I shall never forget the horror of that moment, that sudden dazzling moment of light—that dreadful revelation.

The huge electric fan was turning slowly round and round. It was only then that I realized its true power. Hanging from it, with her hair moving slightly in the breeze—gyrating and oscillating with the halting turn of the blades—was the body of a woman. Her toes were pointing downward barely an inch from the floor. On her face was a look of incredulous horror, as though death had caught her just as she had witnessed another (and even more terrible) of those humorless jests which had become so frequent at No. 12 Potter Street.

As I stared, I noticed something else—something which lent an even more macabre quality to this ghastly spectacle. The face and hands were black—nor was it merely the blue-blackness of asphyxiation. They were covered in grime—soot. Even the white hair was darkened.

It was the body of Mrs. Bellman, but the face and hands were those of a Negress.

For a moment I was so stupefied that I did not even switch off the fan. I gazed blankly at that slight body as it revolved round and round in its grotesque pirouette. Then I noticed that with each revolution, it was moving upward, getting nearer and nearer to the shaft. The cord by which it was tied was being slowly twisted as in a fantastic Maypole dance.

I dashed across the room and snapped off the switch. Then I jumped onto a chair and hacked through the cord with one of my surgical knives. The body fell to the floor in a small, tumbled mound.

I bent to examine it. The skin of the face was almost entirely covered with grime, but I could tell immediately that death was due to strangulation. The cord around the wizened neck was tight—so tight that it was almost obscured by folds of flesh. Instantly, my mind flashed back to the ginger cat, the cat with its murderous bow of red ribbon. My fingers pushed through the ruffled hair. On the back of Mrs. Bellman's head was a large swelling.

As I gazed at that pitiful little figure, crumpled on the floor, I thought of the dreadful irony of those words Mrs. Bellman had spoken to me at our first meeting.

"I've always been a working woman. Doctor Westlake. And I hope to go on working as long as my two legs carry me."

VII

DOWN THE CHIMNEY

I called Cobb at once, but even before I had finished speaking to him, I felt convinced that I could piece together the stages by which Mrs. Bellman had met her death.

The fireplace told the story. In it were some logs and blackened kindling. I remembered the few words she had called after me through the front door about building a fire—that it would make things more cheery. Knowing I would be cold and wet on my return, she had pathetically tried to make the apartment look more cozy. Her murderer must have crept in while she was bending over the grate, while she was setting a match to the first fire in the new hearth of which she had been so proud. A blow from behind, and she would have fallen forward with her head in the fireplace. Hence the grime and soot on her face.

It was easy to reconstruct the rest. A cord had been attached to the neck. The unconscious form of Mrs. Bellman had been propped in a standing position, the cord slung over the hub of the shaft, and then the body had been lifted a fraction of an inch from the floor. No strength would have been needed. The great fan would have done the rest.

A vivid mental picture flashed before my eyes—a picture of the murderer gripping that slim waist, lifting, and watching the thin legs dangling just above the flowered carpet. It was fantastically horrible—and yet so simple. A child, even Agnes Salt, could have climbed on a chair and done it.

I did not want any one else in the boarding house to know of my gruesome discovery. I shot the bolts on the door and sat down to wait for Cobb, not even bothering to remove my drenched clothes. Every now and then my glance returned in fascination to that small, untidy heap on the floor. I hurried into the bedroom for a sheet.

I was just bending to throw it over the body when there was a knock at the door. It was only then that I realized how deathly silent it had been in the apartment. The sound echoed bleakly along the walls—hollow and unnaturally loud.

For a moment I stood motionless. Then the knock sounded again—and again.

"Doctor Westlake!" It was a woman's voice.

I dropped the sheet and spun round to face the door. "What is it?"

"This—this is Delia Davenport. I'm frightfully sorry to bother you, but I've got a devilish headache and no aspirin. Can you do anything about it?"

I glanced at the sheet and then at the door. With sudden decision, I whipped off my coat and rolled up my shirt sleeves.

"Afraid I can't let you in," I called. "I'm changing my clothes. Wait a moment and I'll hand you out some."

I hurried into the bathroom and returned with a bottle of aspirin. Unbolting the door, I opened it the fraction of an inch and thrust my bare arm out with the bottle.

"Thanks a lot." Her fingers met mine. "I see you keep your door bolted. I guess you've found out it's the best thing to do around here."

She laughed and moved away. I could still feel the warmth of her hand against mine, still hear the youthful laughter ringing in my ears. She was so young, so alive—so different from that cold, dead thing behind me.

At that moment the piano started to play in Mr. Washer's room. It was, of course, the inevitable Chopin. There was something bizarre and horrible about its very sweetness. I sat down again, cursing Cobb for being so slow. Once I thought I heard the clank of Miss Sophie's iron heel on the stairs. Someone else shuffled past and perched outside my door. I had a strong suspicion that it was Jo. It seemed as though all the inmates of No. 12 Potter Street were closing in on me—watching, listening, waiting.

It was with relief that I heard the round of gruff voices on the stairs. There were heavy footsteps in the passage and then a knock at the door. I hurried to open it to find Cobb, Doctor Foley, and three or four officers. Jo was standing behind them, his mouth wide open, eyes glazed. I caught a glimpse of Miss Clymer fluttering agitatedly by.

"The police!" she murmured in an awed whisper.

Cobb dismissed Jo with a curt nod of his grizzled head and led the little procession into the room. His kind, elderly face was serious and rather sad.

"Have you done anything, Westlake?" he asked quickly.

"I just cut the body down and covered it up," I said, "Otherwise, nothing's been touched."

While Doctor Foley started his examination, I told Cobb all that had happened at No. 12 since my phone call of the night before. I went into the bedroom and produced the cretonne laundry bag. He took it, handed it to one of his men, and gave swift instructions to the others.

Where before Agnes Salt's apartment had been so quiet, it was now buzzing with activity. The fingerprint man was examining the cord. The police photographer was setting up his apparatus. Two officers were moving about slowly and deliberately.

Cobb had crossed to Doctor Foley's side. As I joined him, the police doctor glanced up.

"Been dead about an hour, I should say." He reconstructed the method of death in a way that fell in with my theories, adding: "Judging by the expression on the face, something had scared her just about the time she was knocked on the head."

"That's funny." Cobb had produced his pipe from the pocket of his tweed coat and was sucking at it reflectively. "You say she was hit unconscious from behind. She wouldn't have seen the murderer. Looks as though something else must have frightened her."

I remembered the red-ribboned cat that had lain on the mantelpiece the night before. "Maybe it did," I murmured. "Heaven knows, she might have seen anything in this room."

Cobb was gazing down at the body. "By the way, could a woman have done this, doctor?"

"Yes." Doctor Foley glanced at me for confirmation and I nodded. "All she would have to do was to hit Mrs. Bellman on the head from behind. It would have been easy to fix the cord to the shaft of the fan."

The door opened, and two white-coated men hurried in, carrying a stretcher. Behind them I saw Jo. He was just shuffling away when Cobb called out to him.

"Stay right there, please. I'll want to talk to you in a moment. I understand you're one of the deceased's nearest relatives."

Jo started, brushed the gray hair from his forehead, and moved back against the banisters.

Doctor Foley had finished his examination now. A magnesium flare flamed as the photographer took his last exposure. Then the white-coated man lifted the small body onto the stretcher.

"Well, I'll let you know the autopsy reports as soon as I get them." Doctor Foley snapped his bag shut and followed the stretcher out of the room.

In the passage I could see Jo staring dazedly after them, staring at the little white mound which was all that remained of his aunt.

Cobb was talking to his men. I heard him ordering one of them to go downstairs and tell the officer at the door to let no one in or out. Another was to check up on all telephone calls sent or received that evening. He instructed a third to stay on guard outside the apartment. Then he beckoned to Jo.

The janitor shambled into the room and stood in front of us, twisting his gnarled hands uneasily. Cobb gave him a long, curious glance.

"I understand that you're Mrs. Bellman's nephew," he said. "Before we start the investigation, I'd like you to tell me anything you know about your aunt's property."

Jo's eyes narrowed furtively. "Say, what you asking me for? She ain't died a natural death, did she? You don't think—"

"All I want to know," broke in Cobb, "is what your aunt intended to do with this house. We can't open her will without a lawyer, and it's too late to get one tonight."

"Well—" Jo's tone was obsequious and at the same time filled with a certain pride, "—I think—that is, she told me she was leaving this place and everything to me."

Cobb was looking at him fixedly. "She told you that?"

"Sure. Only the other day it was. Some sort of an offer came through from a dame that wanted to buy the place. Aunt Eva turned it down and told me she wasn't going to quit —not till she died. After that, she said, she'd rather I had it than any stranger. By strangers I guess she meant her old man. He went off years ago."

Cobb was about to speak when I interrupted.

"Jo," I exclaimed, "do you remember the name of this woman who wanted to buy the house?"

Jo scratched his shaggy head and glanced at me sidewise. "I don't know who it was. Aunt Eva didn't tell me. Besides, I guess she didn't know, either. It was done through an agent."

"O.K." Cobb had scribbled a few words in his notebook. "That's all for the present. We'll take up the question of your aunt's husband some other time."

Jo seemed very pleased to be gone. He grinned nervously, half bowed and shambled out of the room.

After he had left, Cobb turned to me with a shrug.

"Well, we've gotten ourselves mixed up in the craziest affair I've ever heard of—canaries, goldfish, cats, laundry bags, murdered landladies. They don't make much sense to me."

"They make sense up to a point," I replied. "At least, one thing looks pretty certain. They're all connected with one another and they're all part of some devilish plan. The problem is to find the plan. There's a mad sameness about all that's happened, which makes me feel pretty sure one person's responsible for the lot. I wouldn't mind betting, either, that the person is one of my charming fellow boarders. An outsider would never have been able to play those little tricks on Mrs. Bellman. They were all too well-timed."

Cobb grunted. "But who'd want to scare the old lady? And who'd want to kill her, come to that?"

"Yes, motives," I said wearily. "Jo gets the house in the will. He's got a motive all right, but I can't believe he'd have anything to do with it. He's far too dumb to think out anything as picturesque as that red ribbon around the cat's neck or the beastly business with the electric fan."

"Listen, Westlake." Cobb had leaned forward and was regarding me with earnest eyes. "I'm going to start interviewing these boarders in a minute, but I want to get your slant on them first. After all, you've been in this bug house for several days and you must know them pretty well. Is there any one of them that might have a reason for wanting the old girl out of the way?"

"Not so far as I've been able to figure out. They all have their little grouses, but I've got wind of nothing serious. All the same, if you have a good reason for wanting someone dead, you don't generally cry it from the housetops. I suggest we can the motives for the time being and concentrate on opportunity. I think I can help you there—that is, provided we can suppose that one person did everything."

Cobb nodded his approval and pushed forward his notebook, in which he had already compiled a list of the boarders at No. 12. I leaned back in my chair, trying to review in detail the curious events of the past few days.

"In the first place," I began, "I don't think it can be Miss Clymer. On the day I arrived, she was talking to me in the hall a few minutes before Mrs. Bellman ran out to tell me about the goldfish. I don't see how Miss Clymer could have put that bowl on the stove and been in the hall at the same time."

"Miss Clymer," echoed Cobb.

"That's the plump spinster. I'll cross her off for the time being."

"And then," I continued, "there's Mr. Washer. I definitely heard him playing the piano before, during and after the incident with the cat. He was playing, too, when I saw the woman on the roof—playing that inevitable Chopin of his."

Cobb looked amused. "Chopin!" he said. "Didn't know you were a musician, Westlake."

"I'm not," I replied humbly. "I wouldn't have known it was Chopin except that my young daughter has a passion for struggling through the easier masterpieces. Anyhow, you can strike out our friend next door."

Cobb put a light cross against Washer's name.

At this point, I sneezed. Although the electric fan had not been switched on again, it was chilly in the room and I was still wearing the sodden clothes in which I had come back from my fool's errand to Doctor Hammond's mythical patient. I felt all the symptoms of an approaching cold.

"Listen," I said, "let's hold our horses a while until I get that fire lighted. I'm freezing to the marrow."

While Cobb looked on, I made a pitiful attempt to get the fire started. With the assistance of the last few editions of the *Grovestown Times*, I managed at last to get a grudging response from the kindling. Mrs. Bellman's renovated fireplace seemed to be picturesque rather than efficient. The draft was poor. Smoke bellowed out into the room in large, pungent clouds. What heat there was, however, proved cheering. I hurried into the bedroom, undressed, returned in a bath robe and drew my chair near to the meager flames. I had brought in with me my benzedrine inhaler. It cleared my head wonderfully.

"Where did we get to?" I asked.

Cobb gazed in disgust at the haze of smoke which surrounded me. "We ruled out Clymer and Washer."

"Well," I mused, "there was that figure on the roof. Of course, it may have nothing to do with the murder, but I swear it was a woman. If we accept it as part of the crime, that eliminates the men—Jo, Washer, Jay, and Mr. Brown."

Cobb checked off the names.

"And there's Miss Sophie," I said suddenly. "I was up on that roof myself. It's darn difficult going. It would be impossible for a cripple to dash away like that woman did yesterday."

"Yes," murmured Cobb, "that rules out Miss Sophie if she really is a cripple. I guess we can check that later."

I held out my hands to the flames and leaned sidewise to avoid a puff of smoke. "We've got to think of the phone call, too—the one that sent me off on that fake case after dinner. Constance Furnivall couldn't have made it because she was in the room with me at the time. It was a woman's voice, too, which rules out the men again."

Cobb made a few hieroglyphics in his notebook. "How about this sister of Washer's?" he asked. "She seems to be running in and out of the place a good deal."

"I don't see how it could be her. She was in her brother's room when that cat was hung above Mrs. Bellman's door. Besides, a person who didn't live in the house couldn't possibly have had the access to Mrs. Bellman's room. Remember, it's not just these animals. Mrs. Bellman told me there were a number of other little things. That photograph on her wall changed—and pieces of furniture. An outsider couldn't have done all that."

"No." Cobb picked up the pipe and as was his habit, started to suck at it unlighted. "Well, that leaves us only with Miss Davenport and Mrs. Brown. Not, of course, that it means much. Any two of the others might easily have been working in cahoots." He put his elbows on the table and glanced at me. "There's one little thing I haven't told you."

I set a match to a sheet of the *Grovestown Times* and threw the flaming paper onto the smoldering wood. It rested there a moment and then curled up the chimney.

"Yes," Cobb was saying, "After you called last night. I got to thinking about the affair and figured out that it might prove more important than it seemed. There were a couple of men down at the station with nothing to do this morning so I set them on the job of going around the pet shops. They checked up on all recent sales of canaries and goldfish."

I glanced at him in interest.

"They traced them all back—all, that is, except one." Cobb paused. "Three or four days ago a clerk at one of the stores recalls selling a bowl of goldfish and a canary to a woman. He doesn't remember anything about her, but knows she wasn't one of his regular customers."

"Looks as though that's the woman we want," I exclaimed eagerly. "You say the man can't remember anything about her?"

"No. He was as dumb as they come, but I'll have him around tomorrow and let him give these boarders the once-over."

"Miss Davenport and Mrs. Brown," I murmured. "I don't imagine there's a clerk in the world who wouldn't remember Miss Davenport if he saw her. I wonder if this Brown woman—"

I broke off as one of the officers hurried into the room. "It's that call Doctor Westlake received tonight, sir. They've traced it back to this house. Mrs. Bellman must have been on the switchboard at the time."

Cobb grunted. "I thought so. What is the arrangement of phones here?"

"There's an instrument on every floor, but this apartment's the only one to have an outside phone. The rest are worked through the switchboard. They couldn't tell which floor the call came from, of course."

"O.K. That's all."

Cobb turned to me as the man left the room. "Looks as though we're right about narrowing the suspects down to this house."

With the mention of the telephone, another thought suddenly struck me. "That voice over the wire!" I exclaimed. "I thought at the time it was familiar, but I couldn't place it then. I remember some where I heard it before."

Cobb's rather melancholy blue eyes brightened. "Where?"

"It was here—the other day. It was the same voice that called down the stairs to Mrs. Bellman when she was hurrying me to her room to look at those goldfish. So you see, that voice does belong to the murderess—and the murderess does live in this house."

Curiously enough, my own words gave me a strange thrill. There was something exciting in the atmosphere of that quiet, smoke-laden room—something exciting about sitting there with the calm methodical Cobb while gradually the net tightened around the person who had killed Mrs. Bellman.

"That voice!" said Cobb suddenly. "You've heard all the boarders speak, haven't you? Surely, you recognized it."

"That's the darn part of it. I've been listening for it—it was sort of high-pitched and querulous—but voices sound different when you see the person that's talking. So far, I haven't heard anything like it."

Cobb grunted again. "Anyway, we'd better start on those interviews. How about that Davenport woman? She tried to get into the room, you say, when you were waiting with Mrs. Bellman's body."

"You might as well begin with her," I agreed absently. "Whatever she says, it's bound to be original."

He called the officer at the door and sent him to search for the chemically bodied and minded blonde. The man returned within a few minutes, looking rather embarrassed. Miss Davenport in a red silk *peignoir* was clinging affectionately to his arm. The golden hair was slightly ruffled. For the first time, I saw her lips without make-up. The violet eyes glanced shrewdly at Cobb and then flicked to me.

"We certainly are going in for drammer around here, aren't we?" she said. "I was wakened up from my doped sleep. I'll have to take another of Doctor Westlake's aspirins when you're through with me." Without being asked, she perched herself on the arm of a chair. "Mind if I smoke?"

She produced a cigarette and lighted it deliberately. To my surprise I noticed that her hand shook. Apparently, she was less composed than she appeared to be.

Cobb was staring gravely at the scarlet *peignoir*. I had the impression that he was mildly shocked by its scantiness and transparence.

"Miss Davenport," he began, "I expect you've heard something of the things that happened here tonight. Just as a matter of form, we're asking every one to check up on their movements since dinner time."

A frown rippled the girl's smooth young forehead. Then she smiled. "Well, I guess I can tell you without damaging my reputation. After dinner, I helped Jay with a—er—chemical experiment. We had a devil of a row in the middle of it. I got raving mad and stamped off to my room." A swirl of cigarette smoke curled upward, mingling with the wreaths that still trailed from the smoldering logs. "The emotion must have been too much for me because I developed a foul headache. I came here for an aspirin and have been sleeping peacefully ever since. I didn't even know about Mrs. Bellman until Miss Clymer came in a few minutes ago and gave me all the gory details."

She turned to me with a quizzical expression. "By the way, Doctor Westlake, I hope you were lying when you said you were changing your clothes. It's hardly my idea of decency to sit here in the nude and entertain Mrs. Bellman—dead or alive."

Cobb coughed a trifle prudishly. "You seem an—er—intelligent young woman. Miss Davenport," he said mildly. "Have you any ideas about what's been going on?"

"Nothing except that every one's crazy." Miss Davenport crossed her legs, showing a long expanse of stocking. "Either they're queer like Mr. Washer and the Furnivalls, or stodgy like the Browns, or repressed like Miss Clymer. Don't the medical textbooks tell you, by the way, that people who go in for repressing their sex are capable of anything?"

"Well, we aren't accusing *you* of that," murmured Cobb with a furtive glance at her sheer silk stockings. "By the way, Miss Davenport, have you noticed that all the people in the house have been unnaturally interested in this room?" He turned to me. "I don't like to quote Doctor Westlake, but he feels that even you—"

Miss Davenport laughed. "You'll have to think out harder questions than that, inspector. Yes, I'll admit I was inquisitive about this place—darn inquisitive. And who wouldn't be? For months there've been wild rumors around the house that a monster used to live here with Miss Furnivall. I was raring to see it, and, failing that, raring to see its den. After all, I am a student of physiology, and I've never had a break with a monster yet."

"That was your only interest, Miss Davenport?"

The girl grinned at me. "It was nice to meet Doctor Westlake, of course—but it was mostly the monster. And I expect every one else felt the same. I know Miss Clymer would break her neck to pick up some nice dirt. You'd be horrified if you knew some of the things that go on in a good woman's mind."

Cobb did not speak for a moment. He pushed the unlighted pipe between his teeth. "So there's nothing you can tell us that might help?"

"Nothing. At least, there is one thing, if it's not indelicate to mention it before two gentlemen." Miss Davenport screwed up her nose in a rather delightful way.

I remarked that nothing was too indelicate to mention before a doctor and a policeman—especially in these circumstances. She laughed, tossed away her cigarette butt, and produced another from a pocket in her *peignoir*.

"Well, a few days ago I found the toilet wasn't working on the second floor. Jay and I had poured some chemicals down it some hours before and I was scared we'd done the damage. I got Jay and one of those rubber plungers and we put in some hard work." Her violet eyes were staring straight into mine. "At last something came up—the craziest thing you could imagine, yet maybe it has something to do with this. It was a dead canary, and it wasn't the nasty little beast in the hall that Miss Clymer slops over. We went down to look."

"Good." Cobb seemed to be talking to himself rather than to Miss Davenport. "That's another little point cleared up." He raised his eyes. "There's nothing else?"

The girl seemed amused that the canary interested him. She smiled and shook her head.

"Very well. It's getting late, Miss Davenport. If there are any more questions, I'll keep them till tomorrow."

The girl uncurled herself from the arm of the chair and pulled the *peignoir* around her. "You never asked me what my row with Jay was about, Doctor Westlake," she said. "I think it was mean of you because I was dying to tell. But perhaps you know already. There's an account of it in the *Grovestown Times*, and I gave it to Miss Furnivall at dinner tonight."

She crossed to the door and stood with her back pressed against it. "I spat out at Jay in the middle of an experiment because he forgot that we'd been married this afternoon. That's why I got a headache. That's why I had to go to bed with an aspirin on my wedding night. What do you think of that for a crime?"

She smiled at me, turned on her heels, and disappeared into the passage."

As she left, I rose and threw another log on the fire. "Nice girl that," I said. "I don't see her dabbling in murder."

Cobb growled. "Fresh, if you ask me. Still, she's helped us along with that canary. Now I think it's that to see Constance Furnivall. I don't mind telling you, Westlake. When you called up yesterday, I made a little investigation of the boarders here and found out about Mrs. Constance Farrar. I wondered whether perhaps she wasn't up to her tricks again."

Once more the officer was sent away, only to return within a very few minutes.

Constance Furnivall—or Farrar—looked ghastly pale when she entered. I noticed, too that she brought with her a faint odor of brandy. Obviously she had been buoying herself up for the ordeal of meeting the police.

It is to the credit of my friend Cobb that he was more than courteous and considerate with this woman who had spent fifteen years in prison. He rose and placed a chair for her.

"Sit down, Miss—er—Furnivall."

The woman did not seem to hear him. The large dark eyes flamed in her pale face.

"Is it—is it true that Mrs. Bellman has been killed?" she said quietly.

Cobb nodded.

"Very well." Miss Furnivall crossed her arms. I noticed her lips trembling. "I think it's about time I spoke. Before you question me, I want to tell you something—something that has been on my mind now for several months—a suspicion that has kept me awake through many of these hot summer nights." She broke off and added almost in a whisper: "A suspicion that may help you to understand why Mrs. Bellman was killed."

The silence that followed this remark was charged with strained excitement. I saw Cobb gazing tensely at Miss Furnivall. A puff of gray smoke wafted upward from the fire. I followed its slow progress to the ceiling with unseeing eyes.

"Go on," said Cobb at length.

Miss Furnivall began to speak and then paused. Turning, she opened the door swiftly and looked out into the passage. Apparently she knew the ways of her fellow boarders.

"Mr. Cobb," she said, "you know, and Doctor Westlake knows, that I have taken a human life. I have paid for it dearly, but I have an instinct about these things and this is why I want you to give close attention to what I say."

Cobb nodded gravely.

"I believe," she continued slowly, "that Mrs. Bellman was killed because she had found out something about another murder."

"Another murder!" The words shot from Cobb like lightning. "You mean you know of another murder committed in this house?"

"I don't know of one." The woman's voice was sad. "But I do suspect it. You see, I've got no evidence, but I'm almost positive now that Mrs. Salt murdered Agnes—that wretched creature whom I was taking care of."

A log fell in the grate. The noise sounded unnaturally loud.

"Yes," Miss Furnivall was continuing. "I think she killed her own stepchild here in this very apartment."

I shivered despite the fact that I was crouched over the smoky flames.

"I have several reasons for believing so." Miss Furnivall tossed her head defiantly. "In the first place, there was a financial motive."

Cobb looked up sharply.

"Of course, it doesn't necessarily mean a person will commit a murder just because they have a motive, but one day, when I was acting as a nurse for Agnes, three men and a woman came to see her. They came all the way from the Middle West. They were the only visitors she ever had. They explained to me they were the trustees of her father's will. It seems he had been wealthy, and he had, naturally, felt a great responsibility toward Agnes. She was only five years old when he died, and the doctors had told him positively that the child could not live for long. Even so, he left the greater part of his estate in trust for her for ten years, so that while she lived, there would be no chance of her wanting for anything. He stipulated that she should not be put away in an institution. That's why all that money was spent on having me and on this apartment."

"Go on," said Cobb.

"Well, it appears that the day on which they came to see her was her fifteenth birthday. Contrary to all medical opinion, Agnes had lived. But the ten years were up and the trust fund was to stop automatically." Miss Furnivall crossed her strong arms across her breast. "All the money from then on was to go to Mrs. Salt, the stepmother. As a mother, naturally, she was expected to continue supporting Agnes, but she was under no compulsion. Nor would the trustees be interested in the child any longer. There was no one to keep an eye on what happened to her—no one but Mrs. Salt."

"And you suggest Mrs. Salt killed Agnes because—"

"Exactly. It takes a great deal of money to support a child like that—even in an institution. You may think Mrs. Salt had insufficient motive, but I can understand how she must have felt about—about that monster." Miss Furnivall's eyes flickered strangely as though she were remembering something. "I can imagine the horror, the physical loathing she could have had for it. Don't you see, it was not her own child, but the child of the first wife. Sometimes even I myself was almost driven to do what I think Mrs. Salt really hired me for—"

She stopped suddenly and lowered her eyes. Neither Cobb nor I spoke for a moment, then Cobb said:

"You think Mrs. Salt killed her stepdaughter in this room?"

"Yes." Miss Furnivall's dark eyes flashed as she looked up. "Otherwise, why was she always so careful to let no one see her? She made her arrangements with Mrs. Bellman through an agent. She hired me by mail and dismissed me before her arrival. And she came to take Agnes away in the dead of night. She probably gave as her excuse that she wanted to keep the child from prying eyes. No one saw her leave, not even Mrs. Bellman. And I know why they didn't. Mrs. Salt didn't want any one to know that she left alone—that she had murdered Agnes."

Cobb sucked fiercely at the unlighted pipe. "I'm beginning to see what you are driving at. You think Mrs. Bellman started to suspect something about this other murder and—But, no!" Suddenly, he thumped his fist on the table. "We know perfectly well that Mrs. Salt can have nothing to do with this, because we know for certain that the murderer must be one of the boarders."

"Wait a minute," I broke in. "I agree with you. We know the murderer is one of the boarders, but why couldn't she be Mrs. Salt, too? Don't you see? No one ever saw Mrs. Salt. She was a complete stranger in these parts. She could easily be living here under another name. She could have been living here for years and no one would have suspected anything."

Cobb whistled through his teeth. "So she could."

"Yes," I went on. "And that gives us the motive we've been searching for. None of these boarders have a motive as themselves, but if one of them were Mrs. Salt—"

I shall never know why I broke off at that particular moment. I remember the look of eagerness on Cobb's face turning suddenly to surprise. I remember Miss Furnivall standing squarely against the door, her arms crossed, her chin thrust forward.

The room was quiet—horribly quiet. A long tendril of smoke wafted from the fire, bringing with it a pungent smell of burning wood.

Or was it the smell of wood? As I sat there, I seemed to detect something else—something reminiscent of that stale, musty odor that had lingered in the room since my arrival.

We were all leaning forward, gazing at the grate. There was a rustling sound somewhere up the chimney, and a few flakes of soot fell harshly onto the sullen flames. The vague stirring sounded again. Once more soot descended in a sudden stream. I could hear Miss Furnivall's heavy breathing—unnaturally quick and loud. Then for the moment it seemed to stop entirely. It was as though the whole world were still—everything but that slow, tumbling noise in the wide chimney.

The smell was almost unbearably strong row. For an instant it was the only thing of which I was conscious. Then, suddenly, a sharp, hysterical scream split the silence.

It was Constance Furnivall and she was shouting:

"Agnes—Agnes Salt."

In a dash, I saw what she saw. Gradually slipping down into the grate on top of the now almost extinguished fire was a body. At first I thought it must be that of some animal. Then I realized my mistake.

Lying in the fireplace, almost at my feet, were the decomposed remains of a hideously misshapen child.

VIII

HER LAST CHANCE

It is not pleasant to dwell on the happenings of the next few minutes. Finally the body was gathered up and laid in the next room. Doctor Foley had been recalled even before he had finished his examination of Mrs. Bellman.

Cobb had given strict orders that, for the present, the news of this second gruesome revelation should not be imparted to any one outside the officials. Miss Furnivall, who had so dramatically and surprisingly guessed at the crime before its discovery, was sent back to her room with instructions not to mention the matter—not even to her sister.

Doctor Foley called me in at length for a superficial examination of the body. His pale eyes behind the pince-nez were shining with scientific interest.

"Too bad we can't get a picture for publication in the medical journals," he sighed. "The skeletal structure is different from anything I've ever seen before. How do you suppose she got that way?"

I looked down at what remained of that pathetic, twisted body. Some of the purplish skin of the face was still intact. The dark hair was long and coarse, reaching almost to the crooked hands.

"How she got that way?" I repeated. "Oh, acondroplasia, cretinism, epilepsy, injuries at birth—any or all of them might have been responsible."

"Well," muttered Foley, "it's no wonder someone wanted to get rid of her."

It was impossible to tell without a complete autopsy how long the child had been dead. The cause of death, however, seemed obvious. There was a cord tied tightly around the neck. Several feet of it still adhered to the head. The hemp was charred in places and blackened at the spot where some lighted fragment of paper or a spark must have burned it through and thus precipitated our ghastly discovery.

"Not less than three months," Foley was saying. "It's murder all right. I'm amazed you got that fire started at all. The chimney must have been almost entirely blocked."

When we rejoined Cobb and told him what little we had gathered, I noticed that his kindly face was more drawn and haggard than I had ever before seen it. He glanced up wearily as I sat down at his side.

"Well, Westlake, we're not going to get very far until we've gone into the background of these boarders. Tomorrow we can start a search for those trustees. One of them could pick out Mrs. Salt. But it's going to be damned hard to find them. They might be living anywhere in the States, and I expect Salt's an assumed name, anyway."

I lighted a cigarette and glanced at the stretcher bearers who had returned and were carrying the cretin's body out of the room.

"Yes, it's going to take time getting around to Mrs. Salt that way. Let's put together the facts we've already got. It may help."

"O.K." Cobb picked up a pencil. "Let's see what you make of it."

"Well, the beginning's easy to guess at. Mrs. Salt comes to Grovestown and rents a room here at No. 12. She knew the child's fifteenth birthday would soon be coming. I expect even then she was looking around for a suitable place to—to murder her. She finds this apartment and starts to make her plans."

Cobb leaned forward. "Yeah. I guess she persuaded the trustees that the air or something here would be good for the kid. Really, of course, she was getting Agnes away from the place where she was known.

"She sees Miss Furnivall's advertisement in the paper and hires her to look after Agnes. She knows Miss Furnivall must be desperate—possibly even finds out that she is a convicted killer. She's not one that's likely to talk. Perhaps, as Miss Furnivall hinted, Mrs. Salt was even hoping to use her as an accomplice."

I thought of Miss Constance Furnivall as I had seen her but a short time before, her eyes flashing, her arms crossed tightly over her breast. "Sometimes even I was almost driven to do what I think Mrs. Salt really hired me for."

"Very well," Cobb was saying. "She gets Agnes installed here, still living in the house herself, of course, under another name. The fifteenth birthday comes and goes, and the time arrives for the murder. She fakes up the story of a trip to Arizona, dismisses Miss Furnivall, strangles Agnes and puts her in the chimney."

"Yes," I broke in. "You see, the hearth was blocked up then. It was an ideal place to put a body. Mrs. Salt must have gone up onto the roof garden and hung Agnes down the chimney, thinking she would never be found."

Cobb's blue eyes had brightened. Now they clouded over again. "Even so it was a risk—an awful risk. Strikes me Mrs. Salt must have been devilishly clever to figure all this out. I can't see her leaving damning evidence like a body in someone else's chimney. It doesn't—"

"Wait a minute." A sudden thought had struck me. "That tempting offer Mrs. Bellman was always talking about! That offer Jo said came from a woman through an agent. Don't you see? That woman must have been Mrs. Salt. Her plan was to buy the house, and then perhaps, a neat little piece of arson would have made her secret safe forever. That's why she paid the rent three months after she left. By the time those three months were up, she must, have hoped to own the place. Of course, it would have been safer to buy a house before she killed Agnes, but she couldn't. She didn't have the money then. She had to wait till Agnes's fifteenth birthday."

"Good for you, Westlake." Cobb was smiling now. "I'm beginning to see some of the little difficulties Mrs. Salt found herself up against. She planned to buy the house and then discovered Mrs. Bellman wouldn't sell. That's why Mrs. Salt had to start changing flowers and pictures, moving furniture around. She was trying to scare the landlady into thinking she was slipping, trying to scare her into accepting the offer."

"And not only that!" I exclaimed. "She must have learned that the worst possible thing was happening—that Mrs. Bellman had decided to open up the fireplace, ironically enough as a surprise for Mrs. Salt on her return. That must have made Mrs. Salt desperate, and she doubled speed on her attempts to scare the landlady. She even took the risk of buying a canary and some goldfish—just to make things more terrifying."

I paused to light a cigarette "Possibly there was another reason for those grim little jokes of hers—a reason far subtler, far more cunning. You remember Mrs. Salt always tried to change her little tableaux back to normal again so that Mrs. Bellman began to think they had never existed except in her own imagination. Well, I think Mrs. Salt did that on purpose, did it to make the landlady disbelieve her own eyes so that one day, if she came across something that was even more horrible, more unlikely, something, for example, like Agnes's dead body, she would not believe she had seen it."

Cobb glanced up quickly. It was the small points like that which he appreciated particularly.

"And her troubles didn't end there," he said. "When she was fighting with her back to the wall, you came along and rented this very apartment." He smiled grimly. "That must have been, the last straw. In desperation, she makes the final and most horrible gesture. She strangles the cat with red ribbon and hangs it outside Mrs. Bellman's door. Then when you're out of the room, she brings it in here. Now she's not only got the landlady to scare—she's got you, too."

"Yes," I said, sending a spiral of smoke to the ceiling. "I'm getting quite sorry for Mrs. Salt. She certainly has her problems. I can imagine how she felt when she found that cat wasn't going to frighten me out. I can see — Yes, of course —" I glanced up. "I'm beginning to understand the woman on the roof now. Mrs. Salt had made the big decision. She couldn't leave Agnes in the chimney any longer. Very well, she would pull her out and hide her somewhere else. She gets one of Mrs. Bellman's laundry bags —"

"And you arrive on the scene again," put in Cobb, "and scare her away."

Neither of us spoke. I leaned back in my chair, thinking of Mrs. Salt — thinking of that strange, desperate woman who even now must be sitting in her bedroom like all the other boarders at No. 12. I could think of her working feverishly to save the plan against which it seemed, all the forces of fate were scheming. For her, these must have been days of dread, days of mental agony. And this night, I reflected, this must be the worst of all for her, waiting, watching, wondering what was happening here in the room which had once been the safe hiding place of her guilt.

"Try to think of her state of mind," I said, "after she has been chased off the roof. There is one more hope for her — and only one. If she could get into my room, she might be able to draw the body down from the inside. She takes the chance of putting through a fake call to me and gets me out of the way." I inhaled deeply. "At first, the plan worked. But she counted without Mrs. Bellman's efficiency. When she comes into my room, she finds the landlady there, doing the worst of all possible things — lighting a fire."

Cobb nodded. "She had to act quickly. She picked up something — a log, a candlestick, perhaps — and hit Mr. Bellman on the head from behind. But, wait a minute, how about that expression of fright of the landlady's face?"

"Yes," I said slowly, "that's the real reason why Mrs. Salt knew she had to kill her. Mrs. Bellman's face was covered with soot. There was an expression of horror on it. That was because the chimney had started to smoke and she had looked far up it — looked up and actually seen or smelled something."

I broke off glancing instinctively at the charred fragments of log which still lay half buried in soot in the grate.

"Well," said Cobb, "that ends the story of Mrs. Salt. We've figured out everything she thought, every move she made, every move she intended to make, but were still as far away as ever from the most important point. Which of these women at No. 12 is Mrs. Salt?"

"Yes, which of them?" I leaned back, reviewing in my mind all the strange people who, during the past two days, had been so close to me. Suddenly, I sat up and glanced swiftly at Cobb. "I've got an idea," I said. "An idea which, with any luck, ought to put the handcuffs on Mrs. Salt before morning."

"And now—" Cobb smiled skeptically "—I'll tell one."

"But I'm serious. Listen, get one of your men and let me talk to him. Leave this to me."

"O.K. I'll bite."

Cobb shouted, and a man entered almost immediately. He glanced at us inquiringly.

"Doctor Westlake will tell you what we want," Cobb grunted.

"Yes," I said, "we want you to go around to all the boarders and tell them that the police are leaving and that they can go to bed because they won't be needed any more tonight. You can also tell them to keep their windows closed tomorrow morning because a man is coming early to sweep this chimney. We don't want their things to get covered in soot."

I repeated this until the man had gotten it word perfect.

"Don't forget," I said, "let them know the police are leaving." I turned to Cobb. "By the way, why don't you send them away now? There's nothing to stay for."

Cobb looked a trifle embarrassed, but after a moment he nodded. "O.K., Bill. When you're through with that, tell the boys to quit. We'll start in again early tomorrow morning."

When the man had gone, Cobb turned to me. "I sincerely hope you know what you're doing."

"Sure," I said. "The first thing is for me to get some clothes on. Then you and I are going to spend a pleasant few hours together halfway up the stairs to the roof garden."

"And why do we do that?"

I rose. "Haven't you guessed? No one in this house but Constance Furnivall knows we've found Agnes. Bill will tell them all that the police have gone. He'll tell them all that we're starting work on the chimney tomorrow. If I understand anything about Mrs. Salt, she'll realize this is her last chance. Yesterday she tried to pull Agnes up from the roof but I interrupted her. Well, unless I'm very much mistaken, she'll try again tonight. But she won't find Agnes. She'll find you and me."

IX

THE DARK SILHOUETTE

A few minutes later Bill came in to report that everything was ready and the men were about to leave. I heard his heavy footsteps descending the stairs. Outside I heard the police car start and move away. Then there was silence, except for the faint striking of a clock downstairs. The dark blanket of midnight had fallen upon No. 12 and all the ghastly happenings of that evening.

But for Cobb and me, work was by no means over. We switched out all the lights in my rooms and took up our position halfway up the staircase which led to Agnes Salt's roof garden. Above us we could still hear the steady patter of the rain. It was a cheerless night. I sniffed again and again at my benzedrine inhaler in the hope of warding off the cold that was beginning to invade my system.

Neither of us spoke. Our ears were strained for the least sound from that roof. Once Cobb pulled out his revolver and peered at it in the darkness. The barrel gleamed faintly, reminding me forcibly of our strange purpose.

How long we waited, I do not remember, but I know it was long enough for me to reach the conclusion that this plan was harebrained and would never work. "A watched pot—" I told myself. "A watched pot—"

I remember Mrs. Bellman's clock downstairs chiming twice. I remember the rain slackening and then rushing headlong down again like myriad tiny feet on the roof above us. I think I must eventually have slipped off into a light doze, but I never lost consciousness, for even now I can feel the rough brick of the wall against my back and smell that vague, musty odor which still permeated the rank air of that small staircase. Visions of Agnes Salt slipped through my mind—visions of Agnes as she must have been when she was brought up these steps, visions of her as I had just seen her, hunched in the grate in that room below us. A poor crazy monster!

Suddenly I felt Cobb's grip on my arm.

"Don't even breathe," he hissed. "Something is beginning to happen."

I shook myself like a dog and listened. By now the rhythm of the rain had beaten itself into my subconscious mind. Instinctively I could pick from it any alien sound, however slight.

Somewhere a long way off, a victrola was being played. I could feel rather than hear the sharp, syncopated beat. It reminded me with strange vividness that tonight was Saturday, and that all around me there were people enjoying themselves, dancing, laughing.

Cobb's fingers were warm through my coat. This time I heard it, too. Distinct from the throb of the music, distinct from the swish of the rain, was another sound—the slow, stealthy sound of footsteps. They paused, moved forward, paused again. Once there was a slight clatter as though a heel had knocked against a tile.

It was the thought of that heel rather than anything else that brought home to me the grim reality of the situation. Mrs. Salt actually was there on the roof above us. The plan was working. The woman who had so unscrupulously taken two lives was walking into the trap.

"Come on."

Cobb's voice was so low that, even though he spoke in my ear, I could scarcely catch it.

"You go first," he was whispering. "You know the geography of the place."

I felt the cold steel of the revolver as he slipped it into my hand.

Slowly I began to move upward. The footsteps had stopped. There was no time to lose. Mrs. Salt must have reached the chimney. Soon now she would realize that the body had gone.

The chill impact of the rain came as quite a shock to me when eventually I reached the last stair and slipped noiselessly into the deep shadow by the railings which surrounded the roof garden. Cobb's progress behind had been so silent that I was not sure he was following until I felt his hand touch mine. It pressed against my fingers. I could tell that he was asking for the revolver. I loosened my grip and felt the gun withdrawn.

A few yards to our right, looming jet black against the deep blue of the night sky, rose the silhouette of a chimney. I realized instantly that it was the one by which I had found the laundry bag the night before. I realized, too, that it was the chimney connected with the fireplace in my apartment. It was squat and wide. There had been plenty of room, I reflected grimly, for the small, misshapen body of Agnes Salt to have been suspended there.

I do not know what exactly I had expected to see. But when I saw it, I found myself frozen to the ground, completely caught up in the eerie, horrible atmosphere of that scene.

Across the way, the victrola burst out suddenly in a crazy, syncopated rhythm. Someone down in the street laughed. A car rattled by, and the rain swished as a gust of wind sent it skimming across the tiles. Then, as we crouched there, watching, the outline of the chimney's mouth blurred. Gradually something moved above it—something which slowly formed itself into the silhouette of a woman's head.

I must have moved, for suddenly I felt Cobb's grip again on my arm. We pressed more deeply into the shadow as the head moved upward, revealing shoulders and the upper part of the arms. I could see the outline of the hat clearly. There was something essentially feminine about it which made the scene infinitely more ghastly.

Mrs. Salt was in the very act of searching for the body of her stepdaughter.

I do not know how long Cobb and I stood there, watching, but in my mind it seems as though hours slipped by. My eyes were more accustomed to the darkness then, and I could see little movements which earlier would have been invisible. Naturally, it was impossible to recognize any individual feature of that dark, female form, but I saw an arm lifted and plunged down the chimney. I saw it groping slowly from side to side—groping. I knew, for the rope which she had hung there, the rope which had been tied so tightly around Agnes's neck.

The victrola stopped suddenly. There was a sputter of talk and laughter. The wind sighed. Then I saw the arm pause. It had found the rope and was clutching it.

Cobb's revolver flicked upward. From the corner of my eye, I saw it flash suddenly, but I was staring forward, staring at that form as it prepared to pull.

The shoulders hunched. There was one moment of deathly immobility. Then the figure jerked backward, and I caught the outline of a short length of rope as it fell loosely over the mouth of the chimney.

Even then, in that instant of tense excitement, I could imagine what was passing through the mind of Mrs. Salt. I could imagine the horror, the gradual realization that the body had been discovered, that even now the police must be working on the murder of Agnes Salt as certainly as they were on that of Eva Bellman.

The woman stood there motionless. Once again, I saw Cobb's revolver gleam. Then his voice rang loud and sharp across the wet tiles.

"Hands up, Mrs. Salt! I've got you covered!"

For a second, the silhouette did not move. Then with a swift motion it disappeared. Cobb sprang forward and ran along the high railings of the roof garden. I jumped up and followed. As I did so, he shouted:

"Look out!"

Instinctively I ducked, and a tile crashed on the roof at my feet, splitting into fragments. As I crouched there, a second tile hurtled through the air—and then a third.

Cobb had started to scale the railings now. I moved to his side. Ahead of us, threading her way through the stacks of chimneys, I caught a glimpse of the woman. I saw her stumble, throw out a hand to support herself and then dash on. Her skirt blew out, black against the sky.

I shall never know how Cobb and I climbed those railings, but we seemed to be over in a split second. I vaguely remember a ripping sound as the sleeve of my coat caught against one of the spikes. There was a sharp tingling on my arm where the skin had been grazed.

Cobb was ahead of me, scrambling along the sloping tiles, clutching firmly to the side of the chimney. I followed, bent double, my breath coming in short spurts. Then, I saw the woman again—hardly ten yards ahead, moving downward toward the very edge of the roof. She seemed to be making for the house next door.

"We'll get her," I yelled, and, with an abrupt twist, managed to push past Cobb. I stood, clinging to the extreme edge of the chimney stack.

"Mrs. Salt," I shouted. "It's no good. Stop."

At the sound of my voice, the figure halted suddenly. She glanced around as though to gauge the distance which lay between us and herself.

As long as I live, I shall never forget that tableau. I shall never forget that dark silhouette, poised there with one arm stretched out for balance and thrown into vague illumination by the oblique rays from a street lamp below.

"Mrs. Salt," I cried once more.

The figure moved forward again, out of the light. Beneath her I could see the wet tiles gleaming, see their dangerous downward slant. The woman took another step and stumbled. Her hand flew out—clutching, clutching at nothingness. She toppled. Both arms were flung out in a desperate attempt to save herself. Slowly her feet slid downward. I could just see the two heels shining. I gazed at them in fascination as the figure slipped slowly—nearer and nearer the edge of the roof.

"We must—we must get her."

I remember an insane impulse taking possession of me. I let go the chimney and leaned forward. Cobb shouted something which I did not hear. I caught another glimpse of that figure. It was still slipping slowly, as she gripped futilely at the gleaming tiles.

I sprang forward in an instinctive effort to save her, but, as I did so, I felt a sudden shock. Something had struck me hard in the face. The tiles merged into a kaleidoscope of shooting stars. Then I seemed to be falling, falling.

For an instant my brains struggled against unconsciousness. From miles, it seemed, I heard a long, wild scream—like the scream of a desperate animal. It lingered, throbbing in the air.

I remember nothing more.

X

A FIEND

When I came to my senses, I was lying in a room which I had never seen before. At first I was conscious only of the white expanse of ceiling above me and the hard brilliance of the electric light. Then—gradually—faces began to detach themselves and I heard voices. My head seemed to be splitting.

"Feel better now?" Doctor Foley's blurred image faded into the background and was replaced by that of my old friend, Cobb. His blue eyes were tense and anxious.

"Where am I?" I murmured stupidly.

"Still at No. 12 Potter Street." Cobb's smile was reassuring if a trifle forced.

I struggled to collect together my confused fragments of memory. "But what happened? Did I—did I fall off the roof?"

"No, but you tried your darnedest." Even in my half consciousness, I could tell from the grim note in Cobb's voice that something pretty serious had happened. "You got all het up and tried to dash over the slippery tiles. You didn't seem to realize how dangerous it was, so I had to stop you in the only way I knew how. I grabbed you with one hand, gave you a crack on the jaw with the other."

I fingered my face, feeling a large, painful swelling around my lower lip. "Let me thank you," I said ruefully, "for a very unconventional way of saving my life. By the way, what time is it?"

"Five o'clock in the morning."

As he spoke, I began to remember things more clearly: the trap for Mrs. Bellman's murderer, the rain-drenched roof, that figure poised on the very edge of the tiles with wild, clutching hands, that final cry.

"But the woman!" I exclaimed. "What happened to her?"

"It's all over now."

"You've caught her?"

"She's caught herself." Cobb's voice was low. "She wasn't as lucky as you, Westlake."

"You mean—she fell?"

He nodded. "She died instantly. They've taken her to the morgue."

"But who was she?" I pushed myself into the sitting position.

"It was the woman we were after all right—Mrs. Salt."

"And she—she was one of the boarders here?"

Cobb nodded again, and his blue eyes twinkled. "The answer to all your questions will be yes—and no, Westlake. Do you feel fit to hear about it?"

"Good Lord, yes. I'm all right. Give me a cigarette, for Pete's sake."

"In the first place," he began, "I feel I ought to congratulate you, doctor, not only for digging out all the important facts in this case, but also for thinking out a plan which actually worked — worked so well, in fact, that it almost cost you your own life as well as that of — another person."

"You make me feel like a murderer."

"You needn't have *that* death on your conscience. Mrs. Salt wasn't a woman. She was a fiend. She was a diabolical creature who didn't stop at killing fish, fowl and human beings to gain her own selfish ends. She's better off where she is."

"But who the devil was it?"

"I already told you it was Mrs. Salt. The woman who contrived to murder her own stepdaughter so as to be saved the expense of looking after her. There was also the possibility — which must always have haunted her — of having the child's identity disclosed. The woman who tried to buy this house so that she could destroy all traces of her guilt — and then had nerve enough to stay on here and try to frighten Mrs. Bellman into retiring. The woman who called to Mrs. Bellman the day you arrived and who later sent you out on a fool's errand with a fake phone call."

"But the voice," I said. "Why didn't I recognize it?"

"Ah, why didn't you?" Cobb's eyes were still twinkling. "Just think if there's any one around this place whose voice you haven't heard much?"

"Mrs. Brown?" I queried.

Cobb shook his head. "Try again."

The inmates of No. 12 passed in review through my aching head. Not one of them, it seemed, fitted that high-pitched, rather querulous voice I had heard over the phone. Then, suddenly, I realized what Cobb meant,

"You don't — you don't mean Mr. Washer's sister?"

"Got it." Cobb was smiling frankly now. "We've investigated the lady and found that she occupied an attic in the house next door. She wasn't in there much, but it was a convenient spot for any one who wanted to keep an eye on the chimney stack of your apartment. She could climb over here quite easily — that is, when the roof wasn't slippery. That's where she was trying to get to tonight and where she came from that other time when you scared her away."

I was thoroughly awake now and more capable of logical thought. I glanced at Cobb swiftly. "But — there are a thousand buts. First of all, how about that laundry bag with Mrs. Bellman's name on it? And then we decided definitely that all those crazy tricks which were played on Mrs. Bellman could not have been the work of an outsider."

"Could not possibly have been the work of an outsider," echoed Cobb.

"Then what the hell? You don't mean to say her brother helped her?"

"That is a possibility." Cobb's voice was enigmatic and it was hard to tell whether or not he knew the answers to my questions.

"But I don't see how—"

"Suppose we work it out together, Mr. Washer was a rather effeminate man. Our friend, Miss Davenport—that is, Mrs. Jay—hinted some slightly unpleasant things about his—er—characteristics. Let us suppose he wanted for some reason to help his sister by disguising himself as a woman. You yourself saw Miss Washer and noticed a strong physical resemblance. He was artificially sun-tanned, of course, and she wasn't, but a thick layer of powder would hide that. Miss Washer was a visitor—an outsider—and couldn't possibly have played those fantastic tricks on Mrs. Bellman. But Washer could. He could also have disguised himself when necessary in order to give himself—or his sister—an alibi."

"Yes, he could have done that all right, but neither he nor his sister could have killed the cat, for example. They both had perfect alibis. The piano was going continuously before and after Mrs. Bellman came up to my room—and later, while I was on the roof."

Cobb had pulled out this unlighted pipe. "I asked you yesterday, Westlake, if you were a musician. I didn't realize at the time what a sensible question it was. You said you could recognize Shopping—or whatever his name is—because your daughter plays his pieces. But, apparently, you aren't musical enough to recognize the difference between a piano and the same piece played on a good victrola."

"Victrola!" I echoed.

"Yes. Washer had other mechanical devices in his room besides that sun lamp. One of them was an electric victrola—the kind that will play a dozen records without attention, and then play them again. All his records were piano solos by Chopin, the same pieces that he played on his own piano. All he had to do was to switch himself off the piano stool and switch on the victrola. That gave him a swell alibi for any hour of the night or day. It's an old trick."

"It strikes me," I said, "that we're getting rather a lot of criminals, aren't we? You said just now that Mrs. Salt was the guilty party and now you are accusing both Washer and his sister. Is Mrs. Salt twins or triplets or something?"

Cobb laughed. "The answer is again yes and no. Mrs. Salt was the only person who did everything. But she came here originally disguised as a man and then invented a sister for that man—a sister who had a room next door, who could come in and out either by the roof or through the front door—a sister who could provide him with a perfect get-away after he'd disposed of the body."

"You mean—"

"Yes. There never was a Mr. Washer and the Mr. Washer who didn't exist never had a sister. There was only Mrs. Salt."

"For the love of Mike!" I murmured weakly as my aching head fell back against the pillows.

Killed by Time

Inspector Groves, of the homicide squad, banged down the receiver and took his raincoat from its peg. It was still dripping wet.

"Get the boys together," he shouted. "We're going downtown, call's just come through. Sounds like murder."

A few minutes later he was out in the rain, crowding his men into a police car.

"Where to?" asked Collins, the police photographer, as they sped through the morning traffic.

"Doctor Cobden, 329 Somers Street."

Collins whistled. "Not Harmon Cobden, the brain surgeon?"

The inspector nodded. "What do you know about him?"

"He's the doctor who saved the chief's life after the Red House raid. Took a bullet out of his head as easy as clicking a shutter. A great old guy! Hope he's not croaked."

"No." Groves lurched sidewise as the car swung into Somers Street. "It's his son-in-law. Julius van Holdt. Body's just been found in the office by a party called Hazeldean—the doctor's secretary."

As the car drew up, Inspector Groves and his men jumped out and hurried up the steps of a small house which crouched low between two enormous modern apartment buildings. They were admitted by a slight, blonde girl of about twenty-eight. Her eyes, under the rain-drenched hat, were wide with fear.

"Thank Heaven you've come!" she said. "I'm Constance Hazeldean. I found him just after I came in to work this morning. Nothing has been touched. Doctor Cobden is upstairs with his daughter. She's been ill for some time. He'll be down just as soon as he can leave her."

The inspector pressed forward. "Where's the body?"

The girl led them through the patients' waiting room and stopped before the door of the office.

"In there," she said, a little quaver coming into her voice. "Do you mind if I leave you now? I don't think I could stand—"

Groves nodded for her to go and turned to a policeman.

"See that no one leaves the house, and don't let any one in either—not even the reporters."

The inner room was still in semidarkness. From one window streamed a ribbon of light which fell upon the calm, handsome profile of a man lying on a couch as though in slumber. The rest of the room—the desk, the shelves of medical books—were merged in an indistinct grayness. Only the face on the couch stared out in cruel relief.

The inspector threw back the curtains, and the whole room leveled into uniform light. It seemed a very ordinary office of a doctor. There was no sign of struggle or upset. The couch on which the dead man lay stood out about a foot from the wall opposite the door.

In the stronger light, the face of Julius van Holdt was no longer calm or handsome. One eye was closed as if in sleep, but the other—or rather, the place where the other had been—was a hideous red gash, a gaping void. It was as though someone had stabbed persistently and accurately at the eyes with a sharp, thin weapon.

Groves turned to Collins. "Reminds me of that Muloney case," he said soberly. "The bird whose wife stuck him in the eye with a hatpin. Remember?"

The photographer nodded as he and the finger-print man started operations. Meanwhile, Groves proceeded to make a detailed survey of the room. The windows were locked, and a thin layer of dust showed that they had not been opened recently. By the side of the couch was a chair on which stood a tumbler containing a few dregs of liquid.

Groves sniffed without touching the tumbler.

"Better let that wait for the doctor, Collins," he grunted. Then, going round to the other side of the couch, he stared up at a large antique clock, fashioned from heavy metal, which hung on the wall above him. Close under the dial dangled two lead weights, scarred with numberless holes and indentations—some old, some quite recent. He stood a moment, passing a hand over their rough surface, and then a gleam of moisture on the couch caught his eyes. He traced out a small damp patch which left a faint stain on his fingers.

"Funny," he muttered. "That's certainly not blood."

He turned as a little man with a pair of bright, birdlike eyes appeared in the doorway.

"Oh, hello, doctor."

The medical examiner took off his raincoat and started an immediate inspection of the body.

Some minutes later he shut his bag with a snap. "Well, I'm through for the time being," he said. "I'll send for the dead wagon."

"When was he killed?" Groves asked.

"Somewhere between six and seven-thirty this morning, as far as I can tell."

"What with?"

"None of the ordinary weapons—except, possibly an ice pick. I can't say exactly, but there are lots of handy implements around a brain surgeon's office." He picked up the glass. "I'll take this with me for analysis. If anything comes out at the autopsy, I'll phone you."

He hurried out of the room, and Groves whistled for a policeman.

"Avery," he said, "tell Joe to get the dope on all the people in the house. Check up on their movements last night, and between six and eight this morning. It doesn't look like an outside job to me."

After the body had been removed, the inspector started to examine the members of the household. He began with the now-recovered secretary.

"There's not much to add to what I have already told you," she said. "Mr. van Holdt has been sleeping in the office for the past two or three nights."

"Just a shakedown, eh?"

"Yes, the top story is used by Doctor Barry as a laboratory."

"Barry?" Groves cut in.

"He's Doctor Cobden's assistant. Has been for three years. He lives here most of the time as he and Doctor Cobden are conducting a series of important experiments on the brain tissues. Some evenings I help them after the patients have gone, but I never spend the night. Mrs. van Holdt is using the only spare bedroom, so except for the servants' quarters—"

"But," the inspector broke in, "if Mrs. van Holdt was his wife, why didn't—"

"If you want to know about the domestic life of Mr. and Mrs. van Holdt," interrupted Miss Hazeldean coldly, "you'll have to ask Doctor Cobden. There he is now."

As she rose to go, Groves saw a tall, elderly man coming toward him. For all his seventy years, Doctor Cobden was a fine, erect figure. A mane of white hair surmounted a handsome, leonine face. Only his eyes were tired and strained with the look of a man who has seen much of human suffering.

He spoke frankly and to the point.

"Julius married my daughter, Myra, two years ago," he began. "She had not been happy with him, and their life together was seriously impairing her health. For the past month, she has been staying with me under the medical care of Doctor Barry. Acting on our joint advice, she had decided to divorce her husband."

"Then why was he here?" queried the inspector.

The old man hesitated and then went on slowly. "Somehow or other, he discovered a thing that I thought was known only to myself. My daughter is to inherit a considerable legacy from her mother on her twenty-fifth birthday, which occurs next month. Three days ago Julius came round here and flatly refused to leave. He was in bad shape and I could not turn him out. He had taken to drinking freely and it was very embarrassing. Doctor Barry was obliged to forbid him to see Myra."

"Did they quarrel about it?" asked the inspector sharply.

Doctor Cobden gave him a swift glance. "They did have words, but—well, that's hardly to the point. As far as I know, my son-in-law went to bed last night around eleven. Just before that time, he came to my room as he had on the previous nights, and asked for a sleeping draft. He used to say even the ticking of the clock kept him awake. I gave him a pretty stiff dose of bromide. I—never saw him alive again."

"I don't blame him for not being able to sleep under that thing," said Groves, glancing at the clock.

The only servants in the house, Doctor Cobden explained, were a reliable old Negro couple who had been with him for twenty years. Doctor Barry and Miss Hazeldean had been working on an experiment until about ten o'clock. The girl had left shortly afterward.

"Van Holdt was out most of the evening," the old doctor went on, "and, as usual, came home far from sober. I myself went down and bolted the front door. There was no one with him and nothing suspicious occurred."

After the doctor had left, Groves went back to the couch. The medical examiner had removed the mattress, and Groves noticed something white in the center of the floor under the couch. He bent to pick it up. It was a stubbed cigarette butt.

"Queer place for van Holdt to stub a cigarette," he murmured.

He was interrupted by Doctor Barry, who had come down from his laboratory. The tall young man was pale and tense. He said he had heard-nothing during the night and had slept soundly until eight-thirty. He had not left the house, but he admitted freely that on several occasions he had words with van Holdt over the health of his patient.

With his consent, Groves spent a few minutes with the prostrate Myra, who told him that, although she had awakened before six, she had heard nothing at all.

Joe came in just before noon.

"I've got the dope on this van Holdt guy," he said. "He's pretty well known around town. It wasn't hard."

What the detective said bore out the information Groves had received from Doctor Cobden. Van Holdt's reputation was not enviable—especially where women were concerned, and he was desperately in need of money.

"I went over to the apartment house where Miss Hazeldean lives," Joe continued. "She's got an alibi all right. There's a night porter who says for certain she came in before eleven and didn't leave till eight-thirty. There's no way she could have sneaked out at the back. But I did find out one thing. There's been monkey business between her and van Holdt—sure as shooting. Till he came to live here, he was up at her place a whole lot. And," Joe added, "there's something else. Myra van Holdt was engaged to Doctor Barry before her marriage."

After Joe had left, Groves gathered up the slender threads of evidence. Cobden, Miss Hazeldean, Barry and Mrs. van Holdt— all had motives, and there was hardly a decent alibi among them. The only real clues he had found to date were a cigarette butt and a damp patch—both in strange places.

For a long time he studied the couch, the floor beneath, and the clock. He questioned the members of the household about the normal position of the furniture. Then, after inspecting the doctor's surgical instruments, he returned to work with increased enthusiasm. He was beginning to see more than a glimmering of a solution when the phone rang. It was the medical examiner.

"The autopsy's completed," he heard. "No news except that the weapon was possibly poisoned or dipped in some dope. The glass was no help—only a reasonably strong sleeping draft."

"Thanks, doctor!" There was excitement in the inspector's voice. "And, listen, I want you to come over here this evening, just before seven. I'm going to throw a party. Yes, the old gag. Maybe we'll get a breakdown."

Night had settled round the house. Inside, the curtains were drawn. A grim-faced policeman conducted the two doctors and Miss Hazeldean into the patients' waiting room. Myra van Holdt was absent, Doctor Barry having insisted that she was too ill to leave her room. Groves and the medical examiner were waiting by the door of the office.

"Please follow me," said the inspector.

Silently, they all trooped into the darkened room.

All the lights had been extinguished except one tiny, shaded bulb beneath the clock. Here and there one could make out the nebulous forms of chairs, bookshelves, and lamp stands. On the couch lay what looked like a sleeping figure.

Someone gave a little gasp, and then silence—utter and motionless—reigned. Every eye stared at what, for an instant, seemed to be the body of Julius van Holdt. Only gradually did the truth break through to them. It was a dummy. The bulk of it was made from cushions, the head a toy balloon, crudely painted with the markings of a human face!

The house as still as a tomb. Crashing through the stillness came the ticking of the clock. In contrast, the inspector's voice sounded low and hollow.

"Throw your minds back twelve hours," he said. "Imagine it is this morning, just before Julius van Holdt met his death. Everything in this room is exactly as it was then. I have even put the weights of the clock in the same position. In a few moments, you will find out exactly how the murder was committed."

The clock ticked on. It was barely possible to pick out the lines of its black metal frame; but just above the dummy—seeming almost to touch it—hung two indistinct shadows, looking darker against the blackness of the wall. They were the lead weights.

Louder and louder, the seconds shouted themselves by. Nerves grew more tense. Every one breathed quickly, keeping time unconsciously with the rhythm of the clock.

Suddenly there was a little scraping sound as though a mouse were nibbling at the wainscoting.

Everyone strained forward, trying to pierce the gloom. Then, without warning, the silence was split by a sharp noise from the couch—an explosion which cut through the air like a pistol shot. Barry started violently and overturned a chair.

"What was that?" someone shouted, and there was a general cry for lights.

Groves's voice rose calm and clear above the confusion. "Don't worry. It was only the balloon bursting," he called out, and then, putting a hand on the switch, he flooded the whole room with a blinding glare.

The dummy lay straggled on the couch, but now it was only a bundle of cushions and, where the head had been, a few limp strands of India rubber. Just above them, like a great, gray toad, squatted one of the heavy lead weights.

The inspector crossed the room briskly, fumbled under the weight for a moment, and then held up something that glinted coldly. It was a long needlelike instrument—a surgical probe.

"You see now,"—his voice was quiet and efficient—"how the crime was committed. Last night a needle like this one was wedged into a hole in one of the weights."

As they pressed eagerly forward, Groves pointed out the silver edges of a recent hole in the scarred lead.

"The weights drove the needle downward until it pierced the victim's brain," he continued. "You yourselves didn't notice the weapon, even when I switched on the light. And van Holdt, intoxicated as he was last night, would not have noticed it either."

"But how on earth—" the medical examiner began.

"We may be fairly certain," Groves explained, "that the job was done by someone who knew van Holdt's habits. Even if the needle had not been dipped in some anesthetic, his heavy drinking and the strong dose of bromide would have been enough to prevent the pain from waking him. Of course, there was no way of making certain that the needle would strike exactly on the eye, but there was quite a chance of it piercing some vital spot."

He looked searchingly round at the pale faces in front of him.

"Someone in this room did it," he said, and swung back toward the couch. "Do you see this couch? It is back against the wall. I pushed it there myself. Normally, Doctor Cobden tells me, it is kept at least a foot away so that he can get to both sides of the patient he's examining. The murderer pushed it in last night so as to make it possible for the weight to come down over the face—and then pulled it out this morning. I learned that when I discovered a stubbed cigarette *under* the couch. Van Holdt couldn't have reached under that far if his bed had been in its normal position. He would have stubbed it on the floor by his side."

Groves paused dramatically.

The first sound that broke the silence came from outside the room. There was a faint tap, and a policeman pushed back the heavy folding doors. A woman stood on the threshold—a small, tragic figure. It was Myra van Holdt.

Doctor Cobden led his daughter to a chair.

"Mrs. van Holdt," Groves resumed, "we know how your husband was killed. We know also that his murderer wound up the clock and removed the needle before nine-twenty when I came in. Any member of the household could have done it. You all had the means, the medical knowledge, and motives."

Groves's voice rose.

"You"—the inspector swung toward Doctor Cobden—"you admit you strongly resented van Holdt's treatment of your only daughter."

The old man's face clouded.

"You, Miss Hazeldean," Groves said, "were more than friendly with van Holdt up till the time he heard about his wife's inheritance—and then he dropped you. You had every reason to hate him."

"I wasn't the only one," said the girl bitterly.

But Groves was now looking at Doctor Barry.

"And you," he cried, pointing a finger toward the young doctor, "you cannot deny that you felt strongly about van Holdt's abuse of the woman you—"

"Will you please mind your own damned—"

"This is my business," snapped Groves. "There's Mrs. van Holdt, too."

"I didn't do it. I didn't!" Myra van Holdt had risen to her feet and stared wildly around her.

Barry turned toward the inspector.

"Good heavens, man, can't you leave her out of this? She's sick!"

"I make no accusations—as yet," said Groves quickly, and there was a curious gleam in his eyes. "Now, let's get back to the subject of this clock. The person who was calmly able to wind it up when the dead body of Julius van Holdt lay there on the couch is obviously the murderer. Doctor Cobden, please step here."

The doctor came forward.

"Now will you please wind up the clock?" Groves requested.

The old man reached up one of his long, thin arms and, taking the key from a hook, started to wind.

"That's enough," snapped Groves. "Now, you, please, Doctor Barry."

With an impatient shrug, the tall young doctor crossed the room and went through the same movements.

"Thank you." Groves took the key and gave it to the medical examiner.

The little man accepted it.

"Do you mind winding it up, doctor?" Groves asked.

The medical examiner walked over toward the clock and reached upward. He was too short by about four inches. Placing one foot on the part of the couch where the head of the body had lain, he connected the key with the dial.

"Hold it, doctor!" cried Groves.

As the little man stood there, perched in mid-air, the inspector continued.

"This morning I found a muddy patch on the couch in almost exactly the place where the medical examiner is now standing. It was a footprint—the footprint of someone who had been in a hurry—of someone who, like the doctor there, was not tall enough to wind up the clock without stepping on the couch."

"Can I get down now?" interrupted the medical examiner.

"O.K., doctor, and thanks." Groves could scarcely conceal the ring of triumph in his voice. "It was the footprint of a person who was ready to take an enormous chance—of someone motivated by a violent and uncontrolled passion—someone whose feeling for van Holdt had been changed to hate. And—most important of all—it was the damp footprint of someone who had recently come in from the wet streets—of a person clever enough to have an alibi, but not clever enough to remove two pieces of damning evidence."

His voice seemed to smash through the room as he pointed toward the farthest corner. "Would you please show us how you would wind up the clock? You, I believe, were the only person who had damp feet this morning!"

There was no answer. All eyes were turned toward the secretary.

"Miss Hazeldean!"

But again there was no answer, and this time all eyes were fixed on a crumpled mass where a woman lay on the floor in a dead faint.

The Hated Woman

I

A SELFISH WOMAN

Life was easy for Lila Trenton—too easy. And yet she was discontented. Even now, when she had just awakened safe and warm beneath her rose-colored quilt, there were little lines of discontent around her mouth. Her movements were petulant as she fingered the hairnet which preserved the stiffness of her hennaed waves. Restlessly, she stretched her silk-covered limbs, which, despite a slight thickening, were still well molded and voluptuous.

Through the wall she could hear her husband's slow, indecisive footsteps as he moved about his separate bedroom. For the thousandth time she wondered why she had married Paul Trenton. She, the pretty Lila, deserved something so much better than this dried-up, useless stick of a man.

She looked back to the time when she had first met him. Then he had seemed so distinguished, and everybody had said he was going to become famous with those chemical experiments of his. Lila Trenton—wife of the celebrated Paul Trenton. That's what she had hoped to be. Well, he had fooled her. Fifteen years had gone by, and he was still just an ordinary research worker down at the university—never made more than two thousand dollars a year.

Lila Trenton despised her husband because she had money and he had not; because he worshiped her slavishly despite her indifference to him; because she had perfect health, whereas he, who never complained, seemed to look older and frailer each day.

The careful footsteps had passed through the living room to the kitchen. Soon they returned, and there was a soft tap on the door.

"Are you awake, dear?"

A sallow, middle-aged man with graying hair slipped into her room, carrying a cup of tea in uncertain fingers.

"I've brought the tea rather early, dear. I want to be at the laboratory by ten. There are some interesting developments."

"There've been interesting development for fifteen years," snapped Lila as her red-nailed hand reached for the cup. "Oh, Paul, you've slopped it all over the saucer!"

"I'm sorry." Paul Trenton's pale, sensitive face regarded her with anxious attention. "How do you feel this morning, dear?"

"Feel! It's too early to feel anything."

Paul Trenton drew back the curtains and the morning light fell full on his tired face.

"He *does* look old," Lila was thinking not without a certain satisfaction. "Anyone seeing us together would take me for his daughter."

She stirred the tea, crushing three lumps of sugar with her spoon. "You look simply terrible, Paul. I suppose you've been working all hours of the night with those crazy experiments of yours. You never think how dull it is for me sitting all day alone with nothing to do but read magazines and listen to the radio."

"I had no idea you were lonely." Her husband's lips curved in a slight smile. "But you won't be alone tonight, dear. I've asked Professor Comroy for dinner. I hope—"

"Oh, Paul," —the cold cream on Lila's face puckered into lines of irritation—"you know how I hate fixing dinner for those stuffy university friends of yours."

"We can have dinner sent up, dear." Paul Trenton took the empty cup patiently and laid it on a table. "And Comroy is the head of my department. I owe him a great deal."

"Well, it's quite out of the question tonight," snapped Lila. "I don't feel up to it. And I think I've got a cold coming on. Yes, I'm sure I have. I just couldn't cope with that—that old windbag."

She sniffed with what conviction she could and produced a lace handkerchief from under the pillow.

"Very well, dear. I can put him off. And I'm sorry about the cold. Why don't you spend the day in bed and take plenty of fruit juices?"

Lila had been staring meditatively at her expensively mani-cured finger nails. Suddenly she looked up, a crafty expression in her eyes.

"There's no reason for you to give up your date with Professor Comroy, Paul," she said as though making a generous gesture. "Why don't you take him out somewhere to dinner? I don't mind an evening alone."

"Why, that would be nice, Lila. If you're sure you don't mind."

He bent to kiss her, but she pushed him away with bored distaste.

"Oh, Paul, not now! I can't bear you to come near me in your working suit. It always smells of chemicals."

She watched him move into the hall and heard the front door shut behind him. Then, with a curious, inward smile, she slipped her feet into feathery pink mules and hurried to the hall telephone.

"Hello, Larry... Yes, this is Lila. I've got a lovely surprise for you. I'm going to ask you round to dinner tonight... Yes, just us two. It hasn't been that way for weeks, has it?"

There was a short pause at the other end of the wire. Then a man's voice replied hurriedly, awkwardly.

"Well, Lila, I don't know whether I can make it. Business is picking up, and there's a lot to be done around the garage. But ..."

"Oh, of course you'll come." Lila's face had hardened, but her voice was silky smooth. "I know you'll come if your own Lila asks you."

"O.K. But listen, I've got to see you sooner than that." The voice was curt now and determined. "Is your husband there? ... Then will it be all right if I come straight away?"

"Oh, not now, Larry!" Lila gave a playful little scream. "Why, I'm hardly out of bed. I look a fright."

"Never mind what you look like," replied the man gruffly. "I'll be there in half an hour."

"Larry, Larry!" Lila jolted the hook, but the man had rung off.

For a moment she stood by the table. Then she ran to the mirror in her bedroom and started to remove the cold cream from her face.

The image in the glass was entirely satisfactory to her. Although she was over forty, to herself she looked no more than twenty-eight. True, the gray was showing through at the roots of her hair. But she could have a touch-up before the evening. Her skin was still smooth and firm, and her eyes were as clear and lustrous as those of a young girl. There would be no time to heighten the interesting shadows beneath her long lashes. But Larry would be so pleased to see her, he would not notice little things like that.

While she worked at her toilet, Lila Trenton looked almost as young as she felt.

"Wanting to see me at ten o'clock in the morning!" she thought complacently. "These young men are so impetuous."

II

CORNERED

Larry Graves slammed the receiver. As he gazed around the garage which he had bought and fixed up with Lila Trenton's money, his young, almost too handsome face went grim. Swiftly he hurried into a small back room, slipped off his greasy overalls, and wiped the oil from his hands with a piece of cotton waste.

He felt utterly disgusted at the thought of the scene ahead of him. He could see Lila Trenton waiting for him, saccharine, seductive, and yet so predatory—so suffocating. Well, he'd gotten himself into this mess with his eyes open. He'd have to find some way out—anyway. Slicking down his thick blond hair, he took his coat from its hook and moved through the lines of parked cars toward an old roadster.

"Be gone about an hour, Jack," he said as he swung open the door. "Finish fixing the brakes on that Dodd, will you?"

As he drove through the busy morning streets, the words Claire had spoken to him last night kept repeating themselves in his mind. "You're nothing but a gigolo—a gigolo." Well, she'd hit the nail pretty squarely on the head.

He drew up, outside the Vandolan apartment hotel, hurried into the opulent lounge, and, leaning over the desk, grunted a curt.

"Mrs. Trenton, please."

Lila had left the apartment door ajar. She was carefully draped on a divan when Larry entered. The pink pajamas had been supplemented by a diaphanous pink wrap. It would have taken a more observant person than Larry to detect the hard work which had gone to create this tableau of seeming spontaneous charm. She held out both hands and crooned:

"Larry, how sweet!"

"I've got to talk to you," said the young man shortly. He stood motionless by the door, clutching his hat in two bronzed fists. "It's about the garage."

"Come and sit here with Lila."

Mrs. Trenton patted the edge of the divan invitingly and smiled. For an instant, the young man did not move. Then he walked slowly to her side and sat down within the range of her exotic perfume. His untidy, oil-stained suit was in striking contrast to the expensive elegance of her negligee.

"That's better," Lila was murmuring, taking one of his hands in hers. "Now tell Lila all the trouble and she'll fix it."

"There's no trouble, Lila. Business is on the up and up. I'm doing fine. But the repayment on your loan falls due tomorrow. I—I want to ask you to extend it."

"But of course I will, darling. You know I never begrudge money to a friend. Five thousand dollars isn't a matter of life and death to me. I don't mind what happens to it just so long as it makes you happy."

"That's swell." Larry shifted uneasily, "Of course, I'm darn grateful for all you've done, but I want you to know that the garage is a good business proposition. You took a gamble when you lent me the capital to start. It was grand of you, and I'll never forget it. In fact, I'm going to work like the devil to justify your belief in me. I can go on paying good interest, and in time I'll be able to pay back every cent of the loan. But just at the moment—"

Lila patted his cheek and murmured; "Oh, darling, let's not talk about dull business. Let's talk about us–and tonight."

"That's just the point, Lila." Larry rose and passed a hand through his blond hair. "I can't come tonight. At least, not the way I used to. Something's happened and I've got to tell you about it now."

"Happened, Larry?" The curves of Lila's lips straightened into a hard red line.

"Yes, it's a—a girl. I met her last month, Lila, and—well, I guess we fell for each other. I want to get married."

"Married!" The powder could no longer hide the lines around Lila Trenton's mouth. Her voice had frosted. "But, Larry, is it wise to think of getting married when you have—er—other obligations?"

"I know it was crazy of me, but Lila,"—the blond young man sat down by her side again and gripped her arm— "you've always been so understanding. I know, if you'd meet her, you'd realize I couldn't help it."

"Meet her!" Lila pulled her hand back swiftly.

"Yes. I was wondering if I could bring her round tonight. Then you could explain that it really was a business arrangement—that I hadn't taken anything from you under false pretenses."

"You mean she isn't willing to accept *your* explanation," put in Lila sharply.

"Well, she was mad when I told her about you, of course. Didn't like the idea of my having taken money from a woman. But if she could see you, she'd realize how decent, how—er—disinterested you've been."

Lila Trenton rose from the couch. All the softness had left her. She had become harsh, strident.

"My gosh, you expect me to do your dirty work for you, do you? You expect to bring this woman round here to meet me as if I were your—your grandmother! You expect me to give you my money to get married on and then stand back and say 'God bless you, my children!' Why, of all the—"

"It isn't that, Lila. You know it's just—"

"Just that you want me to tell your lies for you." Lila twisted the expensive pearls around her throat. "Listen to me. I didn't lend you that money as a business proposition—and you knew it. I'm not such a fool as to throw away money on stray young men and their dirty garages. I lent you that five thousand dollars because I liked you. As soon as I stop liking you, I want my money back. And I don't like married men."

"But, Lila, I can go on paying the interest."

"Interest! Why should I trust a man like you? Think what you were doing when I first met you! You were little better than a crook. Since you seem to have told that girl so much about me, maybe I should tell her a thing or two about you—tell her that you used to deal in stolen cars, for example. I guess that would interest her—and the police, too."

"But, Lila, that's all over now." Larry's young face looked old and haggard. "You know I've gone straight."

"Strait-laced, I'd say." Lila moved to the mantel and stood there, a sneer on her lips. "You've got all you wanted out of me, and now you tell me you're going to be a good little boy and marry some sweet young thing you met at a church social. Well, let's hope she sings in the choir and gets a salary, because,

Heaven knows, it'll be her job to support you after you get married. I'm through."

Larry strode across the room and stood squarely in front of her. "I know what you are now, Lila. We understand each other perfectly. I know why you lent me the money, and I realize exactly what you're going to do about the garage. Well, you can take it and be damned to you. You can ruin me, but you can't get me to come near this filthy, over-heated place again."

Lila was laughing at him—and her laughter was not pretty. "You look so funny," she cried weakly. "So damn funny!"

"Funny, do I?" With a sudden gesture of fury, Larry's arm shot out and he brought his palm onto her cheek in a stinging blow.

"You—you—" he muttered.

Lila's fingers flew up to her cheek and the laughter drained out of her eyes. In its place there came a new, stranger expression.

"Larry!" she whispered hoarsely. "You struck me."

The young man stood in front of her, stiff and dazed. Then the realization of what he had done seemed to dawn on his face.

"I'm sorry, Lila. I'm all worked up. I didn't know—"

Lila did not take her eyes off him. As he stood there, angry and ashamed, she realized suddenly that she had never seen him so handsome before. In the past she had thought him weak, pliable, but this new streak of firmness intrigued and attracted her. He had just struck her, but she still had the whip hand. She was not going to let him get away from her.

"I'm sorry," he repeated dully.

"You should be," said Lila slowly, "but I think—I think I shall forgive you. That is, if you come and apologize very nicely—when we have dinner together tonight."

Larry turned away. As he moved to the door, she crossed the room swiftly and took from her pocket-book the key to her apartment. She handed it to him, and he snatched it fiercely.

"I'll come back," he muttered thickly.

"That's right," she whispered. "You're going to think it over, aren't you? You don't want to lose that lovely new garage, do you?"

After he had gone, she stared at herself in the mirror. On her left cheek were the red imprints of his fingers. It was a new, exciting sensation to think that a man had struck her. Larry!

She touched the marks gently, almost caressingly. Somehow, she did not even want to cover them with powder.

III

JEALOUSY

Larry Graves could still smell Lila's perfume as he hurried out of the Vandolan Hotel. He felt sick—disgusted with himself and with her. He had been crazy to accept that loan. He saw it clearly now. But at the time it had seemed his salvation. He had not realized there would be these complications—that it would end in this. His mind turned back to the picture of Lila handing him the key a few minutes before. He hated her now with a hatred which was almost physical in its intensity. He saw her as a spider, and himself as a wretched creature struggling futilely in her scented mesh.

He thought of the old days before the garage, when there had been no regular job, nothing but small commission on cars doubtfully bought and sold. Of course, if he had strength enough, he could throw it all up, return the money and start from the beginning again. But Larry Graves knew that he would not have the courage for that—that he would not have the courage to face the investigation into his past which a break with Lila would inevitably involve.

As he got into his car, he was gripped by an impulse which made him half-sick with excitement and apprehension. No one except Claire knew Lila had lent him that money. Lila would not have dared tell because of her husband. She had written a check to herself and given him the cash. He, Larry Graves, had tried to play square with her. But she had not any intention of playing square with him. Why should he be so scrupulous? If only he could get that receipt!

Then as his thoughts ran swiftly along this new channel, he remembered the key. No one knew he had that key. Lila Trenton would be alone tonight—quite alone. He could imagine her there, waiting, triumphant in her victory over him. The remembered scent of her perfume made him feel dizzy. Well, maybe he would go. Maybe she'd get something she wasn't expecting.

But Claire knew. He had told her about Lila last night. He would have to see her again before—before he made up his mind. If only he could get her to understand the way he had felt when he borrowed that money. If only she would see that things weren't as ugly as they seemed. Then everything might still be all right. There might be no need. He released the clutch and sent the car sharply forward.

Claire French ran a beauty parlor a few blocks away from the Vandolan Hotel. She had money of her own—money she had earned. Larry had never thought of that before, but Lila's cynical words brought it back with fresh bitterness. Perhaps that was why she had been so hard on him. She didn't realize how it was when a guy—

Larry pushed open the door marked "Mayfair Beauty Shop," and hurried to the girl behind the cash desk.

"Miss French, please."

"What name is it?"

"Graves."

"Just a moment." The girl disappeared and returned almost immediately. Her voice was flat and impersonal. "Miss French says you must have mistaken the address. The Vandolan Hotel is three blocks east."

"Tell her I've got to see her," said Larry fiercely.

"I'm sorry. She's very busy just now."

"I can't help that."

Larry pushed the girl aside and made for the inner door. He strode down a line of cubicles where women were sitting with electrical equipment on their heads, having permanent waves, face massages, manicures. In a small office at the back he found Claire sitting alone at a desk, busy with accounts. She rose swiftly.

As they stood staring at each other, the physical contract between these two young people was almost as violent as the state of their emotions. Claire was as dark as Larry was fair. And while his features were regular, if a trifle weak, hers had the irregularity of strength—a strength which came from within and did not in any way detract from the elusive charm of her face. Her wide-set, gray eyes smoldered as she spoke.

"I thought I told you last night that I didn't want to see you again."

"But, Claire, we've got to have this thing out. You've got to understand."

"I'm afraid there's nothing about you that isn't very easy to understand."

"After all, Claire, I'm only human. Lila was an attractive woman. You're not a prude. You wouldn't have objected to my knowing her before I met you if it wasn't for this darn money. And can't you see that a loan like that has nothing to do with her and me? It was just a business deal—a perfectly good investment for her. She wasn't doing me a favor."

Clair French sat down wearily. "It's no use, Larry. I can't get worked up over the problems of a man who accepts money from a woman he's having an affair with. It doesn't make the slightest difference to me whether she was getting good value for her investment or not."

"Well, maybe I have made a mess of things, Claire, but you said you loved me. Can't you give me a break—can't you take my word that I'm doing my damnedest to straighten everything out?"

"Are you going to pay her back her money, Larry?"

"I can't yet. You know I can't. And she won't extend the loan unless—"

"Unless you go round regularly—paying your interest," said Claire bitterly.

"She—she did ask me round tonight." Larry drew away slightly. "You know I don't want to go, but she threatened to have me dispossessed, to make me bankrupt if I didn't."

"Well, why not let her!" Claire's gray eyes fixed his squarely. "You can start over again. Other people have to."

"Oh, what's the use? You see, you don't know everything. It's not just a question of the money. I guess I could raise that. I could sell the garage for half of what it's worth. But Lila Trenton would still have her hooks in me."

"You mean there's something else?"

Larry thrust out his jaw. "I'm not handing you a sob story. Heaven knows I've had all this coming to me. But I got out of college in the middle of the depression. I tried to get a job—tried for about a year. Then I got tired of starving. When people came along and made offers that weren't exactly—honest, I didn't see the sense in having scruples. I got tied up with a concern which dealt in cars and wasn't too particular about their titles. Lila's car was stolen, and it was brought around to our place. That's how I met her. She guessed what the racket was, and I thought it was swell of her at the time not to do anything about it. But now she's threatened to tell." He looked down at his feet. "I can't let her do that, Claire—not so long as there's any hope with you. I couldn't ask you to marry me without a cent and with a possible prison sentence hanging over my head."

"You'd have more chance if you actually *were* in prison," said the girl quietly, "than asking me to marry you on that woman's money."

"Well, I guess I can't blame you. That means we're really through."

"I thought I made that point clear last night." Claire turned away. She did not want him to see her face. "I don't give a damn if you bought or sold a million stolen cars. I don't give a damn about your being weak, either. Heavens, we're all of us weak most of the time. It's—it's just that I think your type of weakness is particularly unattractive."

Larry gazed at the back of her head a moment in silence and then turned toward the door. As he reached it, Claire spun round suddenly.

"Larry, are—are you going to see her tonight?"

Larry's hand was in his pocket. His fingers were clasped tightly around the small, steel key. He stared at Claire with a grim, determined look in his eyes.

"Yes," he said slowly, "I'm going to see her tonight. Now that we're washed up, I don't give a damn what happens to me. I'm—I'm going to do exactly what I want to do."

For a few seconds after he had gone, Claire's eyes remained fixed unseeingly on the closed door. Then, throwing herself into a chair, she covered her face with her hands. She did not cry, but her whole body shook with long, strangled sobs.

"Larry said he loved me," she was thinking desperately, "but it's Lila Trenton who still owns him, body and soul. Oh, how I wish she were dead, dead, dead!"

She sat there a while, motionless. Her pale face set in a strained, expressionless mask. Then, suddenly, as though an idea had just come to her, she lifted the telephone receiver. Her fingers trembled as she spun to dial.

"Hello, hello…. Is that the Vandolan Hotel…. I want to speak to Mrs. Trenton."

IV

A WARNING

After Larry had gone, Lila Trenton returned to her room. In the thrill of his violent parting, she had completely forgotten her spurt of anger against him. He would come back. He would have to. The very fact that he would come against his will added a fresh excitement. And she could soon make him forget about that girl, she reflected, feeling assured of her own experienced charms.

She was still enjoying the reassurance of her mirror when the telephone rang.

"Good morning, madam." A girl's voice was speaking with saccharine politeness. "This is the Mayfair Beauty Shop. We are running a special today for new clients and we're eager to get your custom. Is there anything in particular you were wanting?"

"Well, I don't know," said Lila cautiously. "I was thinking of having a touch-up this afternoon. But I usually go to the beauty parlor here in the hotel. It's disgracefully expensive."

"Our specials are extremely reasonable," said the voice hurriedly.

Although her appearance meant more to her than anything else, Lila Trenton was always interested in a bargain.

"I might try you out, but I can't leave the hotel today. I've got a nasty cold."

By this time she had persuaded herself that she really had.

"That's all right, madam. We can easily send a girl over. No extra charge."

"Very well. Make it four o'clock." Lila gave a few details as to her requirements and concluded: "Tell the girl I'm very particular."

"Thank you, madam. And don't worry. We are very particular, too."

Lila had hardly rung off before the phone sounded again. It was the desk downstairs.

"Professor Comroy to see you, Mrs. Trenton."

"Tell him my husband's out," snapped Lila.

"But it's you he wishes to speak to, madam."

"Tell him I'm in bed with a cold."

There was a pause. "Professor Comroy says he will not keep you a moment. It's urgent."

What did the old fool want, thought Lila impatiently. He was to dine with Paul tonight and he couldn't have anything to say to her. It was only curiosity that made her give a grudging "All right," to the telephone operator.

Lila was suspicious of all her husband's university colleagues. She felt they tried to be intellectual and superior. But even though intellectual, middle-aged, and plump, Professor Comroy was a man. Instinctively she hurried to her vanity dresser, bathed her cheeks with astringent lotion, and fluffed the pink wrap around her. She was ready to greet her husband's friend with a sweet, invalidish smile.

"Oh, professor, I'm simply miserable about our dinner together tonight." She pressed a lace handkerchief to her face and held out her left hand. "But you see what a dreadful cold I've got. I don't want to spread it. Please sit over there—away from the germs."

Professor Comroy took the chair that she indicated and leaned ponderously forward. He was shortish, round man with the spectacled face of a benevolent owl. Behind the thick lenses his eyes, usually bright and twinkling, were grave.

"You must forgive my insisting on seeing you when you are unwell, Mrs. Trenton. But I have come to ask a favor—a favor which I feel sure you will be only too willing to grant."

"Favor!" echoed Lila with a slight diminution of effusiveness.

"As I expect you know, your husband has been working for several years on a most important piece of research which has been financed by a special endowment fund. Yesterday I received a letter from the Abel Foundation which stated that the fund was to be discontinued immediately."

"Oh, how terrible!" Lila forgot to control the guarded expression which had slipped into her eyes. "But—but what can I do about that?"

"Your husband has given all his time and energy to that research, Mrs. Trenton." The professor had removed his spectacles and was wiping them deliberately on a corner of his handkerchief. "He has very nearly obtained results which would mean a great deal to chemistry—and to himself. But if we cannot raise five thousand dollars at once, the work will have to be abandoned."

"Poor Paul!" sighed Lila. "But with a big, rich university like that I—"

"That's just the point, Mrs. Trenton." The professor slipped his spectacles around his ears and smiled sadly. "The university is not rich. It is heavily in debt to the city. Besides, even if the trustees were willing to listen to me, they could not possibly put through an appropriation until the end of the academic year."

Lila patted the back of her head but did not speak.

"Your husband is not only a very brilliant man," went on Professor Comroy. "He is also my greatest friend. If I had the money, I would gladly offer it myself. But I'm afraid I haven't. That's why I came to you."

"But I don't understand," said Lila with a tightening of the lips. "Do you mean you want me to put up five thousand dollars?"

"It would only be a loan. There is some rather expensive apparatus to be bought. I'm sure you are as eager as I am that your husband should continue uninterruptedly with his work."

Lila thought a moment. Then she said with sudden, overripe sweetness. "Oh, I'm afraid it's impossible. You don't know how sensitive Paul is. Why, he'd rather starve than feel he was using any of my money."

"I haven't told him that the fund has stopped," said the professor quietly. "He need never know. It can be a little secret between the two of us."

"Well, of course, I'd be delighted, but—but I'm afraid it's quite out of the question." Lila plucked nervously at the down on her cuffs. "Five thousand dollars is a lot of money. What with the depression and everything—I couldn't possibly find it."

Professor Comroy screwed up his bright, short-sighted eyes and he looked from the genuine pearls on Lila's throat to the expensive furniture in the apartment. "I can only repeat," he said at length, "that it means your husband's happiness—the crowning of his life's work. Surely, that is worth making a few sacrifices for, Mrs. Trenton."

"Sacrifices!" Lila rose and stared at him with narrowing eyes. "Really, Mr. Comroy, I hardly feel it your place to tell me how I should spend my money."

"I'm sorry." The professor had also risen, and his cherubic face had lost something of its pleasantness. "But I want you please to consider this matter very seriously. I cannot believe that you are indifferent to your husband's career even if you are not interested in the progress of science."

"Science!" exclaimed Lila scornfully. "Do you suppose I've heard about anything else for the past fifteen years? It's always, science, science, science. He's going to do this. He's going to do that. But he never gets anywhere so far as I can see. There's no reason why I shouldn't be frank with you, Mr. Comroy. My husband has been a great disappointment to me. He's weak—got no push. Why, he's never made more than two thousand a year. I fail to see why I should support him at the university, too."

"Very well, Mrs. Trenton," said Professor Comroy with steely quietness. "I see that it was foolish for me to come."

"It was not only foolish," replied Lila, who was working herself up into a pitch of righteous indignation. "It was impertinent."

The professor crossed abruptly to the door. "There is no need to tell you that I think your attitude a wrong one. Your husband is one of the finest men I have ever known."

Lila shrugged the pink silk of her shoulders and lighted a cigarette.

"And what's more, Mrs. Trenton, I feel I am old enough to tell you something for your own good." Gilbert Comroy's rotund form was standing by the door, and he was peering fixedly at her through his spectacles. "It is easy to feel that you owe obligations to no one. But there will come a time when you yourself may be in need of help; when you see all that you care most for in life falling about you like a pack of cards. It will not be very pleasant then to find yourself—absolutely alone."

"Thank you, Mr. Comroy." Lila spurted smoke from her nostrils. "Thank you for the charming little sermon."

V

WHEN HATING RIVALS MEET

All the rest of the morning, Claire French struggled with the confusion of her thoughts. The night before when Larry had first told her about Lila Trenton, she had felt she hated him; had told herself that she could not even bear the sight of him again. But now she realized she had been deliberately blinding herself. He had been foolish, weak, but it takes more than that to make any real difference. Slowly, illogically, she had felt her anger and disgust shifting from him and settling upon Lila Trenton, the woman whom she had never even seen.

She could not get the thought of her out of her head. While she massaged, shampooed, chatted with clients, her mind was fixed on one thing only—her four-o'clock appointment at the Vandolan Hotel.

Her fingers were trembling when at last she collected her things, packed them in a suitcase, and hurried out into the street. She looked very young and very determined as she gave Mrs. Trenton's name to the clerk and took the elevator to the twenty-seventh floor.

Lila opened to her with a rather querulous "Come in." Claire stepped into the hall and, controlling her voice with an effort, said professionally:

"Good afternoon, Mrs. Trenton. I'm from the Mayfair Beauty Shop."

As Lila languidly shook the folds out of her wrap, Claire regarded her with shrewd, critical eyes. She was handsome, the girl had to admit that. But her looks wouldn't last much longer. Claire, with her expert knowledge of cosmetics, could detect instantly all the little devices which held up the slipping structure of Lila Trenton's beauty.

Not a day under forty, she thought with sudden satisfaction. She eats too much and doesn't get enough exercise.

"I'm not altogether pleased with the touch-ups they give me here," Lila was saying, as she helped herself to a piece of chocolate candy without offering the box to Claire. "I hope you're going to be more satisfactory."

Suddenly a vision of Larry with this woman slipped into the girl's mind. She had to grip tightly to the suitcase to keep herself steady. Her thoughts were racing. Everything that had been so confused before now seemed clear. She knew that she loved Larry—that she would do anything for him. All her high-sounding moral principles boiled down to the one, vulgar word—poweringly jealous of the woman who had played such an important part in Larry's life. It was this moment of honest self-revelation that made her feel calm, assured.

"I'm ready, Mrs. Trenton—ready when you are."

Claire fixed up a beauty parlor in the large, black-tiled bathroom. Lila was patronizing, but gossipy, divulging little intimate physical details about herself.

"It's only at the roots that the gray patches show," she murmured as the hot soapy water trickled around her ears. "Be careful it doesn't get spotty."

"Oh, it won't be spotty." Claire's fingers worked firmly across the other woman's scalp—more firmly, perhaps, than was strictly necessary.

Lila gave an irritated "Ouch."

"I'm sorry, Mrs. Trenton. But it's worth suffering a bit to be beautiful, isn't it? Maybe there's a boyfriend coming around tonight."

"Maybe there is." Lila's voice was glossed with self-satisfaction. "I don't see why all fun should stop when you're married, do you? Particularly when you're a girl and your husband's so much older."

Claire dried off the hair with a towel, put on her rubber gloves and started to work in the henna paste. She was amazed at the almost physical pleasure she felt at having Lila Trenton helpless and unsuspecting beneath her fingers.

"How about a facial when you're through, Mrs. Trenton? The skin around your chin is getting rather flabby."

"Flabby!"

"Oh, it's nothing to worry about. Most women of your age have trouble with sagging muscles. I think I could do wonders to those lines around the mouth, too."

"Listen," said Lila tartly, "I asked for a touch-up. If I need anything else, I'll tell you."

There was an inscrutable smile on Claire's lips. "Oh. I didn't mean it that way, Mrs. Trenton. Really, you're thirty-eight in an artificial light."

Lila jerked her head backward. She was just about to speak when Claire cut in:

"Don't talk, Mrs. Trenton, the henna might get in your mouth."

The atmosphere grew thicker as Claire rinsed out the hair and, selecting a warm, dry towel, wrapped it around Lila's head like a turban.

For a moment the two women looked at each other's reflections in the misty mirror without speaking. Lila's exotic perfume had impregnated the steamy air. As it invaded Claire's nostrils, she felt a vague wave of nausea. Once again she thought of Larry and knew that her control was weakening.

"Hot in here," gasped Lila.

"Yes, it is." Claire's hands fell suddenly to her sides. Her voice, which had been soft, almost sycophantic, was hard as flint. "You fat, useless women always live in a stifling temperature."

"What—what did you say?" Lila was gazing at her in utter astonishment.

"I said that fat, useless females like you always pamper yourselves. You overeat. You—"

"How dare you!" Lila's voice rose to a high, furious scream. "Of all the impertinent, disgraceful—Get out of here. Get out, I say."

"But your hair's not dry, Mrs. Trenton. Surely, with the boyfriend coming in, you want to look your best."

"This—this—I'll report you. You'll be dismissed instantly."

"Lovely," said Claire.

"And this Mayfair Beauty Shop—I shall call up your employers immediately."

"Oh, I don't think they'll mind." Claire was standing by the door, her gray eyes blazing. "And it would be worth it, anyhow. There's lots of things I'd like to say to you, Mrs. Trenton. And lots of things I'd like to ask you, too. How does it feel to be getting old and fat? How does it feel to be cheating on your husband? How does it feel to be giving money to young men because you can't get them any other way? Oh, there are so many things, but I guess you don't even know the answers yourself." Her laughter rose shakily. She was almost as hysterical as Lila herself. "If you knew how funny you looked sitting there with that towel around your head."

Lila was completely taken aback. For a moment her lips could form no words. Then she rose to her feet and shouted stridently:

"Get out! Get out before I call the police!"

"I'm going." Swiftly, Claire assembled her things and packed them in the suitcase. "I guess you'll be able to dry your own hair, Mrs. Trenton. There will be no charge for what I've done to you. You'll—you'll be able to make yourself beautiful for that date with the boyfriend tonight. But before he comes round, take a good look at yourself."

She gripped the suitcase, ran out of the apartment, and slammed the door behind her.

VI

A COVETOUS MAN

For one dreadful moment after Claire had gone, Lila Trenton's anger gave way to a sensation bordering upon panic. Growing old! Could it be true? Swiftly she bent forward and gazed at her reflection in the steamy mirror. Despite the towel around her hair and the absence of make-up, the blurred reflection looked fresh, young, reassuring. Lila breathed a little sigh of relief. The girl was crazy. Of course, that was the explanation. Still, it had been very unpleasant. All that about buying young men! What a ridiculous thing to say. The girl must have a nasty mind—jealous, probably, or sex starved.

She had almost calmed down sufficiently to call the Mayfair Beauty Shop and complain when there was a knock at the door. For some reason she started nervously. The knock sounded again and she cried out an agitated:

"Who is it?"

"Hotel electrician to look at the refrigerator, madam."

Lila crossed to the door. A young man in overalls stood on the threshold. He was dark, strong, rather attractive. Instinctively, Lila smiled.

"Come in," she said, patting the towel around her head. "I was just washing my hair."

The young man grinned back rather too intimately as she conducted him to the kitchen.

"Been working here long?" she asked.

"Just a couple of months, Mrs. Trenton." The young man grinned again and moved his arm slightly so that it brushed against Lila's thigh. "There's not much money in it, but I sometimes get odd jobs on the side. I got a kid brother, you know. Putting him through school."

"How nice of you! Oh, excuse me a moment."

With her best smile Lila hurried away as the telephone rang.

"Hello, what is it?"

"Mrs. Trenton?"

"Yes."

"This is the manager speaking. There is nothing to be worried about, but several of our guests have registered complaints of petty theft the past few days. We are asking every one to keep their doors locked—especially in the apartments like yours which have back doors leading onto the fire escape."

"Oh, all right," said Lila testily. "But why must you bother me with things like that? There's a house detective, isn't there?"

"Yes, Mrs. Trenton," said the voice wearily. "We do all we can to protect our guests, but the detective can't be everywhere at the same time."

Lila put down the receiver and returned to the kitchen. The young man unbent as she entered.

"Well, Mrs. Trenton, the refrigerator's in pretty good shape." His dark eyes were appraising her boldly. Thrusting his hands in his trousers pockets, he sauntered into the living room. "Nice place you've got here. Gee, it must be swell to have money."

Lila was wondering whether her hair was dry enough to look pretty without the towel. She decided to go into the bedroom and see. The young man followed her in.

"Geez," he said, "I wish I was a girl. Maybe then you could use me around this place, Mrs. Trenton. I'm pretty good at housework, too. Used to be a houseboy when I was a kid."

Lila felt a tingling thrill of excitement. The young man was very near.

"Is there anything you'd like me to do for you before I go, Mrs. Trenton?"

His dark eyes were playing on the rose-colored quit.

"Why—er—yes," said Lila hurriedly. "You might light the fire in the living room. I—I want to dry my hair."

"O.K., Mrs. Trenton." The young man had taken out a cigarette and was glancing at her over the match flame. "Got kindling?"

"What? Oh, I—I don't know. No, I don't think so. But there's some wood on the little balcony just outside the back door. You'll find a hatchet there, too."

The young man strolled into the kitchen, and Lila could hear the strong blows of the hatchet outside. For some reason which she could not define, she felt nervous. That crazy girl from the beauty parlor must have upset her more than she had thought.

She actually started when a few minutes later the bedroom door was pushed open and the young man stood on the threshold.

"The fire's ready and waiting," he said.

"Oh! Oh, thank you very much. Did you lock the back door?"

"Sure. I locked it all right."

His gaze moved casually around the room, settled on the dressing table, and then flicked away.

"If ever you need me, Mrs. Trenton, it's easy to get me. Sam Nolan's the name."

He made no attempt to leave. After a second's indecision, Lila rose and slipped past him. She felt his breath warm against her cheek. Once again she experienced that momentary sensation of nervousness.

But the living room reassured her. When she saw the fire crackling cheerfully in the grate, she felt her silly fears disappear and her coquetry return.

"Well, Sam, thanks a lot. And I'll certainly think of you if I want anything."

"Do that, Mrs. Trenton."

He had moved close again. His dark face with its slightly full, drooping mouth was smiling meaningly. A sudden glow swept through Lila. This man was young, attractive. And yet he obviously found her desirable. To think that girl had said she was old!

Sam Nolan was still gazing at her fixedly. Lila flushed. Then the color drained from her cheeks. Suddenly she realized what the boy was looking at. That eager, covetous expression was not directed toward herself. His eyes were fixed, not on her face but on the string of pearls around her throat. Almost instinctively she had moved toward the telephone.

"Well," she faltered, "what are you waiting for?"

The young man jerked his eyes away. "Sorry, Mrs. Trenton. Just daydreaming."

The door slipped shut behind him. Sam Nolan moved down the corridor with a hand thrust deep in his trousers pocket. Between his fingers he was gripping a key—the key to the back door of Mrs. Trenton's apartment.

VII

A CALL FOR HELP

After he had gone, Lila felt the sensation of panic returning. "Why was he looking at my pearls?" she repeated time and time again in her mind. "Why was he looking at my pearls?"

And then the words of that girl from the beauty parlor slid back into her thoughts. "You're getting old. You're getting old."

She gave a little shiver and moved toward the fire, as though its very warmth would bring comfort. She had reached the hearth before she noticed the hatchet. It was standing propped against the wall by a box of logs. The blade shone dully. Somehow, she could not tear her gaze from it. And yet it was just the wood hatchet, she told herself. The young man—Sam Nolan—he had brought it in from the balcony and hadn't taken it back. There was nothing to be afraid of.

Suddenly everything about the day seemed sinister to Lila Trenton. First there had been that scene with Larry; then the professor with his strange warning; the girl from the beauty parlor; and now this boy, Sam Nolan, with his queer looks and hints. Everyone was against her. They were jealous—that's what it was—they were jealous because she had money, because she was still young and pretty.

For a moment Lila Trenton stood motionless, twisting her scarlet-nailed fingers. Then, as usual, she ran to the mirror for reassurance. With trembling fingers she pulled the towel from her hair. She was not old. She—

Lila Trenton's eyes widened. Her mouth dropped half open and hung there. Then she gave a low, strangled sob.

Half blind with panic, she rushed to the mirror in the bathroom. It gave her no comfort. The girl's words were ringing in her ears. "Before the boyfriend comes, take a good look at yourself!"

She stumbled to the telephone and swiftly, clumsily dialed a number.

"Hello, is that the university? ... I want to speak to Paul Trenton.... Yes, yes, it's urgent—urgent! I need his help."

In the pause that followed Lila Trenton twisted the beads around her throat hysterically. Her voluptuous breasts were moving quickly, jerkily. She had never felt this way before—never. For the first time in her married life she was conscious of a desperate need for her husband. He would understand. He would comfort her.

"Hello, Paul, is that you? ... Oh, you must come, darling. Come quickly.... Something awful has happened. I'm frightened—terribly frightened."

VIII

DOOMED!

Gilbert Comroy thought he would never forget the look in Paul Trenton's eyes when he told him about the discontinuance of the Abel Foundation Fund. He had hoped desperately to raise the five thousand dollars so that his friend should never know. He had interviewed trustees, scientific organizations. He had even contemplated the money lenders. But there had been no success.

Trenton was not an expansive man. He never showed or spoke of his feelings. But Comroy had seen that brief instant of disappointment and frustration in his friend's eyes, the momentary droop of his mouth. He knew that there had been taken away from Paul Trenton something which could never be replaced.

He had worked with Trenton at the university for nearly twenty-five years. He had seen him as an enthusiastic, vital young man; had seen him through his disastrous marriage to Lila, through the years of his life with her during which her contemptuous selfishness had slowly, relentlessly turned him from an ambitious young scientist into a frail, broken old man. Comroy had watched the gradual change in his friend with a bitterness that held Lila wholly responsible. His dislike of her was the only violent element in his otherwise mellow, placid existence.

He knew that Paul Trenton had given his all to the Abel Research in a last, desperate attempt to prove to himself and to Lila that he was not a failure. Results were near; success almost with his grasp. But here—as in everything else—Lila Trenton had let him down.

Not only had she failed him, but she had added petty insult to real injury. That afternoon she had called Paul back from the laboratory. That was typical of Lila. Even at the moment when she knew her husband had found the ground cut away from beneath him, she had called him home—called him most likely to do some trivial errand for her.

And he had gone meekly! That was Paul's tragic weakness. He had never got over his blind infatuation for that useless, heartless woman.

Although he looked as calm and benign as ever, Gilbert Comroy felt hatred in his heart when, at seven-thirty that evening, he stood outside the Trenton's apartment at the Vandolan Hotel.

Paul Trenton's face was pale and drawn when he let him in.

"I'll be ready in a few minutes, Comroy. Poor Lila's had quite a shock. She's in bed and there are just a few little things—" He broke off, hurrying back to his wife's bedroom. "She says she doesn't mind being left alone. We can go out to dinner. But she's very upset."

Comroy moved into the living room and stared around him moodily through his thick spectacles. From the open door he could hear his friend's voice, soothing, consolatory.

"Don't worry, Lila, dear. Just stay in bed and drink all the fluids you can. Comroy and I won't be long. We'll be back by ten." There was a pause. Then he added in a louder voice. "Ready, Comroy?"

"Yes. I'm ready."

"Well, good night, dear." Trenton closed the door of his wife's bedroom.

As Comroy followed him out of the apartment, his expression was placid but his thoughts were turbulent. For the first time in his benevolent life, he was consciously wishing evil to a fellow creature—he was wishing fervently that Lila Trenton was dead.

Over dinner at the Davenham Grill, Gilbert Comroy made no reference to the Abel Research Fund. He did his best to chat lightly about unimportant university topics. Trenton listened gravely, but his mind was obviously straying. Once or twice Comroy had the impression that he was trying to tell him something, but it was not until dinner was finished and they were smoking over coffee that he spoke. His drawn, almost ethereal face had taken on a strange determination.

"There's something I want to tell you, Comroy. It's about the Abel Research. I think that it can go on for a while. At least we'll be able to get that new equipment."

"You mean you've raised some money?" asked Comroy, his plump face alight with pleasure.

"Well, hardly." Trenton's mouth twisted in a smile. "You see, I went to my doctor this morning. I've had pain for some months, but I've been busy, never had the time—" He broke off and added softly, "The doctor told me it was too late to operate."

"Is—is it—"

Trenton nodded slowly. "Yes, cancer. It's just a matter of months—weeks, possible. I've got a small insurance policy, Comroy. Just about three thousand dollars. I've left everything to the university. Fleming's a good man. He's been working with me and he could carry on. I think he might get what we want very soon."

"But, Paul, this is terrible!" Comroy felt a sudden constriction of the throat. "You mean there's no hope?"

"Don't worry about me." Trenton stirred his coffee slowly. "I've been pretty much of a failure. I admit it, and now I don't care a great deal. If I felt that Fleming could complete the work with my money, that's all I'd want. Lila has ample means to support herself. And I think she would be willing to pay the funeral expenses."

"Don't talk that way, Paul." Comroy had gripped his friend's arm. "You never know. Tomorrow I'll go to the doctor with you. There's always—"

"No," said Trenton quietly. "I'm happy that it will solve the problem for us. Now, let's forget about it. I'll order some brandy—a little luxury."

While they sat there sipping their old cognac, Comroy's mind was working feverishly—thinking of Lila Trenton. It was she who had done this. For years she had been taking advantage of Paul's almost reverent love for her. She had worn him down, neglected him. This morning she had willingly cut off his career. And now—now he realized that she had been letting him die before her very eyes.

"Another brandy, Comroy?"

"Yes, I think I will."

Trenton glanced up at the clock. "We've got plenty of time. But I'd like to get back at ten o'clock because poor Lila will be alone."

And so they sat together until ten o'clock, those two old friends, thinking their thoughts of life and death. But to the waiters and other diners, they were just a couple of commonplace middle-aged men who could not possible have anything interesting to say to each other.

IX

MURDER

It was ten minutes after ten when finally Paul Trenton and Gilbert Comroy returned to the apartment.

"Excuse me a moment," said Trenton, "I'll just look in the bedroom and see if Lila wants anything. Why don't you go into the kitchen and get yourself a highball? While you're at it, mix me one, too. You know where the refrigerator is."

Trenton moved to the door of his wife's bedroom and, tapping gently, murmured: "Lila, are you awake?"

Comroy made his way through the living room toward the kitchen. Lila Trenton! The image of that woman was still haunting him like an obsession. He glanced at his own reflection in the mirror and was startled at the pallor of his face. God grant he would not have to see her again tonight. If she were there in front of him, he thought suddenly, he could not be answerable for what he would say—or do.

When Paul Trenton hurried anxiously toward the kitchen a few seconds later. Comroy's ample figure was blocking the doorway. His shoulders were bent, his hands hanging limply at his sides.

"Is Lila there?" asked Trenton. "She's not in her room. I'm worried. I—"

"She's here." Comroy's cheeks, usually so pink and unlined, were now a rough parchment ivory. "She's here!"

Slowly he moved aside. The two friends stood together in the doorway, Comroy peering shortsightedly forward, Trenton pressing against the woodwork in a kind of trance.

The kitchen was in a state of utter chaos. The glass panel in the black door leading to the balcony fire escape was shattered. The door of the refrigerator had been flung open. And on the floor, with a hatchet at her side and surrounded by sharp splinters of glass, lay Lila Trenton. She was hunched in an awkward, ugly posture across the gray linoleum. The diaphanous pink wrap was torn and spattered with red. Around her head was a wide, crimson pool. But there was one thing—one thing which added a final touch of macabre horror to that ghastly scene.

Her tangled, untidy hair was not of the auburn tint which Lila Trenton had so carefully and expensively preserved. It gleamed in the hard illumination from the ceiling light—*and it gleamed green, a dull metallic green.*

For a second neither of the men spoke. Then Paul Trenton stumbled forward and knelt shakily at his wife's side. His head was against that crumpled pink silk that covered her left breast.

"She's dead, Comroy," he whispered tonelessly. "Dead. You'd better call the police."

The little professor did not seem to hear. He was clasping his hands in front of him and gazing at the twisted body at his feet with glazed eyes.

"The police, Comroy." Once more Trenton's voice rose, swift, agitated. "And call a doctor, to make sure there is no hope. Quick."

Comroy seemed to gather his wits with an effort. Throwing a last glance at Lila Trenton, he turned and hurried into the living room. In the shock of what had happened, his mind was confused with a thousand terrible thoughts. Visions of Lila Trenton swept before his eyes; visions of her as he had seen her that morning in the pink dressing grown; visions of the hatchet and of the scarlet pools on the linoleum.

"The telephone," he found himself repeating half out loud. "The telephone. I must call the police, the police—and a doctor."

As he reached the passage which led toward the front door, he saw something which at first his numbed senses could not take in. The door of the hall closet was opening slowly. He paused and looked over the top of his spectacles. A man in a gray hat and raincoat had slipped from the closet and was moving swiftly toward the front door.

The sight of another living creature, appearing however unexpectedly, instantly banished the nightmare images from Professor Comroy's mind and brought him back to reality.

"Stop!" he called. "There's been a murder done."

The man's hand clutched the front-door knob. He swung round, his young face pale with fear.

"Murder!"

He stood motionless for a second as though unable to make up his mind what to do. Then, as Comroy hurried purposefully toward him, he threw open the front door and started to run out.

Comroy could not see what happened next, but he heard a woman's voice exclaiming sharply, "Get back in there, Larry." And while the professor's fingers moved toward the receiver of the hall telephone, the young man backed up the passage, followed by a girl. The lines of her face were set and determined. In her gloved hand she held a revolver.

Comroy watched her shut the front door slowly behind her and point the gun at the young man.

"I knew you'd be here, Larry. I had to come, too. I wanted to be sure that nothing would happen." The girl's gaze flicked to Comroy, and instantly her gray eyes faltered. "Who—who are you?"

"I have no idea what all this is about," Comroy said calmly. "Mrs. Trenton has been murdered, and I'm just about to telephone for the police."

"Murdered!" The girl's lips turned pale. Slowly she moved the revolver so that it was aimed at the very center of the professor's expensive vest. "Stay where you are," she said softly. "If you use that telephone, I'll shoot."

Her eyes had flashed back to the young man. "So I was too late. You *did* do it—did kill her, Larry!"

Larry Graves did not seem conscious of what was going on. He was gazing at the girl dazedly. "I waited around the garage all evening, Claire. I hoped you'd call, but you didn't. I guess it was crazy for me to come here. But nothing seemed to matter, and I knew there was only one way to clear up this mess."

"Oh, I'm not blaming you." Claire French's voice was swift, breathless. "But you've got to get away. The police will soon be here. You've got to go."

"But you don't think that I—"

"What's the use? There's no need to lie to me, Larry. But I'm for you. Don't you understand that?"

Both the young people seemed to have forgotten the professor, although the girl was still pointing the gun at him. Gilbert Comroy watched them closely, with understanding gradually dawning on his face.

So he was not the only person who had wanted Lila Trenton dead. There were other lives besides her husband's in which she had been a destructive influence.

"Get out of the country, Larry," the girl was whispering. "The midnight train to Canada. I'll keep this man quiet—stop him calling the police until you've gone. Only hurry."

Larry Graves's square-cut face broke into an expression of grateful relief.

"Claire, you mean you can forgive me?"

"Oh, Larry, how can anything like that matter now?" She broke off and then, impulsively, she laid her hand on his arm. "If you get away, I'll follow. I'll find you wherever you are."

"But you don't think I would leave you here alone!"

Claire turned on him impatiently, almost fiercely. "Go, you fool, while there is yet time! *Go!*"

For a moment the young man stood gazing at her irresolutely. Then he turned and hurried out, closing the door behind him.

X

NOLAN ON THE SPOT

After Larry had gone, the girl passed a weary hand across her eyes. Professor Comroy regarded her face thoughtfully through his spectacles.

"Well, this is a most extraordinary affair," he said. "It is my duty to call the police, you know. Do you still intend to prevent me from doing so with that revolver?"

The girl continued to menace him with her gun. "I—I suppose you're her husband."

"Lila Trenton's husband!" The professor's mouth moved in a slight smile. "Heaven preserve me—no! I'm sure it would be idle to ask whether you or your friend committed this murder. I do think I am entitled to some explanation."

"I'm sorry. I can't tell you anything." Claire French's lips tightened. For a moment she was silent. Then she added suddenly: "But there's one thing I do know. If Larry did kill her, she deserved it. She was a wicked, despicable person. She had no right to live."

"Sh-h!" The professor glanced over his shoulder as faint sounds came to them through the living room from the kitchen. Then, to the girl's utter astonishment, his smile returned. "My dear," he said softly, "I agree with you absolutely."

"You—you mean—"

"I mean that it might be a very good plan if you were to put that revolver back in your bag and leave the Vandolan Hotel as quickly as possible." Gilbert Comroy crossed his hands over his vest. "The police have been kept waiting as it is. I feel they can wait a little long."

Claire was looking into his sympathetic eyes, and, before she knew what she was doing, she had poured out the full story of Larry's relationship with Lila; the instinct of jealousy which had led her to go and see Mrs. Trenton that afternoon; and the scene which had taken place between her and the other woman.

"It was crazy of me," she concluded, "but Mrs. Trenton's the kind of person who'd make anyone do crazy things. That's why I came back tonight. I realized she'd be furious and make things worse for Larry. I've got to save him somehow. So you will help me?"

The professor did not speak for a moment. "It may be difficult. Even if neither of you—er—killed Mrs. Trenton, it's rash to run about with guns and hide in closets. In a civilized world you can't turn life into melodrama without getting into trouble."

"I'm so grateful—"

"Oh, don't be grateful, my dear." Behind his spectacles the professor's eyes were benevolent. "It is unconventional of me to say this. But I feel Lila Trenton's death is—is a benefit to society, and I do not want anyone to suffer for it. Now you'd better hurry up and go. Mr. Trenton is still in the kitchen. He may not feel the same way as I do."

As he spoke, there were slow footsteps in the living room. Paul Trenton appeared, looking very gray and ill. He was holding a hand to his side, and his eyes were glazed. He did not seem to notice the girl.

Swiftly, Claire slipped the revolver into her pocketbook and moved to the door. Then, as her fingers touched the knob, she gave a little gasp and stepped backward. Someone was knocking, loudly.

The sound seemed to bring Paul Trenton back to the reality of the moment. As a swift glance passed between Claire and the professor, he hurried to the door and swung it open. "Are you the doctor?" he asked eagerly.

A policeman stood on the threshold. "Mr. Trenton? Is anything wrong here? I'm Patrolman Davis."

"Why—er—" Trenton seemed unable to form the words.

"The hotel detective arrested a man on the fire escape," continued the policeman, as he stepped into the hall. "Sam Nolan— he was an electrician around here—and for some time they've had their suspicions here that he was a thief. I was called in when the house detective found Nolan on the fire escape, injured. He had a valuable pearl necklace in his pocket and also the key to the back door of this apartment. He's being held downstairs. I came up to find out if you'd missed anything."

"I'm afraid it's not merely a question of missing things," murmured Comroy. "A murder has been committed. You'd better come, look things over, and take charge."

The policeman hurried after Comroy to the kitchen. There, Comroy swiftly outlined the details of their discovery. For an instant the policeman gazed at the dead body of Lila Trenton. Then he snapped:

"Have you called the police?"

"Er—no, not yet. I was just going to when you came."

The policeman moved back to the hall, and for the next few minutes replied rapidly to questions from the other end of the wire. At length he hung up the receiver.

"Captain Lee will be round right away," he said, "Meanwhile, no one's to leave the apartment. It looks as if Nolan had done it, but we can't take chances." His eyes rested on Claire. "How about the young lady? Did she come in with you?"

Comroy looked momentarily nonplused. "No, Miss—er— she had dropped in to see Mrs. Trenton just before you arrived. Naturally, she didn't know anything about the murder."

The policeman grunted.

"Perhaps," continued Comroy, "it would be all right for her to leave."

"Sorry. You'll all have to stay."

As the policeman spoke, Paul Trenton gave a little groan and doubled forward. Instantly Comroy was at his side.

"He's a sick man," he explained. "And it's been a terrible shock. Paul, can I do anything?"

"Tablets," gasped Trenton. "Green bottle in the bathroom."

As Comroy hurried away, the policeman lifted Trenton's slight body and carried him into his bedroom. When the professor returned, Claire was standing by the bedside.

"I'll stay with him," she said.

Leaving the girl with Trenton, Comroy and the policeman returned to the kitchen. Where before the professor had been numbed and stupefied by the shock of that grisly scene, his mind was now clear. While the policeman's eyes darted around the room, he stood on the threshold, thinking.

"Look at that hair!" exclaimed the policeman.

Watching carefully where he stepped, he moved to the body and, tilting forward the grotesquely coiffured head of

Lila Trenton, revealed an ugly wound on the back of the skull. Instantly his gaze flashed to the stained hatchet at her side.

"Easy to see how it was done," he muttered.

"The pearls are gone," put in Comroy. "She was wearing them last time I saw her alive."

"I guess that puts Nolan on the spot."

The professor was looking down at the broken fragments of glass which strewed the floor. Gingerly, he turned one of them over with his foot.

"Don't touch anything," snapped the policeman.

"Look like part of a pitcher," said Comroy reflectively. "And there are some drops of fluid still in it; tomato juice, I think. That explains the open refrigerator door. Mrs. Trenton had a cold and was taking a liquid diet. She must have been getting some tomato juice when she was attacked."

The policeman glanced quickly at the piece of glass and then at the refrigerator. "Yeah. Looks that way. Nolan must have come in through the back door with the key, picked up the hatchet, and hit her from behind while she was still pouring the tomato juice. It's all over the floor."

Gilbert Comroy had moved almost fussily to the back door and was gazing through the smashed glass panel. "This is extraordinary."

"What?"

"You said Nolan had a key to this door." Gilbert Comroy looked thoughtful. "Surely, if he had the key, he wouldn't have bothered to break the glass in the panel in order to get in."

"What d'you mean?"

"I mean," said Comroy, shaking his head sadly, "I mean that I believe you are suspecting quite the wrong person."

The policeman's eyes narrowed. "Well, we'll soon see. But whoever did it, it's a pretty nasty piece of work."

"Oh, undoubtedly, it's—terrible."

Professor Comroy took out a handkerchief and wiped the shiny skin of his forehead.

Poor Lila, he was thinking. And for the first time he felt some vestige of pity for this woman he had always hated. How ironic that she, who had always lived for her appearance, should die like this, with her negligee torn and stained, her face distorted and ugly, and her hair so grotesquely discolored.

XI

"I CAME TO KILL HER"

With the arrival of Captain Lee and his men, the Trentons' apartment became a scene of professional activity. The captain hurried into the kitchen, accompanied by the medical examiner, the finger-print man and the police photographers. Comroy and Claire French were taken to Lila's bedroom to await questioning. Only one room was quiet, that of Paul Trenton, who had yielded to the narcotic effect of the tablets and fallen into an uneasy sleep.

At length, the body of Lila Trenton was removed, and a policeman summoned Professor Comroy into the living room. Captain Lee sat at a table. He was a quiet, middle-aged man with alert eyes and broad shoulders.

"Well, professor," he said with a smile, "I didn't realize who you were at first. My son is in your chemistry class at the university. He thinks the world of you. Too bad we should meet in such unpleasant circumstances."

"Too bad, indeed."

The professor drew up a chair and outlined the salient facts of his discovery, omitting to mention either Claire French or Larry Graves. Lee listened keenly. When Comroy had finished, he said:

"Doctor Jones has made a cursory examination. From the congealing of the blood and the rigidity of the limbs, he thinks Mrs. Trenton died between nine fifteen and ten. That means she was probably killed a very short while before you and Mr. Trenton found the body."

"She died instantaneously?" asked the professor.

"Doesn't need an autopsy to tell us that. Her skull was crushed like an eggshell. Of course, this looks like a pretty clear case against Nolan. He was caught with the pearls a few minutes before ten. I haven't had a chance to talk to him yet because he sprained his ankle trying to get away and a doctor is still fixing it. But before I see him, there are just a few things I'd like cleared up. I suppose I can't talk to Mr. Trenton tonight?"

"He's a very, very sick man," said the professor gravely. "But I think I can tell you anything you want to know."

"Well, Mrs. Trenton was well off. I happen to know that. Do you know how she left her money?"

"As I understand from something Trenton once said," replied Comroy reflective, "his wife made no will. She liked to think of herself as younger than she really was and I believe she felt making a will suggested age. Of course, if she dies intestate, the money, or a good share of it, goes to her husband."

"I see." Captain Lee glanced at his hands. "And you were with Mr. Trenton all evening? It wouldn't have been possible for him to—"

"Quite impossible." The professor shook his head emphatically. "Mrs. Trenton was alive when we left here at seven-thirty, and we were together every moment until we returned. You say she was killed before ten. We were just leaving the restaurant at that time."

"No family quarrel, I suppose?"

Comroy's eyes grew cold. "Paul Trenton was always devoted to his wife."

"Just another matter." Lee's gaze was still fixed on the professor's face. "You say you arrived here at about ten minutes past ten. The police were not notified until ten-thirty. Why did those twenty minutes elapse?"

The professor removed his spectacles and began to wipe them thoughtfully. "Naturally, we were both rather upset by our discovery. But I did hurry to call you. Unfortunately, however, the young lady, Miss French arrived just as I was about to lift the receiver."

"What did she want?"

"I really don't know. To call on Mrs. Trenton, I suppose. But I didn't care to tell her about the tragedy, I was trying to get her to leave when the policeman arrived to report about Nolan's arrest." The color in his face deepened. "That's why there was the small delay."

The captain nodded slowly and glanced at the policeman by the door. "If the doctor's through with Nolan, you can bring him up."

"I was wondering," remarked the professor, "whether you would permit me to stay for this interview. Being an old friend of the family, I am naturally interested."

"Sure, you can stay, professor, only too pleased. Perhaps you can learn something you don't teach at the university."

When he hobbled in with the officer, Sam Nolan was a very different person from the self-assured, impudent young man who had attended to Lila Trenton's refrigerator and built a fire for her that afternoon. His youthful face had lost its easy grin. His dark eyes seemed strained.

"Well, Nolan," said the captain curtly, "you're in a pretty tough spot. Are you going to talk? Of course, you needn't if you don't want to."

The young man lowered his head and said nothing.

"You took that back-door key when you fixed the refrigerator, didn't you?"

Sam Nolan's eyes shifted uneasily.

"And tonight you came up the fire escape to steal those pearls. You let yourself in with the key and killed Mrs. Trenton."

"I didn't kill her!" Sam Nolan's voice was dull and toneless.

"What's the use? You had the pearls on you. You—"

"Might I interrupt for a moment?" put in the professor mildly. "I would like to ask the young man a question."

Captain Lee's eyes widened slightly but he shrugged his assent.

"Tell me this." Comroy looked over his spectacles at Nolan. "Was the glass panel in the back door broken when you came up the fire escape?"

"Why, yes, sure it was."

"I thought so." The professor turned his solemn gaze to Lee. "We all know this man had a key to the back door."

"You think someone else broke that panel and got into the kitchen?"

"That is a possibility."

"I'm afraid you're going a bit scientific on us, professor." Lee's voice was slightly sarcastic as he added: "If you didn't kill Mrs. Trenton, Nolan, maybe you can tell us what happened."

"If I did, you wouldn't believe me." A look of fear had come into Nolan's eyes. Then he shook the dark hair from his forehead and continued fiercely: "But it's God's truth. Yeah, I did steal that key. And I did come up the fire escape to get them pearls. What's the good of saying I didn't? When I got into that kitchen, she was dead already."

"Ah!" exclaimed the professor.

"Yeah. When I got up onto the balcony, the kitchen was all dark. But I wasn't taking no chances. I flashed my light in before I unlocked the door. And she was there on the floor, lying with blood all over her and that—that green hair."

Sam Nolan looked very young and very frightened.

"At first," he went on, "I was going to scram just as quick as I could. I didn't want to get mixed up in no murder. But I could see them pearls sort of gleaming on her neck. Although I was scared, I thought I might as well get 'em. I went in and lifted them. And—and then, as I was bending over her, I heard someone open the front door and call out 'Lila,' so I beat it."

Lee looked interested. "You're sure of that? Was it a man?"

"Yes, a young man. He sounded kind of excited."

"And then," put in the professor.

Sam Nolan gripped the arms of his chair. "You won't believe it. I know you won't. But it's the truth, I swear it. After I was out on the fire escape, I flashed my torch back in, just for a last look." He paused, and added almost inaudibly: "Mrs. Trenton was still there on the floor, but she was moving. At first I thought it was just my eyes and the light and everything, because I knew she was dead. But she moved again. Sort of turned, as if she was going to come after me. God, it was awful. I couldn't do anything, not run, not move—nothing. I could see that green hair and the blood all over her clothes. And she'd been dead, I tell you—dead."

Slowly, Sam Nolan's hands slipped to his sides. "Then I guess I lost my nerve and started to run like hell. On the fire escape I slipped and turned my ankle. It hurt so I let a yell out of me, like a damn fool. That's how the house dick got me."

There was a moment's silence. Then Captain Lee smiled wearily.

"As a story, Nolan, that's not so hot. You say Mrs. Trenton was dead when you came in, and the doctor says she was killed instantaneously. She couldn't possibly have moved."

"But I tell you it's true. Honest, that's what happened."

"Davis!" Lee glanced at the policeman by the door. "Get Mallory to take this bird down to the station house, I'll talk to him again later."

Sam Nolan made no resistance as the policeman slipped on the handcuffs. He rose dazedly and limped out of the room with Mallory.

"These small-time crooks," exclaimed Lee, "when it comes to faking up a story, they have the imagination of a louse."

Professor Comroy's round face was thoughtful. Absently, he tapped a button on his vest.

"Of course," he murmured, "one cannot go against the medical evidence. The boy must have been suffering from some sort of hallucination. But wasn't it possible that the body was being moved by someone whom he could not see? After all, he said he heard a voice in the next room."

"Well, if he isn't lying, I'd like to know who that man was. It couldn't have been you or Mr. Trenton, because it all happened before ten o'clock." Lee turned to the officer. "I'll see the girl now."

Claire French was very pale when she entered. She clutched her pocketbook firmly, and her eyes turned swiftly to Comroy, trying to guess how much he had told. She was reassured by an infinitesimal movement of the professor's eyelid.

"Well, Miss French," began Lee, "there are a few routine questions."

Claire nodded.

"Professor Comroy tells me you arrived here just as he was going to call the police. You had come to see Mrs. Trenton?"

"Yes," said Claire instantly, "I came to see Mrs. Trenton."

"You were a friend of hers?"

"No. I was not."

"Then why—"

Claire bit her lip. "I own a beauty parlor a few blocks away. This afternoon I came round at Mrs. Trenton's request. It was the first time I had attended to her hair. She asked for a touch-up and I used a henna compound. It was not until later that I remembered that this compound, if used on hair that's been dyed already, turns it a sort of greenish color. I was very worried and came to—er—find out if anything of this sort had happened."

"So that explains the color of the hair," mused Lee. "But why didn't you realize your mistake when you were here this afternoon?"

"Oh, Mrs. Trenton wanted to dry her hair herself. The discoloration wouldn't show until after the hair was dry."

"And that was your only reason for coming here tonight?"

Claire inclined her head slowly.

"All right, Miss French. That will be all for the moment."

Swiftly Claire French rose. As she did so, the pocketbook slipped from her lap and fell to the floor with a heavy thud. She bent instantly to retrieve it, but Captain Lee was too quick for her. His lips tightened as his fingers gripped the soft material and flicked open the catch. For a second there was absolute silence. The he said slowly:

"If you were merely going to discuss hairdressing with Mrs. Trenton, was it necessary to bring a revolver?"

Comroy flashed the girl a warning glance, but she did not seem to notice. Her gray eyes fixed the captain's in a level stare.

"I lied to you," she said calmly. "I did use the wrong henna compound, but it wasn't by mistake, I'm afraid I gave way to a thoroughly spiteful instinct."

"And the revolver—was that a spiteful instinct?"

"No." Claire's face had gone cold. "That was more serious. I came here tonight to threaten and, if necessary, to kill Mrs. Trenton."

For the first time that evening, Captain Lee seemed shaken out of his official composure. He was still gazing at the girl when there were swift noises in the hall and a policeman hurried in.

"There's a guy out here who—"

He broke off as Larry Graves pushed past him and strode to Claire's side.

"Larry!" The girl swung around on him almost fiercely. "You fool! I told you to go. Why—why on earth did you come back?"

"Did you think I'd leave you here? I waited for you downstairs. But you didn't come. Then I saw the police arrive. I had to see if you were all right."

"What is all this about?" asked Lee sharply.

Larry was standing very close to Claire. "I don't want Miss French mixed up in this. She hasn't anything to do with it. She didn't even know Mrs. Trenton."

"She seemed to know her well enough to fix her hair and then want to kill her."

"If she said she wanted to kill her, it was a lie, just a crazy attempt to shield me." Larry lighted a cigarette with fingers that shook. "You see, she thinks I killed Lila Trenton. Of course, I didn't, but—"

"Why does she think you killed Mrs. Trenton?" put in Lee quickly.

"Because I was right here in the apartment tonight."

"So it was you who came here just before ten?"

"Yes. I had a key. Mrs. Trenton gave it to me this morning." Larry produced the key from the pocket of his raincoat and tossed it across the table. "I might as well tell you exactly what happened. When I let myself in, the apartment was in darkness. I called Mrs. Trenton's name, but she didn't answer. I thought she was out, so I turned on the light in the living room and looked for her there."

"Did you look for her in the kitchen?"

"Why—no. The door was shut. I never thought about it."

"Did you hear anything?"

"No."

"And how long did you wait?"

Larry jerked his head toward the professor. "Until that man and Mr. Trenton arrived. Then I hid in a closet in the hall. I waited till they had gone into the kitchen, and ran out."

Captain Lee turned to the professor, who was tapping mildly on his chair arm. "Do you know anything about this?"

"Why—er—perhaps I may have heard a scuffling sound, but I was very upset at the time. And then I am slightly myopic. I—"

The detective did not appear to be listening. Once more he was addressing Larry Graves.

"That's the third unlikely story I've heard in this place tonight. You don't expect me to believe it?'

"Of course. It's the truth."

"Well, then, there's one thing you haven't explained. Why did you come to see Mrs. Trenton tonight?"

The lines of Larry's face were set and resolute. He was speaking to Claire rather than the captain and, without knowing it, he used almost exactly the same words as she had used.

"I came here," he said slowly, "to threaten Mrs. Trenton and, if necessary, to kill her."

XII

A FLAWLESS ALIBI

After these two dramatic confessions, Captain Lee had no alternative but to take Larry Graves and Claire French to the police station for further questioning. At length, Gilbert Comroy was left alone. He had pleaded the necessity of spending the night with his friend and had promised to make himself available the next morning.

When the door closed behind the captain, the professor gave a sigh of relief and crossed to one of Lila's mirrors. For the first time in his life, he was eager to see his own face. There should, he felt, be some radical change in his appearance, for he was not used to lying. And he had been telling or acting a lie the whole evening.

The plump, benevolent countenance which looked back at him seemed much the same as usual.

"Well, well," murmured Gilbert Comroy, "I ought to be thoroughly ashamed of myself."

But he wasn't.

He tiptoed to his friend's bedroom and silently opened the door. Paul Trenton was still asleep. One shaded lamp played on his sallow face, smoothing from it the lines of pain and leaving only peace and serenity. Softly, Professor Comroy crept to a chair and sat down.

The hours passed. The clock in the living room chimed two—three—four—five.

Once during the night, the professor's round eyes closed like a sleepy owl's, but he shook them open again and moved into the bathroom for a glass of water to keep him awake.

The pale rays of the February dawn were filtering through the shades when Paul Trenton finally stirred. He moved his head on the pillow and murmured:

"Lila."

Comroy jumped up. "How do you feel, Paul?"

"Gilbert! It's you." A look of remembered pain had come into Trenton's eyes. "Poor Lila. Did they find out—"

"Don't worry, Paul." Gilbert Comroy bustled out of the room and returned shortly, carrying a cup of tea. "Drink this. It'll make you feel better."

As he passed the cup, the hot liquid spilled over into the saucer. "Tut," he exclaimed, "what a mess I've made!"

Paul accepted the tea gratefully.

"Do you know, Gilbert," he said suddenly, "this is the first time I've had a cup of tea in bed since I was a boy."

As he drank it, Comroy told him, as gently as he could, everything that had happened the night before. Trenton nodded sadly.

"Poor Lila," he said at length. "So both of those young people wished her out of the way?"

"The man Nolan is under suspicion, too."

"Well, I only hope that an innocent person will not be convicted."

"Don't worry, my friend. Innocent people are very seldom convicted, despite popular prejudice to the contrary."

"Poor Lila," murmured Trenton again, and his voice was very low. "She was such a pretty girl. And now she's dead. Died before me, after all. Do you have any ideas about it, Gilbert?"

"Yes."

"You suspect one of those three people?"

"No."

Comroy took the empty cup from his friend's hand and set it down on the bed table.

"Things will take their course, Paul, and there is nothing much that we can do about it. I may be an old meddler, but I did tell Captain Lee my own reasons for thinking that two of those three young people were not guilty of murder. Eventually, I feel sure any grand jury would be forced to come the same conclusion, and not indict them."

Almost without realizing it, Comroy had started to speak as though he were discussing a scientific experiment in the laboratory rather than the death of his friend's wife.

"Obviously, there will be no serious charge against Miss French other than carrying a revolver and obstructing justice in a rather theatrical attempt to help the young man. She arrived at the apartment *after* the murder had been committed. Doubtless, she will come to her senses and furnish an alibi for her actions before ten. And although I am no expert criminologist, I cannot help thinking that guilty people are not so eager to admit that they had guilty intentions."

"That is also true in the case of Larry Graves. He came back when there was no need to come back. Besides, from Nolan's story, it can be proved that Lila was already dead when Graves first let himself into the apartment."

Gilbert Comroy rose and drew the shades so that the early-morning light struck across his friend's bed.

"I have no particular sympathy with Nolan," he went on. "A man who steals from a dead body deserves the prison sentence which he will most certainly get. But I do not think him guilty of the more serious charge. There was something about him as he told that tale last night which made me feel he was speaking the truth. And there is one real piece of evidence in his favor, the broken panel in the glass door. Nolan had a key. He was an experienced thief. He would never have broken that glass at the risk of being heard. No, it was broken by someone else, by the person who really did kill Lila."

"And who was that person?"

"I hope that the coroner's jury will reach the only acceptable conclusion." Gilbert Comroy was looking curiously at his friend. "That your wife was killed by another prowler—one who broke into the kitchen, before Nolan arrived. A prowler who I trust will always be described in the official records as person or persons unknown."

There was a long silence. At length Paul said irrelevantly:

"It is curious that Lila was willing to lend that young man five thousand dollars when she would not make a loan to help us continue our work at the university."

"But you have money now, Paul," put in Comroy gently. "You will be able to finish your research."

Trenton smiled sadly. "Yes, if there's time."

"Nonsense, of course there will be time. To live and the will to live are closely bound together, Paul."

"Perhaps," said Trenton dreamily. "And there is always Fleming. He's a good man. At least the university will benefit by all this unhappy business. But those two young people, Gilbert— they are going to have a hard time."

"A hard time works wonders when you are young and in love. They'd had a pretty serious misunderstanding; this will bring them together."

"I hope," continued Trenton quietly, "that you, as my executor, will consider that garage a good investment and continue the loan. I do not want them to suffer."

Once more the bedroom was strangely quiet. At length Gilbert Comroy spoke.

"Paul, I must be frank with you. I have another reason for being certain that none of those three people killed your wife. You see—I *know* who really did it."

"You mean that you don't believe in that 'unknown prowler,' Gilbert?"

"Officially—yes, but actually—no. Of course, I have taken a great deal of liberty with the truth. And I have a certain amount of responsibility on my shoulders. But while I sat here during the night, I gave the matter much thought. I am sure I was justified in everything I did. Can you bear the truth, Paul?"

"As a scientist, the truth should be one thing that I can always face." Trenton smiled wanly as he sank back on the pillows and regarded his friend with questioning eyes.

The professor was cleaning his spectacles. "The medical examiner stated that Lila died instantly from a blow which was struck before ten o'clock. He was right, and there is no need to question his statement."

"Yes?"

"But there was something that the medical examiner could not tell. This crime—as I suppose it must be called—did not begin at ten, Paul. It had already started much earlier in the evening."

Trenton was still looking at him fixedly.

"Sam Nolan told a seemingly incredible tale, but it happens to be true. He did see Lila lying there on the kitchen floor at ten o'clock. And he did see her move."

"Poor Lila!" echoed Trenton tonelessly. "I do hope she didn't suffer."

"Sam Nolan said he saw her lying dead and covered with blood—just as you and I saw her later. But it is easy to deceive the eye. Lila was not dead when Nolan stole the pearls. She was unconscious. And he did not see blood. He merely saw—tomato juice."

"Comroy!"

"Yes," continued the professor calmly, "earlier in the evening Lila was struck with what is usually referred to as a blunt instrument. Let us suppose that in this case it was the flat side of the hatchet. The blow was hard enough to keep her unconscious for a long time. But it did not kill her, and it did not draw blood. If there had been blood, the medical examiner could have told at once that she had been wounded earlier. But in this case, there was no means of guessing."

Trenton's lips parted slightly, but he did not speak.

"The man who struck Lila," went on Comroy after a pause, "knew that he would be returning to the apartment later with a witness. He decided that he and the witness should find Lila apparently dead. Therefore, he poured tomato juice over the floor and over the unconscious body—tomato juice which would give a convincing impression of blood at first and which could later be explained away by the fact that Lila was about to take some fruit juice form the refrigerator at the moment of death."

"And then?"

"The tableau was set. He returned with the witness—and a short-sighted one at that. They found Lila lying there, and the witness was sent to telephone the police." The eyes behind Professor Comroy's spectacles were closed. He was not looking at his friend. "While the witness was out of the room, he completed what he had begun with a blow of the hatchet—a blow which must have killed instantaneously. *The medical examiner—even after an autopsy—could not have told that she had been unconscious for over two hours before she was killed. But the rigidity of the muscles would incline him to set the time of death earlier than it actually occurred.* A lucky occurrence and one which gave both you and myself an unshakable alibi. If any one were suspected, it would be the imaginary prowler—the man who had broken through the glass panel in the door."

"And yet," said Trenton softly, "the man who killed poor Lila could not have foreseen that, instead of an imaginary prowler, there would be a real one. And then those two young people, they complicated things, too."

"They did." Comroy looked long and closely into his friend's eyes. "I guessed almost at once, Paul, but only by instinct. No one else will guess. And yet I am still curious—curious to know what exactly it was that made you decide yesterday to kill Lila."

Paul Trenton did not speak immediately. His worn face had a strange, far-away expression. "It is difficult to tell exactly why one does things, Gilbert. For years now I've known about Lila—known that she despised me, that there were other men, that—well, one need not go into her shortcomings now. About the five thousand dollars to young Graves. But in spite of everything, she was an attractive woman. I still thought I loved her. It was only yesterday that I realized I had been blinding myself."

"But what—what was it that changed you, Paul?"

"When Lila called me back from the university in the afternoon, I'd had two terrible shocks. I had heard about the Abel Research and I'd been to see my doctor. I suppose that in itself was enough to make any one deviate slightly from the normal. And then, when I got home, I—I saw Lila with that horrible dyed hair and her face lined and distorted with anger. It's strange how important little things can be. I think it was that one stupid detail which shifted my whole point of view. Suddenly I seemed to realize that she wasn't young anymore—wasn't attractive."

Comroy was listening in rapt attention.

"We were together in the kitchen," continued Trenton, "and all the time she was talking indignantly about some girl from a beauty shop, I could think of nothing except that one fact: 'She isn't attractive any more.' She wanted to start a lawsuit, spend money to satisfy some little quirk of her vanity. And then, when I wouldn't take it seriously, she told me about your visit and started sneering at my work. I—I tried to tell her what the doctor had said, but she was too busy to listen—too busy telling me how weak I was, what a failure I'd been. She said something—I can't remember what—but suddenly I lost control. Hardly knowing what I was doing, I picked up the hatchet and hit her. I meant to kill her, Comroy, but I've always been a bit of a bungler. I suppose I must have used the flat of the blade."

"You meant to kill her! So you had planned nothing deliberately?"

"No. I did nothing deliberate. And I really thought I *had* killed her. It was merely a vague instinct of self-preservation which made me break the panel in the door and pretend to talk to her in the bedroom when you arrived a few minutes later. The tomato juice was just a coincidence. She had it in her hand when I struck her."

"So when you and I found her there in the kitchen—you still thought she was dead?"

Trenton nodded. "It was only later—after you had gone to telephone the police that I felt her heart still beating. At first I was glad. But then I realized that, if she lived, I'd be charged with attempted murder. That's why I struck her the second time."

For a moment there was deep silence. When Trenton spoke again, his voice seemed to come from far away.

"I thought I was a scientist," he said musingly. "A man whose passions and emotions were nicely under control. But there are some things we don't learn in laboratories—and one of them is how very human and frail we all are."

"There is always a lot to learn about ourselves, Paul. I never dreamed that you would do what you did, and I never dreamed that I would be a willing accessory after the fact."

The light was brighter now. It played on those two middle-aged men sitting together and regarding one another solemnly. Paul Trenton turned his face toward the sunlight.

"It's strange," he murmured. "Somehow I don't feel any remorse for what I have done. People like Lila do not give happiness. Nor can they get it themselves. But I am human enough to wish that I might not be punished until after my work is finished."

"But no one will ever suspect you, Paul." Gilbert Comroy moved to his friend's bed and laid a hand gently on his shoulder. "By a series of coincidences you have given yourself a flawless alibi.

"But you must tell the truth, Gilbert. And so must I. I am little better than a dead man. The doctor told me I had but a few weeks more to live, and there is an unmistakable feeling within me that tells me I am all but dying now. And no living person must suffer because of me. If they do not find out who really murdered Lila before I am gone, I will leave a written confession and put it in your care."

"You can trust me, Paul. Write your confession; but unless it is absolutely necessary, I shall never dare to use it."

"And why not?"

"Because you might set a precedent, Paul." The professor's voice was so low that his friend could not hear. "There are many husbands in the world and many Lilas. I believe that unintentionally you have stumbled upon the perfect method of killing a wife."

Hunt in the Dark

Iris and I were at Coney Island that night. War hadn't come then. And we were celebrating the fact that being married was still wonderful after eighteen months. We were in a gay, frivolous mood. We pushed along the garish boardwalk, jostling against soldiers and sailors and marines and girls and children and Chinamen and half of New York and all of Brooklyn.

"Peter," said Iris, "let's find a Death Plunge or a Suicide Chute or—"

She may have finished that sentence. I don't know. For suddenly everything was changed for me—fantastically changed. Because there, right in front of me, thrown up against me by the shifting tide of humanity, was Marta.

Marta Pauly, the only woman in the world, except Iris, whom I had ever loved this side of idolatry.

She was tragically different—much older than she had a right to be. The exquisite Viennese bone structure was worn and stark. There were streaks of white in the smooth black hair. And her clothes were dowdy. Marta, who had always been so fantastically chic! But I recognized her at once—although it was against all possible reason that she could be there on the uproarious boardwalk at Coney Island.

At the sight of her, fifteen years rolled away and I was back in Vienna—a raw-boned, romantic kid worshipping madly and hopelessly at the shrine of Marta Pauly, the operetta idol of Austria; lovely Marta Pauly, who could have had champagne in every slipper and broken hearts in every pocket, but who had preferred a home and a husband; Marta Pauly, who later had become my greatest friend and whose letters had stopped dead one week after a certain house painter had brought his brave boys to the rescue of his Motherland.

"Marta!" I breathed.

She didn't hear or see me. She was hurrying with a queer kind of tautness through the exuberant crowd. I couldn't let all those memories walk out on me. I grabbed Iris and started after her.

"That woman in the old black coat, it's Marta!"

"Marta Pauly? Your Marta? Peter, it can't be!"

"It is."

She was right ahead of us.

"Marta!" I called it again.

I reached forward, putting my hand on her slender arm, feeling all of Europe coming back as I touched her. She spun round, and her face suddenly broke into life. It was rather horrible because the sudden life in her eyes was fear. Real fear. She made a little wild attempt to break away, then her arm went limp as if she'd given up, as if something so terrible had happened that there was no use in trying to escape.

I couldn't bear to see her that way. "Marta, you've got to remember me. It's Peter—Peter Duluth."

Somewhere, far off, *The Hut Sut Song* was still churning. Voices through loudspeakers boomed enticing overtures above the chatter of the crowds. Gradually, Marta started looking at me instead of some nightmare thing in her own mind. Slowly that pale, care-worn face kindled with a ghost of the old vivid Marta who had Vienna weeping and smiling with her revival of the *Merry Widow*, all through that long, white Austrian winter.

"Peter, my dear! Peter, how wonderful!" The voice was still there, that gossamer, moonlit voice. "Oh, you must excuse me. I feel a hand on my arm; I am thinking of something else and I am stupidly afraid. How could I be so foolish? To see you of all people!" A little laugh, sweet as sleigh-bells in the Dolomites, tinkled as she turned to Iris. "And, Peter, this lovely girl?"

I had often imagined a meeting between Iris and Marta—something fragile and half sorrowful over porcelain teacups. Nothing like this.

"My wife!" I said.

"Your wife!" Marta squeezed Iris' hand. "My dear, I always tell Peter he would find himself the most beautiful wife in America. I am so happy for him."

Iris was liking her. I could tell that. She said, "I always thought I'd be jealous of you. I am."

It should all have been gay, but it wasn't, because, in spite of the magical charm, the fear was still there. I could sense it inside her, immense, all-embracing, screaming for expression.

I wanted to say, *Marta, you're in trouble. Let us help you.* But all I managed was. "I was frightfully worried when your letters stopped. Thank heavens you're here. How long have you been over?"

"For two and a half years, Peter. My son, Karl, and I."

"And you never let me know? Never came to see me?"

She made a wry little gesture, indicating the thread-bare old coat. "I am a woman. I have a mirror. You think I want my Peter to see me like this?"

There was absolutely no self-pity in that remark. That's why it punched right through me like an ice pick. A flat, difficult silence came. And in that silence I noticed that Marta's smoky blue eyes were darting to left and right, scanning the faces of the passers-by with a kind of dread.

Iris noticed it too, for she said, "We can't talk in this crowd. Let's go somewhere and have a drink."

Marta hesitated. I could tell she was struggling with an impulse to get rid of us, but I wasn't going to let her. We were almost at the mouth of Feltman's Arcade. I put one hand on her elbow, the other on Iris', and started guiding them through the crowd. Around us, things were becoming even more gala. Although it was only eight o'clock, the soldiers and the sailors and the soda-clerks were discovering that spring nights and girls go together. Balloons and dolls on sticks and other booty won at the stalls bobbed around us colorfully, as we turned out of the main stream into the dark little alley. We passed lurid posters announcing Rudolph Valentino and Old Time Movies. And then, ahead, a garish, bedizened carousel came into view. It was grinding out the *Merry Widow Waltz.*

The *Merry Widow!* Marta's *Merry Widow!*

With the sound of the music, memories thronged. The dazzle of Marta across the footlights at the Franz Joseph Theater—Marta's first miraculous smile at me in the little *bier haus*—the sun gleaming on Marta's hair in the *Salzkammergut*—that rapturous ski race at St. Anton with the snow tanging Marta's cheeks and making her eyes shine like black ice.

I turned to glance at the gray, careworn little figure at my side. I could have wept.

We reached the restaurant. A tough waiter in elegant tails hovered around us. But it was Marta, with sudden authority, who chose our table. In a corner close to a door and with its back to the wall. We sat down. I ordered beers. That seemed to be the thing to order. When they came I lifted mine to Marta in a toast.

"To our reunion," I said. And then, afraid of what I might hear, but having to say it, "And to your husband. He's with you?"

Marta's eyes met mine for an instant over the beer glasses. "No, Peter. Walter's heart was not strong, you know. And then, the winters in concentration camps are hard."

It was the quietness with which she said it that was so bad. I thought of Walter Pauly, the calm, quiet spoken college professor with his infinite kindnesses to a callow young American who'd been brash enough to fall in love with his wife. Walter Pauly— dead in a concentration camp!

I could still hear *The Merry Widow* from the carousel outside. It was even more poignant now. Beyond it, I could hear the screams of the self-flagellists on the great roller coaster that loomed next to the restaurant.

Somehow I was in no mood for screams. Iris laid her hand on Marta's. Their two utterly different beauties, a narcissus and a faded tea-rose, made a moving contrast. "But your son,"—she was trying to make things better—"Karl, you spoke of him. He's all right."

Marta's voice came so low that I could scarcely catch it. "Karl is gone. They have taken him."

"Taken him! But you said he was with you here in America. Who've taken him?"

She looked up. The mask had dropped now. She didn't try any more to keep that anxiety from gnawing at her eyes.

"A man they call Nikki—and his friends. They came for him last night. They took him away." She paused with a little shiver. "Unless a miracle happens, they will kill him."

Iris looked at me and then back to Marta. "I knew you were in trouble from the first moment we saw you. You've got to let us help."

"No, no. I was wrong to speak to you of Karl, wrong to come here and drink with you. I have no right—"

She half rose. I stopped her. "Marta, you know there's no one in the world we'd sooner help. You've got to tell us."

"Peter, I can't. There's too much danger. There ..."

"We don't care about danger," said Iris.

A faint flush colored the ivory of her skin. "If only I could ask you to help. It might mean so much. It might..."

"Tell us."

Her beautiful fingers—slightly rough and worn now—twisted and untwisted around her beer glass. She wasn't drinking any of it. "It is Karl," she said softly, "Karl and his foolish bravery. He is only nineteen and he thinks he is a grown man, he thinks he can do by himself for America what the police, what everyone, had failed to do."

The little worn hands fluttered over the tablecloth and out of sight into her lap.

"When Walter died, when Karl and I first came to this country it was heaven after Vienna. We had no money, nothing. But we both found work. People were kind. I thought all the nightmares of Europe were over for us. And they were,"—she paused— "until this Nikki came."

"And then—?"

"It was last autumn. He came to see Karl, not me. We had never seen him before, never. They were together for hours. I was worried. And then, when Nikki left, Karl told me. This Nikki was— how does one say?—an agent. Because of our blood, he had been sent to us to persuade Karl to join them in their work, secret, underground work against this country. Oh, I was frightened. I begged Karl to have nothing to do with it, to go to the police. But he is young, rash. And—and he had not forgotten his father. He said that it would be nothing to have this Nikki arrested; he was only a little man, unimportant. He had another, much bigger plan—to pretend to be one of them, to wait and at last to expose them all, when he had the evidence, to the authorities."

A waiter came by, pouring ice water into glasses. He seemed like a creature from another world.

"Nothing I said could stop him," Marta went on. "All through the winter it has been terrible for me. Every night Karl was out with this Nikki and his friends. All the time I am terrified they will guess. And slowly Karl tells me a little here, a little there. He finds out that Nikki is part of only one section of them, who work down at the docks; he finds that, behind all these agents, there is one person, one central brain who controls them all and everything they do, one person who is so secret that not even the agents themselves know him or where he lives. His name alone they know and even among them it is like a legend." She paused. "His name, Karl tells me, is Garr. And it is this Garr whom Karl is after, whom he foolishly was planning to outwit and—and to destroy."

As Marta breathed that name it seemed to take on a sinister life of its own. Garr—!

"And all this time," she went on, "Karl had been making contact with the police—the Federal Bureau of Investigation. Oh, it was very secret. They give him a secret telephone number to call them, but they will never let him risk meeting one of them. You see, they know of this organization well and they know how clever they are. For months they have been trying to catch them. But the slightest move by the authorities—and instantly the whole group dissolves, only to spring up again in another form. It is this Garr. He has a genius. He seems able to feel danger before it is even there. And so, the people at the FBI station here tell Karl to play a lone hand. He is to work secretly and alone—never contacting them—until he make enough evidence for arrests. Then and only then was he to give the signal which would bring in the authorities."

I was listening with a sort of unreal fascination as if I were listening to something in a play.

"And then, Peter, last night"—Marta hesitated—"last night, late, Karl came home. He was all excited. He tells me that at last the time has come. There is a big scheme which starts, he tells me. And, if he plays his cards right, does the right things, this scheme can lead him to Garr. He can at last discover his identity and get all the evidence in the world against him—and give the signal."

She paused, remembered horror taking control of her eyes. "But as he is telling me what he knows, suddenly the door bursts open and Nikki is there with his friends. Karl has not been so clever as he thought. They have discovered that he has been cheating them—and they take him away."

Her voice faltered: "And when they took him away, Nikki waits behind and he says to me: 'If you call the police, if you lift your little finger even, you can say good-by to your son, for we will kill him. And if he has told you anything and if you try to meddle, we will kill you too.' And he meant it, Peter. I know."

There was something appalling about that brutal story, belonging in the chaos overseas, and yet happening right here in New York. Poor Marta! Walter—and then this!

Iris said quietly, "And this scheme which is starting, this scheme which leads to Garr, did Karl tell you anything about it?"

"Yes. He told me a little—what little he knew. It is something big—some big scheme for destruction—sabotage. And it is planned to start here at Coney Island—tonight. That is why I am here."

Sabotage, Coney Island, the FBI, and this shadowy, ominous Garr. How far Iris and I had come from the Parachute Tower!

"It starts here in Coney Island tonight?" said Iris.

"Yes. I do not know really what it is. But it all centers around a woman with a purple hat. This woman has something very, very important which she is to take to Garr. And as I have said, this Garr keeps himself utterly secret, hidden behind a chain of agents. This woman with a purple hat is to be sent, from one agent to another, until she reaches Garr himself. And it begins tonight. Here at Coney Island she is to meet Nikki. Nikki is to give her instructions, to pass her on to the next agent, higher up. He is to meet her at nine o'clock tonight in Potter's Waxwork Museum. He does not know this woman, but he is to recognize her by the purple hat and by the fact that she is to hum the first bar of *The Blue Danube Waltz*. Then he gives her her instructions. That is the beginning. From then, as she gets closer to Garr, the whole plot is to mount, to get bigger, bigger—"

A woman with a purple hat, carrying vital information, humming *The Blue Danube* in a Coney Island Waxworks Museum, slowly creeping through a maze of agents toward Garr! A madhouse story made horribly real by its undertone of tragedy to Marta and Karl!

"That," Marta said, "is all Karl knew. He pieced it together, bit by bit. He listened outside the door while Nikki was given his orders. He had his plan worked out. He was going to come here to the Waxworks Museum, to see this meeting between the woman and Nikki and to follow the woman up, up, until she led him to Garr. He was hoping too to find out what this scheme was, this scheme for destruction. Then, he was to give the signal and at once have this Garr arrested and stop this—this disaster from happening."

Iris was looking at her with a kind of wonder. "And so, when they took Karl away, you—you decided to come here tonight to see whether you could do what he had wanted to do?"

Marta gave a faint little shrug. "Oh, I was desperate. They had Karl. I could not go to the people at the Federal Bureau for help. I realized that. For months they have been waiting for the right moment to come. They could not throw all that away, risk frightening Garr and having him slip through their fingers again— just for the sake of a poor refugee boy. But I knew there was one thing I could do. It was stupid of me, I suppose. I know so little. I have no experience of these things. But for Karl's sake, and for America, who has been so kind to me, and for hatred of this Garr and this Nikki and all they stand for, I came here to Coney Island tonight. I thought that perhaps I might do what Karl had planned to do, follow the woman up to Garr, somehow get evidence. Then I could call, give the signal, and destroy these people and, yes, perhaps save Karl too."

I stared at her—stared at that fragile little thing who had defied Nikki's threat to murder her and who had come alone to try to unearth the elusive Garr and to foil some vast, nameless disaster. In the old days, I'd always said Marta had the courage of ten grenadiers.

"But it's no use." Marta's voice came softly. "I told you that last night Nikki said he would kill me if I tried to interfere. He has already seen me here at Coney Island. I think he followed me from my house; I think he was watching there, to find out whether Karl had told me anything, whether I would try to come here. The moment I came out of the subway station, I caught a glimpse of him in the crowd behind me. And, as I came down through the people, he was always there. I know he is trying to get me out of the way, to kill me before this meeting in the Waxworks Museum takes place. I try to shake him off. But he is clever. I—I was running from him there on the boardwalk when I met you."

And she'd been cool enough to stand there and let a couple of imbeciles chat socially to her when every second might have sealed her death warrant.

"You mustn't worry, Marta." The words spilled out impulsively. "We won't let him get you."

"Me! It doesn't matter about me. You think there is much left in life for Marta Pauly?" Marta's little hand went out to mine. "But, Peter, there's Karl. There's just a chance that he is still alive. Oh, I hate to ask you to help when there is so much danger. But for Karl's sake, and for the sake of your own country, which these people wish to destroy, perhaps—if something should happen to me, you will go to Potter's Waxworks Museum at nine; you will try to watch this meeting with the woman with the purple hat?"

"Of course we will." It was Iris who actually said it. "We'll help you get Karl back; we'll help you fix this Garr and Nikki and all their screwball schemes."

"Sure," I said. And I meant it doubly, for Marta's sake and for—well, for America too. It isn't often you get a chance to prove what you think of people who try to kick your country around. "And don't worry, Marta," I said firmly. "Nothing's going to happen to you."

"You don't know, Nikki," she said very softly.

There was a thick, queerly taut silence. To break it, I said, "This signal Karl was to give when everything was okay, when the time had come for the FBI to step in—do you know it?"

Marta nodded. "It is very simple. It is just to call the secret number—Pine 3-2323 and ask for Leslie. Then, at any time of day or night, they will come wherever you are."

"Pine 3-2323 and ask for Leslie."

"But whatever happens, we must not do that—not until we know where Garr is, until we have enough evidence for them to arrest them all. You must understand that."

"I understand," I said. It was crazy that all this shouldn't sound crazy any more. "And this man, Nikki—tell us what he's like."

"Nikki? He is young and tall and strong, with blond hair. And tonight he is wearing a blue turtle-neck sweater. The sleeves are rolled up to the elbow and on his right arm there is a tattoo—"

Her voice suddenly went. I saw her face go white and cold. She half rose from the bench. Instinctively, Iris and I rose too. Marta was looking across the tables toward the little alley which stretched from the carousel down the open wall of the restaurant to the street. At first I didn't see what she was seeing. And then I did. And it gave me a queer, cold, constricting sensation.

Because outside in the alley, part of that rowdy, haphazard mixture of passers-by—soldiers, stout women with candy bars, Negroes with their girls, mothers and children—strolled a man.

He was a tall, blond young man who walked with an arrogant swagger. He was wearing a navy blue turtle-neck sweater and his sleeves were rolled up to the elbow, revealing on his strong right forearm the violet splash of tattoo-marks.

Nikki.

He passed the window outside. He reached a lower door. He paused. Then abruptly he pulled open the door and entered.

He was there in the restaurant with us—

For one excruciating moment, he hesitated by the door; then he turned his back to us and started moving through the tables in the opposite direction. He hadn't seen Marta.

"I knew he would find me." Marta's voice came in a sharp whisper. "Peter, I must go. You stay here. He mustn't see you with me."

"But—!"

"No, no, Peter. If he knows you are with me—how can you help?"

She pushed up the collar of the pathetic black coat. Silently, before we could do anything, she glided away from the table. There was another door close to us which led out by the carousel and down another little alley toward the great ramp of the roller coaster. Marta moved toward it. The broad, swaggering back in the turtle-neck sweater was still turned to us. Marta reached the door. Her hand went out for the handle. Iris and I stood absolutely motionless. Then, suddenly, Nikki spun round. He stared straight down the restaurant—straight at Marta.

For a second she froze. It was like a little bird and a big hulking snake. Then Marta tugged open the door and ran out. Quickly, Nikki strode back to the door by which he had entered.

They both were lost in the crowd outside.

Iris and I stared at each other. "Peter, we can't let this happen. Come on."

Marta had told us not to follow. We didn't give a damn about that. I put money down on the table for the beers. Iris had already started for the door. I followed. We went out and passed the carousel together.

I saw Marta at once. She was hurrying ahead of us, a forlorn little figure in an old black coat, down the dark alley toward the roller coaster.

There was no sign of Nikki.

Iris and I pressed on after Marta. We hadn't any real idea of what to do. The roar of the roller coaster and the delighted shrieks of its passengers seemed to grow exaggeratedly loud, like the distorted sound track for a movie.

People were moving by us all the time. Vague figures made ominous by the shadows. And then Marta was lost once again in the crowd.

Ahead reared the towering wall of the roller coaster. To the right we could see the little ticket booth in its circle of bright lights. We could hear the harsh voice of the barker drumming up business. A steady stream of people was trickling up, paying their dimes and choosing their places in the showily painted cars that stood there on the rails ready for action.

"Peter, where is she?" Iris' voice was desperate.

Behind us, back by the restaurant, the carousel had started to play the *Merry Widow* again. Damn it! Didn't it know any other tunes?

Iris and I stood in the shadow of the giant roller coaster. The *Merry Widow* played on and on.

"Nikki can't have got her, Peter. He can't ..."

And then we saw Marta. She was in the stream of people going up the steps to the ticket booth. I saw at once what she was trying to do. She was going to take a trip on the roller coaster. She was trying to shake Nikki off that way.

I started forward urgently. "Come on, honey, we're going on that darn thing with her."

"No, Peter." Iris' hand went out to my arm, holding me back. "She doesn't want us to follow. She said so."

"But I'm not going to let that hulking swine..."

"Darling, she's shaken him off. For her sake, we mustn't do anything stupid. Don't you see? In the long run we're going to be much more help to her if we keep in the background. She'll be safe on the roller coaster. Nothing can happen there."

I let her restrain me reluctantly, knowing that she was apt to make more sense than I.

As we stood there, we saw Marta reach the booth, saw her fumble in her purse—a poignant little gesture—feeling for change. She bought her ticket and moved to the bright stationary cars. She stepped into a green one at the end of the chain. Green had always been Marta's favorite color!

It was half-empty. She sat down in the back seat, almost out of sight from the alley, pressing her face to conceal it into the turned up collar of the dowdy old coat, folding her hands in her lap.

The barker's harsh voice sounded over the more distant strains of the *Merry Widow*. "Anyone else? Any other happy customer for the most exciting, the most sensational ride in history?"

We saw the little chain of cars with their laughing, frivolous passengers. We saw Marta still sitting alone at the back of the green car. There was a grinding of machinery indicating that the "most thrilling, most sensational ride" was about to begin.

"Any more for the Hurricane Ride? Any more—?"

I couldn't bear it any longer. Sense or nonsense, I wasn't going to let little Marta be there alone.

"Iris, honey, I'm going. You can stay here if you like—"

I started forward through the crowd.

"No, Peter, come back." Iris' voice trailed after me.

The crowd was thick, the ticket booth seemed miles away. And, as I struggled on, I saw the little cars start slowly to jolt forward. I was too late.

I paused. It was no use going on. I stared ahead toward the moving cars.

It was then that it happened. Out of the crowd at the foot of the steps ahead of me, a tall broad-shouldered figure suddenly materialized. He sprang up to the booth, passed it and jumped into the seat next to Marta, just as the cars rattled past.

And the bright lights above the cars shone down on his blue turtle neck sweater, his blond hair, his heavy arrogant profile, the splaying tattoo-marks on his bare right arm.

Nikki!

It had all been done at lightning speed. Obviously, Nikki had seen her on the roller coaster from the start. He had waited to jump on at the last moment when she had no means of getting off. And I had been too far away. I hadn't had the ghost of a chance of stopping it.

I caught a glimpse of Marta's face when she saw him. I caught a glimpse of his face too. It was like a nightmare.

Dimly, I realized that Iris had caught up to me, that her hand was in mine. We stood there, paralyzed, watching the little cars as they gathered speed, dwindled, and then disappeared, plunging into a dark tunnel before they climbed up, up, on the most thrilling ride on earth.

There was nothing we could do—nothing.

The *Merry Widow* was still playing. We moved away from the great wall of the roller coaster, pointlessly. But we stopped when we reached the carousel. We had to. We stopped there, with our backs to it, staring up the looming scaffolding of the Hurricane Ride—waiting.

"Peter," Iris' voice came brokenly. "This is my fault. It's all my fault. I stopped you. I…"

"Darling, don't say that. You did the sensible thing. How were you to know? Come on, we've got to get to the ticket booth, be there when they come out."

In the distance, miles away it seemed, I heard a chorus of screams as the cars plunged down some headlong descent. And there was always the roaring and rattling of machinery. It grew louder and louder, more and more ominous.

"They're almost at the top of the ramp," breathed Iris. "In a second we'll be able to see them up there."

We did see them then. The little string of cars with their twinkling lights came into view around a bend, way up on the top of the scaffolding, way above our heads.

Iris' hand in mine was as cold as ice. I could think of nothing but Marta up there in that little green car with Nikki. Marta—

The *Merry Widow,* blaring so close, was almost deafening. The cars were right above us. Then, suddenly, there was a scream. It wasn't like the other screams that had been before, excited, titilated. It was a high, thin, solitary scream—piercing through the night air, soaring over the wheezy rhythm of the *Merry Widow.*

And, as I heard it, I saw that dreadful thing happen up there in the air above us. Vaguely, I saw a dark figure topple out of one of the cars and over the edge of the ramp. I saw it, in the eerie half-darkness, hurtling down like some broken, fluttering moth—down, down, past the gaunt skeleton scaffolding, down toward the pavement.

Iris gave a little sob. We started running forward. Other people were running too, shouting hoarsely. We reached the place where the body had fallen. We pushed through the gesticulating cluster of people. A woman with red hair was screaming; two little boys were peering awesomely, their pink balloons wabbling on spindly sticks; a Chinaman watched with slanting, unrevealing eyes. Voices sputtered like firecrackers.

"… fell off the roller coaster … always said those things were dangerous … dead, poor little thing … *Dead …*"

We saw her then. We saw Marta. She was lying sprawled there, her old black coat crumpled around her, her little arms flung upward. Marta lying there dead—undeniably, cruelly dead.

The crowd was crushing around us. My throat was as dry as if I'd swallowed wood ash. I couldn't look any more. I found Iris' arm and pulled her away out of the jostling crowd.

Behind us, the carousel was silent. The *Merry Widow* had stopped.

For a moment, that nightmare end to fifteen years of memories kept my feelings under anesthesia. There was only one acidly clear thought. Marta had chosen the back seat of the last car so that she would be less conspicuous from the crowded alley. But she had walked into a trap. No one looks back on a roller coaster. No one pays any attention to screams on a roller coaster. How horribly easy it must have been for Nikki after his last minute jump onto the car, to pick up that fragile little struggling body in his bare, powerful arms and throw it over the edge of the ramp—with no one to see or care.

"You don't know Nikki," Marta's voice trailed through my memory. I knew Nikki now.

Iris' voice blurred dimly with that memory of Marta's. "Peter, how shall I ever forgive myself? It's my fault. You could have prevented—"

"No, honey. Stop. Don't think that way."

Suddenly the crowd started seething around us, running, hurrying somewhere.

"The roller coaster cars are coming back to the starting place. Nikki will be there."

I felt her hand, cold and taut, in mine. We were moving with the crowd back toward the ticket booth of the roller coaster. Up on the brightly lit platform above the steps I saw the little gayly painted chain of cars sliding into view. I saw the patrons, still apparently oblivious of the awful thing that had happened. They spilled out onto the platform, chattering amongst themselves. With them, boldly evident with his blue sweater and blond hair, swaggered the figure of Nikki.

The crowd from below, hot on the scent of sensation, had started in a tumultuous wave up the steps—to hear the "inside story" from eyewitnesses. Who cared about Marta's little body lying crushed there on the sidewalk now? A short man with a bald head scurried out of the ticket booth. He made a hopeless

attempt to check the incoming tide, to keep the erstwhile passengers segregated. Somewhere far off, I heard the scream of a
police whistle.

"… she fell … lost her balance and fell … she jumped off … I
saw her myself … suicide … " Snatches came across the crowd
to me—snatches from "eye-witness" accounts of people who a
moment before hadn't even known what had happened, people
who hadn't seen a thing but who weren't going to lose out on the
golden chance at the spotlight.

In that crazy beer garden, I kept my eyes glued on Nikki. The
sight of that arrogant, blond young man released my damned-up
emotions. They came out as anger and hatred for this swaggering small time crook who had stolen Marta's son and murdered
her in cold blood. Implacable hatred for Nikki and for that other
figure, hovering like a spider behind the scene, controlling all
these murderous threads—the shadowy figure of Garr. Let me
get my hands on them.

The crowd was quite out of control. And, as I watched, I saw
what Nikki was doing. Very deftly, he was letting the struggling
mass of people push him toward the steps which led down to
the alley.

It was obvious that in this initial period of utter confusion no
one had come around to realize that he was the man who had
jumped into the seat next to Marta. No one as yet connected him,
more than anyone else, with the "accident." A particularly violent spasm in the throng catapulted him halfway down the steps.
In a moment, long before they got around to thinking about him,
he'd be out of danger, out in the whirling crowd where he could
slip away unseen.

Iris was watching him too. Suddenly, in a small, thin voice she
said, "Remember, Peter, we promised Marta. We're not going to
the police—not until we've made them all pay for this, Nikki, the
woman with the purple hat, Garr—all of them."

As she spoke, I saw a policeman battling his way stubbornly
toward the center of the throng. My feet itched to run to him, to
turn Nikki over to him and send him on his way to the electric
chair where he belonged. But I had the same idea as Iris then.
There was only one real way to make our peace with Marta's
ghost, now that a tragic mistake in judgment had put her beyond
personal aid.

Nikki was here in Coney Island tonight to make contact with the unknown woman in the purple hat. That was the main thing. He had killed Marta ruthlessly—because she had been a menace to that meeting's success. And that meeting involved not only the life and death of Karl Pauly but also some vast, ominous scheme for destruction.

Marta had asked us to do our best to see that the plot was foiled.

With Karl kidnapped, with Marta dead, Nikki would feel safe. He had no idea that we knew of the meeting; he hadn't seen us with Marta at the restaurant; he did not even know we existed. Let him go; *let* him think he was safe; let him keep his appointment at nine o'clock in Potter's Waxworks Museum.

And we would be there; we would track the woman with the purple hat until she led us to Garr; when the time was ripe, we would call Pine 3-2323 and send their plots spinning to hell; we would make them realize they couldn't murder our Marta and get away with it.

It was a risk, a wild risk. So what? Marta hadn't hesitated to take it. Pitiful, heroic little Marta … !

We were deliberately letting her murderer escape. But the time would come when he'd wish he'd been clamped into jail right away. Yes, that time would come if the Duluths had anything to say about it.

Pine 3-2323—Leslie.

Nikki had maneuvered himself down the last step now. I saw him mingle into the churning throng, pushing negligently past the policeman. In a few seconds, his tall, blond-headed figure had disappeared into the shadowy obscurity of the fringes of the crowd.

I glanced at Iris. "Don't worry," I said. "We know where to find him at nine o'clock."

There was the grim light of battle in Iris' eyes. She looked very, very beautiful and very determined. "Then you are game, Peter?"

"What do you think? They're all of them going to be sorry for this—damn sorry if it's the last thing I do."

"That," said Iris, "makes two of us."

The crowd was still pushing and jostling around us. There were three policemen now as the center of attraction. Over hats and hair and bald heads, I caught a glimpse of white-coated figures; I caught a glimpse of a stretcher too—a stretcher for Marta. Ghosts of those fear-tormented eyes, that little worn face which had once been so radiant, haunted me. I didn't need to look any more. I was angry enough as it was.

I glanced at my watch. Twenty minutes of nine. I knew where the Waxworks Museum was. Near the subway station. I'd noticed it when we arrived.

Iris slipped her hand through my arm. "To Potter's Waxworks Museum," she said.

So that's the way it happened. Because Aloma, our very vivid cook, had commandeered our apartment for the evening to celebrate the mysterious return of an unexpected husband "after a long absence up-state," we had come to Coney Island. Most people don't let their cooks evacuate them; we realized that. But Aloma was different, she was as essential to us as Mariguana to a moocher—and now our jaunt had led to—this! That's what you get for having a cook with personality!

We threaded out of the alley into a main, glittering thoroughfare. Coney Island swallows up its crimes as it swallows up everything else. Here all was gaiety and unconcern. Cheerful screams came from little cars whirling in a mad circle. Explosions rattled from a rifle range. Marta, her amazing story, and her tragic death, might all have been whiskey dreams in a bar.

As we walked, I reviewed our data. It was miserably thin. The woman in the purple hat had something of vital importance for Garr. She was going to hum the first bar of *The Blue Danube* to Nikki in Waxworks Museum. He was going to give her instructions for her meeting with the next agent.

We crossed the hysterically active thoroughfare and headed in the direction of the subway station, passing gaudy, frowsy little souvenir stores.

Suddenly Iris said, "Peter, what are we going to do? Watch the meeting? Follow the woman with the purple hat to her next meeting—go on till we find Garr?"

"I guess so."

"And Karl! Somehow we must save Karl. But it's too early for that yet. We've got to concentrate on Nikki and the woman with the purple hat. Somehow we've got to—Peter!"

She broke off, swinging me around excitedly.

"Peter—look."

We were standing in front of one of the little cheesy stores, staring into its window. Almost everything was in that window—lurid postal cards, junk jewelry, nutcrackers made like women's legs, little china dolls and animals, all the regular stuff. But I saw at once what Iris saw. Hanging high up in the left corner of the window were hats—large, floppy beach hats.

And right in the middle of the cluster, even more shrill and hideous than the rest, dangled a glaring, fuzzy-brimmed purple hat.

Iris' voice came breathless: "Nikki doesn't know the woman he's going to meet. He's never seen her. All he knows about her is the purple hat and *The Blue Danube*. And he hasn't seen me, either. I can hum *The Blue Danube* and I can wear that purple hat. Peter, I can be the woman he's going to meet. With any luck we can fool him, get him to give *me* the instructions. And I can impersonate the woman with the purple hat all the way up the line to Garr."

I'd known what was in her mind. I didn't like it. Iris is the only thing in this world that I can't do without. I wasn't going to have her impersonate unknown female crooks and fool around with murderers. I began, "Iris, when there's danger, I've got to be the one—"

"—to wear the purple hat?"

"Darling, this is dynamite. You must realize it. I love you. I..."

"You loved Marta too, didn't you? Marta died when I could have saved her. Do you think I'll ever sleep easy until we've done this for her? I'm in it, darling, up to the neck and you better get used to it. So—buy me that purple hat."

I looked at her. I saw the misery in her eyes. I knew then that she'd never be happy again unless she did this thing—as a sort of atonement. I'd sooner have her happy than safe. "Okay."

We hurried into the little store. There wasn't much time before nine. Iris wasn't wearing a hat, which made it easier. A skinny old woman with straggly hair fumbled the purple hat down and handed it to Iris. It cost me a quarter and it was dear at the price. The crown bulged like a pudding and the fuzzy brim had faded to a sickly puce.

"Thank heavens I wore gray instead of my raspberry tweeds. How do I look, darling?"

"Terrible," I said. "Only Aloma could get away with that hat."

The old woman sniffed. "Who's Aloma?" she asked unexpectedly.

"Aloma's our cook," said Iris. "But I can't imagine why you should care."

The old woman sniffed again.

We left.

In Coney Island it takes all kinds of hats to make a world. Among the bobbing heads around us, Iris' monstrosity wasn't as noticeable as it might have been. We hurried on toward the Waxworks Museum. It was ten of nine. My vindictive hatred for Marta's murderer was merged now with sickening worry for Iris.

But she was taking it in her stride. At the prospect of action, she was losing her tormenting sense of responsibility. I could tell that. "It's a perfect plan, Peter. I'll be waiting in the museum. When I see Nikki I'll start to hum *The Blue Danube*. His nerves will be shot after—after Marta, anyway. He'll be in a dreadful hurry to get away, easy to fool. Once I get the instructions from him, we'll be on our way to Garr."

"What about the real woman with the purple hat? She'll be there too, you know."

"You'll have to take care of her, darling. Do anything, just so long as you keep her out of the way while I meet Nikki."

She smiled grimly. "And once she misses out on Nikki, maybe she'll be stranded and have no way of getting any further up the line, to Garr. The whole sabotage scheme or whatever it is that centers around her may be bottle-necked. Don't you see? We may kill all the birds with one purple hat."

That was brilliant, wonderful, crazy—if it wasn't for Iris having to take such an immense risk.

"Honey, you—you really think you can carry it off?"

"Of course."

I guess I'd been resigned to it from the beginning. "All right. Then leave the woman with the purple hat to me. Somehow I'll keep her out of the way."

"Fine."

"And, listen, if you're impersonating her, you mustn't be seen with me. We'd better break up right now and go to the museum separately. I'll go ahead and clear the way. You come on behind. And if it works, scram right out the moment Nikki gives you the instructions before he has a chance to realize what's happened."

"Where shall we meet again?"

I glanced across the street. A flickering neon-light above a little bar said: *Beers and Liquors* in green. "Over there. And don't forget. Get away from Nikki as fast as you can."

Iris saw. "Okay."

We stopped. Iris smiled. She looked wonderful in spite of the purple hat. She really did. I kissed her.

"Take care of yourself, honey. You're very precious."

I left her there, hating it. I hurried away from her through the crowd headed toward the Waxworks Museum.

And, as I turned the corner, it came smack into view, all dolled up with red lights. *Potter's Waxworks Museum of Murderers and Horrors.* It was written up in great red letters sprawled across a black ground. Outside the entrance, in a glass case, a wax lady's naked torso was tumbling out of a blood-stained trunk. Just so people would get the general idea! A man with a droopy black mustache was barking doleful sales-talk to a scant audience, mostly of round-eyed children.

It was five minutes to nine.

I wanted to look back, to make sure Iris was okay. But I suppressed myself. I found a dime and gave it to the mustache. There was a splintered wooden door that said: *Entrance.*

I pulled it open. I moved into the main hallway of Potter's Waxworks Museum of Murderers and Horrors.

There was nothing half-hearted about the Horrors. They smacked you in the eye the moment you entered. It was a long, rectangular room with three corridors branching off, going somewhere. It was dowdily lit, except for the exhibits. They were all dressed up with lights, proudly presented for public approval. To the right, behind one plate-glass pane, savage Indians were scalping helpless white women and children and a very intense, indignant-looking colored nurse who reminded me of Aloma. To the left, white-robed heretics were merrily burning at the stake before a delighted audience of Spanish Inquisitors. In the center, the *pièce de résistance,* naked men and women were being given the once-over with racks, thumbscrews and iron maidens in a Medieval torture chamber.

All good clean fun.

Personally, I was in no mood for wax horrors. I glanced around at the customers. At first I thought the place was crowded — women with babies, sitting on benches, young lovers, with sounder constitutions than I, embracing in the shadowy corners. Then I got on to it. They were all waxworks, too. Cute!

Except for one gawky colored boy, staring at the scalping Indians I had the place to myself. I looked around again, making sure. Yes, that was right.

There was very definitely no woman with a purple hat.

I started getting jittery. What if she was late? What if she walked in just as Nikki was giving the instructions to Iris? There, in that charnal atmosphere, the extent of the danger to Iris made itself horribly apparent. Why had I let her go through with it? Why—?

How to head off this invisible woman with the purple hat, this woman, who, unless I succeeded, could in a thousand unpredictable ways bring Iris' scheme down in ruins around her false purple hat?

It was four minutes to nine.

I started to explore the three corridors. The first, ranged on both sides with super-realistic wax reconstructions of famous murders, was deserted and trailed to a dead stop. The second was the same. Edgy as a cat, I turned into the third. Halfway down, it took a sharp bend. I approached the bend, past the Lindbergh kidnapping and the Gray-Snyder murder, strolling as casually as I could. No one was there. I came to the bend. I turned it.

And, suddenly, there she was.

This corridor came to a dead end too. And, standing there ahead of me, alone, staring at the lurid representation of some hearty hatchet slayer at work, stood the woman.

She was about thirty-five, thin almost to gauntness, with cheekbones and a prominent nose and too high-heeled shoes. I took all that in automatically, for I was looking at the hat on her frizzed-up silver blond hair.

It was a purple hat, a large-brimmed straw, with a purple ribbon around the crown.

She glanced up at me almost the instant I turned the bend. But I had enough sense not to catch her eye. And I kept my face away from her. No one could foretell what would happen later; it might be fatal if she were to recognize me as the man she had seen in the museum.

Acting as if I hadn't noticed her, I stared at the nearest exhibit, not really seeing it at all.

Obviously, she was planning a meeting with Nikki here in the depths of the corridor where it would be less conspicuous. Iris, right out in the front hall, was bound to attract Nikki's attention first. So long as this woman could be kept down here in this dead-end passage, we would be okay.

We were getting the first break.

I found I was quite an actor. Nonchalantly, as if the exhibits were far too boring to merit my attention, I turned from the woman with the purple hat and strolled back toward the bend which would put me out of sight.

I was pretty sure I'd never aroused her serious interest. I reached the bend, turned it. I had my plan then. I was going to take up my stand at the place where the corridor debouched into the main room. From there I could keep a watch on Iris and the "assignation." I could also have the woman covered. If she took it into her head to come out of the corridor at the wrong moment, I'd have to suppress her, by force if necessary. There was to be no chivalry in this fight to the finish.

I moved back past Hauptmann and Ruth Snyder, I was taut now as a bird dog when the rifle's aimed. I reached the mouth of the corridor. There was an exhibit there—*The Cleveland Butcher at Work.* I took up my position, pretending to gloat over its gory splendors. Out of the corner of my eye, I could look straight into the main room.

And, with a twitching of the pulses, I saw Iris at once. The awful purple hat gleamed brightly in the light from the Spanish Inquisition. She was putting on a dandy show, staring at the Burning Martyrs as if she couldn't wait to drop a postal card to mother about them. The colored boy had gone. We were alone in that dismal main room. But, although I was sure she knew I was there, she made not the slightest sign.

I glanced in the other direction, down the corridor. The stretch of it to the bend was still deserted. The woman with the purple hat was still around the corner, waiting there for the assignation which—I hoped—would never come off.

My watch said exactly nine o'clock.

And, precisely at that moment, the entrance door opened and Nikki came in. His punctuality—after the horror interlude of Marta's murder—was rather hair-raising. And in the drab light of the musty room, his huge, swaggering figure with the dark

turtle-neck sweater and the tousled blond head seemed distort-
edly large and somehow unreal. A waxwork come to life.

I thought of Marta again, Marta toppling down, down past
the dark scaffolding. Just to sock him once—just once on that
dimpled arrogant jaw of his! My hands were aching for it.

Calm yourself, Peter Duluth.

I held my breath. He paused on the threshold. His quick eyes
moved straight to Iris and the hat. They lingered there; then
they gave me a casual glance. In the shadows by the Cleveland
Butcher I was nothing more than a vague figure to him. I knew
that.

Very slowly, pausing to look at the Indians, he started easing
his way around to Iris. He was falling into the trap.

And yet the suspense of it was almost more than I could bear.
Because that trap—baited with my wife—could still work in
reverse. If anything were to go wrong, Iris would be the one to
be caught—the helpless victim of that thug who less than half an
hour before had killed Marta in cold blood.

Nikki and Iris—and, more dangerous than a barrel of T.N.T.,
the woman with the purple hat, invisible but agonizingly near,
down the corridor.

Iris' timing was superb. At first, when Nikki came in, she
hadn't looked around. Only now did she throw him one quick,
perfunctory glance. He was moving nearer and nearer to her.
Around them, grotesquely real, the young lovers kissed, the wax
mothers dangled their wax babies.

The silence was stifling.

And then, very softly, with the dreamy unconcern of a little
girl, Iris started to hum. Those lilting notes of *The Blue Danube*
seemed to echo around that madhouse of Horrors. And, with
sudden, gnawing fear, I wondered: *Can she hear? Down there at
the end of the corridor, can the real woman with the purple hat hear?*

Silence came again. Still Iris did not move. Nikki was only
a few feet from her. His great, broad-shouldered figure almost
blotted her from view.

Then he was at her side. He was saying something to her.
I couldn't hear what it was. Iris said something back, low and
quick. I watched out of the corner of my eye, standing there by
the Cleveland Butcher. I saw Nikki smiling at her, smiling with
an insolent Gable leer of approval. I could have killed him for it.

Then he stooped. He bent down to the floor as if he was picking something up. He unbent. He handed something to Iris. She took it, folding her hand over it. He was talking to her again, softly, casually, not looking at her.

With a tingling of excitement, I realized the "transference" had taken place. Iris was winning. She had the instructions now which would lead us to Garr.

In spite of my belligerent hatred for Nikki, relief started, like ice melting inside me.

Then the relief stopped. I felt my heart leap and scuttle around like a mouse. Because, from beyond the bend in the corridor to my right, came the faint, relentless click of heels—woman's high heels on the bare boards of the floor.

The woman with the purple hat. The real woman. She *was* doing it. She *was* coming down the corridor.

Iris and Nikki had stopped talking. But they were still standing there together by the Spanish Inquisition. I wanted to yell out to Iris: *Get away. Get out—quick.* My lungs were bursting with it, holding it back.

And yet, in spite of my extreme anxiety for Iris, I was thinking with a cold, almost impersonal logic. I had it all worked out. That woman wasn't going to reach the main hall while Iris was still there—not if I could help it. There was no point in trying to fool her I was Nikki, trying to lure her back down the corridor that way. She'd know I wasn't Nikki. No turtle-neck sweater, no tattoo marks. Fancy tactics were out. I tensed myself, ready to jump on her when she came round the bend—if need be.

I listened to the approaching footsteps. Out of the corner of my eye, I watched Nikki and Iris. The assignation was over. They must break it up soon. Yes, Iris was moving away from him, heading toward the door.

The footsteps down the corridor seemed deafening. Then, around the bend, appeared that thin, gaunt figure with the ash-blond hair, the match-stick legs and the purple hat. She paused at the bend, glancing at her watch. Then she started sauntering leisurely down the corridor toward me.

Iris was halfway to the exit door, strolling past a wax mother and child. *Quicker, Iris!*

The woman with the purple hat moved closer. Unless she paused, she'd be up to me in a matter of seconds.

Nikki was still lounging in front of the Spanish Inquisition. The pivot—!

I started counting. One—two—three—when I got to ten, I'd let the woman have it. Heaven alone knew what the outcome would be. Sounds of a scuffle in that empty, reverberating museum would be almost bound to attract Nikki. But it would give Iris a chance to get away. That was all that mattered.

Four—five—cold sweat was breaking out on my forehead. The woman came nearer, nearer. And then, while every muscle in my body was taut, she stopped. One of the exhibits attracted her, some fantastic bathtub murder. She stood there, staring with pop-eyed interest at so much blood.

Iris was almost at the door. She was at the door. Her hand was going out to it. She was pulling it open.

And then, as the woman with the purple hat dragged her gaze away from the bathtub corpse and started forward again, Iris slipped out and the door swung shut behind her.

She'd made it!

Elation came like a glass of champagne. Iris was out of the picture, safe outside in the tangled Coney Island crowd. But I was still very wary. Because Nikki was still there by the burning heretics. In a moment the real woman with the purple hat would be in the main hail. In a moment she'd see Nikki and Nikki would see her—a second woman with a purple hat. They'd meet and they'd realize an imposture had taken place. They would realize Iris had tricked them—more successfully than poor Marta or Karl.

On the face of it, that meeting seemed as disastrous as if it had happened while Iris was there. But was it? Marta had stressed the secrecy which kept each agent in Garr's strange network ignorant of the agent next to him. Nikki had slipped Iris something which contained the instructions for the next meeting. Iris had those instructions and was safely on the way to our rendezvous in the bar. With any luck, unless he managed to follow her, Nikki would have no idea where the next meeting was to take place and no means of warning the next agent that Iris was an impostor.

If I could rush her safely out of Coney Island to the next assignation, Nikki and the woman with the purple hat would be helpless.

Or would they? I weighed the alternatives. Try and stop the meeting even though it would mean violence with a doubtful outcome and the loss of my priceless anonymity? Or let it go? I decided. Let them meet; let them do anything they wanted to do. The best bet was to get to Iris quickly.

Somehow, of course, we'd have to find them both again. Nikki might be only a minor cog in a vastly more important machine. But Nikki was also the murderer of Marta and my own pet personal allergy. Our mammoth task wouldn't be complete until he, along with Garr and the others, was under arrest. But that would have to come later.

Later! There was an awful lot that had to come later.

But don't think about that now.

While I stood there by the Cleveland Butcher, letting these haphazard reflections waltz around in my mind, the woman with the purple hat brushed past me. I didn't lift a little finger to stop her. I let her move on and step into the main hall.

Was I making a dreadful mistake?

I didn't turn around. But I heard the click of the woman's heels stop. I could see Nikki without moving. I saw him turn from the Spanish Inquisition and stare straight at the woman. I saw an expression of surprise on his face; then one of sudden, galling anxiety, which gave me untold satisfaction.

There was a long hush in the Waxworks Museum of Horrors.

Very casually, I started moving toward the door, taking the route which was furthest from them, keeping my face hidden. I passed a shadowy wax couple necking in the corner. I came to the Indians. I gave their scalping activities and Aloma a farewell glance. I eased closer and closer to the door, banking on the fact that in the astonishment of their meeting they would have no eyes for me.

I reached the door. Get to Iris—my hand went out to the door. As I felt its rough wood beneath my fingers, a sound came from the vault-like museum behind me.

It was the sound of a woman's voice, shrill and metallic, humming the first lilting bars of *The Blue Danube.*

The assignation which had been planned as the opening gun in Garr's vast and shadowy plot was taking place—a little too late.

First round, surely, to the Duluths. First step, surely, toward Leslie—Pine 3-2323.

I was out in the exuberant bustle of Coney Island again, leaving heaven knew what deviltry behind me in the Waxworks Museum. Here, near the subway station, streams of exhausted revellers, trailing balloons and sagging children, were headed for home. Others—dashing night-owls—were just arriving, making for anticipated conquests on the boardwalk. I pushed my way through them, not caring about them or anything but Iris.

I turned the corner and saw, glimmering across the crowded street, the green neon-sign: *Beers and Liquors.* Glancing back to make sure Nikki wasn't following, I hurried across the street. I reached the swing door of the bar and pushed it open.

I didn't see Iris at first. I felt a stupid panic. Then I found her—sensibly in a dark little booth almost at the back of the gloomy bar. She was sitting there, toying with a drink. She had taken the purple hat off. It was stuffed down on the bench at her side. She couldn't have looked more beautiful. Three or four soldiers at the bar were appreciating that fact.

"Iris."

She looked up radiantly. I slipped into the seat opposite her, wanting to kiss her and restraining myself because husbands just mustn't be that sappy about their wives.

"Peter, it worked. We fooled him."

A waiter came up. I ordered a Scotch and soda. I needed it. Iris said, "But, tell me, the real woman with the purple hat—was she there?"

I told her all about the real woman with the purple hat and all about the meeting between her and Nikki which had taken place after she'd left.

"Maybe I was crazy letting them meet," I said, "but stopping it was such a gamble. And, if you got the instructions, if we can get out of here quick, without their following us, it ought to be okay."

"I've got the instructions," Iris tossed back her dark hair. "Nikki gave them to me." Her mouth was ominously set. "Nikki was quite smitten by my feminine charms. He wanted to know what I was doing next Tuesday night."

"I saw him leering at you, honey. If you knew how much I wanted to sock that guy! But what—?"

The waiter came with my drink then. I paid the check on the spot so that we could make a quick getaway. The waiter went away. Iris glanced around. The admiring soldiers had given up in disgust since they'd seen me. No one was looking. She picked up her pocketbook, opened it and took something out. She passed it to me across the glass sugar shaker and the sticky mustard pot.

"Here it is, Peter. Here's what he gave me."

I had it in my hand. I stared down at it with a sort of awe. It didn't make much sense. It was a small, pentagonal purple star. A smooth, shiny, unattractive purple star. I turned it over. On the back was a pin clasp.

"What on earth is it?"

"A hat ornament."

"A hat ornament?"

"Yes. At least it's Nikki's idea of one. He pretended to pick it up from the floor. He passed it to me and said: *'This ornament dropped off your hat, lady. Better see it's pinned on tighter next time.'* He said that twice. *'Be sure to keep it pinned on tighter next time.'* It must have been a sign—to tell me to pin the star on my hat. It's to be another identification for the next meeting."

"But the instructions?"

"Spring the pin at the back."

I unloosed the pin from its catch. The whole back of the little purple star swung open. Inside was a pasteboard card, folded in two. I took it out, unfolded it, looked at it. It was a regular advertising card for a bar. In fancy print, it said:

> Sammy's
> Bar and Restaurant,
> 254A East 58th St.,
> New York City.

Penciled lightly into the corner were the figures: 11:30 P.M.

"That's the place, Peter. And eleven-thirty's the time."

I slipped the card back into the purple star, snapped the clasp, and handed it back to Iris.

"Two full hours. Okay. All we've got to do now's to get out of Coney Island without them seeing us."

"That shouldn't be difficult."

We got up. I said, "Better not wear the hat. It can be seen a mile off." I picked it up and folded it inside my coat. Luckily, it was that kind of a hat.

Iris was smiling. "The Duluths are pretty smart, aren't they?"

I looked at her, thinking of Marta dead, of Karl, dead too, or held in some unknown hiding place, of the shadowy Garr and the still more shadowy plot with its unknown menaces lying ahead of us. "They'd better be," I said.

We slipped out of the restaurant. We took a circuitous route to the subway station. The jostling, teeming crowds which had been so unkind to Marta were kind to us. We reached the subway station unseen.

With a million and one other people who decided to leave Coney Island at that particular moment, we stuffed into a Seventh Avenue Express and squeezed into seats between a fat woman and a man reading a newspaper covered in meaningless hieroglyphics.

The train jolted, shivered, and started out of the station. The car smelt of garlic. But who cared about that? If we'd really shaken off Nikki and the woman with the purple hat, we were past the first hurdle on the strange and dangerous road to Garr. If we hadn't—

Iris, from somewhere behind the hieroglyphic newspaper, said, "We'll have almost an hour to kill before Sammy's Bar. What'll we do?"

"Go home," I said.

"But, darling, I promised Aloma she could have the apartment till twelve for her party. I—"

"Aloma," I said, "will have to keep a stiff upper lip."

The housewife in Iris became horrified. She broached a subject which, earlier, we had declared taboo. "Peter, her husband might not like us breaking in. He might decide against us."

It seemed almost ludicrous now, but before we went to Coney Island, Aloma's husband, "returned from a long absence," had been the most important thing in our lives. Aloma had made the dread announcement that, if her husband wished it, she would have to give up working for us in favor of unbroken connubial bliss. It had been fear of losing her which had sent us scurrying to Coney Island. Now, in spite of all that had happened, Iris was bringing that fear back with her.

"Darling, if we lost Aloma on top of everything else—"

"Aloma," I said sternly, "has become an object of secondary importance."

Knowing Aloma's uninhibited tastes, my preconception of the dinner party was lurid. When we arrived home at quarter of eleven, I was preparing myself for an orgy of boogie-woogie, scarlet, knee-high dresses and gin. It was a distinct shock when, as I slipped my key into the apartment lock, no sounds of unbridled hilarity issued from within. It was even more of a surprise when we stepped into the hall, to hear the inspiring strains of Beethoven's Seventh Symphony soaring from the living room. Aloma was not by nature a classical music enthusiast. The culture, presumably, was for the benefit of the long absent husband.

"Let's sneak into the bedroom and tidy up," whispered Iris. "We're obviously not elegant enough to crash this party."

In the bedroom, to the poignant strains of the Funeral March, Iris rummaged around for a pair of scissors and started doing something furtive to the purple hat. I changed from my gray suit into blue serge. Ever since she had shown me the purple star Nikki had given her, I had been getting increasingly uneasy about the decision I had made in the Waxworks Museum. Why had I taken it so smugly for granted that Nikki didn't know the locale of the second meeting? It would have been so simple for him to have opened the back of the star and read the directions to Sammy's Bar. If he had done so, he would certainly be there at 11:30, desperately determined to warn the second agent of the hoax.

That wasn't a pleasant thought. And that's why I had changed my suit. Nikki or the woman with the purple hat might have noticed it. I couldn't afford to have them recognize me—if they showed up. Pessimism preyed upon me. There was so hopelessly much to be done; and we were so hopelessly unprepared. We didn't even have a gun.

I wanted to say, "Let's call it quits. Let's drown our sorrows in Aloma's gin and forget." I didn't say it, of course. We'd gone much too far to back down now and nowhere near far enough to call Leslie at Pine 3-2323.

Iris said: "Peter, darling, look."

I turned. She was standing with her back to the mirror, smiling rather sheepishly, the scissors dangling from her hand. On her head was the purple hat, or rather what was left of it. She'd cut off the fuzzy brim; she'd twisted it here and prodded it there. Gleaming in the center of the crown, blazed Nikki's purple star— the identification for the next meeting. By all the laws of reason, the ensemble should have been an atrocity. But there's a sort of genius to Iris. She'd managed to transform that twenty-five cent model into something mad and alluring.

"I had to do something about it. It was eating away my morale." She dropped the scissors and slid her hand through my arm. "Come on, darling. Aloma must have heard us come in, so we'll have to pay a brief social visit—for politeness' sake. Then Sammy's Bar."

When we entered our living room we were greeted by a sight of unparalleled elegance. The Seventh Symphony sighed from the Victrola. Dim lights shone on four immaculately evening-dressed people sitting around a table, playing—not pinochle or gin rummy, Aloma's twin passions—but bridge. Seeing us, Aloma, who was dummy, swept from the table toward us, slinking in ivory satin which had once been Iris' most successful gown. She looked magnificent, gaunt and world-weary with her coffee skin smooth against the ivory satin.

Her measureless Negro vitality was quite obliterated behind this devastating front. I'd never seen Aloma going in for glamour before. It was something.

"Mr. and Mrs. Duluth, how charming!" She extended an elaborately hostess hand. Then, out of the corner of her mouth, the old Aloma hissed, "Fo' Pete's sake, be polite to these people. They're Society."

We were taken to the bridge table. Introductions came. The couple who were Society—a thin, distinguished colored man with spectacles and a haughty wife, bowed and made suitably social remarks. Then, triumphantly, Aloma turned to the other man and announced:

"I have pleasure in presenting—my husband."

Aloma's enigmatically resurrected husband was immense, very tall, very broad, and rather black. He must have weighed all of three hundred pounds and, unlike the others, seemed a trifle ill-at-ease behind his tuxedo. He smiled a dazzling but awkward smile, muttered, "Pleased to meet you," and left the conversation alone to the Seventh Symphony.

Under normal circumstances, I would have been weighing his potential sex-appeal against the awful event of his taking Aloma from us. But all I could think of now was how comforting all those three hundred pounds of him would be back of us in our fight against Nikki and Garr.

"There's nothing like a quiet evenin' with bridge and good music," cooed Aloma brazenly belying her own nature.

"Beethoven!" breathed the wife who was Society.

The chit-chat rippled on from there. After a suitable interval, Iris and I expressed our regrets and made our good-byes. Aloma came with us to the door. Once out of the living room, most of the elegance vanished. She screwed up her mouth in disgust.

"Good music and bridge! I'm tellin' you the truth, Miz Peter, good music and bridge gives me the pain. But I gotta do it, gotta entertain the right people." She added darkly, "For the sake of my husband's prospects on account of him bein' so long absent from the best circles." Her face becoming suddenly rapturous, she asked, "You like him? You like Rudolph?"

"Rudolph's charming," said Iris.

Aloma gave her own ivory satin thigh a lusty slap. "Oh, boy!" she exclaimed.

Her face rather peeky with apprehension, Iris blurted, "Aloma, you—you are going to stay with us, aren't you? You aren't going to let Rudolph—"

"Rudolph figures a wife's place's in the home, but—I ain't made up my mind." Aloma looked important. "I'm jest figurin' for an' against. "

Ominous words!

"I'm plannin' to get rid of those wet-smacks soon." She jerked a thumb toward the living room. "An' then Rudolph and I maybe'll do the town fo' a couple hours."

"When will you know, Aloma?" asked Iris meekly.

"I guess I'll be ready for a decision fust thing tomorrow morning."

"Tomorrow morning."

Here was yet another thing to add to our miseries—the prospect that Aloma might abandon us.

As if realizing our woe and trying to be nice, she said, "That's a trick lookin' hat you got, Miz Iris. Best looking hat I seen you wear."

I gulped. Iris looked proud.

Aloma said, "You gonna be out long?"

"I don't know," I said, wondering rather dourly if we would ever be back at all.

I toyed with a crazy impulse to ask her to get rid of her "wet-smacks" right now and bring the three hundred pounds of

Rudolph along to do the town with us at Sammy's Bar. But I stopped myself. If Aloma knew what nefarious things we were up to, she would definitely plump for Rudolph.

Hand on hip, she stood at the door, watching benignly as we headed for the elevator. "Take care of yo'selves, honies," she called. "And have fun."

Have fun! Those two words hummed around in my ears as the automatic elevator jerked us downward. Murder, sabotage, impersonations, lethal secret agents.

We took a taxi to within a block of Sammy's Bar. Our plans were set. They were simple, reduplicating our plans for the Waxworks Museum. We were to go into the bar separately. Iris, in her role as the purple hat, was to make the second contact which, with any luck, would direct us to Garr. I, in my role as any random citizen, was to sip a beer at a table near the door and watch.

As the taxi jogged through the familiar Manhattan traffic, my uneasiness mounted steadily. I didn't say anything to Iris. Now that it was much too late to call quits with our unknown adversaries, I didn't want to get her worried too. But I had become obsessed with the idea of Nikki. How could I have been so dumb? Of course, he'd opened the purple star and found the address. Of course, he would show up at Sammy's Bar with the real woman with the purple hat in tow—out for Iris' blood.

That was to be my responsibility—at all costs to keep him from getting at Iris.

If she shared my fears, she showed no sign of it. But then, she's always been the Lady Macbeth of our team, taking danger and disaster in her stride. The moment the taxi dumped us on the corner of 58th Street, she melted away into the meager crowd, headed toward the neon-sign which said: "Sammy's." I followed anxiously. The purple hat with its brazen ornamental star would make a perfect mark for any hostile gunman. Why had we got into this? Where was the frail, forlorn little ghost of Marta Pauly leading us?

I saw Iris tug open the swing door of Sammy's Bar and Restaurant and disappear inside. Quicker than I should have done, I followed.

There was nothing sinister about the interior of Sammy's Bar. It was any Manhattan bar. Dim lights, wooden booths, a long wooden bar stretching down one side, with bottles and a bored,

white-coated barman flicking drinks around for a few nondescript loungers. Beyond, there was an inner room, invisible from
the bar itself and in half darkness—a regular restaurant room,
probably—closed at this hour of night. At the end of the bar, a
flambuoyance of scarlet and chromium, stood a jukebox.

As I entered, I was horribly conscious of Iris and her vivid
purple hat moving leisurely toward the bar. I kept myself from
looking at her. I slipped into the booth which commanded the
best view of the entrance and, through the glass window, of the
dark sidewalk outside. I tried to look like a lonely single male
with that eleven-thirtyish need of a pick-me-up.

Snatches of bar conversation, muffled slightly by the low
ceiling, hummed around me. A shrill blonde was complaining
rather ginishly of the stinginess of a "sugar-daddy"; two men
were tossing Roosevelt back and forth; a man and a woman held
contrasting opinions of Tyrone Power. It was all so run-of-the-
mill, and yet in that humdrum milieu were Iris and an unknown
agent of the unknown and sinister Garr, maneuvering to make
their fantastic contact. Amidst those martinis and highballs and
beers, there was Iris and danger!

A waiter came, took my order and brought me a drink. Still
nothing had happened over at the bar. I was sure of it. I glanced
at my watch, 11:31. Something happen! Please something happen soon—before Nikki—!

I kept myself from thinking of Nikki.

Then another thought came. It was even more devastating.
Had Nikki, perhaps, found some way of contacting the second
agent and of warning him before the rendezvous? Did the whole
shadowy chain of Garr's disciples know already of our clumsy
attempt at imposture? Had the real assignation been moved to
some other safer place? And was there here, instead of a gullible
unwarned agent waiting to be fooled by us, some crafty sort of
trap?

That thought, coupled with the sight of Iris there at the bar,
still alone, was almost more than I could bear. 11:32. Why had I let
Nikki meet the real woman with the purple hat at the Waxworks
Museum? Why hadn't I contrived some way, however desperate, to keep them separate?

I saw then how hopelessly amateurish our every move had
been. And it was largely my fault. If there was mortal danger for
Iris now—it was my doing.

These morbid fears racked me as I sat there, pretending to drink, with those pointless fragments of conversation trickling into my unlistening ears.

"... Tyrone Power ... Roosevelt ... artificial pearls, that's all I got for my birthday...."

Then I saw that a man—a man I hadn't noticed before—was strolling from the far end of the bar toward the jukebox. He attracted my attention just because he was something, moving in that stagnant pool. He was a vague, thin little man with no hat and a bald head—an utterly unobtrusive little man. He moved to the jukebox. He took out a nickel. He slipped it into the slot and pushed a button almost immediately, with the authority of a man who already knew, before he reached the machine, what tune he wanted to play.

There was a vague whirring from the machine, mingling with the bar conversations. And then, soft at first, mounting up to a booming pulsing rhythm, issued the familiar and now terrifying strains of *The Blue Danube.*

I saw Iris, at the bar, stiffen instantly. The little man was still lounging by the jukebox, staring with apparent casualness at the list of tunes sprawled across its front. Iris was moving. Nonchalantly, her drink in one hand, she started crossing toward the jukebox, the shadowiest hint of a waltz step in her walk.

Watching her, I felt a sort of dreadful paralysis. Was this the genuine agent making the genuine signal? Or was it a trap? The vast responsibility! To stop her or not to stop her!

Iris was moving closer to the jukebox and the little bald-headed man. No one at the bar was paying her any attention. She was just a woman with a purple hat and a drink going to the jukebox. *The Blue Danube*—the murmuring voices—and then, mingling in with them, Iris' voice, soft but clear—humming.

De-tumptee-tee-tum—tum-tum—tum-tum.

Quickly, with one of those expertly unnoticeable changes of direction, the little man's glance took her in. He never caught her eye. Merely, as she moved toward him, he started away from the jukebox—toward the shadowy room that lay beyond the bar.

To stop Iris or not to stop her! It was the most dreadful decision of my career. If this was a trap, it would mean Iris' life. If it wasn't a trap, it might mean our discovering the whereabouts and the eventual destruction of Garr. Two immensities up against each other. Finally, just because Iris meant so horribly much to me, I let her go. I did nothing.

The *Blue Danube* swam on. The little man disappeared into the room beyond. Slowly, inconspicuously, Iris passed the jukebox. She turned the corner into the backroom. She disappeared too.

Over at the bar Tyrone Power fought it out with Roosevelt. The maddeningly inevitable rhythm of *The Blue Danube* beat on.

The horror of that invisible room beyond. What was going on? What—?

The Blue Danube stopped. It ground out its final chord and then subsided into a swishing sound and silence.

More than anything in the world, I wanted to get back to that inner room, to remove from Iris' shoulders the whole onus of the danger. But I couldn't. For if she was being successful, if the second meeting was going off—my appearance would be a monkey-wrench in the works.

I just sat there, my unsteady hand cupped around my drink, listening to the post-*Blue Danube* silence, staring blankly ahead of me, through the bar window pane out to the drab, ill-lit sidewalk.

A hobo, ragged and unshaven, slouched past, pausing to throw a thirsty glance at a whiskey ad in the window. I watched his shambling progress out of sight. There was no one there—only an empty expanse of sidewalk.

Then faintly, through the glass pane, I heard the click-click of invisible, approaching high heels. The sound linked instantly in my mind with the tapping heels in the Waxworks Museum. I was suddenly taut, waiting for what was to come into view in the framed street scene in front of me. With one of those uncertain intuitions of doom, I knew what I was going to see.

And I did see it. And my excruciating anxiety shifted instantly away from that back room to the sidewalk outside.

For, suddenly, like actors appearing on an empty stage, two figures came into view on the sidewalk outside the window of Sammy's Bar. Two figures, a man and a woman. Inevitably, a man with a blue turtle-neck sweater and a woman with a purple hat.

Their arrival, at the most crucial moment of the second transaction, was a nightmare reduplication of what had happened at the Waxworks Museum. Fate repeating its same trick against us!

In those few seconds while Nikki and the real woman with the purple hat crossed the window pane on their way to the door, I realized what had happened. My early fears had been correct. Nikki had opened the purple star. And, instead of finding some way to send a warning ahead, he had come in person with the real woman with the purple hat—to trap Iris.

And Iris was there, only a perilous matter of feet away, in the next room. In a moment they would discover her and expose her to the second agent—unless I stopped them.

Last time, in a similar situation, I had failed miserably. I couldn't afford to fail this time. And as if through some benign compensation of providence, I found I knew exactly what to do. And I felt quite calm about it.

In the dimly lit museum I had deliberately hidden my face. Almost certainly, neither Nikki nor the woman with the purple hat would recognize me. And if Marta had been right, certainly neither Nikki nor the woman with the purple hat would know Garr.

They were coming in through the door, Nikki ahead, his blond hair dishevelled, his heavy face, which had been so arrogant after the murder of Marta, uncertain and harassed. The gaunt, thin-legged, ash-blond woman came mincingly after him, the brim of the purple hat flapping as she moved. They hesitated on the threshold, glancing around the haphazard assortment of customers—looking, of course, for Iris or the little man with the bald head, both of whom were mercifully out of sight around the corner in the next room.

I rose from my table. I moved toward them, feeling their gazes switch to me. I didn't look at them. I just strolled closer. And then, softly, I started to whistle the first bars of *The Blue Danube.*

I felt their gazes rivet on me. I still didn't look at them. Still whistling under my breath, I pushed past them to the door. I opened it and sauntered out onto the deserted sidewalk.

It was a terrific gamble, depending entirely for its success on the gullibility which the cold-blooded, slaughtering Nikki had already shown. I had nothing but Mr. Strauss' waltz on my side. If they didn't follow me, if they went on into the bar, I would be abandoning Iris to them. If they didn't follow me—

I didn't look back. I moved slowly on down the deserted block. To my overwrought, selective sense of hearing, it seemed as if there was no sound in all of Manhattan. Then—exquisitely—I

heard footsteps on the cement behind me; the thud of male footsteps, the click-click of French heels.

It was working. They were following me, following *The Blue
Danube* like rats following the Pied Piper.

I moved on to the corner of the block. I paused there, as if
waiting for nonexistent traffic to drive by before I crossed. Their
footsteps came after me unbrokenly. A moment later, without
looking round, I could feel their presence at my side—the woman
with the purple hat and Nikki. Nikki—my boyfriend!

I took the leap then in the wildest impersonation attempt in
forty-eight states. In a quiet, ominous voice which, from reading stories equally lurid as this reality, I associated with sinister
master-minds, I said: "You fool! What sort of a mess have you
made of it? A woman with a purple hat came at the right time;
she made the right signals. She was an impostor. You must have
given her the purple star. You should be shot for it."

At the Waxworks Museum I had underestimated Nikki's
quickness and the extent of his information. Was I doing it again?
Standing there, absurdly casual, on the corner of 58th Street and
Third Avenue I waited for his reply which was to mean so much.

His voice came, quick, confused. "L-lis-ten, I can explain. I—"

I had him on the run. Trying to keep triumph out of my tone,
I said: "Explain! Little late to explain, isn't it? For all you know,
that woman may be in with the police—"

"No, no, she ain't in with the police. I can explain—" He broke
off, a tinge of suspicion in his voice. "But who are you? You ain't
Baldy."

"Baldy"—the little man with the bald head who, right at this
very moment was giving Iris the instructions that might lead to
Garr. "Baldy"—the second agent. Thanks, Nikki.

"Baldy!" I echoed. "At least Baldy saw through that woman.
He knew she was an impostor right away. He and the boys are
taking care of her all right. Baldy has some sense."

"But, listen—"

"You can explain. I know. You've said that before. Well, you're
not going to do any explaining here. This neighborhood's as
dangerous as a powder plant now—thanks to you. You're coming with me."

I saw a taxi then. I hailed it. It stopped, swung around, started
for us. My pulses were tingling. Dangerous as a powder plant!
That was an understatement—if only Nikki knew. Any second,

Iris might be coming out of the restaurant. I had to get them away without their seeing her.

All through that remarkable conversation, I had kept my back to them. I had looked neither at Nikki nor at the woman with the purple hat.

As the taxi moved toward us, I said, "You're coming with me—somewhere where it's safe. And then you're going to have a lot of explaining to do. A lot."

The taxi came nearer. *Iris don't come out of that restaurant yet!*

I could hear Nikki shuffling indecisively behind me. Suddenly he blurted, "You ain't Baldy. Who are you?"

That seemed to be the moment. The taxi had stopped right beside me. I turned—rather dramatically. Nikki was standing there, a huge blond figure, his mouth thick and sullen. The woman with the purple hat was staring too, shifting slightly on the spindly legs.

"You want to know who I am?" I paused. I let my glance flick to the woman and then come back to Nikki. For all I knew, I was about to sign my own death warrant then. Maybe Nikki didn't know Garr. But it was more than possible that he knew something physical about him that would disqualify me—that he was old, or thin, or fat, or bald, or something. I held the steady gaze. I said: "I'm—Garr."

The instant I spoke, the woman started and Nikki's face, above the tall throat of the sweater, went a kind of greenish gray. His eyes were rabbit's eyes, the eyes of a rabbit hypnotized by the dread, snake-like name—Garr.

Without the slightest shadow of doubt, the precarious gamble had worked.

Curtly, I jerked my head toward the waiting taxi. The driver opened the door. The two of them scrambled in—cowering. I took a final glance down the street. There was no sign of Iris. I jumped into the taxi, too, slamming the door on us. I gave the driver our home address.

The taxi started and jolted forward into Third Avenue, while I sat there, in the back seat, crammed in with Nikki and the woman with the purple hat.

As we dodged in and out under the looming bulk of the El, I felt a little dizzy. Never had victory come so easily—or brought so many potentialities of danger in its wake. Behind me, in Sammy's Restaurant, I had abandoned Iris, impersonating the sinister Garr himself to one of his own buddies, brashly kidnapping Marta's murderer and a woman who held the key to some vast scheme for destruction.

The Duluths, once they decide to deviate from the respectable norm, are nothing if not thorough.

And Aloma had said—have fun!

On that fantastic taxi ride, there was not a single peep either from Nikki or from the woman with the purple hat. Presumably the very thought of being in the presence of Garr was sufficient to numb their faculties. That was a break for me. In fact, I started to see that my impulsive abduction had been a master-stroke.

For Marta's memory and, now, for our own skins also, Iris and I were pledged to three things. We were pledged to expose Garr and his minions to the police, to rescue Karl Pauly, if he was still in the land of the living, and to deadlock the ominous scheme for destruction which was to have started that night in Coney Island.

Earlier in the evening, even at the brightest moments, that undertaking had seemed wildly ambitious. But now, with any luck, success was all but in our grasp. Back at Sammy's Bar, Iris was getting the lead to Garr. Here in this taxi, thoroughly subdued, I had Nikki, who certainly knew where Karl Pauly was; and the purple-hatted lady around whom the sabotage plot seemed to center and who carried on, her person "something of vital importance for Garr."

Keep them fooled, get them to talk, wheedle the "thing of vital importance" out of the purple hat. That's all I had to do and the moment might come for Leslie—Pine 3-2323.

Play up, Mr. Duluth.

The taxi rattled on. It swerved west of Third Avenue, drawing closer and closer to my apartment. I sat very stiff and poker-faced. The woman with the purple hat, next to me, patted with spasmodic uneasiness at her ash-blond hair and shifted her thin legs. Every now and then when the taxi jolted, the brim of the purple hat flapped against my ear. Each time, she shrank further from me as if she expected flames to shoot out of my nostrils. Nikki's face was still green. Once his unsteady fingers pulled out a package of cigarettes. He glanced at me and, at the last minute, lost his nerve and let the cigarettes drop down onto the seat.

Having Nikki there in the taxi with me, sweating his sweater off for fear of me, was paradise on earth. If they went on being that scared, it was going to be a cinch.

The taxi drew up outside my door. I got out, tossed the driver a dollar bill, and nodded to Nikki and the woman to follow me into the deserted vestibule. As they crammed into the automatic elevator after me, I started hoping that Aloma's pleasant evening of bridge and good music had drawn to its elegant close. Aloma and the three-hundred-pound Rudolph would make invaluable allies in a knock-down, drag-out brawl, but they were hardly the company I would have chosen for this, the most delicate and subtly dangerous enterprise of my life.

I needn't have worried. When I opened the apartment door, discreet silence reigned within. I waited at the door until Nikki and the woman had entered ahead of me. Then I shut the door and led the way into the living-room. Except for a faint lingering of jasmine perfume in the air, all signs of Aloma's revels had been obliterated. Aloma and Rudolph were off, apparently, doing the town.

While Nikki and the woman with the purple hat watched me sheepishly, I crossed to the mantel, preparing myself with the conscious effort of an actor for the epic role I was to play. From now on, I was to be Garr. What did I know about him? Nothing—except that he was one of the cleverest and most dangerous termites in the United States, that his very name inspired terror in his employees and that he was smart enough to have eluded the grasp of Leslie, Pine 3-2323. Okay. I would be Garr; I would be cold and quiet and ruthless and omniscient.

Being omniscient, when I knew so little, wasn't going to be easy!

I turned slowly, facing the two of them. They were still standing respectfully.

"Sit down," I said.

The woman with the purple hat minced to the sofa and sat on its extreme edge, one spindly leg crossed over the other. Nikki hesitated and then dropped into a chair. Their awe of me helped my self-confidence. I gazed straight at Nikki, the man who only a few hours before had murdered Marta. Scare the pants off Nikki for his bungling. That was what Garr would do first. Scaring the pants off Nikki would be pleasant.

"Well, Nikki," I said in a soft, steely voice, "you have a little explaining to do, haven't you?"

He moistened grayish lips, and shifted his great bulk miserably in Iris' gold brocaded chair. I've never seen a more uneasy man. "It ain't my fault," he said. "I get my orders. I'm to go to the Waxworks Museum, look for a dame with a purple hat, and when she sings *The Blue Danube*, I give her the purple star. Okay. I goes to the Museum; I see this dame with a purple hat; she sings *The Blue Danube*. How'm I to know she's a phony? No one ain't told me—"

"It certainly wasn't my fault." For the first time the woman with the purple hat raised her voice. It was harsh and unattractive. It went with the scarlet mouth and the thin legs. She was obviously all out to justify herself too. "I wasn't told in what part of the Museum to meet this man. I was waiting down one of the corridors and this other woman was in the main hall. She's the one he saw first. It's no fault of mine."

"How was I to know she'd be way down one of them corridors?" blustered Nikki.

"It was the most sensible place—" retorted the woman.

A flick of my hand cut them short. "Squabble later," I said.

"When Nikki didn't show up," continued the woman with the purple hat, "I went down into the main hall and I saw him there. But it was too late because this other woman..."

"Yeah. Soon as I saw this dame I realized the other one'd been a phony. But what was I to do? I couldn't contact Baldy before the meeting. You know that. But I'd opened the purple star before I give it to her. I seen the instructions for the next meeting." Nikki tried, rather unconvincingly, to swagger about that as if it had been a master-mind move. "So I figured it was best to take the real dame along to Sammy's place and fix that phony when we got there."

So it had all worked out the way I had imagined. Very icy and being Garr, I said, "You haven't explained how this impostor knew about the meeting at the Museum. You were the only person who was given the instructions—"

"That ain't no fault of mine, either." Nikki ran a hand around the throat of his sweater. "One of the kids we got working with us for our set-up at the docks—he snooped when I was getting my instructions. We'd thought he was okay, but—"

"You mean Karl Pauly," I said.

His jaw dropped at this exhibition of all-knowledge.

"You know about Pauly?"

"Naturally." Here was my chance to get the lead to Karl. "They haven't told me yet what they've done with him."

Nikki grinned. "He won't cause no more trouble." He glanced knowingly at the woman with the purple hat. Her answering smile was discreet. "They got him safe down at the Purple Star."

The Purple Star—wherever or whatever that was! I felt a tingle of excitement. So the purple stars for the purple hat had some significance of their own—a kind of cross-reference. And it wasn't too late to save Karl—not yet. He was still alive—at the Purple Star. Point number one to me.

Still holding the quiet, velvet-glove voice, I said, "You're trying to tell me that this woman was an associate of Pauly's?"

"Yeah. That must be it. You see, this Pauly had a mother—"

Nikki started telling me about Marta. He was in his element now, strutting like a peacock. He told how he'd grown suspicious of her knowing more than she should, how he'd watched her house, followed her to Coney Island, and decided to kill her before the meeting at the Waxworks Museum. His heavy face grew almost animated as he recounted how he had trapped her on the roller coaster, thrown her over the ramp, and made his get-away before the police had even arrived on the scene.

Having to listen to him without socking him in the teeth was a most rarefied form of torture.

"So you see," he concluded, "this dame who got to Baldy— oh, sure, I guess it's kind of too bad, even though it ain't my fault. But you don't have to worry about her. She ain't in with the cops, any more than Pauly and his mother were. I know it. She was just some pal of this Pauly woman who thought she'd get smart. None of them have gone to the cops. They're too scared. You don't have to worry."

So Karl *had* managed to keep from them his FBI contact with Leslie, Pine 3-2323. Good for Karl.

"When I need your advice whether to worry or not, I'll ask for it," I said.

That pricked the flimsy bubble of his arrogance. His speech in his own defense complete now, he crouched in the chair like a great sulky bear, waiting for Garr to pronounce sentence.

I lit a cigarette. I stood with my back to the mantel, staring at him impassively. I was going to enjoy this.

"It's been an unlucky day for you, Nikki. You killed one woman and yet you let another woman trick you. You almost destroyed a very carefully worked out and vital plan. That was unlucky. But the most unlucky thing for you is that, thanks to your bungling, you've had to meet me. You know that I allow very few people to know who I am."

"Yes, but—"

"And somehow," I drawled, "I don't think I'm going to want you to be one of them."

Nikki's face had gone the color of the inside of orange peel. "You—you don't mean—? You ain't going to have them do to me what they did to Anders," he moaned. "You can't—"

I didn't know what they'd done to Anders. I hoped it was something most unpleasant. "You'll find out in time," I said, "just what I'm planning to do."

He cringed like a whipped retriever. I shrugged him away and turned to the woman with the purple hat.

"What's your name?"

She started confusedly and faltered, "Ruby."

I might have guessed it from looking at her. Ruby! Okay, Ruby. This was where I went to town. The whole purpose behind this enigmatic tangle of agents and purple hats and stars had been a meeting between Garr and Ruby. All right. The meeting was now going to come off.

"Well, Ruby," I said, "we finally meet. I believe you have something to say to me?"

I felt very taut. Was it really going to be as easy as this? Was I going to learn the dark secrets of the mysterious plot simply by having Ruby tell me about them?

Ruby patted the ash-blond hair, looked refined and batted her lashes in the direction of Nikki. "Is it all right to talk in front of him?"

"Why not?" I said. And then, because I couldn't resist it, "Just think of Nikki as someone who's going on a long, long journey."

Nikki cringed some more. Ruby looked brisk and business-like and said, "Okay. Well, you got all the facts. Your people from down at the docks gave you the whole dope. How about it? What's your decision?"

That had me rocking for a moment. So Garr knew already everything there was to know about this vague plot. This meeting had been designed not to give him information, but to learn his decision on information already received. What I had thought to be solid ground under my feet had changed suddenly to very thin ice.

Guardedly, very conscious of the hulking and murderous figure of Nikki hunched in his chair, I echoed, "My decision?"

"Yep," snapped Ruby. "What's it to be? Are you ready to play ball? How much cash is there in it for us?"

So long as she kept me on the defensive, I was lost. I saw that. I decided upon a bold counter-attack.

"Before there's any talk of a decision, I want to hear the whole story again from you."

"But that's dumb. You know—"

"I'm not interested in what I know. I'm interested in you, Ruby. There's been one impostor with a purple hat already tonight. D'you imagine I'd risk talking with you until you've proved you're genuine?"

I thought that was rather brilliant for the spur of the moment.

"Genuine? You mean—on the level?" she grumbled. "Of course I'm on the level."

"Prove it."

"But time's so short. I don't want—"

"There are more important things than time," I said ominously. "Go on, Ruby. Tell me the whole story—from the beginning."

It worked. Ruby batted her eyelashes petulantly and crossed her thin legs so that I saw all of them. They weren't the kind of legs you wanted to see all of.

"Okay," she said, "if you want to be that cagey, I'll go through the whole thing. I'll show you I'm on the level. Captain Fisher, he's my friend." She looked knowing. "And he contacted one of your men down at the docks." She shot a contemptuous glance at Nikki. "*His* boss. And your man told Captain Fischer that it was too big a proposition for him to handle, that he'd pass all the dope on to you and that Captain Fischer would have to go to you personally for the final decision. Right so far?"

There was a challenging note in her voice. The uncomfortable idea came that perhaps she was using my tactics as a boomerang—deliberately making up a phony story to test whether I myself was on the level.

"Right so far?" she repeated.

I still had the control. "What's the name of Nikki's boss down at the docks?" I said, as if testing her.

"Swensen."

From the quickness of her reply, and from the fact that Nikki accepted the name without the slightest change of expression, I was pretty sure that my fears were unnecessary. Ruby wasn't interested in whether or not I was Garr; she was too busy trying to prove she was Ruby. Relief slid through my body. Ruby was turning out as much of a push-over as Nikki.

And Swensen. I must remember that name when the time came for the final round-up of Garr and his gang.

Ruby was watching me intently.

"Go on," I said.

"Okay," she said again. "Well, since you're so cagey about being known and won't make a straight appointment with any-one, Swensen told Captain Fischer to get a representative and send her to Coney Island where she'd be started up the line to you. Captain Fischer chose me as his representative—" the blond hair got patted again— "on account of my being his friend and someone he could trust. And I'm here to get your decision. Okay. Satisfied now?"

I couldn't afford to be satisfied for a long time yet. I glanced at Nikki. He had perked up and was leaning forward in his chair. For the first time I started wondering whether he had a gun. Almost certainly he had. That was a nasty thought.

I was wondering about Iris too. In fact, all through that impos-sible session, worry for Iris was gnawing somewhere in back of my mind. Had she made good at Sammy's Place? Had she got the lead to Garr? And if she had, what would she do when she found I had gone? Would she go on to the interview with Garr alone? Or would she come back here? That was what kept me jit-tery as a cat. If Iris were to walk in here now, purple hat and all, Nikki would recognize her, the whole jerry-built structure of my Garr impersonation would collapse and—

I tried to keep that thought out of the way.

Ruby was tugging at her flimsy skirt with elegant fingers. "Satisfied now," she repeated.

Very dead-pan, I said, "Not until you've told me what the proposition is."

"Nothing slap-dash about you, is there, Mr. Garr? I should have brought shorthand notes." Ruby was getting sarcastic. "Okay. Here's the proposition. Captain Fischer's got a ship—the *Purple Star*."

The *Purple Star!* Karl Pauly was on the *Purple Star*—Captain Fischer's ship.

"Right now," went on Ruby, "he's on the transatlantic route, sailing in the convoys. And this trip he's carrying ammunition. The *Purple Star's* just stuffed with ammunition—gunpowder, guns, bombs, everything."

She mounted those sinister words with the caressing intimacy of a radio announcer boosting a sponsored dessert.

"The *Purple Star's* scheduled to sail six-thirty tomorrow afternoon for Halifax. At the moment, she's docked smack alongside five or six other ships. Captain Fischer and I kind of want to put our hands on some money and we aren't any too particular how we come by it. Captain Fischer figured that you, seeing your line of business, might be interested in a little sort of accidental fire taking place on the *Purple Star*. A cigarette tossed away or something and the whole ship blows up and it sets fire to all the other ships and the docks and everything."

She patted the purple hat. "Before you could turn around, half of the docks would be on fire. And who's to blame? No one. Okay, Mr. Garr. That's the proposition, and you're going to have a tough time proving I'm a phony now. So for Pete's sake, let's get down to it. What's the decision? Are you interested and how much is in it for us?"

Ruby sat there watching me as calmly as if she had come to sell me a set of bathroom fixtures. I was staggered. So this was the plot of which Karl and poor little Marta had heard vague rumblings. This was the catastrophe which Iris and I had so impulsively committed ourselves to stop. A munitions ship blown up in the heart of New York! The horror of it had fantastic proportion—and yet it was real. Only too real. I remembered other mysterious fires that had broken out recently around the docks. I remembered, dimly, from my childhood, the Black Tom explosion in Jersey.

All that would be Fourth of July stuff in contrast to this. There was certainly nothing small-time about Ruby and her boyfriend, Captain Fischer.

Both Ruby and Nikki were fixing me with steady stares. The moment for the great Garr to make his great decision had come. I tried to look calm. It wasn't easy.

"All we want is your okay to go ahead, Mr. Garr," said the executive Ruby. "Captain Fischer's got everything set. One word from you and at five sharp this morning the *Purple Star* is blasted to kingdom come. How about it?"

I wondered dimly whether anything as wild and woolly as this had ever happened before to any sober, respectable American citizen.

One word from me and half of New York's docks went up in smoke!

"You've seen the plans and everything," said Ruby. "You know it's a cinch, Mr. Garr. Surely, it's worth a hundred grand to you."

A hundred thousand dollars. So that's all Ruby was asking to destroy the *Purple Star*—mere pin money!

"Fifty grand now," said Ruby. "And fifty grand when the job's done. Okay?"

I was desperately trying to think ahead. I knew the whole fantastic plot now; and I knew where Karl Pauly could be found. There was nothing to stop me calling Pine 3-2323 immediately and turning the macabre and murderous affair over to Leslie. But, if I did, if the plot to destroy the *Purple Star* was nipped in the bud, if Nikki, Ruby, Captain Fischer, and Swensen were all arrested, the shadowy Garr would still elude the net. And obviously, so long as Garr remained at large, only a fraction of the job was done. So long as Garr remained at large, there was always the risk of other Rubys, other Captain Fischers, other *Purple Stars.*

No, however great the danger, I would have to hold off from Pine 3-2323 a little longer. I would have to stall; keep Nikki and Ruby on ice until I could contact Iris and make certain that she had received from Baldy the final instructions that would lead to Garr's hideout.

Stall, somehow contact Iris—

Iris' living-room—so utterly incongruous a setting for these diabolic plots—was preternaturally silent. Ruby was leaning forward on the couch, watching me brightly. I stubbed my cigarette and said casually:

"All right, Ruby. I see no reason not to let you have my decision now. Okay. Go ahead. You'll get the money."

"A hundred grand in cash?" Ruby's eyes went piggy and greedy.

"Yes. One hundred thousand dollars." That was the final fabulous touch, to hear myself placidly offering Ruby one hundred thousand dollars in cash.

Ruby was gloating all over, legs, purple hat, and everything. "Give me the first fifty grand and I'll call Captain Fischer right away. Everything's set for five o'clock, fuses and everything. He's just waiting for the call." She laughed. "There'll be fireworks in New York tonight."

Nice character, Ruby.

I watched her, realizing she'd given me my stalling point. "I'm afraid we'll have to wait a little while." I glanced at Nikki. "Thanks to Nikki, my plans had to be rearranged. One of my men's bringing the money here."

Ruby looked instantly suspicious.

"You don't have to worry," I said. "He should be here in ten minutes."

That was to give me time to think. I was beginning to see what I had to do. When the ten minutes was up and my mythical man hadn't arrived, I would have to maneuver Nikki and Ruby into some place from which they couldn't escape and then make a frantic attempt to contact Iris. The problem of imprisoning Ruby and the probably armed Nikki in a New York apartment wasn't exactly a simple one. But it had to be solved. I couldn't afford to let them get away again. Iris' bathroom perhaps? Or the broom closet in the hall?

Where was Iris anyway? Where to look for her?

Ruby, her self-assurance completely restored by the prospect of fifty grand, lit a scarlet-tipped cigarette and leaned back against the cushions of the couch. Nikki got up from his chair. I'd forgotten how tall he was. He came toward me, towering over me, looking abject.

"Mr. Garr," he began, "since everything's going to be okay now, you ain't—it wasn't none of it my fault. And Baldy fixed that dame. You said so. There won't be any more trouble with her." His great arms hung limply at his sides. "You ain't going to let them do to me what they did to Anders?"

I stared at all those feet of winsome charm, thinking of some of the things I would like to do to him. I said, "We'll take that up later on."

"But, Mr. Garr—"

His hand went out toward me in a gesture of pleading. Then, suddenly, it stopped in midair. I saw Ruby start and sit up straight on the couch. But I saw it only vaguely because I too had heard that dreadful sound which had come without the shadow of a warning.

That sound of woman's heels tap-tapping across the parquet of the hall directly outside the living-room door.

I realized in a flash what had happened. The front door! I hadn't heard her key in the front door. I—

I pushed past Nikki, making for the living-room door, feeling as if the end of the world was coming.

It came.

Before I reached the door, it was thrown open. A voice that was more familiar to me than any voice in the world, was saying excitedly: "Peter, darling, why on earth did you leave? What happened? I've got the directions. We can get to Garr now."

Iris stepped straight into the room.

I stared at her, desperately, hopelessly. Nikki and Ruby were staring too, as she stood there, frozen on the threshold—Iris, slim and beautiful in her gray tweed suit; Iris with that nightmare purple hat, which flaunted two ornamental purple stars now, perched on her dusky brown hair.

Her glance had moved from me and was fixed on Nikki. Very slowly he stepped away from the mantel, understanding, and a sort of evil triumph dawning on his face. One of his great hands went into his pants' pocket. He gave a little laugh.

"So this dame's a phony and you're Garr!" he said. "You're Garr. That's rich. Tried to fool me, did you? Okay. Stick 'em up."

My hands went above my head,

I had been right about Nikki. He did have a gun. Definitely.

That was one of the most disastrous examples of table-turning in history. I had been so near to complete success. Now everything was shattered. And it dragged not only me down with it, but Iris also.

Iris' hands had gone up too. She smiled ruefully at me past the great bulk of Nikki. "Sorry, darling," she said. "That wasn't one of my better entrances."

I tried to smile too. "It could have been improved upon," I said.

Nikki was maneuvering around into a position where he could keep us both covered—a strategic spot in front of the dining-room door. He was a very different man from the whining, woebegone creature of a few seconds before. Nikki was obviously at his best as a man of action.

Ruby, however, in spite of her casual attitude toward bombs, gunpowder and explosions, seemed a little out of her depth at this sudden and violent change in the state of affairs. The red-tipped cigarette poised somewhere in midair, she was staring blankly from Nikki to Iris' purple hat to me.

"I—I don't get it." She was talking to Nikki. "You mean this man isn't your boss, isn't Mr. Garr, after all?"

"Like hell he ain't Garr." Nikki was having fun with his revolver. "This dame—she's the phony who fooled me at the Waxworks Museum. Don't you get it? This guy's a phony too. He's been acting like he was Garr—just to fool us. He's in with this other dame."

Clearly Nikki had an accurate, if inelegantly expressed, grasp of the situation. Ruby grasped it too—and didn't like it at all. Her scarlet lips were a thin, ominous line.

"What sort of an outfit is this where you don't know your own boss?" And then, more ominously, "What about my hundred grand?"

I knew that hundred grand would figure pretty soon.

"Don't worry," Nikki's lips curled in a smile. "There's plenty of time. When I've fixed up these two, I'll get you to Garr; I'll see the deal goes through."

It was my turn to think about Anders now.

Ruby said shrilly, "But how d'you know where this Garr is if you don't even know what he looks like?"

"That's a cinch." Very slowly Nikki started strolling toward Iris. His revolver never forgot me for a second. He stretched out his hand. "Okay, sister. Baldy gave you the lead to Garr. You said so yourself. It's in that purple star on your hat. Hand it over."

I hated seeing that gun so near to Iris, but she was amazingly calm about it. She pulled off the purple hat and threw it to him.

"Take the whole thing and wear it yourself," she said. "It would look cute with that sweater."

Nikki ignored her. He backed away until he reached his former position in front of the dining-room door. Then he tossed the hat to Ruby.

"Take off the stars," he said. "They open at the neck. Find the message."

Ruby's efficient, scarlet nailed fingers started on the stars. She picked one off, sprang open the back and muttered: "That's just the date for Sammy's Place." She pulled off the second star and opened it. She slipped out a little folded card.

"Okay?" said Nikki.

"There's this card."

"What's it say?"

Ruby read: "*Royal Book and Music Store*. Then an address off 42nd Street, too. That's printed. Then underneath in pencil there's: *Ask for a record of The Blue Danube*. 2:30. And after that there's a kind of pencil drawing of a thin sort of fish."

"That's it." Nikki grinned. "That's Garr, he always makes that fish. Garfish. That's his signature. Okay, Ruby. You got nothing to worry about. I'll get you there by two-thirty."

"And I'll get the dough this time?" Ruby had a one-track mind.

"Sure, you'll get it—if Garr okays the set-up." Nikki wasn't paying Ruby much attention. His whole soul was in his fingers and his gun. Killing was obviously what Nikki liked to do best. Iris and I were to him what all-day suckers are to little girls. I could see him licking his chops over us. "I'll get you to Garr. Don't you worry. I've just got to take care of these people first."

Rather awed, Ruby said, "What are you going to do with them?"

Nikki was still watching us with that bright, steady gaze. "I know a place," he said. "It won't take long."

It's strange how one reacts. All through that phantasmagoric night, I had been in a constant state of anxiety at the prospect of danger for Iris. But now that the danger was here with a vengeance, I found there was no room for fear. I knew that Nikki, who had killed Marta in cold blood, was utterly beyond the reach of compassion. I knew, even though we were plumb in the middle of the so-called civilization of New York, that only a miracle could save us once he had taken us to the "place" he knew.

But in spite of that, my mind was amazingly lucid, weighing one threadbare hope after another. Scream out, wake up the neighbors overhead—jump on the gun, take a chance that Iris could get away. Aloma, somehow to contact Aloma—

"Okay." Nikki's voice came softly. "I got you both covered. Any funny business and the dame gets it first."

Ruby, the initial shock over, had opened her purse and was negligently bringing a lipstick and her lips together.

"What do you want us to do?" I said.

Nikki started toward us, very slowly, the gun aimed directly at Iris. He nodded at Ruby to follow. She snapped the lipstick back into her bag and moved toward us too. There was real horror in the two of them coming at us with that dragging, leisurely pace—the huge man in the turtle-necked sweater and the little mincing, red-lipped woman with the purple hat.

"Frisk 'em," said Nikki to Ruby.

Ruby complied—expertly. "No guns."

"Okay." Nikki grinned at us. "You can put your hands down, both of you. Since you've been so smart, I guess you can carry out instructions okay. You're goin' out of this place, see? You're goin' to walk together, and I'm goin' to be back of you all the time—with this in my pocket." He indicated the revolver. "There aren't many people around this time of night. And once we're outside you're goin' to do what I say or the dame's goin' to be sorry. Get it?"

We got it. I glanced at Iris. She was rather pale but as calm and beautiful as ever. I tried not to think about her, tried not to remember that this evening had started out as a harmless, domestic escapade at Coney Island to celebrate the up-and-upness of the Duluths.

What was the point of remembering that now?

Nikki was jerking his head toward Iris. "Move over to the dame," he said.

I moved toward Iris. I was so close to her that I could feel her hand, cold and tense, against mine. Ruby strolled up until she was next to Nikki.

I was still looking at Iris' face. She was looking straight ahead of her at a point beyond Nikki's back. Her lashes flickered.

It was such a slight change of expression that nobody except me, who knew her so well, would have noticed it.

Something was happening. I was sure of it. Something was happening back there behind Nikki and Ruby. But I didn't dare look for fear of interesting Nikki, too.

It was a weird sensation seeing something happening only as a reflection in Iris' eyes. Those few seconds seemed to stretch into a queer eternity.

Nikki's mouth opened to speak. "Turn—" he began.

Then he stopped abruptly, for a deep, booming voice behind him said, "Drop that gun, brother. An' turn around, 'cos I got you covered."

And with that voice, in shrill duet, came another, gorgeously familiar: "You dirty buzzard! Actin' this way in a respectable home. You put down that gun or—"

From then on everything was pandemonium. Ruby spun around and screamed. The gun clattered from Nikki's hands. Slowly he swung round, too.

That was really when I started looking, although I had guessed what had happened the moment I heard those blessed voices.

It really was a magnificent sight. The door from the dining-room was wide open. Standing majestically on its threshold, aiming a revolver straight at Nikki, a vast, irresistible black force in a tuxedo, with a rather mussed tie, was Rudolph. And at his side, an exotic fury still impeccably sheathed in the ivory satin gown, was Aloma.

Suddenly, reaction from the danger came. I found myself quivering all over. I put my arm around Iris. She was laughing a funny little strangled laugh.

And it was too good to be true—much too good. Saved by Aloma and the husband, who had returned "after a long absence," and who, apparently, instead of doing the town had stayed at home after the party to do his courting in his bedroom slippers. Saved by the cook!

I'd always said Aloma was a treasure.

From then on, it was entirely Aloma's party. Rudolph, immense and immovable behind his revolver, stood squarely in the dining-room door, covering Nikki. Aloma swept forward, every well-placed pound of her quivering with indignation. She snatched up the gun Nikki had dropped and flourished it at the completely demoralized Ruby.

"You!" she said. "You little rat, you."

In a flounce of white satin, she backed to Rudolph's side, her revolver aimed directly at the middle of Ruby. Neither Ruby nor Nikki were liking it at all. I didn't blame them.

Iris and I were still in the feeble stage of aftermath. We were still thinking it was funny. Which it wasn't, of course. It was the most miraculous break we'd had on that night of miracles.

Aloma said, "Okay, Miz Peter, what you wan' us to do? Call the police?"

Rudolph shot her a rather bashful glance. He cleared his throat, let his melting brown eyes fix on my face and said in what was obviously his Society voice, "Beggin' yo' pardon, but I feels I should inform you that if the police is to be called I shall be obliged to leave on—on account of difficulties."

Aloma nodded soberly. "That's the truth," she said.

I was baffled by this cryptic utterance, but it didn't matter. I merely said what was only too true. "No, we don't want the police—not yet."

Rudolph was obviously relieved. "What you want then?"

I looked at Nikki. What did I want? This was very pleasant. "We want them kept here for a while—safe. And we don't want them making any noise."

Rudolph took that in his stride. He beamed whitely. "Okay."

Aloma beamed, too. The idea appealed to her savage temperament. "Gaggin' an' bindin'," she said. "Doan' you worry, honies. That's right down Rudolph's alley." She jerked her revolver at Ruby and Nikki. "Come on, you," she said.

She and Rudolph started backing into the dining-room. Nikki and Ruby, hands above their heads, followed reluctantly. In a few seconds the quartette had disappeared into the back of the apartment where, presumably, Rudolph's terrifying "gaggin' and bindin'" would take place.

Alone, Iris and I looked at each other. I couldn't think much about anything except how beautiful she was and how much I loved her. I have a habit of thinking about that at the darndest times.

I went to her, put my hands on her arms and kissed her.

"Hello, honey."

"Hello." She glanced through the dining-room door. "You think Aloma and Rudolph can handle them, darling?"

"From the looks of him, Rudolph could handle anything. I'd hate to be on the receiving end of one of his gaggin' and bindin's."

Iris laughed. Her eyes clouded. "I'm sorry, Peter. I was a dope breaking in like that. I should have guessed when I found you'd gone from Sammy's that—"

"Skip it, honey. It all came out right in the end, didn't it?"

She shivered. "Only just—only thanks to Aloma. I adore Aloma."

"And I adore Rudolph. I won't even resent it if he takes Aloma."

"Peter, all through that horrible business, did you know they were still here?"

"No. I thought they'd gone out on the town the way Aloma said."

"Why d'you suppose Rudolph's so eager not to meet the police?"

"That's one problem I'm not going to bother my head about. We've enough on the fire already without investigating Rudolph's phobias."

"Precisely." Iris was looking purposeful and efficient again. She sat down on the couch. I joined her and took her hand—frivolously, just because I wanted to. "Now, darling," she said, "tell me all—how you got Nikki and the woman with the purple hat here, everything."

I told her that whole melodramatic sequence which had soared to success, catapulted into disaster, and now, thanks to Aloma, was re-established as a triumph.

Iris' reaction when she heard of the plot was as staggered as mine. "The *Purple Star*. Blowing up a munitions' ship in the heart of New York City. What a gal Ruby is. Wham!" And then, "Peter, you're a genius. We know what the plot is now. We know when it's going to take place. We know where to find Karl Pauly. We know how to get at Garr. We know everything."

She told me then what had happened to her while I had been so precariously impersonating Garr. It was nothing exciting. The meeting with Baldy had gone off smoothly. She'd been given the second purple star with the instructions. She'd left the bar; found me gone; waited a while and then come home. That was all.

"*The Royal Book and Music Store,*" she said. "*Ask for a record of The Blue Danube. Two-thirty.* And Garr will be there. Peter, the end's almost in sight. There's only one thing more and then—Leslie, Pine 3-2323."

"What d'you mean—one thing more?"

"Well, darling, there's still Garr. I've got to be there at two-thirty. I've got to make the contact with Garr."

I had very definite ideas about that. We'd had more than our share of excursions and alarms that night; our necks had been stuck out quite often enough. I wasn't going to have Iris plunging on into the very center of the danger.

I put my hands on her arms again. I stared her straight in the face. I said, "No, Garr, honey."

"But, Peter."

"You said it yourself. We know the crazy sabotage scheme. We know when it's to take place. We know how to get at Garr. Okay. Our little kindergarten job's over. Here's where we hand it over to the big boys. I'm going to call Pine 3-2323 right now."

"Darling, are you crazy?" Iris stared at me as if I was crazy. "Don't you see that would spoil everything? Don't you remember what Marta said? They, the FBI, people, they can't do anything until they get evidence. Evidence, Peter. What evidence do we have? We can produce Nikki and Ruby. Okay. But what can we do about them? Maybe have Nikki held for Marta's murder. We can get the *Purple Star* searched; probably have Karl saved. Okay. Maybe we could even get Captain Fischer arrested for kidnapping him. But that's all. This plot, Peter—this vast, fantastic terrible plot, until we get evidence, how can we prove it's anything more than a pipe dream in our own minds? And Garr. We know he's going to be at the Royal Book Shop, yes. But this is the United States of America, remember? It's a place where you can't throw someone in jail just because some other fellow doesn't like his face. We've nothing against Garr for the FBI Nothing at all—yet."

She didn't give me a chance to break in. "That's why I've got to keep this date with Garr. Peter, you must see. It's the crux of everything. Thanks to you, I know exactly what Ruby has to say to him. With any luck, I can get him to okay the *Purple Star* plot. Better still, I may even get him to give me the money—the fifty thousand dollar down payment. Then we'll have him cold, don't you see? We'll have enough evidence to hang him fifty times over. After that we can call Pine 3-2323. After that, we can drive down to the docks with the FBI people and save Karl and the *Purple Star*. After that, we can have the biggest, brawliest roundup since the Indians moved out to Jersey."

I hated having to hear that, because Iris was right about where our duty lay, and I didn't want her to be right. I wanted to start being Peter Duluth with his charming wife again.

"Darling, you must see."

"I see," I said reluctantly. "It's just that I don't want—"

"Peter, we've got to want." She tossed back her hair. "It's okay then. I go to Garr?"

What had I done to deserve this? "Okay. I guess you go to Garr. But—"

"But—what?"

"I'm not going to let you go through this alone. Fooling with Garr's a hundred times more dangerous than with these small fry. You're not having any solo rendezvous with him. I'm coming along."

"But—"

"You can call me anything you like—a bodyguard sent by Captain Fischer, anything. But I'm not going to let you go alone."

Iris looked patient as if she had to handle a well-intentioned but difficult child. "All right, darling, you can come along. I'll think up some story—some plausible story."

She glanced at the rather fancy wrist-watch I'd given her for our first anniversary. "Quarter of two. No time to waste. I wonder if Aloma and Rudolph—"

I'd forgotten about them. "There's been an awful sinister silence. Either they've done the best gagging and binding job in history or—"

As I spoke, Aloma swept in with a rustle of satin. From the triumphant curve of her lip, I gathered that all was well in the back room.

It was.

"You doan' have to worry no mo' 'bout them, Miz Peter. They's in the kitching—fixed for good." A coffee hand on an ivory hip, she stared at us sternly. "You should be ashamed of yo'self, invitin' such company to the house."

After her elegant Beethoven friends, Nikki and Ruby must have seemed rather low-life. "I'm sorry, Aloma," I said meekly. "But it wasn't exactly a social visit."

"You doan' have to tell me that. I listened at the do' for long befo' I fetched Rudolph. I heard. The *Purple Star.* Payin' folks good money to blow up our American ships!" She looked even more admonitory. "Is that any way to behave? That ain't right, Miz Peter, an' that's the truth. Blowing up ships ain't right."

I hastily exonerated our moral characters to her, explaining that we were not fiends intent upon the destruction of New York, but merely rather feeble but well-intentioned citizens trying to prevent a catastrophe from taking place. It seemed to relieve her mind.

"Rudolph sho' will be glad to hear that. He was that worried, I'm tellin' you. Workin' for people that blow up ships, he said, that ain't right."

Rudolph's ethical sense seemed impeccable. In fact, everything about Rudolph was impeccable. Our chances of wooing Aloma away from him had dwindled to nothing.

Aloma suddenly looked self-conscious and arch, if a wild child of nature can look arch. "Guess yo' mad at me, keepin' Rudolph for a tête-à-tête after the party 'sted of goin' out—even though he is my lawful husband. Guess you doan' care for such carryin's on."

"On the contrary," I said, "if Rudolph hadn't stayed we'd be corpses by now."

"Rudolph's wonderful," said Iris. "He could live here if he wanted to." Aloma beamed. Iris went on: "And one of the most wonderful things about him was that gun. How on earth did he happen to have a gun with him?"

Aloma shifted uneasily from one satin slipper to the other. "Jest a bad habit of his, Miz Iris, an' I'm gonna break him of it." She paused. "You heard him say he didn't want no 'sociation with the police. Well—tell you the truth, he's just outta Sing Sing yestidday which accounts for his long absence. An' that's why I gives this party—so's he could get acquainted with real nice people again and rehalibitate his'self."

So! The mystery of Rudolph was a mystery no longer. Oddly enough, it gave me pleasure to find that his character was as tarnished as ours, that he was human, after all.

Poor Rudolph. We weren't giving him much of a chance to "rehalibitate" himself.

"Yeah," sighed Aloma reminiscently. "Five years he done— breakin' an' enterin'. That's why it was a cinch for him fixin' them people in the kitching. That's why, seein' he's on parole, he doan' wanna get mixed up in no mo' shootin' right now." She shook her head sadly. "He's a good man only he sho' does slip." And then quickly: "But doan' let on you know 'cos he's real sensitive."

After all Rudolph had done for us I would have embraced him as a brother even if there had been fifty breakings and enterings against him. I told Aloma so and confirmed her opinion of me as a very sensible and admirable character.

Iris had glanced at her watch again. Abruptly she got up and moved to the mad purple hat, which still lay on the carpet where Ruby had dropped it. Fixing the purple stars onto the crown again, she put the hat on.

Aloma stared at her. "Miz Iris, you ain't goin' out no mo' tonight?"

"Yes," said Iris. "We've got to go to one more place."

"It ain't no mo' to do with them crooks and blowin' up ships?" Aloma was really worried. "You shouldn't have no mo' to do with them."

"We've got to, Aloma." Iris laid her hand on her arm. "Listen, you and Rudolph stay here tête-à-tête again and see those people don't escape." Impulsively she added, "And if we don't come back, look for us at the Royal Book and Record Shop." She gave the address. "That's where we'll be with a gentleman called Mr. Garr."

"The Royal Book and Record Shop." Aloma repeated the words solemnly and moved with us to the door. As we headed for the elevators, she stood watching us, a dark, ominous Cassandra. "You jest head-in' for mo' trouble," she called. "That's what yo' doin'."

It was only too obvious that she had little or no confidence in our good sense. To her, we were two hopelessly naive babes in a very dangerous wood. To her, in fact, we were suckers.

I had a horrible feeling that she was right.

Forty-Second Street, that tireless boulevard, was still bristling with activity as Iris and I moved down it to our final, and by far our most dangerous, assignation—with Garr. Although it was quarter past two, the night here was yet young. Soldiers, sailors, marines, gay young ladies, small-time crooks, drunks, shoe-shine boys, has-beens and will-bes—all the less conventional elements who seem to have so much more carefree a life than sober citizens—paraded up and down in a colorful pageant.

Around them, catering to them, movies still flashed their electric signs; drug stores, haberdashery stores, second-hand book stores, and penny arcades made the night cheerful and raucous.

Somehow, the lusty vigor of Coney Island had reduplicated itself here. It was almost as if we were back at the beginning again—as if the weird and wonderful wheel of the evening was coming full circle.

High-stepping along, wearing the purple hat with an air, Iris was confident, as always. I wasn't, as always. I knew now that we were doing the right thing. Iris had sold me on that. Unless we managed to compromise Garr in some way, he would still be able to slip through our fingers. I wasn't worried about our motives; I was worried about our ability. We'd had tough enough sledding trying to outwit Nikki, the least of Garr's minions. How were we likely to fare against Garr himself, that elusive, terrifying will o'the-wisp whose very name inspired dread in his own associates, that dark shadow who had managed to evade even the far-reaching net of Leslie, Pine 3-2323?

A very dark sailor and a very blond sailor both rolled their eyes at Iris. A shuffling old man with a toothless smile mumbled some begging message to me. There was a street corner ahead. We reached it.

"Down here," said Iris.

We turned off 42nd Street into gloom. One frail bar-sign glowed ahead. Otherwise, all was darkness. No—not entirely in darkness. Beyond the bar, throwing a pale shaft of light across the sidewalk, a single little shop was still awake.

"That'll be it," breathed Iris. "The Royal Book and Record Shop."

The sight of it touched off some fuse of horror in me. I thought suddenly of that vast, consciousless disaster which, unknown to the world, was even now hovering over New York, and which, at five o'clock, unless our puny efforts could stop it, would be rocking the pavements even here where we were moving now. As I had been duped before, I realized the enormity of the responsibility we had loaded onto our shoulders.

At five o'clock, after one word from Garr, the *Purple Star* and all its sister ships of the convoy would soar in a tornado of splinters and flame up into the dawn sky. And we weren't going now to stop that from happening. We were going to give Garr the chance to let that inferno loose!

The dreadful razor-edge between success and cataclysmic failure!

Vague night-figures hurried past us. There was even a policeman—that, to us, most useless of objects. The little shop drew closer. We could see it across the street now, see the haphazard piles of second-hand books in the window and the worn lettering above saying: *Royal Book and Record Shop.*

I started thinking exclusively of Garr, trying to visualize the man whom I had so brashly tried to imitate. What would he look like? A great, hulking bully with cropped hair? No, too obvious. A thin, dark intellectual with stooped shoulders and sad, luminous eyes? Perhaps.

Iris' hand dropped on my sleeve. "Here we are, darling. Let's cross."

The fuse burning slowly nearer and nearer the dynamite! I said tensely, "Don't forget, honey, you're Ruby. Be tough. And I—"

"You're a bodyguard Captain Fischer sent along with me," she said, "in case of any danger. Don't do any talking."

"Okay."

We crossed the dark, empty street. We reached the little drably-lit window of the *Royal Book and Record Shop.* A glance took in a pile of much-fingered detective stories, a pile of reduced biographies; a suggestive column of sex-books, a sprawling heap of records. We moved to the glass door. As we opened it, a rasping, old-fashioned bell squawked an announcement of us. We walked into the shop.

No one was there—in that thin, cluttered interior. Wall-high bookshelves, stuffed with books stretched on either side. Tables heaped with old magazines and books marked: *Anything on this counter 19 cents,* took up most of the space. There were only little corridors for movement. An odor of must and disuse hung on the atmosphere.

A curious setting for the most dangerous man in New York.

And no one was there. In that dead, hollow silence, Iris and I moved between the tables of books. I paused here and there, pretending to glance at something—an old copy of *Leaves of Grass,* a *Strength and Health* magazine from 1936. The throbbing of my own pulses sounded ridiculously loud to me—like something mechanical and apart from me.

Iris looked at her watch. I looked too. Two-thirty exactly. We moved deeper into the shop, our footsteps creaking on the bare boards. We reached a table piled with old jazz records. *Ukelele Lady,* I saw, the topmost title.

If you like a Ukelele Lady, Ukelele —

Suddenly there was sound in the silence, slow, shuffling sounds as of footsteps in carpet slippers. They came from beyond a closed door in the back wall, shuffling nearer and nearer.

Iris' hand went to my arm, then it dropped to her side as the door was pushed open and a man appeared.

He was a small man. That was my first impression. A very small bent figure with a shabby old suit and white, thin hair showing, in the dim light, a pink, benign scalp beneath. As he came toward us, slowly, almost absently, as if his thoughts were miles away from us, I saw the glint of steel-rimmed spectacles.

He came to us. He looked up. He smiled. It was a quiet, unobtrusive face with a strange fluidity to it as if it had never hardened into any particular mould. His eyes, very gray and clear, were smiling too, beyond the flat lenses of the glasses.

Could this possibly be the great—?

"Good evening!" His gaze flicked to the purple hat with its twin stars. He brought his small hands together in front of him with the faintest suggestion of a bow at Iris—a strangely outdated gesture. "I can get you something?"

I tried not to be tense. Iris, with a very passable impersonation of Ruby at her toughest, said: "Yeah. I wanna record of *The Blue Danube.*"

"*The Blue Danube!*" His smile stretched a little. "Yes, yes, I think so." Then he did a curious thing. His eyes, behind the spectacles, moved to me, giving me one quick, appraising glance. "This gentleman is your husband?"

"No," said Iris. "He's just a friend."

"A friend? Good." He stood there a moment, his hands still folded in front of him, his lips still holding the smile. Then, with a little bow, he turned away back toward the door through which he had entered. "If you would be good enough to follow me, I believe I shall be able to find *The Blue Danube* in the other room. I keep the majority of the records there." He glanced back over his shoulder at us. "You won't mind stepping this way—both of you?"

He was shuffling toward the rear door. Some vague atavistic thing in me shouted: *No. Don't go through that door. Don't.* Silly, of course. But then atavistic impulses always are silly. Iris was walking briskly after the man. I followed, hating it, full of nameless dread.

"This way, please."

Still smiling, he was holding the door open for us to pass. I wished he would stop smiling. I wished he was less inconspicuous and harmless and benign.

Iris moved through the door. I went after her. Then he came, the door swinging shut behind him.

We were in a small, windowless room lit by a single ceiling light. Its walls were lined with books. An ancient desk, covered with old magazines, squatted in the center. A second door led to somewhere even deeper within the building. It was any office of any old book-collector. Nothing could have looked more innocuous.

With little bustling movements, he squeezed around the desk and sat down in a rickety chair. His small hands went to the desk, lying there on the magazines. The serene smiling eyes found Iris' face again.

"Now!" he said. "I believe you and your friend have some business with me—other than *The Blue Danube?*"

So he was Garr. Of course he was Garr. I should never have doubted it. Garr, the secret spider weaving the plots in darkness; Garr, the little second-hand bookseller in his dingy, unobtrusive little office.

Iris' hand went to her hip—Ruby with a touch, perhaps, of Aloma. "It's you that's got business with me," she said, "How about it? Time's getting short before five."

"Yes, yes, time is getting short, isn't it? But I still think we have no cause for concern." Garr tapped his fingers against an old-tattered copy of *Vogue*. "I gather you have come for my decision?"

Keep that pulse under control, Peter Duluth.

Iris said, "Sure I have. What's it to be?"

The smile seemed to have spread from his eyes and his mouth until it illuminated the whole, oddly liquid face. "I'm sure you will be delighted to hear that I have decided in favor of it. I have studied all the plans carefully. A great many ships should be destroyed. It seems to be both safe and—ah—effective."

"Good." Iris batted her eyelids. "And the price is okay? One hundred grand?"

He gave a little shrug. "Of course, that is a great deal of money."

"And you're getting a hell of a lot for it," said Iris, which was putting it mildly.

Hold your breath, Peter Duluth.

"I am not denying that." The fingers beat their soft tattoo on *Vogue.* "All right. The price is satisfactory."

"Fifty grand in cash now? And then the other fifty—after it's over?"

"That was the agreement." The little mouse-like hand scurried to one of the drawers in the desk and opened it. Fantastically, he brought out a huge wad of bills, fastened together with rubber bands. He put it down on the desk in front of us. "I think, when you count it, you'll find the amount correct."

My heart was racing. He was giving us fifty thousand dollars. Just like that! It wasn't possible. It was too easy—too devastatingly easy. That money would entirely debunk him in his role as a poor little bookseller; it would implicate him utterly in this fabulous plot.

Take it and scram to the nearest phone.

Leslie—Pine 3-2323—here we come!

Iris' fingers, slightly unsteady, went out toward the money. Before they reached it, Garr's small hand settled over the pile like a wan moth.

"One moment," he said gently. "I believe the agreement was that before I gave you the money you were to make your telephone call to—ah—"

"To Captain Fischer, yes." The words came quickly from Iris.

I'd forgotten about that telephone call, which was to take off the brakes, the telephone call that spelled the doom of Karl Pauly and the *Purple Star.* The thought of it threw me into a flurry of uneasiness. But Iris didn't seem to be worried.

"There is a telephone right on the wall behind you," said Garr in that low, soothing voice of his. "Perhaps you would like to make the call immediately."

"Why, sure."

Iris turned. The telephone was on the wall behind her, half buried by an overflow of books. She moved to it, still acting Ruby. She lifted the receiver.

I realized then what she was going to do and the brazenness of it was magnificent. The time had come and she wasn't going to wait. Right here from Garr's lair, she was going to call Pine 3-2323.

I watched fascinated as her finger picked it out on the dial. P-I 3-2-3-2-3.

The clicking of the dial was the only sound there was. Garr still sat there, smiling impassively, behind his desk. I stood, awkwardly stiff, trying to obliterate myself.

"Hello." Iris' voice came sharp and clear. "Hello."

Slowly, Garr got up from the desk. With that leisurely shambling gait, he skirted it, coming benignly toward us.

"Hello," said Iris. "Is Leslie there, please? I—"

It was then that it happened. Meekly, almost apologetically, Garr had moved to Iris' side. Meekly, almost apologetically, he took the receiver from between her fingers and put it back on the hook.

His smile, as he stared at her, was even more grandfatherly.

"I'm sorry. Perhaps I played out the farce a little too long." His steady eyes glinted to me. "I'm afraid you have rather underestimated us from the very beginning—Mr. and Mrs. Duluth."

Mr. and Mrs. Duluth! Those four softly spoken words were more staggering than an earthquake. He knew our names. All the time, when we thought we were fooling him, Garr.

I looked at Iris, standing by the telephone. Her face was pale with horror. Her hands were twisting and untwisting a little lemon handkerchief. I remembered most irrelevantly, that it had been Aloma's last year's Christmas gift.

Around me, the little overcrowded office lost its stability. Pieces of it started floating across my vision at random—a row of red-backed books, an old-fashioned brass lamp, a black slag heap of records, all of them merging into a crazy, surrealistic background for the figure of that little man with the friendly gray eyes, the gleaming spectacles, the pink scalp peeping through the white candlewicks of hair.

"You should have realized," he said, "that so important a transaction as tonight's would never have been allowed to take place without adequate precaution. Both Nikki and the genuine representative from Captain Fischer have been under constant observation since the beginning of the evening. Every move they or you has made has been reported to me. For some time now, I have found a counter-checking system in these affairs indispensible."

He paused. "It was ingenious of you, Mr. Duluth, to have inveigled Nikki to your apartment by an engaging impersonation of myself. Nikki, I'm afraid, although he is an excellent man of action, is not one of my more imaginative assistants. He was a poor choice for the job. But we have no cause for concern. Both he and Captain Fisher's agent are already being—ah—rescued from your apartment. They should be here shortly and I am quite sanguine that the little affair of the *Purple Star* will go through according to plan—in spite of your obstructive efforts."

I didn't have any words to say anything with. What words were there?

"Yes," said Garr with a note in his voice that was almost sad. "You should have gone to the proper authorities, you know. From the very beginning, I would like to have warned you that this is no line of business for the amateur."

I pushed past Iris toward him. Maybe he'd outwitted us, but I still had a chance to fight our way out of this. That's what I thought. But I might have saved myself the trouble. Before I'd raised my arm to sock him, the inner door opened and three men were on the threshold—three men with guns.

Garr beamed at me. "I admire your spirit, Mr. Duluth, but very little else about you, I'm afraid. Among other things, I believe, you have been eager to meet Karl Pauly. I have made arrangements for that meeting to take place." He nodded to the three men with guns. "Here are Mr. and Mrs. Duluth whom we were expecting. I think you know what to do with them."

What could I do against four men and three guns? They took us through the back door and beyond. Everything was ready.

Mr. Garr was right. His men knew exactly what to do with us.

At some later, indeterminate hour, I opened my eyes. I might just as well have kept them shut because there was nothing to see—nothing but a thick, stifling blanket of darkness. My head ached. There was an unpleasant sickly sweetness in my nostrils. My arms were crushed somewhere behind my back and I seemed to be lying on something very hard. Feebly, I tried to move. My limbs showed little or no co-operation. The reason for this became apparent. My hands, behind my back, were securely tied together. So were my ankles.

I tried to think. At first I didn't do such a very good job. All that came was a vivid mental picture of my grandmother mounted on a scarlet cow charging the Brooklyn Dodgers with a pitchfork. I tried again. Gradually, the phantasmagoria images dissolved. There was nothing but the darkness and the smell in my nostrils.

The smell in my nostrils—

Memory came back then—very distinctly. Garr with his glinting spectacles and his quiet little smile; Iris, her face white with horror, twisting Aloma's yellow handkerchief; and the three men who had come through the inner door. The boys from the back room were in particular focus. Revolvers aimed—rope expertly used—and then the sponge of ether over my mouth. That nauseating sweet scent; a blurred image of Iris and then nothingness.

Nothingness—and now this!

The moments between the ether and now had entirely gone. I had no idea where I was. The darkness was suffocating. A thought pricked me like a red hot needle: *Where is Iris. What have they done to Iris?*

In a funny little voice, throwing it out into the black pall, I piped: "Iris."

Another voice came instantly out of the darkness. It wasn't Iris' voice. It was a man's voice, a voice I'd never heard before with a vaguely foreign intonation. It said, "So you've come out from under at last, have you?"

I couldn't cope with strange voices. That was much too complicated. Again, I said, "Iris."

"She's here," said the strange voice. "At least, there's some woman here, right next to you. I guess she's still under."

Iris right next to me in the darkness! Was that good or bad? Where were we? What—? Why not use that strange voice? It seemed in a mood to give information.

I asked: "Where are we?"

The voice laughed. It was a hollow, cheerless laugh. "On a ship," it said. "Somewhere very deep in the hold of the *Purple Star.*"

The *Purple Star!* I didn't have to know any more. That was quite enough. Suddenly I started realizing about the voice too.

"Then you," I said, "you must be Karl Pauly."

"Why, yes." The voice was startled. "But how do you know? And who are you?"

"That," I said, trying once more to wriggle off my back and failing, "is a very long and a most depressing story."

My head was worse. The darkness started wabbling around. I shouldn't have moved so violently—not yet. Thoughts came. Iris and I had tried, among other things, to save Karl Pauly. That was funny. Ha-ha. Now we were in the hold of the *Purple Star*, stuffed down with Ruby's bombs and gunpowder and ammunition which were all set to explode at five o'clock. And we had tried to save the *Purple Star* too. Ha-ha, ha-ha.

Iris lying there in the darkness next to me, hopelessly remote. Iris—

Her voice came then, weak and piping like mine had been. She said, "Peter."

"Iris, darling."

"Peter, I feel awful. And—and my hands seem to be tied behind my back."

"They are, honey."

"It's—it's very dark. Where are we?"

What was the use of trying to spare her? "In the *Purple Star*," I said. "Right in the bowels of the *Purple Star* with all the bombs. The happy-go-lucky Duluths."

"Peter!"

"And we have a companion. Remember how we were going to rescue Karl Pauly from Garr? Well, he's here too. Pauly, meet my wife. By the way, are you tied up too?"

"'Fraid so." Karl Pauly gave an awkward little laugh. "Been here forever, it seems. But I don't understand. You've got to tell me who you are."

Did it matter who we were? There was nothing I'd left forgotten now. I remembered Garr quietly announcing that Nikki and Ruby were being "rescued" from our apartment. Knowing Garr, they certainly had been. (What of poor Aloma and Rudolph?) And with Ruby rescued, that meant the destruction of the *Purple Star* would continue as per schedule. So why bother to tell Karl Pauly anything that Manhattan's biggest explosion would only make him forget again—any minute now?

The time! That was the crucial thing. Five o'clock was to be the zero hour, our last and least pleasant moment on earth. What was the time now?

"Pauly, do you know the time?"

"No idea."

"I have a wrist-watch," said Iris, who was obviously thinking the way that I was thinking, "only it's somewhere behind my back with my wrists. Maybe I could twist around and one of you could see."

We did an awful lot of maneuvering. Finally we succeeded. Iris had rolled over onto her side. Painfully I rolled over until I was close to her. I could see the little luminous disk, the only shining thing in that impenetrable, musty smelling darkness.

The watch said 4:30. Half an hour left!

Somehow the hard fact of thirty-minutes was worse than the vagueness that had gone before. The utter dismalness of our failure surged over me like a black wave. We had thought so grandiosely that we were a match for the legendary Garr. We were going to show him.

Look at us now!

Iris' voice came: "Peter."

"Yes, honey?"

"We know what's going to happen. So don't let's talk about it. Let's try to be civilized."

Civilized in the hold of a ship with a lot of bombs! "Okay," I said.

She said softly, "And we should tell Karl everything—about his mother, everything."

"Mother!" Karl's voice sounded eagerly.

I told him then about Marta, tragic, courageous little Marta who had been the first victim of this catastrophe. There was some advantage to our predicament after all—for Karl's sake, at least. If you have to hear that your mother is dead, it's less of a shock when there's little or no chance of your being able to survive her long enough to mourn. I told him the whole lamentable story of our own decline and fall too.

Although he was still only a disembodied voice in the darkness, I was starting to admire Karl Pauly. He still had enough spunk to be mad.

"That dirty swine, Nikki," he muttered. "Poor Mother. I—I might have known she'd have tried to help me. I might have known—" He gave a gaunt little laugh. "And you! It's rather late in the day to thank you. But you were—"

"Think nothing of it," I said.

"It's all my fault." Karl Pauly's voice was savage. "I swore I'd get them single-handed. Single-handed! And I dragged you and Mother into it." He paused. "You actually found Garr; you found out what the plot was; you did all the things I never did. And yet we end up like this. In twenty minutes, the *Purple Star—*"

"We said we weren't going to talk about it," put in Iris.

"Sorry." There was a flat, miserable silence. Then Karl said, "But you actually called Leslie at Pine 3-2323 from Garr's place?"

"Yes. But Garr broke off the call in mid-air."

Karl's voice had a slight ring of hope: "But they could trace where the call came from. Just asking for Leslie was enough. They'll be round here. And maybe—"

"I've thought of that," said Iris quietly. "And it's no use. What if they do go around there? All they'll find will be a little bookseller. They won't be able to do anything. They know nothing about us, nothing about the *Purple Star,* nothing about anything. What can they do?"

She was right, of course, and that faint glimmer of hope faded as quickly as it had come. We lay there in the jet-choking darkness. The little gleaming dial of Iris' watch—my anniversary present—swam in front of my eyes, a torturing reminder of reality.

Seventeen minutes to five.

There was absolutely no sound from the mysterious body of the ship above us. Almost anything would have been better than that silence. I filled it with vivid mental pictures—pictures of the unattractive Captain Fischer and Ruby and, maybe, Nikki, tense with anticipation, their plans ready, waiting for the exact moment to light the fuses that would blow us all to perdition and earn them one hundred thousand dollars. They were up there, all of them, so near—so far.

And we, down here in the hold, must be of such complete unimportance to them. Most murderers before the kill have a few uneasy moments about the disposal of the body. None of us were going to leave a telltale *corpus delicti* behind. No, sir.

Suddenly, out of that thick silence, Karl said, "Who's the other person they threw down here?"

"Other person?" said Iris and I together.

"Yes. Quite a while after you two, they tossed someone else down the hatch. He was making an awful racket, but he quieted down. I think he must have got knocked out by the fall."

At that moment, as if a cue was being followed in a play, a faint groan came from somewhere in the darkness beyond us.

"Who's there?" I called, having no idea on the subject.

The groan came again. It was a deep groan with an overtone of indignation. Then, rather dizzily, a booming voice remarked: "Jeepers."

I said again, "Who is it?"

There were vague scrambling sounds. Then the voice said gloomily, "That ain't you, Miz Duluth?"

I knew then. Disaster makes strange bedfellows. "Rudolph?"

"Miz Duluth, they done truss me up like a rooster. I can't move me a limb."

"We're all in the same boat," I said, ruminating on the most painful pun of my career.

Poor Rudolph. My heart bled for him. The gaggin' and bindin' had come home to roost. And it was all our fault.

"I doan' get it," Rudolph was bewailing. "I doan' get it at all. I was back in your apartment keepin' an eye on them two crooks like you said, an' all of a sudden they came in, a whole bunch of 'em. Didn't knock or nothin'; must have picked the lock. They has me covered, takes away my gun, an' they unties the white feller an' the woman an' they holds me up with a gun an' they tells me to come with them or they'd let me have it; an' they all came here to this boat an' they trussed me up an' they pitches me down here; an' I hits me haid. An' me just outa Sing Sing and provin' to 'Loma I could go straight—"

He gave up there. The saga of woe was too woeful for him even to finish it.

Poor Rudolph! This was the straw after the last straw. That this should have happened to him on the eve of his new era of legality under the sponsoring eye of Aloma. What price for rehabilitation now?

Iris said, "But Aloma, Rudolph—what's happened to Aloma?"

There were more grunts while Rudolph was vainly kicking against the pricks. "I doan' know, Miz Duluth. She wasn't there when these fellers came. She was out."

"Out?"

"Yeah. Soon as you went, she says she doan' trust you. She figures you was doin' somethin' you was too dumb to do an' she better go after you, she says. So she went out and she lef' me there alone, an' it wasn't but fifteen minutes or so after that these fellers come an'—"

Rudolph went on reiterating his mournful story. I was hardly listening. For a rap of hope flickered once more—a very tenuous ray, but a ray. Aloma knew about the Royal Book and Record Shop. Aloma knew Garr's name. Aloma knew dimly about the *Purple Star.* And Aloma had gone out into the night to save us.

There was a chance, just a chance that—no, the pencil-thin ray faded. What possibly could Aloma do? What chance was there for a solitary though indomitable colored woman against all the powers of Evil?

The little dial, gleaming in front of me, said ten minutes to five. Rudolph's monologue had stopped and none of us did anything about disturbing the silence. My mind was very clear, but somehow my reactions were numbed. I knew what was going to happen. I knew that Iris, lying there next to me, that Karl, whom we'd never even seen, that Rudolph, that all of us had less than the fraction of a fraction of a chance. Even now, above us, matches must be hovering over fuses.

Garr had won—overwhelmingly. We should have known from the start that he would.

Let's not talk about it, Iris had said, Let's not think about it, either. I tried to go back in my mind to that remote time when the evening had been young.

"Peter!" It was Iris' voice, very soft.

"Yes, honey."

"You love me passionately."

"I do?"

"No one but a dope would let his wife get him into this infernal mess unless he loved her passionately."

"Maybe I'm a dope too, darling," I said.

Iris!

Eight minutes to five. I wanted to touch Iris' hand. That's really all I wanted in the world. It wasn't much to ask. But I couldn't do it.

Meekly Rudolph's voice floated through the darkness, "Miz Duluth, how long do we stay here?"

"Not much longer now."

"Miz Duluth, I'm—hungry."

A funny little stifled laugh came from the place in the darkness that was Karl Pauly. It wasn't really a laugh.

The silence sunk down over us again like a tarpaulin. That profound, unequivocal silence. Surely, before the end, we would hear some sound.

I strained my ears against that utter absence of sound. Was it my imagination? Or was there some vague scurrying noise—miles away, like the sound of distant mice feet? I concentrated on my ears. Nothing but my ears. Surely—

"Listen!" Iris said that sharply.

"What is it?" asked Karl.

"There's a noise. A noise of people moving around, hurrying."

As I listened, that sound became more distinct. Footsteps. It was footsteps—hurrying footsteps coming nearer. The pulses in my temples started to throb.

Seven minutes to five. Garr and his ruthlessly efficient timetable. Now was the time for the fuses. Footsteps of people moving stealthily to their appointed places.

"They're coming nearer," said Karl.

I was suddenly, horribly alive to the imminence of death. I was going to die. Iris was going to die. I didn't want Iris to die.

The footsteps were louder. They sounded almost above us. Images of people creeping forward with matches in their hands. Was it to start here? Was the death stab to the *Purple Star* going to be delivered right here above our heads?

Watch out, New York.

I had to say something, anything, just because the suspense of it was unendurable. I said at random, "I had the funniest dream under ether. I dreamed that my grandmother was riding a scarlet cow and charging the Brooklyn Dodgers with a—"

There was a scraping overhead. Heavy feet stamped.

And then, suddenly, in the blackness above us was a square of light. For an instant I saw vague, trousered legs, lots of them. Then a flashlight pointed straight down at us and I saw nothing but its blinding glare.

Five minutes to five—

There seemed nothing but that dazzle pointed full in my face. Dimly, I caught a glimpse of the dark, shadowy hold around us. Then there was a confused babble of voices above us.

I didn't really try to hear what was being said. The voices meant nothing to me. And then, suddenly, they meant every- thing in the world. Because one of them soared above the others, shrill and female and boisterous and triumphant and it said:

"What did I tell you? Is they there or ain't they there? You should of believed me from the beginnin' without all that fussin' around. Yoohoo, Miz Peter, yoohoo, Miz Iris! Bring out the brass band, Rudolph. Here I come with the G-men."

Aloma! Aloma the treasure.

Iris and I were standing together on the deck of the *Purple Star.* That slap-happy release still seemed like something in a dream. Beyond the rail, vague, crouching forms in the pre-dawn dark- ness, loomed the other ships which, but for Aloma's miracle, would have been blown up with the *Purple Star.* An occasional light, flickering to the left, revealed the gaunt outlines of the docks. Five o'clock over and done with, and all's well.

Around us, moving silently and expertly about their various assignments, hurried FBI men and dock police, magiced out of thin air. Karl Pauly, visible at last as a pleasant-faced kid with a mop of blond hair, was moving around with them. One of the FBI men—Leslie, for all I knew—was talking to us, telling us exactly what had happened.

I found it difficult to concentrate because my arm was around Iris and because the tangy salt air was so pleasant after the sti- fling hold.

"… we got Mrs. Duluth's call at Headquarters. We traced it and went straight around to the Royal Book Shop. A whole squad of us. That was Garr's big slip. He never knew Karl Pauly had been in contact with us; he never knew about that secret tele- phone number. He didn't know what he was doing when he let you make that call."

Iris' profile, against all those cranes and girders and bollards or whatever they were, was wonderful. Iris wasn't blown up in little pieces; she was right there—beautifully intact.

"… but although we went there, we thought it was pretty hopeless. We'd had Pauly's signal but that was all. We didn't know what it meant, although we suspected it was to do with Garr. We arrived at the Royal Book Shop. We didn't have any motive for investigating it. And then, as we came up, we found this colored woman on the street corner arguing like mad with a policeman. She was raising Cain because she said her employers were being held prisoners in the book shop. The cop was trying to get rid of her, figuring she was just a screwball. But she was a godsend to us. She gave us a handle for breaking into the shop. We broke in and we found this little guy and a couple of other men. He was very polite and made out he knew nothing about anything. Of course, we didn't know who he was. And then, suddenly, this colored woman started calling him Garr, giving him hell and swearing her employers were there. We were in that back room, sort of like an office, and suddenly she bent down and picked up a little yellow handkerchief from the floor and started bawling about its belonging to this Mrs. Duluth and proving she'd been there—"

I was beginning to listen now.

"I was all het-up after I'd heard her call him Garr. We wanted Garr more than any man in America. Maybe this was Garr, we figured. And the colored woman had given us grounds for holding him. On the evidence of the handkerchief, we held him and the other men on suspicion of kidnapping, and made a search of the place. We found nothing, of course. And all this time, the colored woman was getting wilder and wilder. That's when she started shooting her mouth off about the *Purple Star* being a ship that Garr was going to blow up. She swore we'd find you all down here at the *Purple Star.*" He smiled ruefully. "I guess we were a bit difficult to convince. But she's a strong-minded lady. She convinced us—and here we are."

He was telling us the rest. They had arrived only just in time; but they had made a perfect haul. Thanks to Aloma, they not only had Garr; they had also caught Captain Fischer, Ruby and Nikki, and their underlings, red-handed, on the ship.

"With Pauly's evidence," he was saying, "we can round up all the other small-time agents. And with your evidence, we can get Garr convicted a dozen times over. You've done us a great service, Mr. and Mrs. Duluth. In one night you've averted the biggest disaster in shipping history and cleaned up a gang we've been hounding for months. You'll be public heroes." He laughed. "As I've always said, in this line of business, you have to be an amateur to get results."

With a certain amount of relish, I thought of Garr's penultimate remark to us, before he handed us over to the boys in the back room. *I would like to have warned you from the beginning that this is no line of business for amateurs.* Mr. Garr, the arch-professional, was now securely under lock and key, while us old amateurs were very much alive and kicking.

Nuts to you, Mr. Garr.

But, through all that hurried, confused explanation, I could think of nothing but Aloma. Aloma, who had saved us from ourselves twice that night, was the real heroine of the hour. Single-handed, she had battled against the incredulity of the FBI Single-handed, she had defeated Garr. Aloma, doubtful of our ability to take care of ourselves, plodding out into the night after us in her satin gown; Aloma fighting with the cop on the street corner for our lives; Aloma, ferociously exposing the quiet little bespectacled bookseller; Aloma bending and picking up that small yellow handkerchief.

The handkerchief—

I turned to Iris. The purple hat, a museum piece now, still perched on her head, she was staring out over the rail across the dim silhouettes of the ships. "Iris, honey," I said, "that handkerchief, did you drop it on purpose?"

She glanced at me. She made a little grimace. "I thought there was just a chance someone might find it."

"But—"

"I didn't say anything about it. I didn't want to raise your hopes."

All the FBI men and the dock police seemed to be collecting around us on the deck now. There is no more comforting sensation than being surrounded with G-men and dock police. They were all grinning and making complimentary remarks. The deck of the *Purple Star,* which, on Garr's schedule, should have been nothing now but so much kindling, had turned into a kind of outdoor reception room.

I wasn't paying much attention to the complimentary remarks. Now that the vast, world-shaking dangers were over, I found myself lost in gloom—because of Aloma. We had ruined her second wedding night with Rudolph; we had utterly undermined her efforts to keep him on the straight and narrow path of virtue; we had all but had him blown into a million pieces. What hope was there now of retaining her services: none. She had saved our lives out of the nobility of her character. But after tonight, she would never want to see us again. Ensconced in some remote

Harlem love-nest with Rudolph, she would forever be beyond our reach.

"—wait till the papers break with this story," one of the G-men was saying.

"Iris," I said dolefully, "this is the end of Aloma."

"—your names will be household words," said the G-man.

Iris wasn't listening. "I know it, Peter," she sighed. "Never mind, darling. We'll just have to love each other that much more."

And then, as she spoke, the ranks of men separated as if before some royal guest of honor. Majestically leaning on Rudolph's arm, Aloma swept toward us. The ivory satin gown was a little frayed, but it in no way detracted from her splendor. Her eyes were sparkling; her hand was squeezed chummily into Rudolph's large dark fist.

She brushed through the congratulations of the FBI men. She came right up to us.

"Miz Iris," she said, "Miz Peter, Rudolph and me's been thinkin' over our future plans like we said we would."

"Yes—" I said gauntly.

Aloma smiled ravishingly at Rudolph. "Rudolph's decided he just can't do without me bein' around all the time."

My heart sank. Iris looked tragic. We steeled ourselves.

"But," said Aloma, "Rudolph's kind of gone on you-all too. An' we was figurin' how maybe—well, there's plenty of room and I could do with someone helpin' around an', maybe Rudolph ain't so hot right now fo' a butler-valet, but under my trainin' and guidance—"

I couldn't believe my ears. I said, "You mean Rudolph wants to come to us as a butler?"

"As a couple," said Aloma conjugally. "That's what we'd be—a couple. An' if it's a question of extra money goin' out, doan' you worry 'bout that. Bein' with people like you after where he's come from's all Rudolph wants."

Rudolph grinned shyly.

It wasn't happening. I pinched myself. I looked at Iris. Her lips were trembling.

"But, Aloma," I faltered, "after the terrible things that happened tonight—"

"Tonight!" Aloma tossed the word back at me. "You know somethin', Miz Peter? Sometimes, aroun' yo' place, ev'ything was so awful quiet, I could of screamed. But tonight—" She beamed. It was the most stupendous beam Aloma had ever beamed. "Tonight. Tellin' you the truth, I haven't had such fun since the time Rudolph busted into the Municipal Trust."

She broke off with an appalled glance at the swarms of dock police and FBI men. Then, hastily slurring it over, "Well, Miz Peter, is it a deal? It'd be doin' us a great service an' it would rehabilitate Rudolph for good an' all."

Rudolph shuffled his feet. Iris was smiling ecstatically.

"A deal?" I echoed, "Aloma, it isn't a deal. It's a dream."

The Woman Who Waited

When the patrolman lugged open the door of the parked car, the body almost tumbled out.

Inspector Macrae's mouth crooked in distaste. Alive, Ellery Trimble had been dandified as an elderly show-window model from his own Twin-Town Department Store, the one big-league emporium in the dual-community of Stuart-Cartersville. He didn't look so fashionable dead. Crumpled over the steering wheel, Stuart-Cartersville's most prominent citizen was just a bundle of clothes, a pudgy travesty of a face and one plump, dangling hand.

There was blood on the cheek. But Inspector Macrae wasn't looking at the blood. He was staring at the insane confusion of silk—*real* silk—stockings which sprawled across the corpse like grotesque, elongated caterpillars.

"Shot with his own gun, you say?"

"Yep, Chief," replied the patrol man. "We found it on the floor by his side and Miller checked with the people over at the store. It's the revolver he kept there in his office. But it ain't suicide. The wound's all wrong. And then them stockings. They must have been ripped out of a package he had with him. We found the torn paper. No one don't throw stockings all over themselves and commit suicide. It's murder."

"Kind of crazy thing a woman might do."

"Sure it was a dame. Miller an' I found a whole trail of dame's foot-prints running away from the car. Look."

The patrolman shone his flashlight down onto the gravel of the private parking lot behind the Twin-Town Department Store, which Trimble had kept for his exclusive use. There, distinct in the gravel, were the imprints of a woman's high heels stretching away from the running board of the car.

"Old Trimble killed by a dame when he was supposed to never have looked at another woman since his wife died!" The patrolman's voice was awestruck. "And on the very day he opened his new store, too."

Macrae grunted. For weeks, every wife in Stuart-Cartersville had been waiting breathlessly for the grand opening of the Twin-Town Department Store's remodeled building. Mrs. Macrae, who had an eagle eye for a bargain, had been one of the first that morning to storm its glass doors.

The Inspector bent gingerly over the corpse and fingered one of the silk stockings. Real silk at that, hard to get as it was.

"Well, what d'you know?"

You know a lot more about a man when he's dead than when he's alive, Macrae decided that next morning. Until the murder, he, like everyone else in Stuart-Cartersville, had known Ellery Trimble only as a model widower who lived a life of respectable ease with his debutante daughter in one of Stuart's most elaborate homes. Investigation, however, had revealed the startling fact that there had been a second Trimble residence — an intimate little apartment in Cartersville, rented under an assumed name, where a well-bribed janitor had observed but kept unpublicized a steady succession of discreetly muffled feminine guests. Ellery Trimble's personality, apparently, had been as dual as that of the community itself, a Jekyll in Stuart, a Hyde in Cartersville.

That a woman should have murdered him no longer seemed remarkable. Now it was merely a question of — which woman?

A lead on the woman came with unexpected speed. One of the salesgirls at the Twin-Town Department Store, a Miss Dora Churt of Hosiery, called headquarters to report that a strange woman had been waiting for Mr. Trimble last night after the store had closed. She and two other employees had noticed this woman. They thought the police should know.

Inspector Macrae reached for his hat.

Twenty minutes later, he pushed through the sensation-hungry crowd outside the closed department store and was let into its crepe-hung entrance by an earnest and elegant young man who introduced himself as Donald Douds of Sporting Goods. As a streamlined elevator raised them to Hosiery, Donald Douds discreetly let it be known that he was one of the three who had seen the unknown woman and that, in his capacity as Admirer-In-Chief to Miss Dora Churt, had persuaded her to call the police. He also made it clear that he was meant for higher things than selling sports clothes.

Passing through a deserted and austerely modern lamp-shade section, they reached Hosiery. Inspector Macrae snorted when he saw the incredible decorations and the huge black mirror which stretched over one entire wall. He remembered the Twin-Town Department Store when it had been a plain, honest, cash-over-the-counter establishment. No trimmings, no fancy Doudses then.

Two women were waiting by the glass hosiery cases to the right of the closed door, which led to Mr. Trimble's private office. One of them was a tallish, pretty girl with light brown hair in a smart jade green suit; the other was older, dumpy, greying with pince-nez and a sensible mouth. The pretty one was Miss Churt; the other was Miss Grace Godson from Table Linen.

Under the loving eye of Mr. Douds, Dora Churt told her story calmly and briskly. Last night, after the store had been closed to the public, Mr. Trimble had come out of his office and asked to look at the dwindling supply of real silk stockings. He wanted some as a surprise present for his daughter. He selected twelve pairs, but Miss Churt had pointed out they were not the right size for Miss Trimble. Trimble had looked rather awkward and had said he would take them anyway. She wrapped them up for him and he carried the package back into his office.

Miss Churt's pretty face was puzzled. "It was then that I noticed this woman. I hadn't seen her come in, but she was standing there at the entrance to Hosiery from Lampshades. She was clasping and unclasping her hands and staring toward the door of Mr. Trimble's office. I didn't think much about her. I was tired after the strain of the gala opening and I wanted to get home. Right then Mr. Douds and Miss Goodson came from the back of the store. They stopped to say goodnight to me. I pointed out the woman and said something about. I hoped she wasn't going to start buying things and holding me up. I wanted to get home. Then, after Mr. Douds and Miss Goodson had gone on through Perfume, the woman suddenly hurried to the door of Mr. Trimble's office and went in. A few minutes later, just as I was leaving, they both came out together. Mr. Trimble called good night to me. And they went away.

Inspector Macrae said: "And none of you saw Mr. Trimble or this woman again?"

"I heard 'em." Miss Goodson's pince-nez quivered on her plump nose as she proceeded in a clipped, telegraphic style. "Left the store after all the others by the back entrance. Took short-cut across Mr. Talbot's parking space; quicker that way. Saw his parked car. Heard voices inside, quarreling. Heard woman carrying on, saying: 'You bought them for someone else. Don't lie to me.' Didn't investigate. None of my business; in a hurry to catch the trolley home. That's all I know."

Macrae watched the three of them. "What did this woman look like?"

Both Dora Churt and Douds opened their mouths, but Miss Goodson got in first. "Young. Around twenty-five. Not tall. Shorter than Miss Churt. No hat. Dark hair. Black dress."

"That's right," put in Dora Churt. "And she seemed very keyed-up, jittery."

"Good figure," added Donald Douds with a faint smirk. "More the petite type than Dora. Personally, I go for them bigger."

Inspector Macrae nodded soberly, "And you have a theory about this woman who—waited for Mr. Trimble?"

"With Miss Goodson hearing that quarrel, it seems pretty obvious." Dora Churt let Mr. Doud's hand stray to her shoulder. "Mr. Trimble bought those stockings although they weren't the right size for his daughter. That means the daughter business was just a line and he was buying them for some other woman. I guess this woman we saw had been a—er—friend of his, heard him buy the stockings, realized he was buying them for some other girl, stole his gun when she was in his office—and killed him out of jealousy."

"Exactly," said Donald Douds.

The less respectable side of old Ellery's life had not yet been made public. "What makes you think," asked the Inspector, "that Mr. Trimble was the sort of man to carry on with women?"

Dora Churt flushed. "I—I guess it's all right to tell. Donald knows. When I first came to work at the old store, Mr. Trimble asked me if I would go over the stock books with him one night at some apartment in Cartersville. It was obvious what he meant and—well, I refused and …"

"I see." Inspector Macrae's face was impassive. "Then that give a pretty clear picture. Trimble was tired of this woman and had started to stray. The stockings made her realize it. She snitched his gun, murdered him in a fit of crazy jealousy, tossed the stockings all over him and made her getaway. All we have to do now is find the woman."

"Disgraceful behavior," snorted Miss Goodson. "Man of his age."

Macrae's gaze had moved carefully over the elegant Hosiery Department. "Perhaps you'd be good enough to let me know just where you were all standing when you saw this—this woman who waited."

Miss Goodson still dominated the picture. She pushed Dora Churt back until she was standing between the counters and Mr. Trimble's office. "Dora was there." Pince-nez wabbling, she gripped Doud's hand and pulled him beyond the mouth of a corridor which led from the back of the store. "Mr. Douds and I came this way. We walked down, paused to talk to Dora." Still guiding Douds, she paused. "Then we saw the girl. Over there." She pointed to the entrance from Lampshades. "We walked on straight through to Perfumery." She and Douds passed on to a third exit beyond. "That plain enough?"

"Very plain." Macrae had moved to the spot where the two of them had paused to speak to Dora Churt. "In fact, I don't think we have to find out anything else at all. Look." He pointed dramatically to the entrance from Lampshades. "The woman who waited for Mr. Trimble. You see her? She's come back. She's standing right there at this moment."

As the two joined the Inspector, Miss Goodson squeaked, "Yes, that's the woman!"

They stared toward the entrance from Lampshades. Standing there, it seemed, right by the doorway, was a woman's figure—the figure of a girl who seemed to be shorter than Dora Churt, a girl who seemed to have darker hair, a girl who seemed to be wearing black.

Then the tableau altered, for Macrae left them and moved to Dora Churt's side. Suddenly, standing next to the woman who had waited for Mr. Trimble, was a shorter, darker image of Inspector Macrae himself.

"Smart." The Inspector's voice was relentless. "Very smart, Miss Churt. Smart to build up a story about an imaginary woman who had your own motives for murdering Trimble—jealousy because he'd been having a secret affair with you and, from the stockings, you discovered he was switching to another girl. Smart to call the police and tell them about that imaginary woman. But smartest of all to fool two perfectly good witnesses into believing they had actually seen this woman who didn't exist."

Douds gasped. Dora Churt's face was very pale.

"But I—I still don't…." began Miss Goodson.

"The newly-decorated store only opened yesterday and everyone was strange to it. Miss Churt knew that if she stood in the right place and pointed out a woman by the entrance, both of you wouldn't realize that the woman was in fact only her own reflection in that unfamiliar black mirror. The distortion of the mirror made her reflection seem shorter than she is; the blackness of it made her light hair look darker and her jade green dress look black."

Macrae grinned. "The world's going to lose a promising murderess in you, Miss Churt. Pinning the crime on your own reflection. Well, what d'you know?"

This Way Out

He had done it. For eighteen long, bitter months he had been living for this moment. He had expected to feel a huge sense of relief. But there was nothing like that. If he felt anything, it was a faint disgust.

Steve Glenn glanced down at the man sprawled across the gray and green carpet. Tony hadn't put up much of a fight. He had crumpled under the first or second impact of Steve's fist. That was part of what was wrong. Blood trickled from Tony's mouth, and a bruise darkened the skin around his left eye. There was a splash of scarlet also on the prim white of his tuxedo shirt front. He looked such a trivial thing to have wrecked Steve's life—a puppet Don Juan stuffed with sawdust. That was part of what was wrong, too.

"Celia," Steve murmured.

Maybe by saying Celia's name, he could restore the mood which had brought him to the apartment. It didn't work. Celia seemed infinitely far away. And Tony Dort seemed—nothing.

Steve felt in the breast pocket of his worn army blouse for a cigarette. He pulled out a twisted, empty package. He threw it on the floor and glanced around him. There were no cigarette boxes. He dropped on one knee and felt in the breast pocket of Tony's tuxedo jacket. His probing fingers found a wallet and a thin platinum case. He took a cigarette and slipped the case back in Tony's pocket.

He'd got cigarettes from worse places in New Guinea, Leyte. He'd rifled them from dead Japs. Who hadn't? But this was different.

"I beat him up," he thought. "Then I bum his cigarettes."

Steve's unhurried brown eyes, trained to observe every detail, shifted their gaze around the room. It was almost cloying in its luxury, like a playboy's apartment in the movies. Automatically, he compared it with the room he had known for the past three years in the Pacific—from the palm-covered octagonal tents in the Byak to the bare scrubbed building in Fort Dix where, a few hours ago, a solemn young major had handed him his honorable discharge.

A silver framed photograph of a girl stood on a table by the couch. She was a cool, metallic blonde, whose eyes were set a little too close together. The photograph was signed: "Eternally—Janice." He wondered whether this was the girl who had come after Celia. Or the girl after the girl after Celia.

He was glad there wasn't a photograph of Celia. How would she have signed it? "Eternally," too?

Tony moaned and half rolled onto his side. His eyelids flickered. In a couple of minutes he'd be conscious. Steve could at least spare himself the anti-climax of a second squalid scene. On an impulse he only half understood, he bent and wiped the blood from Tony's mouth with his handkerchief. Then he picked up his hat and left the apartment.

The civilian-thronged, brightly lighted streets of New York were still new and confusing to Steve. Like all soldiers, he was an arch conservative. Like all recently discharged soldiers, too, he clung to the habit of self-discipline. He knew where he was going. He had planned it all ahead of time and, even though the evening was working out so differently from his expectations, he kept stubbornly to his original idea.

A couple of blocks down the avenue was a bar where he and Celia used to drop in for a night cap after a show. He was making himself go there alone, because killing his memories of Celia was just as important as giving Tony what was coming to him.

He pushed through the doors of the Clover Bar. It was a dumpish sort of bar, but Celia had always liked eccentric places, colorful characters. Everything was hauntingly the same. The glaring scarlet jukebox was grinding out Bing Crosby. Bright ceiling lights fanned down. Although it was only eight o'clock the bar was already crowded. Steve found a place at the extreme end. His reflection, tall, tanned, surprisingly grim, glared back at him from the bottle-lined mirror behind the bar.

The barman moved then and saw him. His face broke into an incredulous, delighted grin. He came hurrying down the bar.

"Well, well, if it ain't my old pal Steve. How's tricks, Sergeant?"

He held out his hand. Steve took it in his own strong brown fingers. The barman looked down at the abraded skin on Steve's knuckles.

Charlie laughed. "Beating up civilians already?" His face sobered. "Gee, it's good to see you. Furlough?"

"Discharge," Steve said.

"Happy days. That calls for one on me. Still the same? Rye and water?"

Steve nodded.

Charlie poured a jigger of rye. "How's the wife, Steve? You know something? She's still the best looking babe ever come in this bar. Never forget her. Just thinking about her makes a guy feel good. She okay?"

"Celia?" Steve grabbed the jigger of rye. "Sure. She's okay. She's around."

Someone shouted for a beer. Charlie grinned and hurried away.

Around. The word stabbed Steve like a knife. That was Celia now. Around. Around every night spot with any guy who had the price in his jeans. One word and you had her. *Around.*

Insidious memories crowded into his mind. Celia, grave and absurdly young in her white bride's dress on their wedding day. Celia on horseback, laughing, her silver blond hair streaming. Celia, as he'd last seen her before he was alerted for overseas shipment. That was the time he had given her the compact. He could see her hands curving around it, that exquisite, white gold compact studded with tiny emeralds which he had persuaded Roy Chappell to design especially for her. He could see her eyes, wide, solemn, gazing up into his.

"Darling, it's beautiful. A compact. It'll be a compact between us, a compact that we'll never change until you come home."

A compact between them!

From the jukebox, Sinatra was singing an oldie—"Night and Day." Celia had always stolen nickels from his change to play "Night and Day, under the hide of me." Steve swallowed his rye. He made himself think of the letter he'd received in New Guinea. Even now, after more than two years, every word was indelibly etched on his memory.

"I'm terribly sorry, Steve, darling, but pretending is bad, isn't it? We've fought against it, both of us. I swear we have, but it's no use. I could get the divorce. It won't be difficult. And Tony will divorce Virginia at the same time. Baby, life is dreary, isn't it? But I can't help it, because this is the real thing ..."

The real thing. How could he have been such a fool as to have signed the divorce papers? He'd regarded himself a tragic, heroic figure then. Stepping aside for Celia's happiness. Yet he'd known Tony for years. He should have realized that Tony was poison to women, and that he'd never have let himself be divorced from the social and financial security of Virginia, that the "real thing" would turn out to be just another shabby affair with a broken heart for Celia.

Around. The word stole back. There had been plenty of sympathetic friends to write Steve and tell him how very much "around" Celia was, after Tony was through. Around with rich playboys like Goody Taylor. Around and drinking plenty—and not only drinking.

With a bitter grimace Steve put down his empty glass and walked out of the bar.

II

Beating Tony up hadn't worked. The Clover Bar hadn't worked. Steve felt even more confused, and inexpressibly lonely. It meant so much to him not to be weak, and yet a burning desire to see Celia just once more had him in its grips.

He was passing a store that sold men's clothes. He paused, gazing without interest at the civilian jackets on their stiff, rounded dummies. He'd have to buy some suits soon. Tomorrow, maybe. He could see his own reflection in the window. The Purple Heart gleamed with the other ribbons on his chest.

The Purple Heart. He had been wounded for his country and he was supposed to be a hero. Heroes come marching home from the wars. Ticker tape streams from skyscrapers. People cheer. Wives throw themselves into their husbands' arms, laughing, crying. That's how heroes come home in books.

He stood alone on the sidewalk, staring into the store window.

That's what was wrong, he thought. I've been kidding myself I was the hero of a book. Beating Tony up—that was something like a book. I've got to wise up to myself. I'm just a little guy who get roped into a war and then got thrown out again. I'm just a little guy whose girl wanted someone else more than she wanted me.

Suddenly he felt shame for having done what he'd done to Tony; leaving him there on the floor, bleeding. Maybe he should go back, call a doctor. The idea was so utterly unlike anything he had expected that he could not absorb it at first.

But it brought a strange excitement, as if he was saving something from the wreck. He had a key to Tony's apartment, a hangover from the dim, dim days before his marriage when he'd been Tony's friend and had been given the run of the place.

Tony's apartment house was quiet as a Sunday evening. No one was in the vestibule. He had the self-service elevator to himself. Following his only half understood impulse, Steve used the key to let himself into Tony's top-floor apartment.

The lights were still burning Tony was still lying there motionless.

Steve moved toward him. No, Tony wasn't quite in the same place. He was nearer the fireplace.

There was more blood on Tony's shirt-front than Steve remembered. It was trickling down toward his pants in a sluggish stream. That was queer. There hadn't been any wound in his chest. It had just been the blood that had splashed there from his mouth.

Steve bent down. The hair at the back of his neck stirred. There was a wound now in Tony's chest—a neat, round wound that had cut a neat hole in the starched shirt.

His hand slightly unsteady, he felt for Tony's pulse. There was no motion in the cold, limp wrist.

Steve faced this thing as he had had to face so many other unfaceable things in the past two years.

Tony Dort was dead.

Someone had shot him through the heart.

It was second nature to Steve to do the safe thing at the right moment. Instinctively, without thinking, he went to the door and slipped the locking chain into place. He moved back, staring down at Tony. He wasn't feeling much of anything. This wasn't a time to feel.

His brain coped with the bald facts, precisely one fact after another. At eight, he had left Tony lying unconscious on the floor. Unconscious, not dead, not seriously hurt even. It was just after eight-thirty now. In the past half-hour, Tony had revived. He could tell that because the position of the body had changed.

In the past half-hour, someone had come in and shot Tony.

The bar carpet stretched on each side of the corpse with no hiding place. There was no gun visible. That definitely made it murder.

Steve started to feel a little then. Not for Tony. The vague, cosmic desire which had brought him back had vanished into limbo. He was feeling for himself, because his thoughts were sending out danger signals.

When you find a body, you call the police. If he called the police, the police would come. They'd ask him to explain himself. He'd say Tony had stolen his wife when he was overseas and that he'd beaten him up. He'd say he'd left him unconscious and gone off to a bar and then come back. Why? For some crazy feeling, half pity, maybe, half shame.

It was obvious what the police would say about that story.

He thought of the fingerprints he must have left on Tony's platinum case when he took a cigarette. He pulled out a khaki handkerchief. Quite steady, he leaned over Tony, slipped the case from his pocket, wiped it and replaced it. He looked around. Shiny surfaces were everywhere—surfaces he might have touched.

He moved through the room, running the handkerchief carefully over tables, chair backs. He might be removing the murderer's prints with his own. He knew that and didn't care.

He was standing by the fireplace. Something gleamed, half hidden under a chair's slip cover. During his first visit he had stood exactly in this place when he'd lunged out at Tony. There had been nothing gleaming under the chair then. He was sure.

A gun, he thought. Maybe there's a gun and it's really suicide, after all.

He stopped and picked up the thing that gleamed. He held it in the palm of his hand. He stared at it.

The thing in his hand was a compact, a small white gold compact encrusted with emeralds.

The compact he had given Celia.

Steve was used to hard knocks. He'd thought he could take them on the chin. But suddenly he was nearer to breaking than he'd ever been in his life.

Celia's compact was here, under the chair. It hadn't been there when he left the apartment for the first time. Celia had been here after he was gone. Celia!

All the things, to whose loss he'd thought adjusted himself, came rushing back. Waking up in the morning and Celia being there. Celia laughing her sudden, spontaneous laugh at the movies. Celia who had been his wife and who'd walked out on him when he'd been away.

Celia had murdered Tony!

Steve made himself say it, and he saw it as something inevitable, like a complication in a Greek play. He saw, too, that he couldn't hate Celia just by telling himself to hate her, that he couldn't put the past behind him, write it off.

Whether he wanted to or not, this was still his problem. Whatever the cost, however barren the gain, he would stand by Celia.

A cigarette would have helped, but now he was reluctant to take another from Tony's case. He put the compact in his pocket and started to investigate the room again. This time he took infinitely more pains. Celia was always careless, he remembered. He wiped every surface he had not wiped before. He came to the telephone. Maybe Celia had used the telephone. The handkerchief hovered over the instrument.

It started to ring.

III

Because the danger was Celia's danger now, Steve was less steady. The stakes were so dizzily high. Let the telephone ring? What if it was someone who had a date with Tony? Someone who knew he was there, who would investigate?

Steve took the receiver up in his handkerchief.

"Hello," he said in a blurred, neutral voice.

"Tony?" It was woman's voice, hard, bad-tempered. "This is Janice. What on earth's happened to you? I'm coming right around."

"Tony's not here," said Steve.

"Not there? Then—what? Who are you anyway?"

"A friend of Tony's. He lent the apartment to me for the night."

"Where's Tony then? He was supposed to meet me at Sardo's for dinner. I've been waiting an hour. I'd better come over."

"It's no use. Tony's been called out of town."

"I suppose it's Virginia acting up again. That woman's a positive menace. Why doesn't he divorce her and have done with it?"

"Don't ask me," said Steve. "I wouldn't know."

Janice laughed suddenly. "You sound cute. What about pinch-hitting for Tony and buying me a dinner?"

"Sorry. I've got a date."

"Okay. Just give Tony hell if you see him before I do."

Eternally Janice rang off.

Steve put the receiver down, wiping the stand. He'd done the right thing. If he hadn't answered, that girl would have rushed straight over.

He turned off the lights. Quietly, he slipped out of the door, locking it and putting the extra key in the pocket of his blouse. He took the stairs down. There was less chance of being seen.

There was no one in the vestibule. And there was no one on the street as he emerged from the apartment building and strode along the sidewalk.

Three blocks farther on, Steve hailed a taxi. His voice sounding unnaturally gruff, he gave the driver Celia's address. It was the first New York taxi he'd ridden in for three years. The worn upholstery, the little vase with no flowers in it, the muffled radio muttering sports news, made him feel more at home than he'd felt since his arrival at Penn Station. The familiarity of it was bitter, though.

If life had left him alone, he'd have been in a taxi like this, driving home to Celia as his wife. Not driving home to a woman who had no more use for him, to find out whether she had committed a murder.

The taxi stopped outside a large apartment house with an opulent red and white striped awning. Steve paid off the driver. The building was new to him. Celia had moved there after he'd left. The newness seemed hostile. So did the silent, uniformed elevator man who took him eighteen flights up. Soon he was standing outside a strange door.

He wished he wasn't so afraid of that first moment of seeing her. He couldn't help her if he was afraid. At last he moved closer and pressed the buzzer.

The door opened on a girl, slight and very young in white lounging pajamas, with tawny hair loose to her shoulders. She stared at him for a moment. Then she threw her arms around his neck.

"Steve, darling. It's you. I can't believe it."

She clung to him. Her warm lips were on his cheek. He could smell the faint fragrance of her hair. He'd been so sure that Celia would open the door that he could not immediately adapt himself. For one instance moment he felt it was Celia—Celia as she used to be.

The girl drew him into the apartment and shut the door. She looked up at him brightly, tossing back her hair.

"Steve, you don't remember me. Have I grown that much?"

He remembered Dennie, of course. Although Celia's kid sister had been a gawky fifteen-year-old when he left, he'd recognized her after that first haunted moment.

"Hi, Dennie, baby."

He kept his hands on her arms, looking at her. It hadn't been all imagination. She was staggeringly like Celia. It threw him further off balance that she could have changed so much.

"Steve, this is wonderful. I never dreamed you'd come." She flushed slightly. "How long a leave is it?"

"Not a leave, Dennie. Discharge."

Steve hadn't planned on Dennie being there. He wasn't quite sure how to handle her. He glanced around the room. It was lovely. Celia had a way with rooms. Soft colors, soft lights. There were freesias too in a tall white vase.

Trying to sound casual, he asked "Celia around?"

Dennie wasn't looking at him now. "No, she's out," Impulsively she added, "Steve, do you think you ought to see her?"

His sense of danger was growing by the minute. You never could tell in New York. Tony's body already might have been found.

"She's different, Steve. She … Oh, I don't know how to say it. It won't do any good seeing her."

Her young eyes were watching him earnestly. She was pitying him and that was one thing he wouldn't take from anyone.

"What do you think I'm going to do when I see Celia—faint?"

"Steve." She ran to him and clutched his hand in her warm, soft fingers. "Don't be bitter, Steve, please. Oh, it's been the most ghastly thing that's ever happened. Tony was a terrible mistake. You and Celia … It was so right. The two of you … You'll never know what the two of you meant to me. Steve, don't make it hurt you more than it has already."

Steve tugged his hand out of hers. "If I want advice for the lovelorn, I'll buy me a newspaper. Where's Celia? That's quite a simple question, isn't it?"

Her lips were trembling as if he'd struck her. He felt suddenly ashamed.

"Sorry, baby." He patted her arm. "Army life's hard on manners. Give me a little time."

"It's all right, Steve." Very softly, she added, "Celia's at the Topaz Club with Goody Taylor."

"Goody Taylor? I thought he'd been embalmed years ago. When did she leave?"

"Around eight."

He felt a tingle of hope. Tony had been killed between eight and eight-thirty. Celia had been with Goody Taylor since eight.

"Steve." Dennie's voice was husky with anxiety. "Promise me you won't do anything. Promise."

But Steve was halfway to the door.

The scent of the freesias seemed to follow him all the way down the street.

IV

Steve pushed his way through the evening crowd on the sidewalk to the entrance of the Topaz Club. A liveried doorman, conscious of the social importance of the door he guarded, loomed in front of him.

Steve had never been here before. In the old days Celia had hated smart places. Dumps with lugs, she'd called them. He passed the doorman into a lush foyer.

He gave his garrison hat to the check girl. The manager was talking to a woman in low-cut evening gown and a colonel plastered with gold braid. When he saw Steve, he left them and drifted inquiringly forward.

"It's okay," said Steve. "I'll find my party."

He moved down a short flight of steps into the club. White baroque mirrors gleamed on burgundy walls, throwing back a kaleidoscopic reflection of faces, dresses, hands holding drinks. It was a small room with a pocket handkerchief of a dance floor. A discreet orchestra was playing as if it was afraid of being heard.

A dump with lugs. Celia was right. The Topaz Club was just the Clover Bar with a penn'orth of interior decoration.

Waiters were hovering near him. Steve paid them no attention. His brown eyes studied the crowded room, searching for
Celia. He hadn't planned on meeting Celia in a place like this
where there was less privacy than at a Turkish bath. He had pic-
tured them alone together in her room. It would have been possible then.

Celia, he thought, I know you've killed Tony. But I've covered
your tracks. Tell me everything. We'll figure out some way. I'll
swear you were with me all evening.

Suddenly he heard Celia's laugh. It sounded clear, spontaneous above the babble. No one who'd heard Celia's laugh could
ever mistake it. Steve looked in the direction from which the
laugh had come, and he saw Celia. She was at a table in a corner
across from a plump black and white man with a red carnation
in his buttonhole. "Goody" Taylor.

He'd known it would be bad seeing her, but it was worse than
he'd expected. He felt as if he'd been punched in the stomach.
It was because Celia looked exactly the same. Celia, who was
so changed, shouldn't look the same. But there she was, her silver blonde hair swept up, the skin of her bare shoulders dusky
cream above the smoky blue of her gown. Her profile was exactly
as he remembered it, delicate, magical, her white throat curved
slightly backward as she laughed.

Something in him exulted. She couldn't possibly be sitting
here laughing if she'd murdered Tony less than two hours ago.

The intensity of his gaze must have reached her, for abruptly
she turned from Goody and was staring straight at him.

For a moment her face was blank. Then it broke into a radiant
smile. She rose. She drifted through the tables. She came straight
to Steve. She put her bare arms around him and kissed him.

There was no awkwardness in her, no embarrassment at the
interested glances thrown at them. In the past Celia's utter lack
of self-consciousness had been one of the things he loved. Now,
with all that had happened between them, it seemed jarring,
almost exhibitionistic.

"Steve, darling!" she cried. "It's great to see you."

She was different. He could see it now that she was close to
him. She was just as beautiful, but there was a shadow. There was
something strained, haunted in her gaiety. She's been through
hell, too, he thought.

"Hullo, Celia," he said.

For so many months he'd struggled with what he'd say to Celia when he met her. This was how it had turned out.

Still smiling, she slipped her hand into his and started to draw him through the tables. Her voice chattered on, fashionable, meaningless.

"Steve, what is it? A leave? Why didn't you write me?"

They reached the corner table. A magnum of champagne, in a silver ice bucket, stood between two glasses. Goody Taylor, plump, florid, like a cynical baby, stared up at Steve from small, bored eyes.

"Goody," said Celia, "you know Steve."

Goody stretched out a pudgy hand. "H'yah, Sergeant. Any friend of Celia's is no friend of mine."

Celia laughed. "Goody, don't be clever. This is Steve, my ex-husband."

"Oh," said Goody. "People in uniform always look so depressingly alike."

Celia said, "Sit down, Steve, and tell me about the Pacific."

"Maybe you'd like to hear about the Pacific—alone," Steve suggested.

Goody darted him a quick, suspicious glance.

Celia said, "Of course, darling." She patted Goody's arm. "Be a baby. Go flirt with some of those dismal models of yours. Just for a little while. Steve and I—we haven't seen each other for a long time."

Sulky, but obedient, Goody rose from the table and waddled away. There was some champagne in Celia's glass. She titled the glass to her lips. Steve noticed her hand was unsteady. She was feeling then. In spite of the brittle front, it did mean something to her, seeing him.

He said, "How about moving on to some place less infested with Society?"

"No, Steve." She shook her head almost violently. "I like it here."

"You used to hate these places."

She didn't reply. An awkward silence fell between them. Desperately Steve groped to find a way to cope with this almost impossible situation. Suddenly Celia laughed.

"There must be something for an ex-husband and wife to talk above. Do you still like your eggs soft boiled at breakfast?"

She poured more champagne. A little splashed over the rim of the glass.

Steve said, "Do we have to talk about eggs? Or us, for that matter?"

"Why not?" Celia's smile was studiedly casual. "After all, we don't have to be tragic about it. Other people get divorces, too."

"Do they? Nobody told me."

"All right, darling" Celia shrugged her exquisite bare shoulder. "I was a heel. If that's the way you want it. I walked out on you. I made a mess of my life. So what?"

"Celia!"

"I'm sorry if it caused you grief and pain in the Lesser Hebrides or wherever you were. But I'm not sorry for myself. I was born to make a mess of my life. I enjoy it. It's fun."

"You've changed," Steve murmured quietly.

"Oh, no, darling, it's just that you never really knew me. I've always been a—what's the polite word for it? Butterfly, isn't it?"

She fluttered her hand through the air, imitating a butterfly. A man at an adjoining table thought she was waving at him. He smiled. She smiled back. She was deliberately trying to hurt Steve. He could tell that. Maybe it was easier for her that way. Just as the champagne made it easier. If it did, it was okay with him. He was watching her hand, half-hypnotized.

Could that slender hand, so familiar to him, possibly have fired a gun at Tony and killed him?

V

The silence had come again. Because he could bear it and the suspense no longer, he tugged the compact out of his pocket.

"Remember this, Celia?"

His eyes never left her face. The change in her expression that he had dreaded did not come. She looked town at the compact and then up at him questioningly.

"Of course I remember it, Steve. Where on earth did you find it?"

"At Tony's."

"Steve!" For a second her eyes were off their guard. "You weren't difficult with Tony?"

"I wasn't difficult."

"I mean you mustn't blame Tony. This isn't a Victorian set piece with a black-mustached villain. If he hadn't double crossed me first, I'd have double crossed him."

Steve was still watching her. "Yeah. I understood you were through."

She laughed. "You make it sound so portentous. Tony was just a thing, darling. There have been plenty of other things since Tony."

She had wrecked their marriage for a "thing." Something as frivolous as a meringue. That's what she was saying. She knew how to turn the knife in the wound, all right.

He said, "Then you haven't seen Tony lately?"

"Oh, here and there, maybe at parties and things. But no, I haven't really seen Tony in weeks. Why should I? Darling, why do you keep harping on Tony?"

"A guy's got a right to harp on something that lost him a wife, hasn't he? Besides, I was wondering. If you haven't seen him in weeks, how come your compact was in his apartment?"

This was the moment. She twirled her empty glass languidly. "That's easy, darling. I gave it to him."

Steve's fingers closed tightly around the compact. He remembered his abraded knuckles and hid his hand quickly under the table.

"Months ago, Tony was in one of his periodical jams with his wife," Celia went on. "You know Virginia. He had to think up a present for her in a hurry. I gave him the compact."

She had given Tony the compact which had been the symbol of Steve's love. Instead of it hurting, that news brought Steve a wild exhilaration. Celia had given Tony the compact months ago. It wasn't hers any more. Then it wasn't she who had left it at Tony's apartment.

"Maybe I was a heel about that, too." Once again her voice was challenging, daring him to find a weak spot in her cynical armor. "But I can't abide sentiment. When a thing's smashed, it's smashed. You can't tie it together with little pink ribbons."

"Then Virginia must have left it at Tony's apartment?"

"I suppose so," Celia laughed. "If you've snitched it Virginia will think Tony's given it to one of his current girl friends."

So she didn't do it, Steve thought. She didn't kill Tony.

"Celia, if you were in trouble—real trouble—you'd tell me, wouldn't you?" he asked impulsively.

"Trouble?" Her creamy forehead wrinkled. "Yes, dear, I think I would. You're a wonderful guy in trouble. But then I don't trouble easy."

"No prospect of trouble at the moment?"

Her red lips parted in a smile. "The rent's paid, if that's what you mean."

He wondered why she was trying to make him hate her. Probably because she had more than enough men in love with her already. But he was seeing himself very clearly then, and he knew he would have gone on loving her even if she had killed Tony. Now he'd go on loving her anyway. There wasn't anything he or she could do about it. The magic was still there.

"Darling." He felt Celia's hand on his arm. "Don't let's be stuffy anymore. It's our tune. Remember?"

He realized the subdued little orchestra was playing "Night and Day."

Celia rose. "Let's dance, baby."

Steve shook his head. He didn't want her to know the wound in his leg had left him clumsy.

"Oh, Steve, don't be a bore." Celia looked petulant.

"Sorry," said Steve. "So I'm a bore."

An unknown young man was moving through the tables towards them.

"Hello, Celia."

Celia smiled at him ravishingly, "Hello, Don."

"Like to dance?"

"Sure. I'd love it." She waved her hand absently at Steve. "Bye darling. Look me up again sometime."

She drifted away on the young man's arm. Soon he caught a glimpse of them among the crowded dancers. Celia was clinging to the young man tightly, her cheek tilted up to his.

Almost immediately Goody Taylor came back to the table. He settled into a chair opposite Steve.

"So she's given you the air again, ex-husband."

Steve was watching Celia. He didn't bother to reply. Goody Taylor leaned forward and tapped him the arm.

"Listen to me. Soldiers coming back from the war don't come back to girls like Celia. Forget her. Celia, find yourself a nice little number with a gingham gown and a light hand for blueberry muffins."

Steve's brown eyes moved to Goody's face then. It would have been so easy to knock him down.

"Yeah. Competing with you would be kind of rough, wouldn't it?"

"Me!" Goody's laugh was light and half-mocking. "Don't be unkind. I'm just an old fat guy with a ready hand for paying a check—and no gingham gown. It's Tony. Celia can kid herself, but she's never going to get Tony out of her blood. Not till he's neatly tucked away in a long, plain box."

Steve wasn't really listening. All he was thinking was: So Goody's in love with her, too. He felt tired. He got up. Giving Goody a vague glance of farewell, he headed toward the door. What to do now?

As he glanced back at the dance floor, he saw Celia. She was still dancing with Don. He was holding her very close.

Steve bought his hat back from the hat check girl. He headed for the door to the street. Behind him a voice called:

"Steve!"

He turned, hoping absurdly it would be Celia. But it was Dennie. She was wearing a low-cut black evening gown with a single gardenia, attached to a black choker ribbon, gleaming against the bare skin of her throat. He had never seen her in evening dress. Somehow it touched him. She looked so very young.

"Hi, Dennie." He smiled at her gently. "So you chased me with the smelling salts after all."

"Steve, I had to see you again."

He fingered the gardenia at her throat. "Pretty snazzy, aren't you?"

"Roy Chappell bought it." She put her hand on his sleeve. "I was scared to come alone. So I called Roy. He'll do anything for Celia, even tote her kid sister to the Topaz Room." She hesitated. "I had to come because I've got something important to tell you."

He thought, Maybe the police have found the body. Maybe Celia's name was in a phone book or someone told them.

"Okay. But let's move out of here. I've had enough glamour. There's a milk bar across the street." He smiled again to keep her from guessing he was anxious. "An orange drink. That's more your speed anyway, fifteen-year-old."

"Eighteen, Steve." She returned his smile uncertainly. "One minute. I'll tell Roy where we're going."

VI

When Dennie rejoined Steve they crossed the street to the milk bar. It was bare, white and clean. A taxi driver was dunking a cruller in a cup of coffee at the far end of the counter. Steve chose seats near the door and ordered two orange drinks. The counterman brought them and strolled off to talk to the taxi driver.

Steve was thinking of the murder. The compact belonged to Virginia Dort now. He tried to visualize Tony's cool, impersonal wife shooting him.

Another thought sneaked into his mind. What if Celia had been lying? What if she hadn't given Tony the compact to give to Virginia?

In a tight little voice, Dennie said, "Was she—very awful?"

"Celia?" He shrugged. "She was having a good time, I guess."

"She's not really that way," Dennie blurted. "She's deliberately doing it, deliberately making herself as cheap and horrible as she can so you'll hate her."

"Psychology?" queried Steve quietly.

"Oh, Steve, she loved you. You know she did. This thing with Tony was something mad, something outside of herself. She never really stopped loving you. She always keeps your photograph in her room." Dennie was twisting her fingers together. "Listen to me, Steve. Things could be the way they used to be between you again. I'm sure. It's just that she thinks she's no good. She thinks she's poison for you."

After Goody's cynical, "She'll never get Tony out of her blood," Dennie's passionate young loyalty to a dream was moving. Celia, who had given his compact to Tony, still loved him! It sounded nice. But that was all.

Steve watched Dennie's pale, intense face. This was the important thing then. The kid thought that just by trying hard enough she could make everything be the way it used to be.

He thought again. What if Celia didn't give Tony the compact?

He said, "You love Celia, don't you?"

"Of course I do." Dennie's lips were trembling. "I love her almost—" She flushed. "I love her more than anyone in the world. And so do you."

"Maybe. But that doesn't make me kid myself."

"I'm not kidding myself, Steve. I know what I say is true. Oh, if you only could—" She broke off with a little sob. "It's all Tony's fault. Oh, how I hate Tony."

"Enough to kill him?" Steve said softly.

She looked up. Her eyes flickered. "Why did you say that?"

"No reason."

"Steve." She gripped his arm. "Something's wrong, isn't it? I thought so, ever since I first saw you. Steve, have you seen Tony?"

"I've seen him."

"Where?"

"At his house."

"Why did you go? You haven't done anything? You didn't— make a blunder?"

"Kill him, you mean?"

She was watching him with a growing sensation of horror.

He thought, Why not tell her? A murder's a murder. Soon everyone will know. Something's got to be done. Nothing's been done yet.

Dennie loved Celia. Whatever happened, she'd be an ally, and he had an instinctive need for an ally.

Steve said, "Okay, baby. Drag out the smelling salts. Tony's dead."

He thought she'd be able to take it, and he was right. The horror was still in her eyes, but she kept a firm hold on her feelings. She glanced down the counter at the two men who were absorbed in some discussion of their own.

"You, Steve?" she breathed. "You went there and—did it?"

Steve shook his head. "I might just as well have killed him, but I didn't."

"You found him dead?"

"Yeah. Shot."

"And you called the police?"

"No."

"Steve, why not?"

He couldn't tell her about the compact. That was something to close to him, too tied up with his bride.

"Because—because I was afraid, maybe for Celia."

"Celia!" Her fingers were clutching his. "When did it happen?"

"Between eight and eight-thirty tonight."

"Thank God. It couldn't have been Celia. She was on her way to meet Goody." Dennie flushed again. "Not that it could be Celia anyway. Of course, it couldn't. Steve, you know that."

"I guess I do now. I was just scared, that's all."

"And you haven't called the police." Dennie stared at him fixedly. "What if someone saw you going here? Since you didn't call the police, they'll think you did it."

"That's a chance I took," Steve said grimly.

"Maybe they're after you already. What are you going to do?"

"Somehow I guess I'm going to find out who really killed him."

He saw he was committed to that then. He was in too deep to let chance take its course. The first step would have to be Virginia. He'd have to find her and ask her about the compact.

The little voice nagged, What if she denies ever having had it? What if she says Celia's lying? He tried to suppress the thought.

"Yeah," he said. "I'm going to do something about it right now. I'm going to Virginia."

"Virginia, Tony's wife? Why, has she—" Dennie glanced at the door and broke off. "Roy," she whispered. "Please, please don't say anything in front of Roy. He's so smart. He'll suspect."

Roy Chappell came toward them and sat down on a stool beside Dennie. Steve had known Roy slightly for years, but he had always thought of him as Celia's friend. For as long as he could remember, Roy had been around Celia. Some husbands might have resented this passionate obsession, but Steve hadn't. Roy with his frail, humpbacked body and shock of gray hair was no serious rival. His adoration for Celia was as unphysical as the adoration for beauty which had made him the most famous jewel designer in New York.

"So young Lochinvar is back from the wars." Roy's brilliant eyes met Steve's with a faintly sardonic smile. "That compact I made for you turned out to be love's labor lost, didn't it? Too bad. It was very beautiful."

"It was," said Steve.

"Poor lovely, lost Celia." Roy's lips tightened into a severe line. Then, with a sudden change of mood, he asked, "Well, what have you been doing with my ewe lamb here—whisking her off from me and buying her guilty orange-ades?"

"We were just talking, Roy," Dennie said quickly.

"So I imagined." Roy's gaze shifted back to Steve. "About Celia? Don't listen to Dennie about Celia, Steve. Dennie's too young. The young have too much hope. If you want to talk about Celia, buy me an orange-ade and I'll give you a speech."

But Steve wasn't listening. In his mind was a picture of Virginia Dort holding a gun, then carefully aiming it and firing it.

"Some other time, maybe, Roy. I've got to shove along now." Steve rose.

"A date?" Roy asked quizzically. "You're not wasting much time, soldier."

"No," Steve said, "I'm not wasting much time." He patted Dennie's soft, bare shoulder. "So long, baby."

"I'll see you later?" she asked anxiously.

He looked at her for a long moment, his face tight with weariness.

"Sure. When I'm through."

"At the apartment. I'll be waiting. I'll have Roy take me home."

"Okay."

"Steve." She clutched his hand. "Be careful. Promise?"

"Sure."

"Careful?" Roy's bright gaze fixed upon Steve's face. "You're not going to see Tony by any chance?" His voice rose sharply.

"Tony? No. Why?"

"I thought you might be just foolish enough to try it. That's all." Roy's gaze did not flicker. "And it would be foolish, you know. Very foolish, indeed."

VII

Steve found Virginia Dort's address in a drugstore phone book and headed uptown. He knew he might be running into danger. The police might already be there. But he was still enough of a soldier to have certain contemptuous indifference towards civilian danger.

He was half-kidding himself that he had turned detective to help clear himself. It wasn't really that. It was the little nagging voice that was sending him to Virginia. Until he actually heard Tony's wife admitted Tony had given her the compact, he couldn't be entirely sure that Celia was safe.

And if Celia wasn't safe, life wasn't worth living.

He had his plan worked out. Obviously he couldn't confront Virginia with the compact. If she was guilty she'd know he must have found it at Tony's and would lie. There was another way. Virginia was essentially conventional. The proprieties were important to her. That was once reason why she had never divorced Tony. He would go to her as Celia's ex-husband, asking for the return of the last present he had given his wife. It would be rough on his pride, but his pride had been so battered already that a little more humiliation wouldn't hurt it.

Virginia's apartment house was like herself, discreetly correct in the discreetly correct East Seventies. A uniformed maid asked him to wait in the hall and took his name though a curtain into an inner room.

It was quiet. No police were around yet, that was certain.

Virginia came out quickly. She was still handsome in a fine, chiseled way, but she looked older, less amiable. Her thin arms drooped from an expensive sleeveless gown of dark red crepe.

"Hello, Steve."

She held out a small hand, stiff with rings.

Steve was very conscious of hands that evening. He looked at hers and wondered.

"I wish I could whip up a brass band for the returning hero. All I can offer, I'm afraid, is a drink and some strictly hen bridge."

"I can't stay. I just thought I'd come up and say hello."

Virginia's green enamel eyes flickered. "How nice. And I'm dummy right now so I do have a minute. In fact, if need be, we'll let the bridge fiends scream their heads off. After all, I've been at it with them since eight."

Since eight. It was after eight when Tony was killed.

Virginia smiled and put her small hand on his arm.

"Okay, conquering hero, let's go somewhere and sit."

She led him into a formal library. She sat down on a gold brocade chair. She looked up at him clearly.

"You don't have to be polite with me, Steve. You've come about Celia, haven't you? I'm sorry. I think she and Tony behaved abominably. You were rather foolish, you know, letting Celia go ahead with the divorce. You ought to have realized Tony wouldn't go through with his part of the bargain."

"Because you'd always veto a divorce?"

"Oh, no, my dear. I'm not the villain of the piece." Virginia laughed, tilting back her head. "I'm awfully useful to Tony. He uses that 'I'm going to divorce Virginia' line on all his girls and he knows he's absolutely safe." Her face softened. "Too bad it got into your life, though. I liked you. I liked Celia, too." She paused. "Have you seen her?"

Steve nodded.

"That was silly of you, my dear," Virginia fitted a cigarette into a red holder. "I know nobody likes advice on these subjects, but I'm going to give you some. Keep away from Celia, Steve. You're a sweet guy. You've probably even got illusions and things. I had them once, before I married Tony. But illusions and ideals don't thrive around people like Tony and Celia."

He was trying to investigate a murder and everyone gave him advice for the lovelorn.

"Don't kid yourself that there's a chance to patch things up with Celia!" Virginia's finely molded lips curled behind blue smoke. "Tony's through with her, yes. But she's no good for anyone else. No girl who's been Tony's girl is any good for human consumption afterwards." She touched his sleeve. "Forget her, Steve."

"The way you've forgotten Tony?"

Virginia laughed. "My dear, you think I'm still nurturing a hopeless passion for him? Tony and romance went out of my life, hand in hand, almost before the ink was dry on the wedding certificate."

"But you still see him." There was a line here.

"Tony? I haven't seen him in weeks." Virginia shrugged. "We communicate almost exclusively through lawyers and month separation checks. Of course, he occasionally puts in an appearance if he's needed at a function. Sometimes, too, he sends me presents. If his conscience is particularly guilty at the time."

She'd given him his opening.

"As a matter of fact, I've come to see you about presents." He looked down at his hands. He didn't have to see her face when he said this. "Before I went away, I gave Celia a sort of farewell present. Okay, so I've got illusions and things. I guess maybe I'm a hick by your standards. But I'd like that present back."

"Present, Steve? Why should I know anything about any present you gave Celia? Ask her about it."

"I did ask her." Steve made himself look up then. Virginia was watching him in polite, apparently sincere bewilderment. "She gave it to Tony and Tony gave it to you."

"To me?"

"It was a compact. A white gold compact set with emeralds. Roy Chappell designed it."

If she denied having it, would it mean she was lying? Or would it mean Celia hadn't told the truth? He cut the thought, staring at her. To his infinite relief, her face cleared.

"So that's what it was. I happened to see that compact once in Tony's apartment. I said I thought it was awfully good-looking. Tony offered it to me. A charming gesture, I knew perfectly well it belonged to one of his girlfriends. I refused it, of course. But a month or so later one exactly like it came through the mail for me. There was a note from Tony, explaining that he'd persuaded Roy Chappell to make a copy."

"So it was a copy you received."

"That's what Tony said. It looked exactly the same as the other one.

Which was which? Had he picked up the copy at Tony's? Or the original?

Steve said casually, "And you've got the copy?"

Virginia opened her small silver purse and held a compact out to Steve. He stared at it. It was identical to the one he had in his pocket. He hadn't banked on this. If she was speaking the truth, she couldn't have dropped the other compact at Tony's tonight.

But what if Tony had given her the original and she'd had it copied herself? What if she owned two copies of the compact? Who could prove her story? Roy Chappell, of course. If he'd made a copy, he'd know who had ordered it.

"Take it, Steve." Virginia was pressing the compact into his hands. "If I'd known the mess behind it, I'd have died rather than accept it in the first place."

Steve shook his head. "Thanks Virginia, but a copy wouldn't mean anything to me. I'm that corny." He paused, and then brought out the sentence that mattered. "You don't happen to know who has the original, do you?"

"If I know Tony, and if Celia gave it to him, I'd say he'd have kept it for a rainy day. One of those rainy days when a girlfriend has to be made to feel good in a hurry." Virginia laughed shortly. "I understand his current girl is called Janice something. She probably has it."

Eternally Janice, who had been stood up at Sardo's.

"Happen to know her name? Where she lives?"

"My dear, I've given up keeping track of my rivals years ago. I believe she lives in Scarsdale, Pelham, or some place drearily adequate like that. Married, I understand." Her small hands suddenly clenched into fists. "Steve, baby, how can you take all this? You loved Celia. Probably you still love her. If I were you, I'd have killed Tony."

Steve started. Virginia's face was pale.

"I'd have killed him if I was Celia, too," she went on. "Oh, I've warned you off Celia, but that doesn't mean I hate her. Celia's just another girl who got a raw deal. Better than the others, too. It is Tony who's the rotter. I outsmarted him. I married him and now I'm in clover. But if he'd done to me what he's done to Celia, I'd have felt just the way she does."

"Celia feels—what way?" Steve asked quietly.

"My dear, I don't know how she feels now. But right after the break up, she wrote him a letter." Virginia paused and then went on, "It sounds filthy telling you these things, Steve, but you might as well have it straight on the jaw and be done with it. Tony showed me that letter. It amused him, letting me know how het-up his girlfriends could get about him. It was mad, hysterical.

"She said that he'd ruined her life, that she'd never be able to look you in the face again. All that. Tony said he was always going to keep it with him in his wallet so that if ever he was found dead in bed, they'd know what hit him."

VIII

Hope, sudden, unexpected, surged through Steve. Celia had written Tony that he had ruined her life, ruined her for him, Steve. He remembered what Dennie had claimed about the way Celia felt. Maybe, insanely, in spite of everything, there was still a chance that things could be patched up. The thought was engulfed by another, much stronger one.

Maybe Tony still had that letter in his wallet. Steve had removed the compact, fingerprints, but if the police found the letter it would lead them straight to Celia.

He said. "And Tony's still got the letter?"

"I imagine so." Virginia was watching him anxiously. "Steve, dear, did I talk out of turn?"

He looked up, trying to grin. "It's okay, Virginia. I can take it."

"Darling." She leaned forward, running her hand lightly over his hair. "My heart bleeds for you. You've had the rottenest deal in the world." She rose then, tall and slender in her clinging red gown. "Will you think I'm a heartless heel if I remind you that I do have guests and I do have a bridge game? I really should go back, you know."

"Sure," said Steve. "Sure, Virginia. I understand."

She went with him to the door. Impulsively she slipped her arms around him and kissed him on the mouth.

"Why is it the nicest people always take the worst beating? You are an attractive guy, Steve. Know that? I'd give my teeth—which I still have, thank God—to be able to solace you right now. But you wouldn't have any part of me, would you? I'm just a dried-up old hag with my neck gone. It's too late."

"Everything seems to be too late," said Steve.

"Not for you, my dear. A couple of years from now when you're walking down the aisle with some ravishing new thing on your arm, think of me, baby. I'll still be here playing bridge with a bunch of old crones. Oh hell! Good night, Steve."

"Good night, Virginia," he said, and left...

What he had to do now was really dangerous. He knew that, but the exhilaration that had come at Virginia's kept him from giving it much thought.

Who owned the compact—Virginia, Janice, or some other girl? None of that mattered now. All that mattered was Celia's letter. If he didn't get Celia's letter before the police got it, the pack would be howling at her heels.

There was only one way to get the letter.

He hailed a taxi. As it rattled downtown, he thought what he would do if he found the police already at Tony's apartment. He'd try to get in and retrieve the letters anyhow. It would be a terrible risk of course. As soon as they knew he was Celia's ex-husband, he'd be Suspect Number One. Why not be Suspect Number One?

His mind had been so settled earlier in the evening, before all the happened. When you're through, you're through, he'd said. Things were different now. Maybe he and Celia weren't through. He gave himself up to seductive fancies.

"Celia, you still love me. I still love you. Baby, don't let's throw everything away out of pride. Other people get divorces and marry again."

Faintly he seemed to hear her answer. "Do they, darling? Nobody told me."

"Here you are, Bud." He hadn't noticed. He paid the cab driver. The taxi drove away.

There was no police car outside Tony's apartment house. No sign of excitement or confusion disturbed its sedate façade. Steve's pulse quickened. Maybe he wasn't too late.

For the third time that night, he took the self-service elevator up. He was grateful for Tony's shady private life which had made him select so unobtrusive a dwelling place.

He paused outside the closed door of Tony's apartment, listening. There was no sound. He brought out his key and opened the door softly onto darkness.

He paused on the threshold, feeling the darkness, alert for a trap. Satisfied, he turned on the lights.

He surveyed the room. Tony was still lying sprawled across the carpet. The room looked exactly the same. Or, did it? Heavy cream curtains were drawn across the window alcove behind the body. Had they been drawn before? For once, Steve's jungle-trained memory betrayed him. He wasn't quite sure.

He stared at them for a while. Then, with a shrug, he moved to the body. He knelt down at its side. He felt in the breast pocket and drew out the wallet. Its contents were stuffed in untidily, money bills in crumpled balls, a bent draft card. That was odd. Tony had always been a neat man. Steve searched silently. It didn't take long.

There wasn't a letter from Celia in the wallet. There wasn't any letter from anyone.

For moment he stared at the messy wallet. He took out his handkerchief, wiped it and put it back in the dead man's pocket.

What if someone had rifled the wallet after he, Steve, had left?

He thought of the cream curtains drawn over the alcove behind them and he knew then, with a sudden flash of memory, that they hadn't been drawn when he was there before.

He crouched, quite still, the blood tingling in his veins. Quickly, with no warning movement, he spun around and tugged the curtains back.

A girl was crouching on the window seat—a pale, very young girl with upswept hair and a trailing black evening gown.

"Dennie," he said.

The girl looked up at him from wide, frightened eyes. Then she rose and threw herself into his arms.

"Steve, I was scared. I heard someone outside the door. I just had time to turn out the lights and get behind the curtains. I thought maybe it was the police."

Her slender body was trembling against his. He hated her being there. Dennie was too young to be here in a room with a murdered man. He stroked her hair.

"Baby, you were crazy to come."

"I had to, Steve." She drew away, looking up at him. "There was a letter—a letter Celia wrote Tony when they broke up. I knew he always kept it on him, and suddenly, after you left me, I remembered it. I thought if the police found it, Celia might get into trouble."

"I heard about the letter from Virginia. That's why I came, too. Baby, you shouldn't have come here yourself. You should have told me."

"Why?" Dennie's eyes were blazing. "Why should you take all the danger? I love Celia, too."

He grinned. "Independent, aren't you?" His face went grave. "You made a hash of that wallet, searching it. Did you get the letter?"

She nodded.

He said. "Give it to me."

"No, Steve. I don't want you to read it."

"I won't read it. Just give it to me."

She took a folded letter from her purse. Steve put it in the pocket of his blouse, unread.

"What did you do with Roy?"

"I left him at home in the apartment. I said I'd be right back."

"Did anyone see you come in here?"

She shook her head.

"How did you get in anyway?"

She flushed. "Celia had a key. It's a hangover from—well, I knew it was in a drawer. I got it and came around." Her eyes moved to Tony's body. She shivered. "Steve, did you find out anything from Virginia?"

"Enough to prove Celia didn't do it."

"Oh, I don't mean that. I mean did you find out anything to make it safer for you?"

Steve shrugged. "Who cares about that?"

"I do."

"You? Why?"

"Because I love you." She said it that simply, like a grave little girl. "I've loved you ever since I can remember. I'd do anything, I'd kill myself—if it would make you happy."

That was the second time that evening Steve had been close to breaking. It wasn't the surprise of what she said; it was her sincerity. He knew she meant it, and the perversity of life got under his skin. Celia loved Tony; Steve loved Celia; Dennie loved Steve. He felt a sudden, savage hunger for the old world of mud and death in the Pacific. At least you knew where you were in a foxhole. Nobody loved anybody there.

"Dennie."

He bent to kiss her forehead. She pulled herself away.

"Don't, Steve. You don't have to be sorry for me."

He stood close to her, staring down at her. He felt weary, spent.

"Maybe not. But at least I've got to get you safely out of here."

The apartment buzzer from downstairs suddenly started to shrill.

IX

Dennie stiffened in nervous apprehension. Steve remained quite still, listening. Then the buzzer shrilled again.

"The police," whispered Dennie.

Steve shook his head. "The police don't come by magic. Someone has to discover the body first."

The buzzer whirred again. There was a moment of keyed-up silence. Then, fainter, the buzzer for one of the other apartments sounded. There was an answering burr.

"They've got it," Steve muttered. "They rang another bell. Baby, if they've got a key to this apartment, we're in a spot. And Tony was generous with his keys."

He glanced down at the body on the carpet. Quickly, he crossed to it, lifted it up like a sack, and dumped it into the window alcove. He drew the cream brocade curtains. There was a dull red stain on the carpet. He grabbed a chair and pulled it over the patch.

A key sounded in the lock of the front door. They heard footsteps in the hall. Steve gripped Dennie's hand.

"Steady, baby. Don't do any talking."

"Tony?" a voice called.

Then a woman walked into the room—a blonde with cool amber eyes, set a little too close together. She was wearing a mannish gray tailored suit, but there was nothing mannish about the movement of her hips and her appraising stare.

Steve recognized Eternally Janice without having to check with the silver-framed photograph.

"Hello." She studied Steve with a frankness that made him uncomfortable. "I suppose you're the guy who answered the phone."

Steve didn't reply. The girl's gaze moved to Dennie.

"Who's the infant?" Her eyes arrowed. "Aren't you the fabulous Celia Glenn Tony's always talking about? No, you can't be. You're too young."

"I'm her sister," Dennie said awkwardly.

Steve cursed inwardly. Things were bad enough without Dennie taking them worse. Now, when the news of the murder broke, Janice would be able to tell the police she had found Celia's sister in the apartment hours after the murder. The situation could hardly deteriorate further—unless, of course, Janice were to discover the body right now. The girl shrugged and dropped into a chair. "I could kill Tony. I suppose he's not back yet?"

"No," Steve said. "I told you. He won't return until tomorrow."

"What a bore." Janice lighted a cigarette. "By the way, am I the hostess or are you the host? In any case, I need a drink."

Dennie glanced at Steve. He nodded.

"Get me one, too, Dennie," he said.

Dennie hurried out into the kitchen. Janice stared after her and then smirked at Steve.

"Isn't she a little young, soldier?"

"To the snide," said Steve, "all things are snide."

"You're not polite."

"I don't have to be."

Steve was watching her closely. Had she murdered Tony, remembered about dropping the compact, and come back for it? She appeared tough enough to carry off harder assignments than that.

Before he got rid of her, there was one thing he could do.

He pulled the compact out of his pocket and held it out to her.

"I guess you came back for this?"

Janice looked at the compact. Then she looked at him. "What's that supposed to be?"

"Your compact?"

"My dear, you flatter me. I don't add up to that many dollars and cents in Tony's life." She seemed bored with the compact. She stared around the room and suddenly rose. "Why on earth have you got one set of curtains drawn and the others open? It gets on my nerves."

She started straight for the window alcove. At that moment Dennie came in with the drinks. She saw where Janice was going and gasped.

Steve said, "Watch out for those drinks, Dennie."

He grabbed Janice's arm and pulled her toward Dennie.

"Here. Your drink."

"Thanks," Janice said wryly.

Steve said, "Draw the other curtains, Dennie. The lady's sensitive."

Obediently Dennie pulled the drapes across the other windows.

Janice sipped idly at her drink. She seemed in no hurry to leave.

Steve said, "There's no point in waiting for Tony, you know."

Janice smiled sweetly. "My dear, don't say you're trying to get rid of me."

"Could be."

"I'm sorry, darling, but I'm spending the night. I'm not dragging my weary bones back to Pelham."

She thought she was spending the night. Steve watched Dennie out of the corner of his eyes. She looked all in. He'd hoped he wouldn't have to be violent. Things always seemed to break wrong for him.

Very quietly he said to Janice, "I'm sorry, too, but you are dragging your weary bones back to Pelham."

She stared. "Of all the nerve. Do you know who I am? I'm Tony's best friend."

"I don't care whether you're Tony's mother. He loaned me the apartment for the night and I'm taking it for the night—alone."

Janice put down her drink. The twist of her mouth was ugly.

"Listen, soldier. I don't know what dreary battle fields you've been losing your manners on, but this is New York. And if you think you can turn Tony's apartment into a dump with a girl not old enough to know better, you're wrong."

"It wouldn't be the first time this apartment's been a dump. But, since you're interested, Dennie's leaving with you. And that's right now." He moved toward her. "Do you want to get up out of that chair under your own steam or shall I drag you out of it?"

Janice laughed suddenly. "Drag me out of it. I dare you."

Steve leaned over her, picked her up by the collar of her gray jacket and jerked her to her feet. She started struggling. He held her off at arms' length as if she were a bad- tempered, ineffectual kitten.

"I'll call the superintendent," she panted.

"And I'll explain your relationship with Tony to him," Steve said blandly.

He started pushing her toward door. Dennie, white-faced, moved after him. Steve opened the door and dumped Janice in the foyer. He pressed the button for the self-service elevator.

"You!" Janice was muttering furiously. "Wait till I tell Tony—just you wait!"

The elevator came. Steve opened the doors and swung Janice inside. He patted Dennie's arm.

"Call the lady a taxi, baby." As she passed him into the elevator, he whispered, "Wait on the corner. I'll be right out."

The elevator doors slammed. Steve went back into the apartment. He washed the glasses and put them back in the kitchen. Then he took the body out of the window seat and put it back more or less as had been on the floor. It was better for it to be in its original position. It would cause less questions.

Questions. Steve's lips moved in a faintly self-mocking smile. He was certainly leaving a raft of questions in his wake.

And most of the questions were going to have him for an answer.

With a twisted smile, he left the apartment for the third time.

Dennie was waiting on the corner.

Steve said, "You got rid of her?"

Dennie nodded. "She took a taxi, but she was muttering about coming back. Steve, I think she will."

"Yeah." Steve's voice was grim. "I wouldn't put it past her—unless she killed Tony herself. She was the type who would have the gall to come back with a policeman and claim her rights."

He saw a passing taxi, hailed it, and gave Celia's address. At least he could take Dennie home.

X

In the back seat, she slid her hand into his. Neither of them spoke. Steve was very conscious of her nearness. A haunting image of her face when she told him she loved him rose in his mind. In contrast with the tangle of his own feelings, her simplicity was infinitely moving. How good a home-coming like that would have been, with Dennie loving him as she did, and without his bitter longing for Celia.

Suddenly Dennie said, "If she does come back, Steve, she'll find it."

"Sure."

"And she'll think you did it. You answered the phone earlier when she called. She'll know you were there at the time it happened. She'll know you threw her out because it was behind the curtains. She'll tell the police."

She broke off, her fingers clutching his more tightly.

"Steve, don't you see the danger you've made for yourself? There's got to be something you can do."

What could he do? Roy Chappell would be waiting at Celia's. He could ask Roy whether it had actually been Tony who ordered the copy of the compact. If it had been, that probably cleared Virginia. But what then? He couldn't pursue Tony's infinite brood of girlfriends around New York until he finally found the one who had been given the compact.

Wearily, he saw that he was in too deep now to struggle out. That's what happened when you handled a civilian problem like a soldier's problem. At least he'd done what he could to shield Celia. That was all that really mattered anyway. From now on, he'd just have to sit back and wait for the police to catch up with him. Either they'd believe his story—or they wouldn't.

Roy Chappell was sitting in Celia's lovely living room, studying a portfolio of drawings. He got up when he saw them, pushing his slight, humped body up with some difficulty.

"You're the most remarkably active couple I've ever known. What have you been doing? Playing hide and go seek in Radio City?"

Dennie moved out of the room. Steve sat down and smoked a cigarette. He watched Roy who had settled back in the chair again and had picked up the drawings.

"I've been visiting Virginia," he said.

"Virginia Dort?" Roy glanced up. "Really, that was a rather peculiar thing to do, wasn't it?"

"She has a copy of the compact you made for Celia."

Roy held up one of the drawings, studying it. "Yes. I made it for her."

"Wasn't that rather peculiar of you? Making a copy of Celia's compact for Tony's wife?"

"Extremely peculiar." Roy was still looking at the drawing. "But since Celia was sordid enough to give the compact to Tony, I thought the only polite thing for me to do was to be sordid, too."

"Tony ordered the copy for Virginia then."

"He did."

"And who got the original?"

"Really, Steve, why this elaborate quiz?" Roy did glance at him then. "I should have thought the compact was rather a dead issue for you now."

"Dead issue is right," said Steve.

"There's my advantage over you. I never had Celia, so I never lost anything." Roy put the drawing back into the portfolio on his knee. "Now's the time for my speech about Celia. I've got it all ready. Want to hear it?"

"No," said Steve.

After a moment Dennie came in with the drinks. Steve thought, Virginia was telling the truth then. Not that it mattered. Roy had been right without realizing it when he'd said the compact was a dead issue. The police wouldn't ever know about the compact. All they'd know was that he had been in the apartment at the time of the murder and had returned there later and hid the corpse.

The scent from the freesias reached him. If it ever came to a question of himself or Celia, he'd take the blame, of course. Funny how he'd changed. Earlier in the evening, he hadn't been concerned about what happened to him. It will be different now. And it was Dennie's fault, and Virginia's. If only they hadn't give him that goading hope that maybe there was a change for him and Celia to start over again.

It would be so much easier to be without that hope.

Dennie was watching him desperately. He knew how the kid must be suffering for him, but he could bring himself to feel about it. The freesias were back at their old trick, conjuring up unbearably sweet memories.

And, as if his memories had sprung into flesh and blood, Celia was suddenly there. He heard her laugh in the hall. Then she came in with Goody Taylor.

She'd been calling something over her shoulder to Goody, but when she saw Steve she stopped dead on the threshold. She'd had too much champagne. He could tell that from the hectic sparkle in her eyes and the rather vague smile that played over her lips. Her beauty was almost like a physical pain for him. He got up. They stared at each other. Her smile went. Something, strong as an electric current, seemed to be passing between them. Steve had forgotten there was anyone else in the room.

"Steve." Celia's voice was very quiet. "I—I didn't know you'd be here."

"Any objections?" he said.

"I didn't know." She moved a little closer. "Steve, I don't like things I don't know. I don't know what to do."

"Do you have to do anything about me—baby?"

"Steve." She came to him. She out her arms around him. He shivered. Her hand moved up to his hair. "It's shorter. It goes with you." Suddenly she was crying. "Your hair, it goes with you."

"Celia." His arms tightened around her. Something was wrong with his throat. "Celia, baby."

She pulled herself away. Her eyes were still glistening, but she was not crying any more. She tossed her head, laughed and spun around to the others.

"Life, life, life. There's nothing so lovely as life. Goody, sit down and have a drink. You're always sitting down and having drinks. Roy, too. And Dennie. Why, it's a party."

Roy looked up from his drawings. "I'd call it a wake, Celia."

Celia laughed again ringingly.

Steve said, "Celia!"

She laid her hand on his sleeve. "Yes, darling? What?"

"Couldn't we talk, alone?"

"You don't want to talk to me alone. Baby, you don't know how terrible it is talking to me alone."

Goody said, "Stop making an exhibition of yourself, Celia."

Celia laughed again. "Exhibit A." She pointed to herself. "I propose that this young woman be added to the already existing evidence as Exhibit A."

She shrugged her bare shoulders. "Oh, I'm bored with all of you. Terribly, terribly bored." She waved vaguely and started for the door. "Good night, ladies. Good night, sweet ladies. Good night, good night."

Steve started after her. "Celia."

"No." She turned on him savagely. "No, Steve. No."

Her gaze fell on Roy. Impulsively, she tossed her gold evening bag to him.

"The divine bag you gave me, darling. Something's happened to the clasp. Fiddle with it."

With a meaningless smile at Steve, she hurried out of the room.

Dennie, her face very white, said, "I'll go after her."

She left. In a few moments she came back. She shook her head. "It's no use, Steve. She's locked her bedroom door."

XI

There they were, all of them, sitting around. Steve dropped back in his chair and picked up his drink. His head was throbbing.

Roy had slipped Celia's bag down on the chair at his side.

"Get Goody a highball, Dennie," he said. "We might as well all drink to the corpse."

Dennie brought Goody a drink. Roy raised his glass at them.

"To a very beautiful lady who died young."

Dennie said fiercely, "Shut up, Roy. You make me sick."

"I'm sorry, Dennie. I forgot that youth likes its bitter pills sugared. Let us say to a very beautiful, very sick lady"—he nodded at Steve—"in need of a cure."

Goody had slumped down comfortably in his chair. He yawned. "Don't you ever get out of the charnel house, Roy?"

Steve listened vaguely. He was wondering whether Janice had gone back to Tony's apartment yet. Since she knew he'd been with Dennie, she'd send the police here to Celia's after him.

Should he give them the compact and say, "Find the owner of this and you have the murderer?"

If he did, wouldn't everything inevitably swing back to Celia? Wasn't the only way to protect Celia to take the blame himself? To take the blame for a crime he hadn't committed, in order to protect Celia who hadn't committed one either? He felt confused, spent. Celia had done that to him. Those few agonizing, tantalizing moments with Celia.

Goody was saying something. He didn't know what. Suddenly the apartment buzzer sounded. Steve's fingers gripped his drink. This was it.

Dennie had half risen. She was staring blindly at the door. The buzzer hummed again.

Goody said, "Answer it, Dennie. It can't be anyone drearier that we've already got here."

Dennie's eyes met Steve's. He nodded. Dennie went to the door and opened it. Steve didn't look around. He was waiting to hear the sound of heavy boots and gruff voices. The police in books always came that way.

He didn't hear anything for the moment. Then Dennie's voice said, "You!" Another female's voice, clipped and cool, replied, "Yes?"

There were tapping heels. He looked up then.

Eternally Janice had come in the room with Dennie doubtfully behind her.

Janice's amber eyes surveyed the group. Their gaze settled on Steve. She smiled. It was a brief, ominous smile.

"I thought I'd find you here."

She turned to Goody then. "Hello, Goody." She jerked her head at Steve. "Who's this man?"

"Hello, Janice. What on earth are you doing here?" Goody's calm stare moved to Steve. "He's Steve Glenn." "Want to be introduced?"

"No, thank you. We've already met." Janice's voice was growing a little shrill. She swung round towards Steve. "So you're Celia's ex-husband. I might have realized. This explains it all, doesn't it?"

Steve watched her steadily. "If you've got anything to say to me, there are other rooms in this apartment."

"What's wrong with this one?" She laughed. "We don't have to be private about murder, do we?"

Dennie said, "Janice, please."

"Please what?" Janice whipped around on her. "Please be kind to your poor brother-in-law? Tony was such a naughty man. He deserved to be murdered? Is that what you're trying to say?"

Dennie's hand moved in a gesture of hopelessness. Roy stared.

Goody said, "Janice, what in the name of grief are you babbling about?"

"Just listen, Goody." Janice was glaring at Steve. "I went back, as you've probably gathered. You hid the body behind the curtains while I was there, didn't you?"

Steve said quietly, "You're doing the talking."

"At the moment. You'll be talking soon enough. You were there earlier in the evening when I phoned. You'd just murdered Tony then, hadn't you? The hero's first returning gesture. Kill a lot of Japs and then come home and kill the man your wife walked out on you for. It's a wonderful philosophy, isn't it?

"A guy gets a seat in the subway ahead of you so you kill him. A couple of characters have first row seats for the theatre. Kill them and take in a show." She laughed again. "Patent the process, soldier. Patent it quick before you're in a place where you can't take trips to Washington."

Steve was listening almost impersonally. He hadn't expected it to come quite this way. But here it was. He wondered how soon she was going to tell him she'd called the police.

Goody and Roy were both firing questions. He didn't pay any attention to them. Neither did Janice. The girl was still standing in front of him, her hands clenched at her sides. Nemesis, he thought. Nemesis is a blonde with her eyes too close together.

"Okay, soldier," she said. "Talk."

"You're doing the talking. Remember?"

"Okay. So you killed Tony. Later, I guess, you remembered something you'd left there, some clue or something. So you and your little helpmate"—she tossed her head at Dennie—"went back to smooth things over. Check?"

Steve didn't say anything. Janice's eyes suddenly narrowed.

"It did happen that way, didn't it? Well—maybe that crazy Celia shot him. Maybe you're just playing the noble husband with a broken heart protecting the dream girl who went sour. You and Dennie picking up after big sister. How about that? Did you kill him or did Celia?"

What he'd dreaded most was always the thing that happened.

He said, "What's the point of talking to you? Why not wait for the police? I guess you told them to come here?"

"The police?" Janice tugged a cigarette out of a case and lighted it. "I didn't tell the police to go anywhere."

Steve stared incredulously. "You haven't called them?"

"I haven't called them—yet." Janice sat down on the arm of a chair. "I wanted first to know what you were planning to do."

"What I'm planning to do?" Steve repeated, his face bewildered.

"Exactly," Janice puffed smoke. "I have no objections to being frank, even though you are coy. I happen to have a husband and a certain reputation in Pelham. I'd a lot rather it didn't come out that I was at Tony's apartment tonight. You can understand that, I'm sure."

"How does that fit in with what I'm planning to do?"

"Simple. If you go now to the police and confess, you'll have a much better chance. Don't you see? A plea of war nerves, the disillusioned veteran, the civilian snake who broke up his Eden. Come clean and you'll have all the sob sisters of America behind you." She paused. "And if you confess, then I needn't bring evidence against you."

For someone whose lover had just been shot, Janice was showing an admirable flare for self-protection. Goody was listening in a stupefied silence. Roy had picked up Celia's bag and was clicking the clasp open and shut as if there was nothing more important to attract his attention.

Steve said, "And if I don't confess?"

Janice shrugged. "Painful though it'll be to Pelham, I'll have to tell the police exactly what I know. I'd be quite good on a witness stand." She leaned forward, her red lips a tight, unyielding line. "Okay, soldier. From now on you're on your own. What's it to be? Confession and no Janice? Or no confession and Janice ready with a nice little noose to slip around your neck?"

Dennie got up suddenly and came to Steve, standing behind him, putting her hand on his shoulder in a warm, friendly gesture.

Steve moistened his lips "What would you say if I told you I didn't kill Tony, and neither did Celia?"

"I'd say: 'No? Not really? How nice.'"

"It's the truth." Steve looked down at his hand with the bruised knuckles. He didn't really know why he was telling her this. "I beat Tony up. I admit that. I left him. Later I went back because I was afraid maybe I'd hurt him badly. I found him murdered. I didn't call the police because I knew they'd think I'd done it. Later I went back again with Dennie to make sure I hadn't left any traces." He paused. "That's all I know. Someone else killed Tony." He raised his eyes to hers. "What do you think of the story?"

"It's true," blurted Dennie. "I swear it's true. You've got to believe that."

"In the old days," said Janice "when people heard stories like that they used to say, 'Tell it to the Marines.'"

"You don't believe it?" she asked, her voice faint with strain.

"I don't believe it." Janice was tapping her toe against the carpet. "Well, what's it to be? Time isn't something we can ignore. Do you call the police and confess? Or do I call the police and let them fight it out with you and Celia?"

XII

Steve wished the evening hadn't taken so much out of him. It was cruel that the great decision had to come when he was least equipped to face it. Dennie's hand on his shoulder was curiously steadying. He glanced up at her. She smiled faintly. If he let Janice call the police, there was just a chance that the real murderer would be found, that he and Celia could be cleared. But if the police didn't believe him, it could mean disaster.

Janice said, "Well?"

Steve opened his mouth. He never knew exactly what he had been planning to say, because he didn't say it. Roy Chappell spoke instead.

The famous jewel designer had tossed Celia's bag down on his chair. He rose. In spite of his slight misshapen body, he looked strangely impressive. He was watching Janice from eyes bright and hard-surfaced as one of his own gems.

"I rather think this dialogue's gone on too long. After all, there are other people in the room."

Janice turned to him suspiciously.

He said, "There's at least one question I should like to ask you."

"Which is?" Snapped Janice.

"I would like to know just how spiteful you are."

"Spiteful?"

"The aspects of your character which you have so far revealed have been singularly unattractive. That is what makes me feel that you are probably as spiteful as you are vulgar and self-interested and sordid."

Janice looked flustered. She flared, "When I want homilies from humpbacks, I'll ask for them. This is hardly the moment."

Roy smiled then. "I'm afraid it is the moment. You will please tell me whether your spite against Celia and Steve is sufficiently strong for you to go ahead with this false accusation—even after you've heard the truth."

"The truth!"

Roy's smile widened. It was an infinitely sad smile.

"If you care to listen to me, I can tell you who really did murder Tony."

Janice gasped. "You mean—you know?" she cried.

"I mean just that. Don't you think it might be a good idea to hear the truth before you call the police?"

Janice dropped back onto a chair arm. Her vitality seemed to have left her. Everyone else was passive, too. It was as if Roy were a magnet, drawing to himself all the strength that was in the room.

"I've been accused of being a homiletic humpback," he said, "Maybe there's a homily in this story somewhere. I don't want to bother with it. I hate tales with morals. It's a feeble little story at best, moral or no moral. And it begins with me."

He slid his hands into his pockets. He was calm and yet, behind the calm, there was an odd, veiled excitement.

"Tonight I'd been working hard in my workshop. I'd been thinking how thankless it is to create beautiful objects and get nothing for them. Nothing except money. My thought processes are not particularly interesting, I suppose. But this thought process made me think of Tony Dort.

"I'd done a job of copying for him some time ago. I dislike copying my own work and I dislike doing favors for Tony, but I'd done it and he hadn't paid me. Tony wasn't the sort of man who knew the price of everything and the value of nothing. That sort of man, I feel, should always be made to pay for things that are really priceless—and pay promptly in cold, hard cash." He shrugged. "This, I suppose, is an elaborate way of saying I went around to see Tony."

His gaze moved to Steve. "I reached Tony's apartment house just as you were leaving. I don't imagine you noticed me. I hadn't seen you for several years. You are, if I may say so, a very fine figure of a man. The sight of you made me think enviously—and here come my thought processes again—of what I would give to have been born with your body instead of this miserable, twisted frame."

"Come, come," snapped Janice. "We don't have to get psychopathological."

Roy's eyes glinted. "You are a very offensive young woman. As it happens, my psychopathological thought processes are vastly important because they set the mood for my meeting with Tony. I found him in an ugly temper. That was reasonable enough as he had just been beaten up. I found him also looking singularly unappetizing. Tony wasn't the sort of man who should look unappetizing. His only excuse for existence was that he was pleasing to the eye.

"Tonight he was not pleasing. He was bruised, battered, untidy. Hamlet, I believe, told his mother to look at two pictures, one of his dead father, one of the murderous man she had married. Hyperion to a satyr, he said. I thought of Celia with Steve and Tony. Hyperion to a satyr, I thought. And it disgusted me that Celia should have shown such bad taste to have chosen the wrong man."

Roy looked down at his fine, sensitive hands. "You all probably know that I have been devoted to Celia for some years. She was very much in my mind tonight. I was probably more angry with. Tony for what he'd done to Celia than I was insistent upon his paying the bill. In any case, our conversation rapidly degenerated into what I believe is called 'words.'

"I'd been wanting to have words with Tony for some time. What I did say and what he said back are not relevant. What is relevant is that he became sufficiently incensed to produce a revolver from a drawer and threaten me."

"We started to struggle. I have some knowledge of ju-jitsu. Many humpbacks do, I understand. It give us an illusion of strength. I practiced my strange Oriental arts on Tony. Unfortunately, the gun went off. It shot Tony—quite dead."

He paused for a moment. The scent of the freesias came to Steve, achingly sweet.

"I don't pretend I'm sorry I killed Tony," Roy Chappell continued. "In fact, I feel rather pleased with myself. I don't pretend, either, that I was planning to give myself up. I wasn't. But since this female"—he nodded at Janice—"is so bent upon making herself obnoxious with accusation against completely innocent people. I have no recourse but to tell the truth."

Roy paused again. His eyes found Steve's. He felt in his pocket, produced a gun, and tossed it down on a table in front of him.

"The murder gun. That's the right expression, isn't it?" He looked questioningly at Janice. "Any objections if I call the police right way and get this over with? I imagine I have quite a chance of knowing self-defense. And if I'm less lucky—" He shrugged. "What is it about jewel workers that makes them so violent? Me and Benvenuto Cellini."

The realization of it all was coming through to Steve slowly. He was like a man who's been lost in a desert with no water. He was afraid of gulping the truth down in one swallow. He snapped at it. Roy had killed Tony. Roy was going to confess. Miraculously, everything was going to be all right.

It *was* going to be all right, wasn't it? The compact. Roy hadn't mentioned the compact. Steve put his hand into the pocket of his blouse, pulled out the compact and tossed it to the table by the gun.

"You left this at Tony's, too?"

Roy picked up the compact.

"It was probably the most beautiful thing I ever made."

"But you left it at Tony's?"

Roy looked up. "Didn't I explain? Tony owed me for the copy I made of his. Knowing Tony's vagueness about debts, I'd been holding the original until I got his check. Tonight, however, when I became angry, I forgot I was the cool-headed business man. I threw the compact back at him." He put it down again on the table. "I'm not fond of it any more. It was made for Celia. The moment she gave it to Tony, it lost its symbolic significance. It became—just a compact."

No one spoke. In the intense silence, Roy started to move to the phone. Dennie's hand was still on Steve's shoulder. He felt it tense.

"Don't." Dennie threw the word after Roy. "Stop. Don't call."

Roy half turned, smiling at her tenderly over his shoulder. "Why not, my lamb?"

Dennie was watching him with a kind of wild indecision. She swung to Steve.

"Steve, please. I've got to talk to you alone."

Steve stirred uneasily. "Alone?"

"Please. And Roy, promise me that you won't phone. Not till Steve and I come back."

For a long moment Roy stood still. Then with a faint shrug of resignations, he dropped into a chair.

"All right. I will wait a few minutes. Wait for you, Dennie. A little child shall lead me."

XIII

Dennie gripped Steve's hand. Steve rose. She drew him out of the room and down a passage into her bedroom.

"What is it?" he asked. For a moment, back there in the other room, he had been happy. For a moment, life had been indescribably kind. Now he was worried again.

"Steve," she whispered, "why didn't you tell me about the compact from the beginning?"

"The compact?" He moved nervously. "Why should I?"

"Steve, it makes all the difference in the world." She put her hand up to her face. "How can I tell you?"

"Dennie."

"I've got to." She said that fiercely. "Don't you see how I've got to? I can't let Roy lie."

"A lie? Baby, what are you trying to say?"

"He's lying, Steve. He couldn't have killed Tony."

Steve's mouth was dry as ashes. "Why?"

"Because of the compact. It's true Tony had the compact copied for Virginia. But the rest is a lie. Celia never gave it to Tony. Tony lied to Roy that she had because he knew that was the only way he could get Roy to copy it."

"But why?" Steve's thoughts was whirling. "Why would Tony lie? Why would he want a copy for Virginia?"

"Because Virginia had seen it one day at his apartment and she liked it. Because he had to square Virginia. Tony never thought above principles or sentiments. He had to have a present to please Virginia. He knew that compact would please her. So he tricked Roy into making a copy."

"And the real compact?"

Dennie was shivering. "Steve didn't you believe me when I said Celia still loves you? She'd have died before she ever gave your compact to Tony. It was in his apartment that day, yes, just because she'd left it there. But she never gave it to him. She treasured it more than anything in the world."

"Then Tony never had it? Roy never had it?"

"Of course not." Dennie's voice was almost inaudible. "No one ever had it—except Celia."

"And tonight?"

"She had it tonight." Dennie's face was stricken as she stared up him. "I saw her put it her purse before she left. She took it with her tonight."

They looked at each other. Neither of them spoke. Then, suddenly, Dennie threw herself into his arms.

"Oh, Steve, Steve!"

He pushed her roughly away. "Where's her room?"

"Next to this."

He ran out. She came after him. Steve turned the handle of Celia's door. It was locked. He raised his fist to pound on the panels.

Dennie warned, "No, Steve. The others will hear. There's a balcony that leads from my room to hers."

Steve ran back into Dennie's room. He vaulted out onto the balcony. The window to Celia's room was open. He stepped inside. He felt no reality. It was as if he were moving in a dream.

A single light was burning by the bedside. Celia was lying in bed. Her eyes were closed. Her wonderful silver blond hair foamed over the pillow. He tried to look at her. He couldn't really.

He went to the door and unlocked it. Dennie moved in. Together they crossed to the bed.

"Celia!" Dennie whispered. "Celia, wake up."

Steve glared at the bedside table. It was the only way of keeping himself from thinking. There was an empty glass. And propped against it an envelope. There was a word on the envelope in Celia's large, erratic writing.

Steve.

He picked the envelope up. He opened it. There were several sheets of paper inside.

"Celia!" Dennie called again.

Steve put his hand on her arm. "No. Wait."

He started to read the letter. He passed the sheets to Dennie as he finished with them.

The letter said:

Steve, darling:

When I did it, it seemed so right, so inevitable. I thought it would be easy to explain, but it doesn't seem easy now. Nothing about me's easy to explain, I guess. How could I have gone on loving you all the time I was crazy about Tony? I don't know, but that's the way it was. Even when I realized he wasn't going to divorce Virginia, that he had fooled me, I was half relieved because it gave me the crazy hope that I could get back to you and the way life used to be.

It *was* a crazy hope, of course. I saw that right away. You'd never have wanted me after Tony. That's really why I hated him—not because he'd walked out on me, but because he'd brought out all the shoddiness that was in me and made me lose my chance of ever having you again.

Do you understand a bit? This evening, just as I was getting ready to go out with Goody, Tony phoned. He asked me to come to his place. I wouldn't have gone if he hadn't mentioned your name and threatened me. But I went and he was wild with anger. You'd beaten him up, he said. I could tell that from the way he looked and, darling, I was so glad I could have laughed out loud. But it wasn't really the time for laughs because he was seething. He accused me of setting you on him.

He said he was going to have you arrested for assault with intent to kill. He'd get you behind bars, he said, if it was the last thing he did. That frightened me for you, darling, because you were still in uniform and maybe he could make trouble for you. But that wasn't the real thing. The real thing was his face. That horrid, angry little face. As I looked at him, I thought, This is what wrecked my life. Our life.

And I couldn't stand it. It was like a physical sensation, a dreadful physical loathing for him and for myself. I knew he had a gun in the bureau drawer. While he ranted on, bawling out filth against you, I got the gun. I didn't care about anything except stopping the noise he was making. I killed him almost before I realized I'd pressed the trigger.

And the moment I'd done it, I knew it was right. You see, it wasn't just killing him. I was killing myself, too. Because you'd beaten him up, I knew you still felt something for me. Darling, I couldn't bear to think of you loving me, carrying me around like a virus in your blood. So I did this thing to get rid of me, too. I didn't want to cover my tracks. I just put the gun in my purse and went off to meet Goody. Any moment the police would catch up with me, I thought.

And when they came, I was going to say, "Okay. Here I am. Take me, champagne and all."

But the police didn't come, baby. You came. And when you showed me the compact, I knew I must have left it there—I was always careless, wasn't I—and that you must have known Tony was dead. That was the worst moment of all. I know you so well. I knew that if you thought I'd done it, you'd try some awful, chivalrous thing like taking the blame yourself. I had to prevent that, so I lied about the compact.

You see, I thought if I said I'd given your compact to Tony you'd despise me so much that it'd kill your love for me. Baby, I tried to do everything, so that you'd think I was the scum of the earth and be free of me.

But what's the use of saying that now? I almost spoiled it as few minutes ago when I came in and saw you there. And I'm spoiling it completely now, aren't I, by telling you I love you. Because I do, Steve. Maybe, in some queer fashion, what I did and what I'm doing is the only way I really could prove I love you.

The gun's in my purse. I gave it to Roy. Maybe he's found it by now. If not give it to the police when they come. As for the compact, keep it baby. Pink ribbons. Among my souvenirs. Did I say all that revolted me? Oh, Steve!

If you don't want to keep the compact, give it to Dennie. Dennie's worth a thousand of me. Lately I've been hoping that perhaps you and she ... Oh, well, if it's to be, you'll find out for yourselves.

Good-by, Steve. When you read this, I'll be asleep. Very much asleep, if the pills can be trusted. Let me be, won't you, baby? Let me sleep on.

Celia.

P. S. Remember that old corny play we saw? Remember the line: Thank you for having loved me? Thank you, Steve.

This was how it felt to be lost, thought Steve. Dimly he was conscious of Dennie drawing the last page of the letter from his limp hand. Contact with her finger brought a fleeting comfort. But wasn't a real comfort. Nothing could be a real comfort.

During the evening there had been moments of wild, racing hope, moments when he'd thought he was on top and could thumb his nose at doom. They hadn't been real, of course. Steve saw that now. He'd been licked from the start. He, who'd sworn he'd never kid himself, had walked about with blinders. He'd refused to see what had always been obvious, just because he didn't have the strength to face it.

"Roy found the gun in her purse." Dennie's voice trailed through his thoughts. "He realized then—and he was trying to take the blame. He loved her that much."

Who didn't love Celia that much—too much?

Steve forced himself look at Celia then. "Pale beyond porch and portal." Who'd said that? Some poet. Her smooth arms lay outside the covers. He felt for her wrist. There was the faintest stirring, like the echo of a pulse.

"Celia!" He almost shouted her name. "Celia!"

He leaned over her to shake her.

But a hand touched his arm. Dazedly, he saw Dennie. Standing there, staring up at him, she didn't look like a kid any more. She looked like Celia—so hauntingly like Celia that it confused him.

"No, Steve."

"No?" He echoed her word, not really understanding what she had said to him.

"Don't wake her. This is the only way, Steve. Let her be. Let her sleep on."

Sources

"The Frightened Landlady." *Street & Smith's Detective Story Magazine*, December 1935

"Killed by Time." *Street & Smith's Detective Story Magazine*, October 1935

"The Hated Woman." *Street & Smith's Detective Story Magazine*, February 1936

"Hunt in the Dark." *Short Stories*, October 10, 1942

"The Woman Who Waited." *The Shadow*, January 1945

"This Way Out." *Mystery Book Magazine*, March 1947

Hunt in the Dark

Hunt in the Dark and Other Deadly Pursuits by Q. Patrick, edited by Curtis Evans and Douglas G. Greene, with an introduction by Curtis Evans, is set in Palatino Linotype and printed on 60-pound Natures acid-free paper. It was published both in full cloth and in trade softcover. The cover is by Gail Cross. *Hunt in the Dark and Other Deadly Pursuits* was printed Southern Ohio Printing and bound by Cincinnati Bindery, and published in April 2021 by Crippen & Landru Publishers, Cincinnati, Ohio.

The Puzzles Of Peter Duluth by Patrick Quentin. Lost Classics Series.

Anthony Boucher wrote: "Quentin is particularly noted for the enviable polish and grace which make him one of the leading American fabricants of the murderous comedy of manners; but this surface smoothness conceals intricate and meticulous plot construction as faultless as that of Agatha Christie." Full cloth in dust jacket, $29.00.

The Cases of Lieutenant Timothy Trant by Q. Patrick. Lost Classic Series.

Full cloth in dust jacket, $30.00.